Basketball & Ballet

Published by SDH Books

Made in the United States of America
Cover Design: Ennel Espanola
Project Editor: Paulette Nunlee of 5-Star Proofing
Author's Photo: Derrick Pearson of One Way Photos
Author's Make-up: Vadia Rhodes
Interior Design: Milmon Harrison Designs

ISBN-13: 978-1-7337217-2-1

Library of Congress Control Number: 2020905477

Basketball & Ballet is Book 2 in the California Love series.

The author may be reached at:
SDH Books
P.O. Box 340012
Sacramento, CA 95834
www.sdhbooks.com

DEDICATION

To all the "Sistas" & "Brothas"
willing to try love again:

May it be splendid!

Basketball & Ballet

SUZETTE D. HARRISON

CHAPTER ONE
EIGHTY-ELEVEN CAVITIES
Yazmeen Williams

For the first time in a long while, I wore white. The absence of dark colors was my testifying that my depression days were gone goodbye. I was done with that Morticia Addams life. I felt free. Like me. With all my imperfections and idiosyncrasies. Re-connected to my best—okay, *better*—self, I felt floaty, semi-angelic. Thank God for panty girdles gripping the hips and beating them into submission. Wearing white was merciless and told all my big booty business.

"You sporting three or four Spanx?"

I had to swallow hard to keep from spitting virgin daiquiri across the waist-high, bistro table at my golden-eyed, *bestest* ever friend. "Joy Matthews, stay out the business."

My favorite nut had the nerve to laugh. "Tonight, my business is your booty. As is your ridonculousness. How many, Yaz?"

"Two. Okay!" I answered only because chick could be merciless, as she'd been since meeting at Howard University's Freshman orientation. I was a dance major. Joy was business. Tall, voluptuous, with gorgeous eyes, I'd been drawn to her wicked humor and unique boldness. We instantly connected. Learning her mom and my parents resided in northern California was kismet. We'd been pre-assigned other dorm mates freshman year, but thereafter we were off-campus roommates, becoming sisters versus friends.

"Yaz, I swear you waste your sexy."

"And you, sweetie, your sanity."

We laughed, knowing I wasn't lying. After graduating with highest honors, my girl interned her way into a Fortune 500 gig but left that cushy position, enrolled in culinary school and pursued pastry passions. I supported that one-hundred. Joy was insanely gifted and could bake both our big butts off. But truth? Boo was reality T.V. kind of cray-cray.

"I agree on that sanity," Joy chimed. "But I'm not the one whose muscle-butt is on lock like it might wiggle away my righteousness."

"That's because your righteousness is a myth."

"As is your last orgasm."

Dipping fingers in my glass, I flicked liquid at my ride-or-die since college, knowing she was partially right. I wasn't scared of sexy. I was petrified.

My libido had led me so wrong in life. Not that I was a happy ho: I was a twenty-eight-year-old virgin until four years ago. But my sons were proof I'd done some sneaky-freaky. Now? I was a repurposed virgin focused on raising three-year-old twins. Between being a divorced mom, administrative assistant for my church, and a part-time Zumba (and dance) instructor, I had zero time for being saved-and-sensuous. I was content living as a born-again Christian committed to locking her legs until 'I Do.' Which I wasn't saying again *anytime* soon. One joke of a non-child-support-paying ex was sufficient. I had negative interest in anything same-sex, but drama with my children's father made me painfully disinterested in all things men.

"Yaz…chillax. Enjoy the moment." Joy was my bestest for a reason. Girlfriend could tell me my thoughts before I finished thinking them.

"I'm living my best life."

"*Righhhttt.* That's why you've refolded that napkin forty-eleven times."

Tossing that mangled mess on the table, I scoped my situation of adult socialization. Despite being a trained dancer, clubbing wasn't my thing. I typically attended church-sponsored functions and avoided dance floor, back-that-thang-up-sexual-simulations. Not that church folks didn't come to mixers horny for unholy hook-ups. We did. But most of us had the commonality of Jesus to tame that flesh with. Tonight, beneath Club Neo's pulse and beat, I harnessed Yazmeen. Just like I'd been doing the past three-hundred-and-sixty-five days times three. Unfortunately, in our private party room were several mildly appetizing Man Club members.

"Yaz, Corn-on-the-cob dude's coming for you."

Whipping around, I saw the "fluffy" brother whose dance invitation I'd declined headed our way in a bright yellow beeline. I wasn't bent about his being fluffy. I loved eating, too. Only Zumba and rigorous dance kept my bootyrificness in check. It was his banana yellow, Curious George handler hat-suit-shoe combo baptized-in-body-spray that had me stressed.

"Halloween's a week away," Joy stage whispered. "Guess he started early."

"Hello again, lovely ladies."

That barrel of body spray hit the back of my throat with an asphyxiation-by-fragrance goal. Afraid to inhale, I held my breath and let Joy do the honors.

"Hey, Lemon."

"Le*Mon*," he corrected, eyeing my legs, making me wish I'd worn something longer than an at-the-knee, flouncy-hemmed dress courtesy of a recent thrift store shopping spree. "You ladies enjoying the evening?"

"Your yellowness makes it better."

I kicked Joy beneath the table. She kicked me back. We stared each other down, trying not to laugh.

"I'm known to brighten a lady's nightlife," Lemon-LeMon told Joy while grinning at me, gold-toothed grille shining.

I suddenly needed Ray-Bans and the restroom. "Excuse me, please."

"No, you sit and let me get your drink," he offered, mistaking my need to breathe as a desire for a refill. "What can I get you?"

Besides Axe-less air?

"Thank you, but we're good," I wheezed, then sneezed.

"Lemme grab myself something real quick and I'll be back..."

"I'm Petula and that's Quaneeva," Joy lied, offering the fake monikers we'd used in our college party days when escaping unwanted male attention.

"Queen Quaneeva, mmm-mmm-*mmm*, I see ya!"

He'd barely left before I pinched Joy's arm. "You're wrong!"

"Girl, you want him to have your real 4-1-1? Excuse me, Lemon!"

I snatched her arm out the air. *"You better not!* And it's Le*Mon*."

"It's yellow and round, and probably bleeds curd and lemonade."

I snorted back a laugh. "I hate you. Go sit somewhere else."

"Boo, I'm good coochie-sitting and keeping you from conceiving citrus-flavored infants."

"Joy, lock your jaw," I suggested, thoroughly enjoying a Saturday evening doing something besides ironing church clothes, or snuggling with my babies and watching animated movies starring helium-sucking sounding characters while gorging on animal crackers and apple juice with no gin. As if second nature, my feet and body tuned into the rhythms of Club Neo's bass and beats. I danced while seated.

A multi-level building offering a different musical vibe on each, Club Neo was a perfect place to host a celebration for someone as eclectic as LaVelle—Joy's cousin, and part two of my twins' co-godmommy team.

"Only Velle's dumb tail would plan her own surprise party then show up late to make an entrance."

"Joy, that's your cousin," I needlessly reminded, admiring the work LaVelle's faux-prise party coordinator had put in. Guests were vibing, drinking or enjoying appetizers while waiting on the birthday lady. Again, I noticed Velle's crew included some eye-fine brothers. Thankfully, most were boo'ed up. My *extreme* aversion to playeritis left them off limits which was what I preferred seeing as how a man was nowhere on my She Needs List.

"Velle's family only because I wasn't consulted before crackhead kin were distributed. *You*, on the other hand, chose to make that crackhead co-godmother of the twins."

For Joy "crackhead" was a term of endearment.

Head bobbing in sync with the old school R&B rocking the room, I gave my girl a stare. "One day you'll stop being salty about sharing godmommy status."

"Hold your breath on that possibility and you'll wake up jumping rope with Jesus."

"Joy?"

"Yaz?"

"Sweetie...*shut up!*" Popping a palm in her face to halt her comeback, I shushed her with a vengeance. "Shhh! Velle's here."

Our private room featured smoked glass walls allowing us to see out, while outsiders couldn't see in, letting LaVelle play out her fauxprise to completion. She stood on the opposite side patting her perfect hair as her husband, Ronnie, opened the door for her diva-ish entrance.

I snickered when Joy whispered, "This chickenhead's about to beat out Betty Davis."

True enough, entering the room amid a unified shout of "Surprise!" LaVelle's mouth opened in pantomimed shock. Hand on blessed breasts pushed high above the low-cut neckline of a curve-hugging dress, LaVelle's face featured pure pleasure and fabricated amazement. "Oooh, y'all came out to celebrate my twenty-fifth birthday?"

I hit Joy's leg when she quipped, "That must be in canine count."

LaVelle pranced into the room, unfazed by the clap-back. "Be glad I'm on a cut-a-cousin fast or I'd come for you, Joy Matthews!"

Lord, these two!

They'd walked with me through the inferno and fallout of my fake "marriage" to one of Satan's seeds. These women would get in the mud and go to war with and for you, then wash you off and bandage your wounds when the war was through. I adored them despite their insane ways.

Joining the family and friends piling on genuine love despite the faux-prise pretense, I waited my turn to squeeze LaVelle and coo birthday blessings in her ear. "Happy birthday, honey! Malcolm and Malik told me to tell their Mimi they love you even though you wouldn't let them come to your party."

LaVelle's laughter was carefree. "Yaz, I love my godsons, but tonight's all about the *turn up*! I'll see my babies at tomorrow's post-birthday dinner after church."

"You'll have to if you want your gift. They're holding it hostage."

"Sounds like them." When LaVelle leaned in, whispering, I took no offense. "That's enough twin talk. Tonight, your mom button's on pause. Work that round-the-way-girl booty and get me a brother-in-law."

Squeezing my hand, Velle moved on, meeting and greeting guests, leaving me laughing. Thanks to lifelong affirmations from my she-bear of a mother, I was fine with my size eight body and size twelve behind. Balancing womanhood with motherhood, on the other hand? That was a delicate act.

Not tonight, Yaz. This is a no-toddler zone...

Grabbing my tiny clutch and empty glass, I scoped the bar at the back of the room, ensuring LeMon was nowhere near, before heading for a refill.

Keep it sugar-free.

For me the alcohol-free piece was automatic. Courtesy of my first beers in college, I was well-versed in the fact that I suffered *severely adverse* reactions to the smallest amounts of alcohol. But that sugar thing caution was all for me. Former dancer, fitness advocate or not, I had a sweet tooth to the extreme and limited tonight's indulgence. Not due to caloric concerns, but because—I'd learned through detox and with-drawal—sugar would trigger the King Kong-sized headache I'd beat down to a cute critter with the help of over-the-counter meds and a cool bath. A critter I could deal with; Kong I couldn't.

Addiction ain't pretty.

I wasn't crack addict-hardcore. Legally prescribed medication had been my dirty little secret. Thankfully, God rescued me courtesy of Inez Williams. My elegant mother had never laid those kinds of hands on me, but finding me popping pills, crying behind my ex like some ignorant little delinquent, she'd slapped me so hard I slid down the wall like white women in movies.

I didn't raise my children so some upside-down ignoramus could reduce them.

Trust, Mama would never need to lay *those* hands on me again.

About that ignoramus, a.k.a. my ex-half-a-husband who took me through twenty degrees of hell and back again? Until five days ago Le Troll, legal name Royal, had been missing in action an equal number of months. Guess he got a little Lazarus in his leg and rose again. Now? Royal's new life goal was blowing up my phone trying to talk his way into his own addiction: money. Seeing as how I was struggling to raise "two twins" (as Joy hated hearing folks say), I'd be his private teller on the forty-fifth of November. Or hashtag, never.

Inwardly laughing, I—in an effort to avoid LeMon—hurried to the opposite end of the bar and into the web of the flirtatious mixolo-gist showing thirty-two teeth for me.

"Told you you'd be back, pretty lady."

"That you did." My smile felt as real as the Kardashians.

"Can I put something extra in that sexless daiquiri this go 'round, and make it sweet as you when it goes down?"

Guess it was my Mack Monster magnet night. "Water with lime is fine." I gave myself two points for acting human and over the age of five.

Looking me over and chewing his bottom lip like he'd never heard of the #metoo movement, he served my drink with a side of supposed-to-be sexy. "If you change your mind...I'm ready."

My mind'll change when you take that earring out your tongue. Look-ing like a decorated demon.

As a mother of multiples, I'd developed peculiar patience. But right then it felt tried. Dude didn't get a pass for being easy on the eyes.

Looks no longer lit my life. I'd been there. Done that. Had beautiful twins and make-believe child support to show for it. Drink in hand, I reminded self my therapy included being nice to men.

First Lady would be proud of me.

A licensed family and marriage counselor with an advanced degree in psychology, my pastor's wife, First Lady Richardson, ran a successful practice before accepting her husband's invitation to co-pastor their modest congregation that grew into one of the largest megachurches in the region. Refusing to forfeit her licensure, she served the church in a counseling capacity. An amazing woman who managed wifehood, motherhood, and being a clinician, First Lady was a force of nature who'd helped pull me up when—five months pregnant and less-than-a-year-married—my ex-monster decided I wasn't what he wanted. The wounds were real, but I put the work in. When her then administrative assistant relocated, First Lady offered me the vacant position. Dance was my first love, but between gigs and expecting twins, I'd accepted the position with modest pay but excellent benefits. First Lady and I segued from therapy to life coaching to avoid a conflict of interest. Now? I was good, enjoying drug-free living with zero need for a penis.

Well…not tonight, but maybe one day?

Love and I were done, but lust still had a say.

Tickled by my foolery, I navigated back to my seat, smiling when seeing the nearest arrival hugging the birthday woman. The epitome of tall, dark, and delicious, my bestie's boo had his one-dimple grin on display while exchanging pleasantries with his fraternity brother—LaVelle's husband, Ronnie. When I approached, Quinton Daley aimed that dimpled smile my way.

"Hey, Sis. You look lovely." His hug was brief, brotherly.

"You're pretty tolerable, too."

Quinton's laugh was smooth. "How're the boys?"

"My parents're watching them, which means they've probably eaten enough sugar to give me diabetes."

"That's what grandparents do." He laughed while scanning the room. "Where's my woman?"

I lifted my drink in Joy's direction.

When my bestie looked up and found herself the center of attention, we exchanged a loaded look. Joy's was indifferent. Mine bordered on smug triumph.

Quit fighting like a fool and let this man love you.

Intuiting my thoughts or not, Joy rolled her eyes before focusing on Quinton.

"We'll catch you later, Yaz."

My heart melted at the softness claiming my girl's face as Quinton crossed the room. After years of random sexing and claiming she didn't need or want it, love was reeling in my B.F.F.

The old romantic me my ex-monster hadn't completely killed felt giddy seeing Quinton greet her with a kiss. Snatching my cell, I fired off a text.

Mess over this & I'll toss you off the Golden Gate Bridge. #serious.

Watching Joy, I said a silent prayer that as it softly landed, she wouldn't play the fool and pitch love over a cliff. Ecstatic for her, I held no nonsensical notions about love landing on me again. Truth? Love didn't find me the last time. I married without it.

I taught Hip Hop to inner-city kids. I led Zumba for hip-shaking women. A trained dancer, rhythm and movement were intrinsic parts of me, making it difficult to be still. The Nico and Vinz joint bumping through the speakers had me wanting to dance freestyle like I hadn't in a while. Like a woman without cares or choreography. Just pure motion fed and led by the soul, the body. Feet tapping, I was mentally concocting a series of swirls and twirls when I lost my ability to live.

Breathe, Yazmeen. Breathe.

I tried. With my mouth big, wide, and open.

Bubble-eyed and breathing like I had adenoids and emphysema, my respiratory abilities suffered courtesy of the Dear God Almighty Goodness entering, causing mild commotion.

Coming from a football family, I recognized his name only because of my baby brother, Taj's, obsession with basketball. I vaguely recalled Taj ranting about his early retirement. One of Taj's favorites, I semi-sort-of remembered he was good in the game. But I did not recall him looking you-got-my-vulva-twitching kind-of-orgasmic.

Jesus, that eye candy's giving me eighty-eleven cavities!

I'd need multiple root canals come morning.

When Quinton passed my perch at the bistro table to embrace the buzz-causing brother as if acquainted on a deeper, friendship level, I caught enough sense to shut my mouth and dab drool from my lips in a dignified-as-a-dog fashion. I barely registered Quinton's introducing him to Velle, or Velle shrieking, "I'm your numero uno fan!" I was only mildly conscious of folks swarming the entrance in true sports fan fashion. What had me feeling like living a panty-less life was the incredible object of their attention.

B-ball tall, beautifully built and broad shouldered, he was bronze-skinned, with deep black, close-cut hair. His perfectly groomed moustache-goatee framed thick, lickable lips that made me want to feed him a steady, ready, naked diet of Yazmeen Williams. He. Was. Delicious!

Dear Black Jesus, he's serving my abstinent eyes visual orgasms.

Obviously accustomed to "fandoration"—as Taj called the affection showered on athletes—that commercial-worthy smile was on full display as he flawlessly worked the room. Despite LaVelle hanging off his arm like an unexpected appendage, he was into the meet-and-greet as she made breezy, wheezy introductions.

I panicked like an asinine preteen when Velle pulled that Sweet Wonder away from a half-dressed woman looking at him like she was ready to strip tease.

Lord, no! Do not let them come towards me!

With Velle redirecting that lusciousness my way, obviously the Lord wasn't listening.

Nervously sipping my lackluster drink, I told myself to act the thirty-two I was, not thirteen.

You are good and grown, not some titty-jiggling groupie.

That reminder did little to calm nerves that were suddenly jittery. The closer he came, the more I was amazed and dazed. By the pure light in the whiskey brown of his eyes connecting with mine. The glint of the diamond in his left ear. The subtle sexy of his scent. The majesty of his height, and the utter lusciousness of...

Them there lips! Lord, lemme lick 'em.

Unsure if the words actually exited my mouth or were a mere thought, I was too lost in his stare to care as LaVelle made introductions.

"This is my girl, Yazmeen Williams. Yaz, former Titans' point guard, Tavares Alvarez!"

Remembering I'd been raised to be a dignified Black woman, I acted half-human, extended a hand and accepted his.

Ice angels in heaven needed to tend to me. The touch of his hand unleashed an internal heatwave that threatened to melt my braided extensions. And my hold on celibacy.

That fire was immediate yet slow, intense. Heat took its sweet time sauntering up my arm to explode, sprinkling hot petals, in my chest. I tried but failed to extricate my hand from his firm, sizeable grip. Slobbering in the back of my throat, I let his hold linger and sat mesmerized by the man wearing, with absolute ease, designer threads and ultra-sexiness.

"Pleased to meet you, Yazmeen."

I never understood the need to throw panties at performers until his velvety baritone hit the bottom of my belly, and stripped all cobwebs from between my legs. "Likewise," was all I could manage.

LaVelle pulled Tavares one way despite his hand remaining fixed about mine as if reluctant to leave. I felt the delicious pressure of his gently pressing my fingers before releasing me.

Lord, I am so disturbed and unnerved.

I had to squash a ludicrous wish that my tongue was long enough to lick the back of his neck.

Amused by the foolery, my smile faded when Mister Luscious looked back at me. Fresh warmth surged through my saved and sanctified center as our eyes connected and he held my gaze, appearing unwilling to turn away.

I turned, instead, towards the table where water waited. Sipping greedily, I did my best to douse a heat my born-again, Spirit-filled, celibate self had zero business feeling.

Sitting here acting like Rahab, Jezebel, and Mary Magdalene.

Careful not to mar my makeup, I patted my face with a beverage napkin, feeling like a discount freak in sheep's clothing.

Humored by my ridonculousness, I couldn't help wanting to snatch another glimpse of his magnificence. I slowly glanced up only to encounter my best friend. She sat across the room, one arm at her waist, the other hand at her lips, eyes shrewdly swiveling between me and Mister Luscious. When her eyes lit up like she'd discovered something, I mouthed in annoyance, "What?"

Joy's handing me my earlier smugness had me sucking my teeth and returning my attention to my church-worthy drink. But for my mind-altering reactions to the tiniest drop of alcohol, I would've run my behind to Brother Bartender for something strong enough to heal a heat that needed extinguishing.

Suppressing a desire to simply sit and watch that man work the room, I grabbed my glass and headed for Thirty-Two Teeth and his bartending. I needed a water refill. No lime. Just ice. Anything to cool a sexual heat I'd never experienced in life.

Girl, you're pitiful and your panties are perspiring.

I inhaled deeply before slowly exhaling. I wouldn't beat up on myself. Or give Mister Alvarez undue credit. Yes, the man was Jesus-take-every-wheel kind of wonderful, but my fleshly friction wasn't solely because of him. Being "bothered in the britches"—as my Grams would say—was a byproduct of three years of abstinence.

Right?

Subtle as I could, I slid a peek in his direction only to find him—head and shoulders above others—returning my stare.

Lord, that heat thing!

The way he looked at me. The way I visually undressed him. We blistered and burned something somewhere.

Slapping my sinner-istic self into subjection, I headed for the restroom, hoping my clutch held extra pantiliners for the ungodly gush between my saved and celibate legs.

CHAPTER TWO
TEMPTATION IN A DRESS
Tavares Alvarez

Preferring to steer clear of fan follies, I'd stalled on Quinton's invite despite needing to chill. Being a venture capitalist side-hustling in real estate development and *Athletes & Academics*—my give-back-to-the-community project—my schedule was loaded. A brother was pressed if not stressed. But the sultry rhythms of my father's Latin music pulsing through the club had me dialing it down and glad to be there.

My heritage was mixed, and Carlos Santana was *Papi's* music. The kind I grew up with. It was as familiar as *Abuela's* menudo and *Mami's* black eyed peas, and *ponsit*. But I wasn't appreciating Santana's syncopated beats mirroring my pounding response to Miss Williams. Why did a ridiculously beautiful stranger have me on twelve shades of insane? I wasn't new to lust. But my gut-grinding, mind-tilting reaction was a whole other kind of raw and real.

"You ever think about going back? Or you good with being gone?"

It was rude not maintaining eye contact with the questioner, but my attention was on stray. I managed an intelligible, well-rehearsed answer to a variation of an oft-asked question while observing that sable goddess across the way.

I'd been good to the game, and the game had been good to me. But life was life. It moved on when it wanted. And when it did, I was ready. What I wasn't ready for was the woman wrecking my focus.

Babygirl is thirty-eleven flavors of flawless!

Posted up on one of the sofas strategically placed about the room, I was beyond stealing glances. Straight up, I was taking notes and scoping.

Plate in hand, I ate on autopilot, preoccupied with sable skin looking lustrous in the room's ambient lighting. The braids intricately designed atop her head, high cheekbones, almond eyes, and soft-looking lips completely drew me in. And the way she moved even while seated?

Fluid as a dancer. Still, on the real? There was nothing ballerina-esque in her build. Babygirl was opposite of the long, lean, barely-there women who'd overloaded my back-in-the-game days. This woman was what Papi called 'hurricane ready.'

Those curves and swerves ain't going nowhere.

She was fit-thick. Sexy-goddess-kind-of-solid.

Swapping my plate for the drink atop the sofa table, I sipped away the hot choke in my throat. On the real, I meant to stop eye-jocking, but I was stuck, inhaling her in.

Up top, Yazmeen Williams was tight and right. Snatched at the waist, she had seriously sensuous hips that I needed to grip. But when she slipped from her chair to join a group exiting the room, liquid splashed from my glass she had me so shook.

"Well...*dammmnnn...*"

I asked God's forgiveness for coming out of pocket, but I wasn't ready for the fullness.

"Yo, T., you alright?"

Glancing at Quinton, my "bwoi" since childhood, I flat out falsified. "I'm straight."

I wasn't. Trekking Yazmeen, I was swerved by heaven-kissed curves, that flirty, flared thing-of-a-hem floating above truly shapely legs that flowed into thick thighs, and a backside that straight blew my right mind.

Baby Boo had cakes for days!

La negra tiene tumbao...

The flavor of my father's favorite Celia Cruz tune oozed across my mind as I watched, liking entirely too much the way she, indeed, moved that high and mighty, proud and round behind like a Black Queen who need not step aside for anyone or anything.

"How y'all doing?" LaVelle Coleman appeared, blocking my view of booty and beauty. "Everybody getting enough to eat?"

Feeling like feeding a certain appetite I hadn't in half-a-decade, I refocused on the night's honoree. Like the brothers seated about me, I offered reassurance that everything was everything.

"Keep enjoying yourselves, but I need to steal my man." LaVelle didn't miss a beat grabbing her husband. "It's my birthday, baby, you gotta groove and grind with me." Pulling Ronnie to his feet, she issued a warning. "Some of y'all have wives and boos waiting on you. Stop collecting dust and go dance."

LaVelle's challenge elicited humorous comebacks and laughs.

"I still can't believe *the* Tavares "T-Alva" Alvarez is at my party! I told you I'm your *all*-time number one fan, right?"

Despite years on the court, genuine adoration could still bring on a blush. "Yes, Miss LaVelle, you did."

"About twenty-twelve times, bae. Come on before you scare the man," LaVelle's husband playfully checked her, maneuvering towards the door. Laughter accompanied the shuffling and shifting of bodies as brothers stood to search out their women.

"It was good talking with you, Tavares!"

Returning the handshake of a man who'd rattled off question after question about my career, I exchanged dap and pound with other brothers extending courtesy, kindness. As folks exited, I scanned the room, confirming what I already knew. It was absent of Miss Williams. I swallowed disappointment with the aid of an Arnold Palmer. After years of living off liquor, lemonade-on-tea was as strong as I was getting.

"T-Squared Acquisitions still making real estate moves? And how's that V.C. life, and the facility coming?"

Refocusing on Quinton, I placed my drink on the table and sat back. Stretching my legs, I rubbed my chest and assured him my community development business, T-Squared, named for myself and my twin sister, was still moving and grooving, restoring properties in low income neighborhoods before gentrification consumed them. The difference with T-Squared was we sold those properties back to our communities versus displacing residents. My venture capital hustle? It was all about investing in minority-owned start-ups and promising companies. "I went for that facility in San Rafael to keep it accessible to us. It's coming. A little slower than wanted, but we finished the refurbishing and basically have all components in place." *Athletes & Academics*, the brainchild I'd birthed before retiring the jersey two years ago, had grown beyond the small accommodations my church afforded. What started as youth outreach had grown into a full-fledged commitment. It required more time than initially anticipated but was my way of giving back some of the good I'd gained. "We're waiting on the inspector to come through and approve us for opening. We have thirty-five young bloods enrolled with twenty waitlisted."

"Growth's a good thing."

"Praise God, it is," I agreed. "A brother's hustling, but I can't complain."

"Well, I appreciate you coming through considering what's on your plate. I owe you."

"Kid, you always do." Laughing, I dodged Que's playful punch. "On the real, you know I got you." Pressing a fist to his, I dismissed tiredness from a full day of dealing with contractors and reviewing business proposals before navigating that congested Bay Area-to-Sacramento weekend traffic. True friends did what we do.

Que and I went back to childhood days when my family lived in Philly. We'd shared teen years and a road to manhood. Adult journeys took us in opposite directions, but our bond was blood. Through Quinton's college sweetheart surviving a brutal gang rape only to take her own life; through all my mess with Kryshelle, we'd had each other's back without judgment. Que's temporary relocation to Sacramento brought us in close proximity again. We were brotherhood unbroken.

"'Ey, I'm meeting a local developer tomorrow, plus the fam has a function, so coming a day early and staying overnight isn't putting me out any." Leaning forward, I braced my arms on my thighs and pinned him with a look. "So…what's up with this little work-around?" Grinning, I swirled a hand in a circular motion. "You milking this set-up of me being here as a surprise to LaVelle as some kinda way to juice your life up with Miss Joy?"

"Bruh, I needed reinforcement," Quinton joked.

Our shared laughter was deep, quiet.

"She's got you grinding?"

"T., that woman's making a brother put the work in! Truth? She's worth it."

"I just met her, but she feels real. Joy's a beautiful woman."

"That she is."

Sipping my drink, it was good seeing my friend open to love again. "I've never been one to squash a game so, bruh, do what you do. Just be clear about letting God work whatever *He* wants in her life first. When the time's right, if it's His will, He'll gift you to each other."

My words were a slap upside my head, making me wish I'd had better wisdom back when. Wisdom would've kept me walking. Away from Kryshelle's fakery and foolishness. Instead, I'd opted in on green contacts, butt-length blond weave, and surgically-made breasts.

Man's born dumb and dies dumber.

Abuela's homily stopped me from stomping myself. I'd lived. I'd learned. My pain was my past, and I prayed I was better for it. Plus, I didn't walk away empty-handed. I had Aniyah, my best blessing and five-year-old princess. As Quinton updated me on his work, part of me wondered if my better self would ever find a woman who wanted the real Tavares, raw flaws and all, and not my wallet.

One day. When God wanted and willed. Until then, I was content. Even if my mind was relentlessly stuck on a beauty who'd long ago left.

Watching her work that dance floor like she meant business, I felt rhythm-less. Heated. Needy. And *real* greedy. Like I hadn't had sex in fifteen versus five years and was about to die if I didn't. Laughing at myself, I considered my environment in an effort to escape fantasies of doing things with Yazmeen Williams guaranteed to bust a bed.

Club Neo was interesting. I'd flowed floor-to-floor checking the musical vibe on each. The R&B had been smooth. The EDM was much for my mellow. But the Latin groove moved me as I sat on the sidelines of level three lusting after Yazmeen.

Positioned as I was on raised seating about the room's perimeter, I had a nearly clear and unobstructed view. I felt stalker-ish observing her without her awareness. But a brother couldn't be blamed. Miss Williams was mad mesmerizing.

You've been female-free far too long.

Five years to be exact. Five years of disciplining my flesh. All because I'd had enough of women like Kryshelle and the fakery of the dating scene. And because my relationship with the Lord meant more than random pop-offs and booty-getting.

Trust! A saved and sexless life was about as easy as walking barefoot on hot butcher knives. But grace kept me, helped me manage abstinence while negotiating the natural needs and challenges of a healthy body and strong sexual appetite. But sitting, watching an exceptional example of God-kissed femininity, I had a noteworthy arousal and uncomfortable curiosity.

God help a born-again brother. Please!

Miss Yazmeen Williams was way too intoxicating. When shaking her hand, I hadn't peeped a ring and assumed she was a miss, not someone's missus. At least I prayed she wasn't, seeing as how babygirl had me all caught up and wanting to backslide a bit.

T., find an ice block and sit.

I was straight tripping, lusting on a woman like I hadn't in all five years since opting on abstinence. Reminding myself that lust was a sin didn't ease my groin or what was wanting to be an erection.

Back down, beast! I'm not here for the south rising.

Snorting at my craziness, I forced my focus elsewhere. That lasted two minutes before my eyes decided they knew best and made their way back to temptation in a dress.

Easily, she stood out from the crowd of dancing bodies getting busy. Maybe it was the all-white. Or the fact that she moved as if she and music were one; and together they were oxygen, life, and blood. Her soft, sensuous movements triggered one thought.

Ella es una hermosa mariposa.

She was a beautiful butterfly. Unquestionably.

Pleasantness took a dip when a tall, young brother moved in. Until then, she'd been dancing freely without a man. When she smiled up at new dude, allowed him to take her hand and lead her into a spin, my jaw spasmed.

That is not your woman.

"She could be." I headed for the dance floor, wanting the angel light of her smile solely for me.

I'd developed an immunity to the stir and whir my former pro-baller status sometimes caused. I wasn't fazed by the buzz of recognition or folks lifting cell phones for photos. My attention was anchored on one woman. Posting up behind her, I was there when she came out of a spin and stumbled into me so that our bodies collided.

Her hands bracing my chest was instinctive. Steadying her waist with my hands was deliberate.

"I'm so sorry..." Her gaze was friendly, open, until traveling upward.

Light shifted and played in her eyes as a slow, creeping warmth spread where her hands spanned my chest, wherever our bodies connected. The lovely lady's nearness was luscious. Dangerous. I should've stepped back. Instead, I stared into her face, unable to look away.

"*T-Alva!* Yo! Is that you, dude?"

I barely glanced at young blood who'd been her dance partner. "It is. Mind if I cut in?" Hand at her back, I shifted her in the opposite direction without waiting for an answer. "Hello, again. Yazmeen, right?"

Man, quit 'acking' ignorant. Her name's engraved on your brain.

"Yes, and hello to you, too, Tavares." On that warm, velvet voice, my name sounded worthy of satin sheets and The Isleys.

"I hope I interrupted something."

Her laughter was silky, sultry. "You obviously did."

"Good." Grinning down at her, I liked her nearness and the soft notes of her scent. Being "tri-racial" I hated when folks referred to me as exotic. But it was the only way to describe her fragrance. "May I join you?"

She hesitated momentarily. "I'd like that."

Claiming space on the dance floor, we eased into a light and simple salsa—matching the music, and easily adjusting to each other's rhythm. I liked the way she held my gaze and let our bodies naturally sync. But I wasn't feeling the loud music that had me practically yelling.

"You're a very smooth woman...I like your sensuality...and the heat in your body. I mean...you move like you could bring it...*not in bed*...on the dance floor." I over-corrected, "All I'm saying, Miss Yazmeen is...you flow...like a real dancer. Not that you're fake or anything."

I wanted to punch myself for babbling.

That angel smile was gracious. "I understood your meaning."

I grinned at my own idiocy. "How long did you study ballet?"

My question brought a strange look to her lovely face. "Why do you think I studied classical dance?"

"Your sexiness has a certain elegance." There I was blurting again. I hurried on, hoping she wasn't offended, or didn't consider me God's goofiest idiot. "Why does my question surprise you?"

"Most folks don't look at me and think Misty Copeland."

"Most folks didn't look at Misty Copeland and think ballet, but she changed the game."

"True."

"So, how long?" I reiterated, earning her soft smile with my persistence.

"From the age of five through college. So, seventeen years."

"Why'd you stop?" Taking her hand, I led her in a series of fast spins that she flawlessly executed.

She came out of the final turn, wide-eyed. "You know something about Latin dance!"

"My dad would disown me if I didn't." Her sultry laughter lit something lethal just below my abdomen. "About that ballet...you stopped because...?"

"Life said 'enough.'"

Her answer held an untold story, but I didn't push while indulging my senses with her nearness. Still holding her hand, I thumbed its softness until she gently freed herself from my grip. Something in this woman called me to touch her, once and again.

Song after song, we gigged. Salsa. To merengue. And more. When a slow, sensuous beat sizzled across the air, she backed away, claiming a need for rest. "You're wearing me out, Mr. Alvarez."

"'Tavares', and I doubt that." Clearly, she was a trained professional who could wipe my behind across that floor without a sweat. "But if you'd like to take a break..." Lifting a hand, I indicated leaving the crowded space, respecting whatever her reasons for preferring to avoid dancing that slow, grinding beat with me. She proceeded. I followed, like I was moth and she was flame, flunking my half-hearted attempts to not watch her luscious behind swishing and those God-have-mercy hips swaying.

Heavenly Father, You mind taking a communion break and giving me twenty minutes? That's all I need. That, a bed, condoms. Lubricant. And these right here hips stroking it.

For the second time that night, I asked God's forgiveness and gave my game some act right.

Finding an isolated spot in a quiet area conducive to conversation, I felt hot attraction in more ways than needed. Removing my jacket, tie, and unfastening the top buttons of my shirt, I tossed the gear across the sofa and rolled up my shirt sleeves while leaving enough safe space between us as I sat, scoping our surroundings. "This is good. We don't have to holler to be heard. Thank you."

"For?"

"Indulging an amateur. I enjoyed dancing with you." Yazmeen had me triggering. This time something in the vicinity of my chest responded when she offered the full warmth of her smile.

"It wasn't a hardship."

"Speak for yourself." Acting all animated, I whipped the pocket square from my discarded suit jacket and dabbed my face. "Keeping pace with you was killing me."

Yet again, a strange sensation skipped across my chest when she tossed her head back, offering that sexy, slightly husky laugh. Her head angled like that, I wanted to taste the long column of her neck, to suck and lick that satin skin.

"Don't ballers have legendary stamina?"

Her innocent challenge conjured visions of us in bed, in some wicked contest of who could outlast the other and climax last. *"Just damn."*

"Pardon?"

"My apologies." Patting my mouth with that pocket square, I made a dismissive gesture. "Ignore me."

"That's an impossibility." I couldn't help grinning when she rushed to cover embarrassment caused by her slip of the lip. "You actually did work up a sweat. And you missed a spot."

She reached for my silk square. Releasing it, I willingly surrendered to her leaning in, patting perspiration from my hot forehead until the side of her breast brushed my arm. She jerked back as if experiencing the same flash of fire I felt.

"Pardon me for invading your space." The husk in her voice confirmed she'd been equally affected by the flare.

I had to thank God for the lack of a tie at the neck of my open shirt. A brother needed oxygen. "Apology unnecessary and not accepted. You really smell delicious."

T., you sound like a horny fourteen-year-old fool.

Truth was true. When she'd leaned against me, I'd deeply inhaled the sweet spice of her scent. She smelled tropical. Like something I wanted on my tongue, my lips.

"I'll give my sister, Sasha, your compliments."

"She deserves them because?"

"She has a line of body care products. Sasha's Essentials. They're the only products worthy of my skin. Did that sound like a walking advertisement?"

Rubbing my hands down my thighs, imagining the pleasure of smoothing potions and lotions over the beautiful brown of her bare body, I chuckled a bit. "It did, but it's all good. I like you, Miss Yazmeen." Sitting forward, arms braced on wide-spread legs, I had to breathe deeply before going all in. "If I'm out of pocket, it's not my intent. May I see you again?"

Her face wasn't only exceptionally beautiful, it was highly expressive, showcasing a slideshow of emotions as she struggled for an answer. "Tavares, I'm flattered—"

"No flattery necessary. Like my *Abuela* says, 'truth is true'. You're an alluring, fascinating woman. I'd like to get to know you."

Her touch was gentle when she placed her hand on mine. "I appreciate your interest."

"But?"

Silence swirled between us before she offered a non-answer. "Thank you for sharing your evening with me."

Accepting defeat wasn't easy, but it was my only option.

Grabbing my jacket, I assisted her to her feet while standing. "My evening was blessed because of you." Feeling her shiver when I kissed her hand had me wondering how responsive the rest of her would be if I kissed her everywhere, every way I wanted.

Squashing hot thoughts, I played at being magnanimous. In reality, I felt fifty degrees of defeated. That didn't keep me from acting the gentleman. With a light touch at the small of her back, I navigated us through the crowd to the private room where LaVelle was being serenaded "Happy Birthday" in too many keys to name or tame.

I was surprised by Que's Joy taking a knife to what I thought was a purse. Turned out to be some red velvet deliciousness that I accepted when a slice made it my way. I sat back and enjoyed, giving my mouth the sweet the rest of me wasn't experiencing.

This woman...

I double-dog dared myself not to look. But my eyes stayed on stray as if I had no control of my neck. Head kept swiveling in the direction of a woman who'd essentially told me to kick bricks. She wasn't interested.

My past randomness was something I regretted, but it taught me to move on when my interests weren't reciprocated. With virtually unlimited options, I never pushed my way into a woman's world. I respected a "no," and never pressed a female. So, I didn't get my mental insistence. I must've enjoyed punishment. Or maybe it was prolonged abstinence and horny hormones fouling up my intelligence. There was no other explanation for my dumb determination. It bordered on imbecilic. I admit it. Still, all I knew was I was about to put some prayer and energy on making sure I saw Yazmeen Williams again.

CHAPTER THREE
OPERATION DODGE-A-DUDE
Yazmeen

I loved my church despite having married my ex-troglodyte there. We had a vibrant congregation that reflected our Pastor's and First Lady's spirits. Down-to-earth people who'd offered unwavering support when my free-ninety-nine marriage went sideways, our leaders were as genuine up-close as they appeared to be when ministering. I knew firsthand as a church employee, and "life coaching" client of First Lady.

Large but not intimidating, our nondenominational, rainbow coalition congregation probably reflected heaven. Even so, we were predominantly African-American with one of the best church bands in town.

Enjoying my family's contribution, my little ole chest poked out with pride. I loved seeing my cousin Jamal at the keyboard giving his talents back to God. Jamal played with secular artists occasionally, but this was where I saw and heard the sweetness of his gift.

The praise team—led by a sister with a little Tata Vega in her vocals—had me all energetic despite minimal sleep thanks to LaVelle's party and my naked-nasty dreams.

Tavares Alvarez went to bed with me—in my mind, at least—and refused to leave.

I woke up twice last night rebuking nocturnal nasties featuring His Fineness, and calling Lucifer all kinds of lies. Made absolutely zero sense acting all heffa-and-ho-ish over a man I'd barely met. But I had until, disturbed by the ludicrous dampness between my legs, I'd cleaned my business, grabbed my Bible and put some Proverbs 31 on my flesh.

It took two rounds of that and some scary, apocalyptic passages in Revelation to set me straight again. But I finally got that dreamless sleep with the help of the Virtuous Woman, and the four horsemen.

That was last night or, better stated, this morning. Thankfully, I was back to being sexless and sanctified in the sanctuary, feeling purified in the presence of worship so sweet I couldn't help lifting—questionably—holy hands.

Lord, You are too good to me.

Despite my struggles and needs.

Being a *divorced* mother of toddler twins, my challenges were as real as the next person's. Coupons were my favorite cousins, and I'd turned thrift store shopping into an art and science. Not a month passed that my money wasn't funny or my change didn't have to be rearranged, but that couldn't alter my heavenly Father's grace. God and I didn't agree on everything, but we loved each other fiercely. Despite my hills and valleys, He was excellent in all of His ways. Grateful, I poured appreciation on my worship and praise.

Obviously, I wasn't the only parishioner feeling the Father's presence. Folks were into His adoration. Saints were crying and bowing, taking love next level. The praise team leader and singers were useless, personally caught up in worship. By the time First Lady took the podium, we'd been to spiritual nirvana and back.

I knew my face was a hot, crying wreck and a mess when reclaiming my seat. That sent me on an expedition through my bottomless purse for a tissue that wasn't contaminated by Twin cooties to wipe my Mary Don't You Weep-ing eyes. Mascara and high worship didn't mix, and I probably looked like a Raccoon for Christ.

Finding my cosmetic bag, I snapped open my compact and mentally hissed at myself.

Girl, you look like a domino in reverse.

White tissue bits plastered all over my Brown Girl face, I took care to correct my dotted-up situation, thankful as always for the presence of the Lord and the "me time" of Sundays.

Loved my babies to infinity, but one of the benefits of attending a progressive church was an excellent children's ministry. Malcolm and, even my shy guy, Malik loved it, leaving me ninety minutes to sit and participate in grown folks' service each Sunday. Just then, First Lady was trying to read the opening scriptures, but that worship was still on elevate. Tossing my compact back into my bag, I had a hand in the air, blessing Him when the monitor images panned the sanctuary and I saw a woman entering who resembled my "bestest."

I wish.

My B.F.F. was clear about never stepping foot in a church again unless she was "crunched in a casket." That girl had me and Velle praying she'd yield her heart to the Lord, sooner versus later. Last night's post-party fiasco had me praying even harder.

Cruising back in the party limo Velle's husband rented, we'd arrived at their place to find someone had gone Jazmine Sullivan on Joy's vehicle with a brick. Her windows were busted, and a nasty note was left that had me worried the anonymous vandalizer was that freak-a-deak stalker she'd recently acquired at that companion club, part-time job. Top that with the fact that something happened between she and Quinton that had him hard-jawed and exiting. But all of that was last night's story. Right then and there, I did a double-take seeing a woman entering the row and looking too much like…

"Joy?"

Amazing how we could pray only to act ignorant when God answered.

Seeing Joy navigate the persons between us until she was sitting beside me, I was struck double dumb. Snatching myself back to reality, I squeezed her so hard I cracked her back while asking what she was doing there. She couldn't fathom an answer.

Lord, the power of prayer!

"I gotta tell Velle."

Only after texting did I consider the fact that Velle and Ronnie were seated several rows ahead accompanied by someone Joy might not want privy to her presence. When Velle whipped her head around and visually located us, LaVelle's tapping her husband and Quinton and pointing in our direction was automatic. My girl stiffened when Quinton slid her some tight, attitudinal look. Squeezing Joy's hand was me offering consolation on a situation that had obviously gone bad. Too happy to have my girl beside me, I prayed God would right it again.

The offering collection finished, the choir serenaded us with a beautiful ballad that spoke of God's incredible mercy. That slow jam had my eyes extra misty as I sat beside my bestie. I was about to be up on my feet, hands raised in praise when Joy pinched my leg so hard I needed to either slap her or scream. I did neither thanks to the fact that what she was animatedly indicating left me scatterbrained.

My mouth was mile-wide watching a party of two entering late and making their way to where Quinton sat, finger discreetly in the air like some kind of traffic conductor.

"Yaz, you see this?"

My favorite college professor insisted dumb questions didn't exist. Joy thoroughly debunked that.

How could I not see the couple claiming the empty seats Quinton had obviously saved? Even if I was sight-impaired, my body was registering. Warming. Thanks to the newly arrived Tavares Alvarez.

Really, Lord? I just put some holy on my horny and had myself happily saved and sanctified again.

Apparently, the doors of God's house were open to orgasmic-looking men.

Sacramento had no shortage of churches. If the man needed Jesus, couldn't he find Him elsewhere?

My normally even-keeled, level-headed self was suddenly salty.

Because?

I hated when self asked questions when self had the answers.

Because! My sacred space felt intruded upon.

Better told, I didn't like the instant squirming or burning resulting from the man's presence. The sight of him was like a boomerang for the brain, taking me back to last night and how, on occasion, our dancing brought us so close that I felt his solid muscles against mine. That, combined with his touch, his scent, his *everything* had been uncomfortably next level sexy. When I declined his desire to know me better and he, like a gentleman, kissed my hand, I swear his lips on my skin had me ovulating.

It was ridiculous, the effects a total stranger elicited. I'd never responded to a man like I had Tavares. Not appreciating the reinsertion of His Fineness in my face, I forced myself to slowly exhale like I'd learned in meditation.

"Yaz, you alright?" Joy's whisper snatched me back.

Forgive me, but I lied in the house of the Lord. "Yes."

I so was not. I wanted to do like the Prophet Elijah and get sucked up in a God-sent whirlwind. Eyes closed, I was shaking, wishing the man was a figment of some hyper heffa imagination. But, no, not so. When I looked again, he was still there, his too edible image commanding space on the big screen monitors at the front of the sanctuary.

Tavares Alvarez, the very real embodiment of my happy ho dreams, had come to church with me.

"You know her? Is she a member?"

Just like that, Joy's whisper-hissed inquiry harnessed my heat.

Thanks to past experiences and two hell-sent exes, I had a massive aversion to anything smelling like infidelity. Their relationship was none of my business, but Sir Sexy and the woman in his presence were clearly well-acquainted. That had me acting detective-ish, trying to analyze a sister.

Mesmerized by Tavares' unexpected presence, I'd only caught a glimpse of her. Still, she seemed familiar. Maybe that was because she reminded me of Joy. Tall. Plus-size, voluptuous. Caramel-skinned. That's where the similarities ended. Opposite of Joy's short and fashionable flare, sister had wild, curly, beautiful big hair. Unlike my bestie, Miss Companion seemed genuinely pleased to be in the house of the Lord.

Is she his boo?

If so, I gave him props for being with a sister who didn't fit stereotypical images of what, presumably, was an "acceptable" B-Baller's babe. Evidently, he wasn't shallow, and appreciated beauty beyond a size two. Maybe I'd misjudged him last night in thinking he was merely toying with some sort of sister-of-substance fantasy when expressing interest in me.

Pump your brakes, Yaz. He's her man.

I had no intention of doing anything about my physical reaction to him. His being with someone made him absolutely off limits. Truth put me back in proper position and allowed me to refocus as Pastor launched into an empowering sermon about God's divine timing and the seasons of our lives.

I did good, focused on the Word, minded my born-again business despite the camera person having a love affair with Tavares' image.

A sister must be manning the camera today.

It was ludicrous, a tad too obvious how that camera panned Sir Sexy again. And again. Humored by the ridiculousness, I froze finding myself the new object of the camera's affection.

My image on blast, I glanced his way, observing the impact.

I saw it: that moment he recognized me on the big screen.

Even from the back, I noticed his shoulders lifting, straightening before his head swung around so fast, he must've self-inflicted whiplash. He even did that crane-the-neck-looking-past-other-folks thing in his attempts to verify that who he saw was truly Yazmeen. Despite the distance, when our eyes connected, I felt that unneeded, unappreciated heat in the house of The King.

Really, I needed to break that visual connection, but couldn't.

I sat stuck and staring at that incredible, edible mountain of a masterpiece until his boo thang glanced back to see who or what had his attention. That snapped that.

Scrounging through my purse suddenly became my life's work. Needing to occupy my time and not be the subject of a couple's curiosity, I was searching for nothing.

Finished wasting several seconds of my life, I squared my shoulders and dared to look up only to find Joy watching me. Her crooked smile was annoying. "Yes…?"

Girlfriend quietly busted me. "I hope y'all have fire extinguishers in here 'cause you and *Señor* Alvarez 'bout to burn up before the benediction."

Putting Joy on ignore, I fixed my mind on Pastor's message and dutifully dodged every fiery-dart-distraction of a man I didn't know, didn't want, and definitely couldn't have.

Benediction barely said, I pulled Joy from the sanctuary and left her in the lobby waiting on LaVelle while I retrieved my children. My actions were quick, fast, and in an unholy hurry.

Yazmeen, what's your problem?

Self had nerve asking, as if not understanding my zero need to interface with Tavares Alvarez ever again. His being with someone should've doused all heat or interest. Problem was it did but didn't. Not appreciating lingering thoughts of him, I wanted to avoid encountering His Fineness and reactivating any unrighteousness.

God loved me, and blessed Operation Dodge-a-Dude to be a success. I managed to introduce Joy to Pastor and First Lady, exchange hugs and love with Velle, and was hustling my tribe of "two twins" and a best friend towards the exit without a T-Alva sighting when my second-born busted my disappearing plans.

"Mommy, I have to potty."

"Malik, honey, can you hold it until we get to Titi's?" With Joy's car down due to her busted window episode, we were taking her home. Not wanting to deal with Quinton, she'd opted out of LaVelle's post birthday dinner. Sure, my girl lived twenty minutes away, but I was willing to run red lights and do sixty in school zones if necessary. Anything to leave church and avoid running into him. And seeing as how it was Sunday, school zones were free of kids. It was a win-win.

"Mommy, I can't."

"Are you sure, Malie?" I invoked my baby's nickname as added enticement.

When Malik crooked his finger, I leaned down so my son could whisper-spit in my ear. "I don't gotta pee pee, Mommy. I gotta do number two, and I can tell it's gonna be big."

Gazing into the beautiful brown of my baby's wide eyes, I longed for the days of diapers, and wished he wore Depends. "Malcolm, sweetie, do you need to go, too?"

Preoccupied with his Titi Joy, my firstborn couldn't care about waste removal.

Handing Joy my car keys and explaining where my SUV was parked, I smiled down at my youngest. "Little Mister, make this quick."

Clutching my hand and skipping happily, my precious child had the nerve to tell me, "Mommy, I poop at my pace."

Touché, and flush away.

"*Uncle Jamal!*"

"Hey, Malie!"

"Malik, don't run in the lobby." My motherly caution was practically ignored as my son, finished with his bathroom business, propelled himself rocket-style at my cousin.

The youngest offspring of my deceased uncle, Jamal and his brother, Bryce, had spent so many summers with my family that he was a big brother to me and an uncle to my children. Seeing Malik bending Jamal's ear, talking a mile-a-minute, I was thankful that, despite their flaky father's shortcomings, my sons had strong Black men to love them. "Hey, Cuz."

"Whaddup, Yazzy?" Malik in one arm, Jamal embraced me with the other. "You look good, girl."

The pumpkin-colored, flare-legged pants and waist-cinched jacket with flowing tails in the back was one of my favorite thrift store finds. "Thanks. You were burning those keys today!"

"Yeah, I was getting it. I'm 'bout to blow up, so touch me while you can," my cousin kidded.

Laughing, knowing first hand my cousin was a humble man, I wrapped my arm about his and turned, intent on exiting the edifice. Instead, I was paralyzed, frozen. In the foyer, near the front doors, a cluster of youth had crowded about one very tall, delectable individual. He stood in their center, temporarily oblivious to the fandoration for staring across the distance at yours truly.

Something hot ripped through me. Just like that, I was back in Lusty Land.

Sir Sexy is off limits.

I forced that truth on my horny hormones, but my body did that warming thing that only this man unleashed. I stood there staring like an unblinking owl with no home-training.

God was going to get me for wanting to lick my lips and do things with my hips, but I couldn't help it.

This man!

I disliked him. Better stated, I hated that he made me feel eighty shades of sensuous and delicious without obvious effort, like I'd readily lay down abstinence and defy my morals to get some of that lusciousness. Suited up with a silky-looking tie at his neck, and yet another color-coordinated pocket square adding just the right flair, he was debonair. Scrumptious. Watching him had me high from an overload of man candy goodness.

I need insulin.

"Yazzy?" That extra in my cousin's tone indicated maybe he'd called me more than once. "What's up?"

My head snapped back like I'd broken a trance.

Glancing again at Mister Luscious, I saw him scrutinizing all narrow-eyed, miscalculating my little situation. Jamal holding Malik, me with an arm about my cousin's, must've transmitted "happy nuclear family." I went with it. If Tavares thought Jamal was my man maybe he'd lessen his sex appeal and stop intentionally enchanting me.

And he's doing that how, Yazmeen?

By simply breathing.

Clutching Jamal's arm, I tried steering us towards a side exit. "I'm good. Let's go."

That's when simultaneous happenings happened.

"Daddy!"

Malik squealing and squirming out of Jamal's arms perfectly synced with my cousin's, "Whoa! Wait! I was sitting at the keys thinking, 'dude looks like T-Alva' when he walked in. That's 'cause it is him!'"

Malik took off one way. My cousin headed in Tavares' direction. And I felt a tap on my lonely, shook shoulder.

"Excuse me, aren't you India's sister?"

I'm sure I looked as ignorant as I felt trying to master multi-mayhem. Jamal had pushed his way through the quasi-throng to introduce himself to Mister Luscious while my son jumped into the arms of his fickle, flea-ridden father.

Who comes to church after *it's over?*

Royal's late entrance was as ludicrous as he. As usual, he was sagging and swagging, looking like an unpaid video extra wannabe. From experience, I knew every piece of Royal's expensive gangsta get-up cost more than I'd seen in child support in years. Royal's champagne taste and Cracker Jack income were long-lived.

I could've bought the boys a year's worth of shoes with the amount he spent on his.

Telling myself that ex-spouse-icide was a sin, I focused on the person who'd tapped my shoulder questioning my connection to kin.

Lord, it's about to get real.

With my sister India owning a natural hair care salon and being active in multiple community organizations, she seemed to know half of Sacramento's Black populace. With our looking so similar, coming across someone who knew her wasn't a rarity. But this encounter God could've kept. He obviously had jokes and felt the need to spank me for pandering to my flesh. I couldn't do a thing except hope my Judas smile looked guiltless while staring at, none other than, the companion of His Fineness. "Yes, I am."

"I thought so! I'm her client. Reina Kingsley." Her speaking voice was lyrical, musical as if gifted with singing abilities. "It's so good seeing you again."

Honey, if you knew the dreams I've had about your man you'd WWF clothesline my neck.

"Yazmeen Williams," I offered, inwardly laughing at the Lord's way of tossing water in my face. Meeting Reina Kingsley up front and personal proved a perfect antidote for any stray Tavares Alvarez imaginations. Her sweetness squashed wayward shenanigans and set me on the straight and narrow again. "We've met?"

"Not officially, but I remember you and your other sister being in the audience with India at last year's jazz festival," she explained, undisturbed by my rude distraction.

Conversing with her while keeping an eye on my child, praying he didn't catch a doofus disease from his father, wasn't easy. "I apologize...I'm trying to watch my son."

"No worries."

Watching Royal pimp-limping towards me, Malik in tow, I half gave Reina my attention only to do a double-take as if seeing her for the first time. "Wait, Reina, that's why you seemed familiar!"

That jazz festival set had been a last-minute gig for both of them, but when asked to fill in for a friend, my cousin-brother, Jamal, had agreed to play keys for a promising artist. And that same velvet-voiced singer just happened to be with Tavares?

I didn't believe in coincidence. This was a divine butt-whooping.

"Is this your church?" she questioned, gazing around the foyer. "It's beautiful. And wasn't that Jamal Williams on the keys? We did that festival together last year." Reina was sweet, with a gentle, open friendliness, but the girl could talk and fast. "Wait! *Williams.* You're related right? Speaking of, let me introduce you to my cousin, Tavares."

"Whaddup, Yaz?" Royal's arrival interrupted my processing Reina's revelation, as well as my serenity.

"Mommy, Daddy's here!"

Wishing I had selective blindness to block Beelzebub's baby, I simply responded, "I see." Refusing to be rude, I added, "Royal, this is Reina Kingsley."

"Why you ain't answering my calls?" Royal rudely ignored Reina's greeting. "You realize I got money to make? Do the video."

My whole world fogged up with Royal's foulness.

Reaching for Malik, I propped him on my hip to keep from kicking his father in the neck. "Let's not revisit that." I'd been crystal clear when declining a demand dressed like an "invitation" to dance in a rap video. Been there. Done that. Wished I hadn't. "Reina, it was really nice seeing you, but—"

"Where's Malcolm?"

I just couldn't with Royal's unnecessary rudeness. Putting him on ignore I exchanged goodbyes with Reina, intent on exiting church crime-free. Instead, pivoting in the direction of my vehicle, I collided with a wall of muscle that felt delicious in its familiarity.

"Hello, Yazmeen."

That sexy baritone deserved a blue ribbon for dipping me in dangerous liquid and doing sixty-eleven, illegal nasty things to me. His steadying hold at my waist had my body acting as if it deserved to be touched, and held, and live life centered in the strength of his embrace. I felt like a fool for wanting another woman's man only to remember Reina calling Tavares her cousin. That was a green light not good for me, my salvation, or celibacy.

"Hey, young man."

I escaped wanting and wishing when he removed a hand from my waist to extend it to my son, leaving me to experience the void of his touch.

Overprotective mother that I was, I actually appreciated him acknowledging my child and introducing himself as if Malik mattered. Not that I was in the market for a man, but most brothers became track stars and did a Jesse Owens in the opposite direction when discovering I had twins or, conversely, ignored my sons as if nonexistent.

I'd taught my children stranger danger. They knew not to divulge personal information. Surprisingly enough, my shy guy—who typically hid behind me when meeting someone—looked at me, silently wanting permission to return Tavares' greeting. When I nodded, my son shook his oversized hand.

"I'm Malik." My baby pointed at me. "And that's Mommy."

Tavares' deep rumbling laugh got lost in Royal's stepping up, all swollen as if I was his current not his ex. Tavares extended a hand, prepared to introduce himself.

Pulling me back as if that hand was contaminated, my children's sperm donor all but spat on it. "Nigga, I don't need to know you, and neither does my son."

Royal's rankness was mortifying. And tongue-tying. Looking at Tavares, I couldn't even apologize on Le Troll's brain-dead behalf. I merely managed to grab Jamal's arm, feeling my cousin tighten up at Royal's ridiculousness. We were in the church foyer and not about to WWF.

"Reina. Tavares. It was a pleasure seeing you, and I regret that you were subjected to…this." Knowing His Ignorance would follow, twin on my hip, I turned my cousin away from Reina—whom he'd been chatting with—and towards the side exit before either of us could jab Royal's jugular.

"Yazmeen!"

Royal and Tavares calling my name in perfect sync had me stalling. Royal's rendition was nails on chalkboard. Tavares' silky smooth felt simply golden.

I made the mistake of glancing back to find them grid-locked in a stare-off, mugging each other like, "Boy, who *you* calling?"

I left that test of testosterone untouched.

Walking fast in my own rendition of Sophia stomping through *The Color Purple's* cornfields, my head said I was leaving church before assassinating my ex. Truthfully, I was accustomed to his foolishness. What had me pressed was *that man*, the one who made it hard for my panties to stay moisture-less. *He* made it necessary for me to hone my skills as an escape artist.

God be my strength. I had to keep Tavares Alvarez *far* from the range of my existence.

CHAPTER FOUR
MISSING
Tavares

W hat's up with Thug-a-Mug?"
My cousin laughed as if the humor was all hers. Personally, I saw *nada* funny about dude's rancidness. He wasn't salty. He was pure acid.

"As if I know," Reina responded. "Maybe he didn't like you stepping to his woman."

"Is she?"

"What?"

"His woman?"

Headed to the whip, my cousin stalled at my question. "I don't know Yazmeen like that, Tav. Why're you asking?"

"I'm curious."

Reina stared up at me like my face was a crystal ball she could easily read. "Tav, you're crushing?"

"I'm curious." As to why the Suge Knight wannabe was tight about me approaching Yazmeen. I mean, I understood. The woman was special. Extra enticing. I would've puffed up at another brother pressing my good thing, too. But unless she was his boo, he had no cause to flex like a class act fool.

When first noticing her across that foyer, he hadn't even factored into my focus. Had he, I wouldn't have—as Reina said—stepped to her. Being a third leg in other folks' relationships wasn't my thing. But I *had* approached, and per her facial expressions and body language, Thug-a-Mug wasn't particularly welcome in her intimate orbit. Didn't mean he hadn't been. Based on the fact that her son looked exactly like him, he obviously had. That was impetus enough for me to step back. I wasn't anti-women-with-children. I was anti-dramatics. And dude was that.

Still, not much for coincidence, short Suge didn't keep me from considering my running into Miss Williams a divine occurrence. Hadn't

I prayed before crawling into bed at *Abuela's* last night, 'Lord, if seeing Yazmeen again lines up with Your perfect will then let it happen?'

I knew better than forcing fate, so I'd left that prayer in the Lord's lap and got to snoring. Walking into God's house and seeing her that morning had me wide awake. As had her hip-switching exit.

Dude's rankness had her fleeing that foyer, hips rolling fast and furious, sinking me in an ocean and needing Dramamine from all that yam action.

Now, opening the car door for my cousin, I was staring into space, hot memories messing with my wayward member.

"Hola, primo! Qué pasa con usted?"

What was up with me? My disloyal libido that insisted on doing its thing.

"I'm straight, Cousin." Answering in English, I waited for her to get in my whip. Instead, she stood there staring.

"Oh my God, Tav. You *are* crushing." My cousin had the nerve to squeal before hugging me, all congratulatory.

"Get in the car, Rae, or you're walking." Closing the door when she complied, I moved to the opposite side of the Cayenne and took a deep breath before sliding in, hoping to put whatever my cousin had peeped on disguise. I obviously failed because Reina picked up like she hadn't left off.

"This isn't fake news. You're feeling Miss Williams."

"Fine, Rae. Say what you want." I couldn't deny an attraction, but I didn't need family in my face about it.

"Trust, I'm saying it. You're interested, which is major seeing as how your never-been-opened-nose is spreading."

Fastening my seatbelt, I reversed from the parking space, wishing my cousin was exaggerating. She wasn't.

Having "lost" my virginity at sixteen—and after a life as a pro-baller—I'd had much sexualizing. I'd been in and out of beds and in between legs, just never in love. Now my life was "from feast to famine." Like a monk's vow of poverty, celibacy had me on lock these past five years from all things feminine and sultry. Until Yazmeen. She broke my well-constructed No Booty barriers and was sitting in my lap, front and center, winking at me. At least mentally.

Babygirl had me wishing she was. On my lap. Literally. Grinding. That galactic behind doing its thing. With all her sensual dance movements. Straight giving a brother pleasure and peace.

Shifting into drive and glancing at the edifice we'd just left, I caught a glimpse of a cross above the multi-doored entrance.

I'd gone to church for fellowship and the Word only to leave fighting an erection.

My family was loud. We were Puerto Rican with swirls of African American here and there. My siblings and I put some Filipino on the table as well. Representing highly vocal cultures, we always had much to say in whatever tongue we chose: Spanish, English, and Spanglish. We did it loud and fast, holding simultaneous conversations that would give an outsider a headache. Such was *La Familia Alvarez*.

Stuffing my face with my aunt's black bean salsa and fried plantains, I argued sports stats and player strengths and weaknesses with cousins. Mind you we were supposed to be finalizing plans for my grandmother's "Celebration of Life" versus arguing and eating.

Abuela had been diagnosed with stage four lymphoma eleven years ago and given a life expectancy of eighteen months. Having lost our grandfather to renal failure the year prior, the Alvarez clan wasn't having it. Our Catholic contingent did that Hail Mary, while the Santeria-practicing went to chanting. We charismatic Christians dug into prayer and fasting. Faith was faith and, combined with chemotherapy, my grandmother was the miracle that lived. God had been good and gracious. Now, His healing power had us celebrating a decade of *Abuela's* complete remission.

"*Cállete! I need you thick-heads to shut up and listen!*"

Reina's shout-out was accompanied by my aunt's fingers-in-the-mouth dog whistle. We shut it down and paid attention.

"Okay, listen up, *mi familia*. We meet the photographer at the McKinley Park rose gardens at nine o'clock next Saturday. Use your white people watches and be on time." My aunt's reprimand left us laughing.

"Come on P.C.T. if you want and full payment for the shoot will come from your pocket," Reina added, eyeing those notorious for strolling in if and when "the Spirit hit them." Thus, the P.C.T.—People of Color Time—comment.

"If you crazy Alvarezes act right, the whole shoot should take an hour, ninety minutes top. The photographer'll have the proofs online next Tuesday," my aunt explained. "View the proofs. Email me your vote by nine that night, and you only get one vote. Not two. Not ten.

Uno! ¿Comprehende?"

Surrounded by a fraction of my grandparents' thirty-four grand-children, my aunt explained the winning pic would be ordered immediately after the voting deadline which would be strictly enforced in order to have the picture of my grandparents' grands mounted, framed, and presented at Abuela's "Celebration of Life" fiesta in three weeks. "Reina, we're good on the vendors, right?"

My cousin ran it down in typical rapid-fire Reina, weaving in and out of English and Spanish, ending with, "I promise I confirmed *uno, dos, tres* times, *Tia*. Everything's good…"

"Except?"

That sheepishness on my favorite cousin's face was a giveaway that everything wasn't copacetic. "The cake."

"What about it?"

"I can't find the baker."

"Didn't you meet up and pay her in full already?"

"I paid…online, but when I went by for the scheduled taste test, she wasn't in…as in her storefront has been out of business two years."

"Aye, Dios mío. Reina…"

"*Tia*, I've called, and emailed, and instant messaged her and—"

"Nada?"

"Nothing."

I felt for Reina sitting there looking like she'd lost her best puppy along with our family's money. My heckling cousins didn't help.

"Cuz, you got mobstered?"

"She Cake Boss'd you, boo."

"Alright, alright." My aunt had to holler over the laughter to get us back in line. "We'll deal with cake crimes later. Right now we need another cake artist. Any ideas?" *Tia* asked, looking around the room.

"And keep in mind we want a gloriously gorgeous, one-of-a-kind custom cake that screams *Abuela* and tastes like heaven. So, don't suggest any of your cross-eyed, non-baking, no-talent-having-big-titty girlfriends," Reina quipped.

"'Ey, Rae, peep this." Scrolling my photos and locating a pic of Miss LaVelle's edible Luis Vuitton red velvet deliciousness, I handed Reina my phone only to find myself fending off sudden thoughts of last night's decadence. Of dancing with one sultry, sexy woman who had me feening for the feminine like I hadn't in five years.

Running into Yazmeen in the sanctuary that morning was new for me. Not that I'd been all about heathens or atheists, but my past hook-ups didn't include sister saints. Their calling on Jesus was limited to bedroom business. I knew nothing about her spiritual life, but discovering Yazmeen at church was refreshing. Promising? It fueled my interest in her and had me feeling foolish and fifteen: adolescent, yet daring. Like I was ready to wade through Thug-a-Mug infested swamps for her time and attention. Which was atypical for me. As a pro-athlete, I'd never had to exert much effort for a woman's time, body or mind. Even if I was wanted for the wrong reasons, interested females made their desires clear. I entertained it all in my carnal-before-Christ days. My random ways had changed. And now *I* was ready to chase a woman. I could deny my cousin's observations if I wanted, but truthfully I *was* crushing.

"OMG, Tav, are you serious?" Reina's excitement brought my mind back to family matters. "That's a *cake*?" Reina's disbelief gained her a cluster of cousins "oohing" over her shoulder. "I thought it was a purse. Who made it?"

"Que's lady friend, Joy."

"You have her contact?"

"I could get it *if...*" My cousin looked at me like I was stupid for falling silent. But a brother had strategy.

"Tav, quit playing before I choke you."

My grin was ten shades of impish. "Let *Tia* move on with the meeting."

Rolling her eyes, my cousin momentarily acquiesced before texting.

Get Joy's #. Plz!

She included a happy face emoji to sweeten the plea.

I let it sit a minute.

It's all about that exchange, Rae-Rae. I get Joy's # 4 u. U get Yazmeen's digits 4 me.

"Really, Tavares?" Reina's outburst had our aunt locking her in a look. "Sorry, *Tia*. Go 'head with what you were saying." That put our texting on temporary pause until my cousin came at me.

Told u I don't know Yazmeen like that. Just get Joy's # already!

Reina's punctuating her text with several angry emojis had me chuckling.

"Are you two finished?" *Tia's* busting us out, hands on hips, in true aunt fashion had folks laughing.

"Lo siento." Apologizing, I eased off the sofa and headed for the bathroom. I swear when I finished and opened the door, my cousin was standing there. "Dang, Rae, back up and let a brother breathe."

"You're gonna need new lungs if you don't hurry up and call Quinton. *Por favor.*"

"You threatening *and* begging and pleading? The conditions of that exchange have already been set. Get me Yazmeen's."

"OMG, Tav, are you not listening? I. Don't. Know. Her," Reina responded, adding fake sign language gestures with each word.

"You know her cousin Jamal right?"

"Wrong. I sang a set with him last year so that means I know *of* him. There's a difference. We're barely acquainted."

"Use your female powers of persuasion."

That had Reina laughing hard. "I will when I get some."

My cousin was out to lunch when it came to men. She obviously hadn't noted the way Jamal Williams was gazing in her grille in the church foyer. Reina was an attractive Afro-Latina oblivious to her beauty because she was plus-size and had struggled with weight most of her life. "Aiight, Rae. Stay 'sleep 'til you wake up one day," I muttered in Spanish, wishing Reina an epiphany. "Can you move out the way?"

"I will when you get Joy's number."

"Like I can't climb out the bathroom window."

We both laughed, knowing the truth behind that.

In our teenage days, on one of those weekends at our grandparents', my little cousin had talked me into taking her to a house party down the block. We asked permission. Our grandparents denied. Smelling ourselves, Reina and I climbed out the bathroom window instead. When we got back after midnight, we climbed through that same window and found *Abuelo*, belt in hand, waiting on the other side. I was already over six feet tall, but that didn't keep my grandfather from blazing my behind.

As if sharing similar thoughts, my cousin rubbed her backside. "I only have to think about it for my booty to burn. That was *Abuelo*. He was full of love, but he didn't play. He was all about his family."

"We takes care of we," I murmured, repeating one of my grandfather's favorite mantras.

"Yep," Reina agreed, hiding her face against my chest when her eyes got misty.

I hugged her a moment before asking, "You good, Cuz?"

Sniffling, she raised her head. *"Sí.* Now, get Quinton on the line for me."

Laughing and pulling my phone from my pocket, an incoming call interrupted that progress. Recognizing the assigned ringtone, I answered in Spanish. *"Hola, Señora Carmen—"*

That's all the greeting her frenzied screaming permitted.

Spanish was my second language. I was most definitely fluent. That didn't help me understand the ish that turned my blood cold and had me screaming, *"What the hell do you mean my daughter's missing!"*

CHAPTER FIVE
UPTIGHT CHURCH GIRL LIFE
Yazmeen

M ama! Where's everyone?"

"Yazmeen Renee, were you raised in a cave?"

Laughing at Mama's rebuke, I followed her voice to the family room. "Hey, you."

"Hey, yourself. Since when do you enter a house hollering?"

"Since today?"

Mama looked over her glasses at me. "Don't be smart-mouthed. Your backside's never too big to beat."

Snickering, I kissed Mama's forehead and perched on the arm of her oversized chair where she sat like a puzzle queen—sudoku book in one hand, pencil at the ready. "Mother, push up your glasses."

Inez Williams had a bad habit of leaving her reading glasses dangling on the end of her nose as if nostrils needed to see. When she didn't move, I properly positioned her glasses. Her eyeballs probably thanked me. "Are you winning?"

"It's about strategy and mental agility, not winning, Yazzy. What do you see?" Mama raised the book for my viewing.

"A bunch of numbers liable to drive me crazy. Today is not my day for a headache."

Mama shot me a look. "Leave my house. You're no help."

"Yes, ma'am, when you give me my children."

"Honey, take them. I never liked them no ways."

That had me flat out laughing. My mother was that cookie-baking, sweater-making grandmother crazy in love with her grandbabies.

"What's wrong with you?" Shifting sideways, Mama stared intently. "You've been walking around giggling all week. You on that dope again?"

"Oh my gosh, Mama! Old things. Let 'em go already."

We could laugh now that I was three-years sober thanks to therapy that became very necessary after being abandoned by my ex-half-a-husband.

We didn't even make a full year. Before our first anniversary, when I was five months pregnant, Royal put us in a situation from which there was no return. True, I didn't love him. But that whole set-up he left me for? I was so done that I almost wound up on complete bed-rest for the duration of my pregnancy. When my babies were born, they were the only light in my life. Loving them was the air I breathed on a daily. Even so, I experienced what I thought was serious postpartum depression. When it lasted overly long, I sought medical intervention and was diagnosed with clinical depression, and prescribed medication.

Contrary to professional opinions suggesting a person can't be addicted to antidepressants, I developed an acute dependence to the point that I couldn't make it through the day without popping those pills.

Being a first-time mother of newborn twins had me so busy that I forgot to refill my prescription. Finding that bottle empty, I'd sprawled on the bed all (as Joy would say) Betty Davis-ish, snotting and crying like a lunatic. That's how Mama found me, pitiful, ripe from three days of not showering, sobbing over half-a-man I'd never loved and didn't need.

"Come on, baby, let's get you washed up."

Helping me from bed, Mama walked me to the bathroom. But when my clown act escalated with me sobbing about leaving this world and my babies being better off without me, Mama laid hands on Yazmeen.

That woman slapped me back into sanity, flushed those pills, and put some soap action on my funky. Afterwards, she got a quart of ice cream, two spoons, and crawled into bed with me—holding me as I cried in between eating. Mama was my shero for real.

I grew up in a military household. Daddy was a decorated air force officer whose career called for frequent relocations. Usually our family went with him. But a few times Daddy was deployed to the opposite side of the world leaving Mama to hold it down. That—and the fact that she was merely amazing—was why my two sisters, my brother, and I had crazy love, respect, and regard for Inez. Being on the other side of grown, my reliance on Mama had morphed into a beautiful woman-to-woman relationship that I didn't take for granted. That didn't mean, at times, Mama wasn't "the most." Like then, how she was laser-eyeing me as if searching for drug dust.

She felt my temple, my neck, as if body temperature would snitch on addiction. "Mama, you're doing too much."

"I'm doing what a mother does: checking her child for drugs."

"And your diagnosis?" I managed not to roll mine when Mama bent to stare into my eyes.

"You're clean. Constipated, but clean. Come get some of these greens."

Snorting with laughter, I followed Mama into the kitchen. "Did you make it to yoga today?"

"I did." Mama was all smiles while removing a container of leftover collards from the fridge. "I'm not sure I like this big yam yoga. It had me sweating like ten pigs."

"Mama, it's *bikram*, not big yam." A correction was unnecessary. My highly intelligent mother liked to play with words, which was probably why my youngest baby, Malik, sometimes struggled with his. Grabbing a banana from the fruit bowl on the granite-topped chef island, I hopped onto one of the barstools stationed there.

"I like big yam better."

Smiling at Mama's playful wink, I admired her beauty as she moved about the kitchen, chatting and repacking leftovers into a care package for my benefit. At fifty-six, my mother was amazingly fit. Elegant. Long and lithe, genetics were in the mix, but my mother's dedication to health and fitness also contributed. Having lost one too many friends to avoidable diseases, Inez was determined to treat her temple to long life. About the face, my older sister, India, was Mama's twin, but all three of us girls inherited our mother's health perspective, sable skin, thick hair and height. The differences took over from there. Though long and willowy Mama was an E-cup to our Cs. She was slim with curvy hips, whereas my sisters and I'd inherited what Grams dubbed the Williams' women triple threat: abundant booty, thighs, and hips. For real, a Williams family reunion looked like a Brazilian butt-lift convention.

"Are you anywhere close to starting that Zumba class for seniors? We silver foxes want to work our swerve, too."

"Mama, don't repeat the slang you hear from Taj. Speaking of, where is he? And where are my children?"

"Your daddy took Malcolm and Malik to the store. Your brother's at basketball practice."

Just like that, my mind shifted. Mama's voice became background noise as the mention of basketball sent my thoughts in a delicious man's direction. Without rhyme or reason, throughout the week Tavares Alvarez and my mind had orgies that had me changing panties and rebuking things. Right then, I was warm and wiggly, remembering the smooth deep of his voice. The ultra-sexiness of his scent. The touch of his hands as we danced. The sensuous shape of his full lips that I so wanted to slowly, leisurely taste and lick like a mouth Popsicle on a stick.

"*Yazmeen.*" Mama's voice interrupted lust. Hands on hips, she gave me a look. "I know you haven't heard a word, so don't pretend."

"Ma'am? I missed something important?"

"Every word from my mouth is relevant."

Sliding from my seat, I discarded my banana peel and grabbed bottled water from the fridge while apologizing with a laugh. "What were you saying?" Sipping, I reclaimed my seat.

"You're strange-acting. What has you twisted?"

Toying with the bottle cap, I shook my head at Mama's youthful jargon. It was the collateral damage resulting from her and Daddy having a sixteen-year-old. We constantly teased my baby brother, Taj, that he was the "oops" proof that Daddy's soldiers and Mama's eggs were still communing. "I'm good, Mother Dearest."

The sound of the garage door lifting curtailed my mother's comeback. "Here come Frick and Frack."

"*Mommy!*"

When the door leading to the garage opened, I spread my arms and welcomed the twin hurricane that blew in. "*My babies!*" Malcolm reached me first, flinging himself at me so that the barstool wobbled. "Whoa, soldier." I sprinkled kisses all over Malcolm's face as Malik wiggled himself up into my embrace. "How was your day?"

"It was great," Malcolm supplied as I treated Malik to his own set of kisses. "Guess what?"

"What?"

"Mister Snackers is coming home with us!" the twins answered in tandem.

"That gerbil thing-a-ma-jig?"

"He's a hamster, not a gerbil, Mommy," Malcolm corrected. "And Ms. Katie says the whole class gets a turn to take Mister Snackers home each weekend starting next month."

I bit back a laugh hearing Mama mumble, "Sounds like Ms. Katie wants her weekends free of rat-sitting."

"MoMo, Mister Snackers isn't a rat," Malik insisted, folding his arms over his chest.

Uncrossing my son's arms, I invoked his nickname when gently correcting, "No pouting, Malie. Exactly when is our weekend with Mister Snickers?"

In perfect sync, the twins hollered, "Snackers!" before bursting out laughing.

"Snickers. Snackers. Crunches like a cracker. Go help your grandfather." My father struggled through the door, arms loaded with a box taller than the twins. The boys scrambled from my lap and ran across the floor in a race to be the first to help. I smiled, wondering if they'd be as eager when the terrible teens hit.

"Hey, Babycakes! Whatchu know good?" Talk about women shopping all you want. My father had collector-itis.

"Hey, Daddy. I know that better not be something for Malcolm and Malik."

Placing the large box in the middle of the kitchen, Daddy offered an innocent look.

"Mommy, looka what G-Daddy got me and Malkie," Malik exclaimed with three-year old ecstasy, using his brother's nickname while carelessly plopping bags on the kitchen floor before rushing to the box containing prized loot: a pint-sized basketball hoop set.

"I see, sweetie. Daddy, why're you buying toys when Christmas is around the corner?"

"This *is* for Christmas! My M-n-Ms are just opening it in November."

"We like going to the store with G-Daddy. MoMo says he don't have no impulse control."

"Malcolm, honey, it's 'doesn't have.' And no, he *don't*," I concurred, joining my mother's laughter and conceding the futility of fussing. Unlike how my siblings and I were raised, our parents were overly indulgent when it came to their grandchildren. "Boys, go get your backpacks. We need to head home."

"Aww, man, Mommy. We wanna stay and help G-Daddy put up our basketball hoop."

"Are you pouting again, Malik?" I bit my tongue to keep from laughing at my son's hanging lip.

"No, Miss Mommy, ma'am."

"I didn't think so, because my babies are good listeners and do as they're told...when?"

"The first time," answered the twins.

"Thank you. Do as I asked. Please." I watched my babies sulk from the room before pointing an accusatory finger at my daddy. "I blame you."

"When's the last time I told you you're my favorite daughter?"

Mama giggled. "Lord, this man."

Easing from the barstool, I pulled my keys from my pocket and crossed the kitchen to kiss Daddy's cheek. "You're a bad influence." The rumble of his chuckle felt so right as he hugged me.

"You dropped something."

Peering at the floor I found the half-grin of a thin-lipped Benjamin Franklin. I scooped up the folded bill. "*Daddy*...why're you giving me money? I don't—"

"Babycakes, eat a slice of humble pie and say, what, the first time...?"

"Daddy, you and Mama do enough for us already." I ignored my father's turning on me the instructions I'd just given the twins. Retired from her days as a music teacher, Mama picked the boys up from day-care, watching them until I got off work. Daddy was an ever-ready handyman for whatever went wrong in my townhouse. I was blessed with parents who constantly gave and gave, again. "I appreciate this, but the boys and I are fine."

"Yazmeen." Mama's tone reduced me to pre-teen days of butt whippings.

Sighing, I grinned. "Thank you, Daddy." When he tapped his cheek, I kissed it. "Have I told you lately you're my favorite father?"

Lifting the box, Stuart Williams pointed at his wife, his chest stuck out. "I'm the only fertilizer for them there eggs."

"I just threw up in my mouth." I shivered as my father strutted off.

"Yazzy, take this bag and go home so you can eat and rest," Mama instructed, grinning at her husband's cockiness as the twins barreled in.

"Mommy, G-Daddy promised to have our basketball court ready for us when we get home from school tomorrow."

It tickled me that my babies insisted on referring to daycare as "school." I considered their enrollment a necessary stepping stone in social development; particularly for Malik, my sensitive, shy guy. Mama had insisted on caring for the boys, but I felt her early retirement should be about Inez. After raising four children, she deserved her time. We compromised. "MoMo" picked the boys up weekdays at two, leaving Mama time to enjoy whatever silver foxes do. "That's good, baby. Come here so I can zip your jacket."

"I'm a big boy," Malcolm announced. "Watch me do it."

Accustomed to splitting my attention, I praised Malcolm's accomplishment while listening to Malik advise I needed to complete a "vermission" slip before they could bring home that rat-thing, Mister Snackers.

"*P*ermission slip, Malie," Malcolm corrected his twin, younger by mere minutes. Placing his brother's hands on his own cheeks, Malcolm instructed, "Say it with me, Malie. P-p-p. *P*ermission." When Malik enunciated correctly, Malcolm hugged his twin triumphantly.

I exchanged a look with my mother, moved once again by my sons' soul-ties. Arms about each other's, backpacks in hand, my boys stood smiling and confident.

"Well, that right there is a perfect reason why tomorrow's Friday," Mama announced.

I had to move aside as my squealing sons raced to wrap themselves about their grandmother's legs. Friday was ice cream-after-school day.

Once upon a time, Fridays were designated for them and their father. Royal would pick the twins up from daycare and spend several hours with them. That stopped too long ago to tell, and Royal's presence in our sons' lives had become increasingly inconsistent, his behavior more and more malignant. Mama reclaiming Friday as ice cream day helped divert the boys' attention and lessen their disappointment.

"Good night. Sleep tight…" When Mama paused, the boys joined in. "Don't let the bed bugs bite. But if they do, make bug stew before they make it out of you."

Peppering her grandsons' faces with kisses, Mama handed me my care package. She had no idea my gratitude.

Most Saturdays, I did my best to cook and freeze meals that we could eat throughout the week. But these past few weeks at work had been extra busy preparing for the church's holiday season. Plus, between Zumba and my dance troupe, I was stretched east to west.

Kissing my Mama's cheek, I moved towards the front door. "Good night, Daddy!" From somewhere at the back of the house, he echoed the sentiment. "Let's go M-n-Ms."

Moments later, the twins strapped in, I steered my Honda CRV through my parents' quiet Silver Bend community in Elk Grove and headed towards my townhouse in the Calvine Commons. I'd intentionally chosen the Calvine area for its close proximity to my parents and its affordability. Raising two sons on make-believe child support and no alimony wasn't easy. Of necessity I haunted thrift stores, religiously used coupons, and my ability to sniff out a garage sale had Joy dubbing me The Yard Sale Queen. I survived on frugality.

Remembering my father's monetary blessing, I pulled it from my purse.

Lord, thank you! Daddy, bless you.

Unfolding it, I was doubly surprised to find not one, but two Ben Franklins.

With the changing seasons and their constantly growing bodies, my babies had needed new jackets. And shoes. I wasn't opposed to buying gently used clothing at yard sales or thrift stores and laundering them until like new. But they deserved unworn shoes on their feet, and quality wasn't cheap. We were only a week into November and already I'd had to shuffle bills and highjack Peter and his disciples to pay Paul. And still my ends weren't meeting, leaving me with more month at the end of my money. Daddy's generosity would help hold us until my mid-month payday.

"Mommy, put on Ba-Dee-Ya."

"Please," I corrected.

"Please," my sons sang in twin-ified harmony.

Stopped at a red light, I scrolled my phone's music app until the opening bars of Earth, Wind, & Fire's "September" filled my SUV's interior. Beating the arms of their car seats to the syncopated beats, the twins joined Maurice White's flawless delivery of an R&B classic. Docking my phone in its dash-mounted holder, I admired their antics in the rearview mirror.

Lord, I love my babies.

They were the gift my twelve-cent marriage couldn't rescind. Infected by their joy, and despite a long day at the office, I found myself joining in.

We were hollering at the top of our lungs, enjoying that first round of the chorus when the tune was interrupted by an incoming call. "The Imperial March," Darth Vader's signature song, rang sinisterly.

"Daddy!"

Might've been wrong for assigning it as Royal's ringtone, but devils deserved unified theme music.

Removing the phone from its mount, I handed it to the twins. I usually ear-hustled conversations between my sons and their father, but tonight my mind was all A.D.D.-ish. With a moment for self, my thoughts immediately drifted. To a toy basketball set. And a very real man.

Not tonight, Tavares!

I was disinterested in squirming and burning. Plus, when out on the dance floor, I'd noticed that shoe length. And on a man that fabulously fit? He'd be dangerous to my uterus. My insides were precious, so thanks, but no thank you and amen.

Snickering, I had to honestly admit that, for the first time since being single, I regretted turning down a man.

Other than my delicate anatomy, what could it hurt, letting Tavares get to know me?

We could keep it casual. But with him, I imagined that even casual would be crazy. He was openly interested and genuinely attentive. That right there was fresh air and highly flattering. Might have me rethinking. Not to mention, despite celebrity status, the man was comfortable in his humility.

Lord knows, I've had enough of asinine arrogance.

"Mommy, it's Daddy."

Yes, Malcolm, that!

"Thank you, baby." Retrieving and mounting the phone, I positioned my earbuds wishing up a vaccine of anti-ignorance pills. "How may I help you?"

"Yeah…about last week. If I'm strong and wrong it's 'cause I don't need no men around my sons."

"Obviously, seeing as how you haven't been here." I prided myself on treating my children's father as something better than—in my grandmother's words—'doo-doo in a diaper.' After a year of imaginary child support and manic misbehavior, I wasn't in the mood for Royal's monkey-mouthed theatrics. Christian kindness aside, I felt no need to front good feelings. Especially after he'd showed his whole baboon behind last Sunday.

"Pull back, Yazmeen! Why you actin' all tight when I just apologized?"

I must've gone temporarily deaf, because an apology I'd missed. "Royal, let's move on."

"Yeah. Lemme take the twins to North Carolina for two weeks to visit my mom for Christmas."

I looked at the phone as if it was stupid. A man who hadn't consistently seen his sons this past year, and who couldn't afford monthly child support suddenly had airfare for three and wanted the twins for two weeks?

I had to body slam an urge to scream, *"N****, please!"*

Money aside, the twins didn't exactly have a bond with their paternal grandmother. Whatever familiarity existed resulted from my efforts to connect via calls and video conferencing. Other than that, they'd never met in person. I didn't fault her. Living in North Carolina on disability insurance and raising three grandchildren left on her doorstep by Royal's broke down brother, there'd been neither ability nor need for Miss Jones to fly in for our hush-and-rush exchange of vows in Pastor's office. God is my witness: I'd never aspired to be an ex-wife or a baby mama. I didn't do chaos or drama. But the foolery had me wanting to strap up and jack a Negro in the neck. I said a quick, silent breath prayer instead. "Let's table this for another time."

"Listen, yo! I said I'd catch up on those coins when I can. So, post up a minute without acting all siddity."

If ever I 'posted up' waiting on Royal's imaginary Monopoly money, the twins would still be rocking baby bibs and infant onesies. All tight and choked, feet busting the seams.

I wanted to stab him with a fork and my feelings.

I wanted to kick myself for not filing for child support, officially.

Simply wanting out of my dollar discount marriage, I'd agreed to terms I regretted. Namely, our handling our children's welfare without court intervention. Royal had semi-shown up those first two years, spending time with them or providing irregular monetary assistance. This year, however, he'd been all miss and no hit, leaving me with financial burdens while struggling to explain his absence to two beautiful little boys who wanted him. I was done with the sugary spice and everything nice persona I periodically adopted just to have a tolerable partnership with him. Turning onto my street, I decided come morning I'd start legal proceedings for child support like I should've done when we first separated.

"Royal, I had a busy day at work and would appreciate putting this on pause."

"So now it's all about you and your convenience? How about my needs? Neither one of us would be hurting for nothing if you'd quit being selfish and do this video like I been telling you to."

Jesus, hold my mule so I don't cut this fool.

Glancing in the rearview mirror, I was real aware of a little audience of two. I lowered my voice and increased the volume on the rear speakers to limit Malcolm and Malik's overhearing.

A make-believe music producer-slash-promoter, in Royal's unsolicited opinion, I was wasting my life working as my church's administrative assistant. Seeing as how it paid the bills he wasn't helping with and provided excellent benefits, I refused to react to his broke man barb and responded to his convenience quip instead. "No, this isn't about my ease, but about what's good for our sons and us not acting ignorant in front of them. And the video dancing? Not happening. So, again, let's pump the brakes and resume this discussion this weekend."

After my anti-Royal rabies shot and vaccination.

"That light-skinned, basketball nigga you was pressing up on got you acting all contrary, huh?" He chuckled like the demon seed he was "Or…is it that you still living that uptight church girl life and ain't had good dick in a minute and need me to come give you some?"

"Say 'good night' to your father," I instructed my sons, returning the phone to speaker mode and pulling into my driveway while praying a five-word prayer.

God, I need a gun.

Spending the next hour serving dinner, bathing twins, packing lunches and laying out clothes for the following day, I was able to push thoughts of Royal Jones away. After a bedtime story, prayers, and the boys were in bed, unpleasant thoughts came banging back.

Lord, was I really that horny? Or did I have a brain hemorrhage?

Truth was when Royal and I met, I was livid over a dance opportunity gone bad, my father was suffering complications from gallbladder surgery, and I'd just been dumped by my first love, Darrien Jackson. It was a perfect storm that—aided by a long night of dance, three Raspberry Cosmopolitans, and a half-pint of I still can't remember what—landed me on my back. Thanks to the alcohol, the details of giving up my virginity are still sketchy. But I obviously did because I woke up pregnant.

Basically.

Smiling at my sleeping babies, I tucked in blankets and kissed foreheads, knowing that I'd come to wake them up tomorrow only to find them snuggled about each other in one bed. My stupidest action had produced the purest beauty life could give. Malik and Malcolm were why I was able to forgive myself; and forgiving self was the only way I could live.

They look just like him.

Scandalous as he was, Royal was eye candylicious. Our sons a middle blend of my rich brown and Royal's butterscotch complexions, they'd inherited their father's loose curls and intense eyes. Heading for a shower, I earnestly prayed they hadn't inherited any of his *qualities a la canine.*

His Highness called.

My text was simple. Within minutes, a response chimed.

Tell that mufu I have a silver bullet with his mugshot engraved on it.

Joy's lunacy had me laughing.

Right! And that Quinton situation?

The mess they'd stepped into the night of LaVelle's party that had Quinton leaving like Speedy Gonzalez? All because my girl wasn't ready for a man who was clearly ready for her.

We're working on him.

I sucked my teeth. "Felecia, please!"

Work on u, 2.

Chick sent back a halo-wearing emoji.

"Keeping you on the prayer list," I commented to myself, opting out of a shower. Despite the lateness of the hour, I chose my favorite cherry vanilla bath bomb and treated myself to the luxury of slipping into the caress of hot, fragrant depths. Releasing the cares of the day on a long, airy breath, I lit my lavender candles to aid the atmosphere and my clarity.

True, being employed as a church administrative assistant wasn't in keeping with my dreams, but Pastor and First Lady Richardson were extremely good to me. My position was stable. My babies had health benefits and a roof over their happy heads. It was out of my realm of dance, but therapy had helped me make peace with the truth that sometimes dreams were placed on pause in exchange for living.

Relax.

Soft jazz playing on my phone, I obeyed my own advice and leaned back, reciting soothing affirmations before offering heaven a brief prayer of thanks for the day's blessings.

Maybe it was that basketball hoop Daddy gifted the twins. Maybe it was being naked in warm water with Marion Meadows blowing his sax in my ear. Seduced by a cocktail of warm water and smooth jazz, my mind went rogue. Straight to Tavares Alvarez.

Really, Yazmeen?

I'd met the man twice in life and was acting like a fiend, had been subject to ridiculous thoughts and curiosities all week. Truthfully, I was tired of them. And him.

Naw, boo, you're tired of wrestling.

True. But I refused admitting an interest. I couldn't afford to.

Swishing my hands through scented bathwater, I wished I was free to float, to drift and shift. I was a former dancer and single mom who taught Zumba two nights a week to make ends meet. I had a hip-hop troupe. Church. Family. And life coaching. Lusting after a retired, larger-than-life sports celebrity was nowhere on my She Needs list. Despite knowing this, I laid in that tub thinking on that man until doing what I shouldn't. I popped out of that warm water and searched the internet.

Leaning beyond the tub to avoid accidentally dropping my phone in, I dried my hands before typing his name in a search engine.

Results were immediate.

Playing stats. Multiple interviews and articles. A career timeline that proved a dossier. And a recent write-up on his mentoring organization—*Athletes & Academics*—whose mission was striking a balance between academics and athleticism for up-and-coming athletes.

"Impressive…"

Overall, the press coverage was positive, but I made the mistake of hitting the images.

"Omigosh, she's a cutie!"

A little girl—maybe five or six—with big brown eyes and an enormous afro puff atop her head, had her arms around his neck. They shared the same complexion, but other than the open laughing-smile cracking their faces, he didn't dominate her features. Clicking the photo instantly linked me to a Father's Day feature in a men of color magazine.

T-Alva and Aniyah: demonstrating that daddy-daughter affection.

Agreeing that the love was obvious, I wanted to read the article only for it to be blocked by a subscription-required pop-up. Disinterested in subscribing, I clicked back to images that proved prolific.

He ain't never missed a woman!

There was no more Aniyah. Just female after flawless female. Formal events. Casual outings. Some poses more intimate than others. Images flowed across my phone making one thing unmistakably clear: T-Alva liked his women and women liked him. Sure, some might've been stand-ins for the paparazzi's pleasure. Still, he had more flavors than there were months in a year; but each shared clear commonalities. His women were supermodel tall, lettuce-eating-thin, light bright citizens of Weavy Wonderland.

These sisters were my picture-perfect, polar opposites.

So, why front an interest in me?

I was five-eight, deep down brown, and had never been a size three, even pre-puberty. My eyelashes were mine. I didn't have talons. A gel polish manicure was my extent of posh. I'd never known silicone. Other than my braided extensions, my curly-kinky hair was my own. This fabulous flock of ultra-beautiful females was proof that, for him, I was some kind of curious diversion.

"Well there you go. You're not his type."

That photographic evidence freed me, proving some fake immunity against lust and need. Closing the app and laying aside my phone, I eased back into my bath, hating on none. I was okay with the fact that I'd never be them. They'd never be me. Embracing my own brand of beauty, I let my mind drift until it landed on Pastor's sermon last Sunday about our lives' seasons and divine timing.

Maybe my Tavares encounters are simple alerts that my seasons are changing.

Contrary to what I lived and claimed, perhaps my attraction to him hinted that I'd be open to love again. One day.

Wiggling deeper in the tub, I murmured dismissively, "That's fine. But I *won't* choose him when I decide not to be man-free."

CHAPTER SIX
A PUNK FOR PUNISHMENT
Tavares

I*'m 'bout to catch a case.*

Texting my lawyer, I told her to get my defense ready as my oldest brother, Juan, scooped me from LAX and tore up the 105 freeway.

I'd never been violent, but I had things working against me. That trinity of crazy culture in my blood and the bullheaded Taurus in me predisposed me to the edge, easily. Add the fact that a fool was playing with my daughter's safety?

"Baby bruh, Aniyah's my niece and we takes care of we, but you can't clown out."

I made no promises. Juan knew my stubbornness and type-A personality. When I was fixed, I was fixed. Couldn't nothing or no one but God get me off a decision. And right then, even God might've been wrestling for my attention.

Posted up on the passenger's side, I felt big bruh's scrutiny. Ignoring it, I watched Southern Cali whip by, jaw grinding, chest tight. "Who the hell—Lord, forgive me—leaves a five-year-old in a strip club dressing room while ho'ing with two dudes in the bathroom?"

"Kryshelle."

I glanced at Juan before sucking my teeth and shaking my head. "I swear I must've been on crack!" Or close. My own ho-ing and drugging had me holed up in a hotel six years ago with a woman I didn't even know.

Before accepting the Lord in my life, I'd sniffed my "socially acceptable" share of white lines. White lines, liquor, and lust at a club led to that sexing-a-stranger-in-a-hotel weekend that came with consequences. High as hell, I either chose to buy the B.S. about her being on the pill or failed to put condoms on it. Truthfully? That part there, I never clearly recalled thanks to my dumb a$$ drinking days and snorting like I couldn't be caught by anything because I was T-Alva-Almighty.

Sexed out by Sunday, we went our separate ways.

A month later, real sick of wilding, I left the liquor and the white lines, responded to an altar call at my sister's church, fell on my knees and gave the Lord my life. When Kryshelle tracked me down three weeks later, telling me I was going to be a baby daddy, my world spun backwards. There I was Mister New Christian caught by past indiscretions.

Hard as it may sound, I pushed for a paternity test. I knew of athletes "getting strapped," usually for cash. They laid up. They paid up. I'd been dumb enough; still, I didn't know or trust Kryshelle and, truthfully, wasn't trying to hear about a pregnancy. Conversely, I couldn't abandon what might've been mine to a woman I learned was a *real* drug-head.

I paid for Kryshelle's residential rehab. She cleaned up and when Aniyah was born—healthy, *thank God*—and the paternity tests came back 99.89% positive, I stepped up and fell deep in love with my princess. Now, five years later, I was burning road to Santa Monica to snatch her from the foolery of a female who'd given her life but never love. "And before you say it, you were right. I was soft for sleeping on that joint custody thing," I admitted.

"Naw…baby bruh…you were being decent."

I'd met and genuinely liked Kryshelle's mother, Miss Carmen. A widow whose only other child had been lost to gang violence, she—a non-English-speaking Dominican immigrant—had worked three jobs to keep Kryshelle's lazy, unemployed behind fly and fitted. Aniyah's birth was light to her overloaded life. Miss Carmen's pleas that we share custody, positing that Aniyah needed a maternal presence on the daily, felt reasonable. Kryshelle's voluntarily terminating her parental rights two weeks after Aniyah was born sealed the deal. I paid Miss Carmen's living expenses and was financially responsible for my child. My sole stipulation? Kryshelle, who was back on that stuff, was to have zero contact with Aniyah.

"So, how'd she end up with her?"

I snorted to keep from cussing. "She took her. Point-blank period."

"As in snatch, grab-n-go?" Juan yelled.

"As in hell yeah! Or…might as well have…" A crying Miss Carmen admitted she'd resumed allowing Kryshelle's visits, hoping time with Aniyah could help "cure" the former's drug addiction. "Apparently, she put on some act right the past few weeks." But Miss Carmen never left the room and kept Aniyah close by during these down-low visitations I knew nothing about. "Kryshelle's there. Everything's everything. Miss Carmen falls asleep and wakes up three hours later. Aniyah's ghost. Gone. Kryshelle's not answering her cell. No one's heard from her. That's when Miss Carmen calls me."

That busted up the business, ended that meeting of *mi familia*. If I was on one-hundred, running to my whip and rolling for the house to pack that heat I was licensed to carry, multiply that by ten. My cousins were right behind me, most of them missing that piece of paper permitting them to be in possession. It was like somebody flipped the light and scattered things that come out at night. *Tia* had her hands full trying to hold that tidal wave of whip a$$, but somehow, she managed while my cousin, Reina, booked my flight, called Juan—the one most likely to keep me calm—which helped back down that vigilante posse.

While I was inflight, Reina connected with my southern Cali contacts and the cliques I knew Kryshelle ran in trying to get a line on where she was holed up, hiding. I was fully prepared to call law enforcement if things came to that, but it wasn't an Amber Alert kind of abduction situation, yet; and I preferred keeping my daughter's likeness off the airwaves, well-protected.

By the time I'd landed and took my phone off airplane mode, I had messages and voicemail popping hot like corn. The one that stood out the most was from one of my B-ball bruhs.

"Yo, T-Alva, your girl's working that pole like a mufu."

And that's what led me to find my five-year-old at the high-priced strip club where her "mother" and I first met.

That was five nights ago and my jaw was still clenched. I could go zero-to-sixty in ten seconds remembering it. I repeatedly reminded myself to focus on God's grace. Despite the egg donor-incubator's foolishness, I—unlike parents of too many abducted children—was blessed to roll up at one o'clock in the a.m. and find my daughter alive, unmolested, and eating pancakes. Yes, in the manager's office at a strip joint, but safe.

"Daddy!"

When I walked in, she'd abandoned those flapjacks and flew at me. I must've hugged and held her five full minutes, barely breathing. I finally let my brother take her from me just so she wouldn't be in on the bidnezz of my talking to the manager and getting the info on Kryshelle's hiding Aniyah in the dressing room closet so she could work her shift. Or getting busy with two dudes in the bathroom in exchange for crack, and all the other ish.

"Daddy, you didn't do this one right!" Posted up on her bathroom step stool and brushing her teeth, my five-year-old's fussing put me back in the present.

"What's the problem, Nubs?"

"This braid keeps coming loose."

I wasn't one of those brothers posting social media videos of themselves giving their little girls ten thousand cute hairdos. My hair game was weak and limited to questionable afro puff-ing. This bedtime, supposed-to-be-a-braid that I'd already redone four times was unraveling. Again.

"Daddy, you need braid therapy."

Laughing, I grabbed a ponytail tie from my daughter's vanity top organizer and slapped that puppy on. "There. How's that?"

Spitting toothpaste in the sink, Aniyah rinsed her mouth and side-eyed my braid calamity. "Daddy...you have other nice qualities."

This girl.

"Guess you're glad Auntie Reina's sending us to her hairstylist, right?"

"Right!"

Squatting down so she could hop on my back, I turned off her bathroom light, my dog, Mister Bojangles, mirroring my steps. A bedtime story and a prayer later, I put my daughter in bed and kissed her forehead.

"Daddy, can Bo sleep with me again?"

Since day one, my daughter had had her own bedroom and belongings at my place. But as of this week my home was hers permanently. Furniture was off-limits to my massive black and white American Bulldog who looked like a Pit and could and would take a grown man down. He'd been trained as a guard dog and was good on his grind, but I'd also trained him—using verbal commands and hand signals—to differentiate foe from friend. He posed zero threat to the innocent. With Nubs, Bo was all marshmallow, and per my child therapist uncle, ensuring Aniyah's sense of security and well-being during this transition phase required flexibility. I caved. "Yes, but he still stays off all other furniture, Nubs. Agreed?"

"Agreed." She held out her hand and we pinky-promise shook on it before she patted her mattress. "Come on, Bo."

To his credit, Bo eyed me first for permission. When I signaled 'yes,' dude jumped on the bed, practically knocking me off in the process. "Well, dang."

"Ooo, Daddy! That's an unacceptable word."

"It isn't."

"You don't let me say it."

"Then unacceptable it is. Ready for your new school?"

Hopping out of bed, she ran to her closet. "I'm ready for my new backpack!" Slipping it on top of her PJs, she slid back into bed.

"So, you're sleeping with it?"

"Yep." She was grinning so hard I couldn't crush her goals.

"How about we take it off and put it next to you?"

She complied after a split-second consideration. When my baby and her multicolor backpack showcasing some bubble-eyed girls with stubby bodies and big hair were both tucked in, I turned off her bedside lamp and made sure the nightlight was plugged in. Aniyah was Alvarez all the way: daring and fearless. But she'd had nightmares and wet the bed once or twice after that locked-in-a-closet-at-a-strip-club nonsense. Thankfully, both the bad dreams and bedwetting had stopped, but she still had a nightlight and sleeping companion needs since moving in permanently. Otherwise, to my overprotective eyes, she seemed her same self. A nightlight, backpack buddies and canine comfort were easy concessions. "Alright, Nubs, sweet dreams."

"Why do you call me 'Nubs'?"

She knew the answer but liked the story. "When you were *really* little—before you were a professional talker and all—you'd hug my neck so tight I'd be choking." She giggled when I pantomimed a lack of oxygen. "But then you'd kiss my nose, and say, 'Ah nub oo' instead of 'I love you' and that made the choking worth it. Now, go to sleep or no banana pancakes in the morning."

The thought of missing out on one of her favorites had her fake snoring, and me laughing.

"'Ey...Nubs...can I ask you something?" I turned the lamp back on. "Any reason you didn't tell me your mom had started coming around again?"

Averting her eyes, she stared at nothing before answering. "'Shelle said you'd be mad at me for being happy to see her so I shouldn't say anything. And the night she took me, she said she just wanted to spend time with me."

Like Nubs knew how she got her nickname, I knew how that night went down. But, testing her memory for any changes, I asked her to tell it again.

"When *Abuelita* fell asleep, 'Shelle said we should go somewhere and let her rest. So, we went to her new apartment."

"How was that?"

Nubs shrugged. "Okay, but not that clean. We watched cartoons and that was fun until we both fell asleep. Then it was dark and 'Shelle woke me up screaming that she was gonna be late for work and lose her job if she took me home first. That's why she took me to that panty people place. She promised if I had another nap in that closet and didn't make any noise, she'd take me out for pancakes after her job."

Satisfied that nothing had changed in her story, I sat a moment before responding. "Aniyah, look at me. I'm glad you love 'Shelle. She's your mother." Kryshelle was a consistently inconsistent absentee parent and substance abuser. Still, I didn't want to teach my daughter hatred. "But I also need you to know that you and me, we tell the truth to each other. That's the way we Alvarezes roll. Right?"

"Right. Sorry for not telling you."

"You're forgiven. Just don't do it again." I added a rib tickle at the end.

"Ah nub oo, Daddy." Giggling, she was as adorable as when toothless and just learning to talk. "And thanks for my bracelet!"

Custom made, I'd picked it up yesterday. It was girly cute and innocuous with butterflies and her birthstone; but not only was it engraved with my contact; it included a microchip locator. After almost losing my daughter, I didn't care about invasion of privacy arguments. I'd be able to locate my child if ever separated from me again. "You're welcome, *Princesa*, and I love you, too." Scratching Bo behind one ear, I doused the light, left the door slightly open, and headed for my office thanking God, yet again, that my daughter bore no obvious scars of her egg donor's shenanigans.

Trust, I'd taken her to her pediatrician for a complete exam, as well as notified law enforcement before leaving L.A. Not only had Kryshelle violated court orders limiting her contact to supervised visitations, but chick (whenever she resurfaced above ground) was looking at child endangerment charges for driving our daughter on a revoked license with no insurance while smoking what Aniyah called "that icky smelling, white pebble-looking stuff." And while last I knew Kryselle was unemployed, I kicked myself for wasting hours looking all over L.A., instead of hitting that strip joint from jump.

Grabbing a sports drink from the built-in mini fridge, I plopped onto my desk chair with the very ugly thought that *anything* could've happened to my child at that club. Upscale and catering to ballers, shot-callers or not, the environment was what it was.

"But God…"

I killed fear with the triple assurance Aniyah's doctor had given that, physically, my daughter was undamaged. That alone had helped me cave to Juan's wisdom of allowing Aniyah time with Miss Carmen before boarding that Bay Area-bound plane. Her grandmother had been her constant and, despite what went down, I owed them their goodbye moment. Besides, even though I'd lawyered-up and Miss Carmen agreed Aniyah's being with me full-time was best, I'd needed to walk away with written consent to avoid bogus kidnapping charges anyone might wanna play with.

"I did wrong, Tavares. I believed my daughter. The scary thing is my heart so wants her to do right that who knows if I wouldn't believe her again?"

Her words flowing in rapid Spanish and decorated with tears, Miss Carmen admitted being a mother with tunnel vision and that Kryshelle was her addiction. The matter would still have to be actualized in court, but notarized documents granting me full versus joint physical custody in hand, I'd relaxed long enough to let Aniyah pack her pink and purple suitcase. Not that she needed any of it, but my daughter deserved the chance to load up the creature comforts she liked best.

Now her room's a hot mess.

A mental picture of her nation of dolls and stuffed animals had me grinning. My housekeeper loved Aniyah to life, but that menagerie mayhem even had her fussing.

"Alright…focus." Sipping my drink, I opened a database on my laptop and scoured the info Reina needed me to review. Besides being fam, Reina was also my personal assistant. Paid with benefits. My previous assistant, Char Simpson's, relocating to Detroit nearly coincided with Reina's prior employer downsizing and outsourcing two years back. Reina stepped up, helping as needed. My cousin could botch up a cake order but my girl was good on her grind. What was supposed to be a fill-in situation until I found a replacement wound up being Reina's full-time gig. Living in Sacramento, she—except when attending board meetings and events—telecommuted.

"Man…these figures aren't making sense."

Put on your glasses.

Finding my second set of eyes, I plopped them on my face, knowing my contacts were whipped and in need of a new prescription. Or maybe it was eye fatigue. Nubs and I had gone from being together on holidays and off-track periods from her private, year-round charter school, to co-residents. Being self-employed, I had the advantage of modifying my schedule to our benefit. I'd been financially responsible for my daughter from day one. Our time together was regular, not rare. Still, this Daddy-on-the-daily was straight up different. No complaints. Simply said, the Mister Mom Life was an adjustment.

Between T-Squared Acquisitions making real estate moves, and getting *Athletes & Academics* up and legit, a brother was already juggling and trying not to drop balls. Now, making best efforts to give my daughter a "normal" life, I paired back on travel and had Reina reconfigure my schedule so I'd be fully present to help Aniyah embrace her new normal. According to my child therapist uncle, that was best accomplished through consistency in simple things like a schedule, meals at the table, and a bedtime routine of a bath, teeth-brushing and prayers before we posted up for a story. Our lives had been reloaded.

Glancing at my calendar, I saw I was five days in and already exhausted.

"Dude, you got at least thirteen more years of this." I chuckled, knowing that with Nubs and her larger than life self, those years would be interesting. For real.

The chime of Reina's incoming text rerouted my attention.

Lex is available Tuesday. Uncle Julio says 'thanks' on that airfare. Oh & check your email.

Lexington "Lex" Ryde, six or seven years my senior, had been an NFL rookie with star potential two decades ago. Unfortunately, his career was tanked by injuries sustained in a motorcycle accident. A smooth brother who'd already overcome a boatload of life's ish, Lex picked himself up and turned a love of cars into a world-class, multi-million-dollar transportation service. My fellow venture capitalist, Lex was the definition of resilient. He was a perfect fit for *Athletes & Academics'* board of directors. He just didn't know it yet.

Uncle Julio, my father's oldest brother, had been disabled by a stroke and was living on a fixed income. Making sure he and his family were able to attend Abuela's upcoming "Celebration of Life" was a no-brainer. My parents had drilled into us kids that family was everything. I wasn't stupid about who I helped, when or why. My daughter had a trust fund, and I'd set up scholarships for my nieces and nephews. Thanks to a daggone good financial manager who wisely invested my game day earnings as well as ongoing product endorsements and speaking engagements—my money was straight, and helping wasn't a hardship. As long as I had, fam did, too.

Tell Unc he's the man. Confirm with Lex. And thanks 4 flowing in the p.m.

An early riser by nature, my work routine had been off since my daughter's move-in. Adjusting my schedule meant a change to Reina's as well. We'd been pulling late hours but would resume the regular when Aniyah returned to school next week.

No worries. Tell my baby Auntie Rae said 'hey!' And don't 4get a gift. Be original, not a man, & make it something other than dead presidents.

I laughed at the dis because it was legit. Money typically comprised my gift-giving. But Reina was right. We were celebrating our grandmother beating cancer and being in remission ten years. I needed to get my game up.

I've no idea what to buy.

Bulbs for her garden, a vacation, and a donation to her favorite charity? All gifts I'd previously given. Call a brother clueless and ashy.

"Dang..." Peeping my hands, they looked like I'd been playing in flour and sand. All that constant-hand-washing-'cause-you-got-a-kid had me in desperate need of lotion.

And just like that my mind snapped to a place my tumultuous week had kept me too busy to frequent.

Sasha's Essentials. They're the only products worthy of my skin.

"Miss Yazmeen Williams..."

My dry, ashy hands spun my mind onto the smoothness of her sable skin, had me remembering. Her scent. The lush of her lips. Her absolute enticement.

"Man, you bugging."

Launching an app on my phone, I distracted myself with arming my home security system. I'd bought Bojangles, a glock, and tricked-out the house with a state-of-the-art safety system a la James Bond after dealing with a psycho chick who showed up outside my previous property with a banana pudding, wearing nothing but a G-string, talking about God told her we were supposed to be married. That followed by a break-in had me selling that house in the Oakland Hills. Tiburon was now home to these here Alvarezes. The property was pricey, but the safety, serenity, and beauty of northern California's coast was worth the cost. With Aniyah's move-in, the gun was on lock, leaving me to rely on my high-tech system, the security company I'd contracted with and were available at a moment's notice, and Bo's canine senses as a first line of defense.

Putting my laptop in sleep mode, I pushed away from my desk and went to my daughter's room for one last check-in. Both Aniyah and Bo were sawing logs. "So much for the protection of a dog."

Partially closing her door, I detoured to the kitchen looking for something to hit my belly before turning in. With kid-friendly food dominating the shelves, I grabbed four snack-sized bags of white cheese popcorn, a handful of turkey jerky, sports drink and headed for bed.

Sprawling across it, I turned on ESPN, snapped open that corn, and got to crunching. Remembering Reina's instructions, I grabbed my phone and pulled up my email. Scanning the notice she'd forwarded, I flopped onto my back.

"Yasss, Father God, You *did that.*"

The official letter was forthcoming, but to compensate for hold-ups and errors on the processor's part, we'd received a courtesy notification that *Athletes & Academics* had secured non-profit status. I closed my tired eyes, tremendously pleased that I'd have good news to share at next week's board meeting. Shooting Reina a victory text, I zoned back onto ESPN. That focus lasted all of a minute before drifting back to one very beautiful, brown-skinned woman.

"Man, she *ain't* interested."

Turning off the flat screen, I lay, listening to the muted sounds of the Pacific Ocean, wondering when I'd caught a dose of doofus. Twice now, Yazmeen Williams had entered my orbit, only to leave as easily as she pleased. My stubbornness obviously didn't process the disinterest. It was doing its thing and wanting what it wanted.

Removing my eyeglasses, I placed them on the nightstand, telling myself to move on. I had a daughter to raise and no time for dating. Praising single parents who held it down on the daily, who raised children with little to no help, and maybe dealt with crazy, I dragged myself off the bed intent on showering. The sound of an incoming text interrupted.

Here! Now quit holding Joy's # hostage.

Reina had sent a new contact.

Opening it was like a gut punch. Cuz had come through on our agreement.

I'd promised to get her Joy's number for *Abuela's* cake, if she came through with the contact for Yazmeen. She had. Texting her Joy's info, I wondered what to do with Yazmeen's.

Was I really that out-of-circulation that I didn't know how to call a woman?

Stripping and stepping into the shower, I needed that blast of hot water to clear mental cobwebs. My initial efforts to know Yazmeen hadn't met with success, and that subsequent Sunday outside the sanctuary was a ripe mess. My knowledge of her was limited, but something in me said she was a single parent.

"Five days in and suddenly you're a single parent detective?"

Shaking my head, I admitted that didn't mean she was unattached. Based on her reaction, if she was boo'ed up, Thug-a-Mug wasn't it. Even so, she'd already demonstrated that knowing me wasn't a priority. Straight up, I respected that. But the bullheaded Taurus in me obviously had a dose of optimism it didn't need, asking if she ever green-lighted me, would I be interested in the possibility?

"Heck yeah."

You're a punk for punishment.

Laughing at my own expense, I let hot water drench my head, washing away thoughts of Yazmeen. Or so it seemed.

As if they'd patiently waited in the wings through my recent mess and mayhem, full-blown images of her stepped up and claimed center stage, her very scent swirling in the shower's steam.

The trickery!

That steam was floating and gloating, pulling me into some crazy kind of hypnosis. Had me imagining her touch, the sultry sway of her hips, the seduction of her movements. Yazmeen's stimulating fragrance played with my senses and had my body responding. Made little sense, the effect the woman had on me. I'd encountered women who came at me, spitting game from the get-go. Yazmeen? Her seduction was uncontrived. Effortless. She hadn't even come for me. Yet, she had my attention completely. My head felt clouded, a certain body member grew thick. Like she was there with me, and we both wanted physical fulfillment.

"Naw, man, squash that. We ain't doing this."

I had to look down at self and cut the throb off.

Teeth clenched, I turned the water to cold and endured that chill until the beast calmed, and I could step from the shower without my stuff standing at attention.

Grabbing a towel and drying my face, I peeped myself in the mirror, wondering what kind of exhaustion had seeped into my brain. I'd never had a woman come up on me like that.

Glancing back at the shower behind me, it was like that steam was still there, dancing. Fluttering. A butterfly with gossamer wings.

Mariposa.

She was an ethereal butterfly seducing me, effortlessly.

"Get your life, Alvarez."

Slathering on some anti-ashy, I headed for the built-in in the walk-in closet and pulled PJ bottoms from a drawer. With Nubs in the house, I'd changed my nude-at-night habits.

Sliding into bed, I said a prayer knowing God wasn't insecure about my not being on my knees when I talked to Him. Offering sincerest thanks for His countless blessings, I turned off the lights and tried settling in. But that shower incident had my mind rolling. Reaching for my phone, I glanced at that newest contact.

Should I call? Should I not?

"Dude, you're thirty-five. That's too old for juvenile ignorance."

Daring to dial, after several rings a recorded, professional greeting sounded. Realizing it was for the administrative offices of the church I'd visited with Que a few weeks back, I started to hang up, thinking I'd misdialed, only to pause when hearing Yazmeen Williams as one of the "press number __ to reach" options. "Oh, you clowning, cousin!"

Reina had provided Yazmeen's work number. Disconnecting, I shot her a text.

You're fired.

She shot me a laughing-crying emoji back.

Dropping my phone on the nightstand, I settled in bed, allowing the sounds of the Pacific to sing me to sleep. Tumbling deep, I eventually, inevitably, found myself a willing prisoner of sweet but sultry, Yazmeen-centered dreams. Sprawled out like the world was mine, I welcomed that seductive butterfly and hot, sensuous nocturnal trips that were everything naughty and definitely nice.

CHAPTER SEVEN
BRAIDS & BUSTED LIPS
Yazmeen

"Yazzy, where's your big booty at?"

"Behind that preposition," I answered instead of reminding India that—after five children—her bootyrific behind out-rounded mine.

"Come help me braid this head."

"Put a 'please' on that."

Across the phone, my bossy big sister's laughter was light, bright. "Pretty please with cheese. Boo, come through and help me finish."

"Nope."

"Because?"

Military brats who'd grown up relying on each other's hair care skills when living in foreign lands, my braiding abilities were almost as legit as my licensed cosmetologist sister's. That didn't make me interested. "India, that's *your* profession not mine. *And,* I just finished Zumba. I'm hungry, sweaty, and a hot shower's calling. Plus, I have *Step-N-Style* in the morning."

After dancing practically all my life, studying the art form in college, and pursuing a dance career that never went where I wanted, I was still devoted. Approached by a sister at church who was a community center director interested in offering dance classes as a means of youth intervention, I initially agreed on a trial basis. With the center located in Meadowview, the class inevitably catered to underrepresented youth who brought crazy passion that enriched my whole attitude. That "trial" class had morphed into *Step-N-Style*, my dance troupe who were now—nine months later—still going strong. We'd recently placed second in our first competition. Now, my kids were on fire for more.

"Girl, I've seen you get out of bed after three hours of sleep and dance like you were possessed by the ghost of Alvin Ailey, so you'll be fine come morning. Besides, everyone's left for the day. That makes me the only one at risk of being offended by your funk. And forget the hot shower, Yazzy. Get a hot man. Speaking of: one of Kyle's cousins is visiting—"

"The lies of your life! I will never ever again do time with one of Kyle's creatures." I'd previously made the mistake of letting my brother-in-law set me up with a distant relative visiting from out-of-state. That led to a date with a five-foot-two-inch, ninety-seven-pound man recently released from a mental health facility. Missing two fingers from his left hand and needing a mother for his six children, he'd proposed over a dinner of hog maws and chitterlings. "Kyle's on *that* list."

India had the nerve to laugh. "Yazzy, you know! If it's not related to his t-shirt business, my honey lacks small detail skills and overlooks pertinent info. Anyhow…why were you at Zumba? You don't teach on Fridays."

Accustomed to my sister's nosiness, I didn't bat an eye while entering southbound I-5.

"I subbed for someone." Add my babies' recent increase in daycare costs to the rubber check Royal mailed a few days back and extra income was first on my She Needs list. Zumba it was and braiding it just might be. "India, why're you still at the shop when you and Kyle have tickets to see Jill Scott tonight?"

"Now you understand why I need help?"

"Call Sasha."

"That preg-a-saurus is good for two-and-a-half braids."

Where *Sasha's Essentials* was concerned, baby sis was about the business. Anything else was extra with which she couldn't bother.

"Do crochet braids or interlocks, India, and cut your time in half."

"Just not. Parents pulling those interlocks-on-tracks into ponytails has these babies walking around looking like curtain heads."

Changing lanes and setting cruise control, I laughed through a yawn. "You're stupid."

"Possibly. Come on, Yazzy. Help your favorite big sister. We'll be finished in an hour. Promise."

Seeing how it was six-thirty, I could conceivably help braid a head and still be home by eight. With the twins—and India's tribe of five—spending the night at my parents,' I had nothing but time.

To do what?

My girls were busy. A flight attendant, LaVelle was out-of-state. Joy was working that shady part-time job of hers that had me praying. My lack-of-choices quickly considered, I capitulated. "Give me ten minutes."

"Thanks, boo. See you."

Disconnecting with a sigh, I wished my options were less pitiful and more pleasing than ice cream, a marathon of *I Love Lucy*, and whether or not to click "add to cart," finalizing the purchase of a vibrator I'd recently developed an elicit interest in. Hot, hungry and maybe funky, I opted to help braid a head instead, embarrassed by the notion of a battery-operated boyfriend.

Sasha's pregnant self was there when I walked in. Seated in the waiting area across from India's station, baby sister was scarfing down garlic fries, her newest prego crave, clearly finished with her contribution of two-and-a-half braids.

"Hey, Sasha. Hey, India!"

My older sister hollered back above the noise of the blowdryer loosening the curls of the child client in her chair. The back portion braided, the massive undone remainder brushed forward and completely covering the child's face had me glad God gave me boys and barbershops.

"Hey, Yazzy. You look...committed to fitness."

Removing my attention from the little person whose mane I was about to help tame, I peeped my fit and found zero wrong with it. We Williams women were stylish, but Sasha was that face-beat-hair-on-hit-always-ready-to-work-the-runway chick. Sporting capri-length exercise pants, a hoodie wrapped around my waist, a top that was little more than a sports bra, and my box braids in a ponytail atop my head, I looked Zumba-ish.

Grabbing a handful of Sasha's fries, I fed my committed to fitness face. "We can't all be divas all day."

"It's November and cold as cane, but at least your half-naked fit is cute and color-coordinated. But dang!" Acting offended, Sasha leaned sideways. "Your deodorant died."

"And your wig's alive," I retorted, finding perverse pleasure in running oil-and-garlic-coated fingers through baby sister's store-bought hair.

"*Yazzy!*" Snatching her wig off, baby sis chick took to fussing, waving that wig with emphasis. "This is twenty-four-inch, one hundred percent Remi human hair on Swiss lace. Do you know how much it cost? A grip!"

"Felt like it." Jumping out of Sasha's reach, I headed towards the restroom to wash my hands before putting them on that child client's head only to have my whole life spin.

"My apologies if I was gone too long."

Hear me when I tell you the baritone the November wind blew in had my whole body whipping around, not merely my head.

Jesus, take me please!

Confronted with a mountain of magnificence, my body flashed so hot a yeast infection was likely imminent. Staring and stuck on stupid, I barely heard India's reply.

"No, you're fine."

"Ooo, can I make you mine?"

Sasha's whispered silliness did nothing to undo my struck dumbness. Unable to move, I stared at all that yum booted in Timberlands, loose jeans, a hoodie featuring a black and gray collage of African American greats, and designer glasses that left Tavares Alvarez looking like every sexy thing I did and didn't need.

"Hi, Daddy."

That animated voice fed me some reality.

Glancing back, I saw India's child client smiling from beneath her wall of hair.

Lord, for real?

Even cuter in person—and thanks to that Father's Day article I'd read—hair out of her face, I recognized Aniyah Alvarez.

"Hey, Nubs. I have your juice." His Fineness spoke, but he didn't move. Rather, he stood slowly scoping me, those whiskey brown eyes missing nothing.

Jesus, we need to talk about the games You play. Got me up here looking and smelling like leftovers from six yesterdays.

I felt even funkier when he thawed and walked past me, handing my sister a bottled beverage, the subtlety of his cologne like a clean mountain breeze. His sexily whispered, "Hello again," made me want to hide my ovaries.

"Your iced coffee, Miss India."

"You really didn't have to, but thanks. Let me introduce you to my sisters."

"Huntee, yes, *please*."

With His Fineness busy inserting a straw in his daughter's juice box, I pinched Sasha for her foulness and whisper-hissed. "Quit acting up and put your wig on, Missus Married-and-Pregnant."

Slinging fake hair like Cher, baby sis was quick in resituating it.

"The one in the chair is—"

"Sasha Calloway, the baby and the beauty. And you are Tavares "T-Alva" Alvarez, our little brother's all-time NBA favorite. Wonderful to meet you!"

"The honor's mine. Are you *the* Sasha of Sasha's Essentials?" he asked, shaking Wiggy Wonder's hand.

Baby sis sat momentarily stunned before getting all screechy and lit. *"You're familiar with my products? Who told you about them?"*

"A beautiful butterfly." His focus remained on Sasha. Just the same, I felt the warmth of his words flow my way.

"I'm flattered. Thank whomever told you. Have you tried my Essentials yourself?"

Girlfriend could work a nerve with the gushing and product promotion, but—four years my junior—Sasha had busted her butt building her brand and deserved every moment's attention. Truth? I was absolutely proud of baby sis and her accomplishments.

With Daddy's military travel taking us to foreign lands, finding Black products was often iffy. Of necessity, Mama resorted to concocting skin and hair care products for our family; and taught us her recipes. But Sasha was the one who loved being in the kitchen helping Mama and developing her own concoctions. During her college days, baby sis made and sold body butters to earn spending money. She was so successful with it that she changed her major from art history to business with a minor in chemistry. By the time she graduated, chick had a solid customer base and a bona fide business.

Taking advantage of her holding Tavares hostage, I slipped into the restroom to wash garlicky grease off my hands, wondering why I kept encountering this man.

The bigger the world gets, the smaller it is, was something Grams, my paternal grandmother, often said.

Drying my hands, I decided to run with that and not add extra meaning to anything. My world was small, and Tavares kept bumping into it. End of story.

That's what I told self when peeping my post-Zumba image in the bathroom mirror, wishing I had mouthwash and my makeup bag.

Hoodie removed from my waist, I had it on when I returned and headed straight for India's station. Thankfully, Sasha and His Fineness had moved to the waiting area and were chatting like old friends.

"That man's in trouble. That girl has the gift of gab."

Agreeing with big sis, I focused on the little person in her chair. "Hi, Aniyah. I'm Miss India's sister, Yazmeen."

She waved while asking, "Is that why she calls you 'Yazzy?'"

"It is."

"Can I call you that, too, if I put 'Miss' in front of it?"

India and I exchanged a smile. "Absolutely. Is it okay if I help braid your hair?"

"Yes, ma'am."

I fell in love with Her Cuteness just like that. Eyeing India's work, I selected enough extension hair to match. "Do you normally wear braids, Aniyah?"

Sipping juice, she shook her head. "Daddy only does crooked afro puffs. My hair needed help."

India and I laughed. "Well, sweetie, help is here," I offered, getting busy and ignoring the presence of the man who felt as if he were beside me, versus across the room.

I'd been proud of self the prior week for escaping all thoughts of him. They came, but I banished them. Him here in the flesh was crazy kind of torturous. The man possessed way too much presence. It was more than his height and size. He was magnetic, and I didn't like it. Braiding away the distraction, I focused on being India's apprentice.

As if that'll help you forget him.

I tried. That lasted three whole minutes.

"You're for real, right?"

His rich, responsive laughter to Sasha's outburst had me ear hustling.

"Miss Sasha, bet. I'm stopping by your shop."

I looked up in time to see them fist bump before Sasha pulled her business card from her oversized Coach bag and handed it to him, smiling all fan girlish. "If you don't, I'm coming for you." They laughed as Sasha pushed her prego self from her seat. "Tavares, it was so good chatting with you."

"Likewise."

"Hey y'all, I'm heading home to hubby." Rubbing her tiny baby bump, Sasha sashayed over. Saying goodbye to Aniyah, she simulated kisses when pressing a cheek against India's and mine.

"Text us when you get home safely," India instructed, forever the oldest. "Tavares, you okay? You're welcome to sit over here with us if you want."

"I'm good, Miss India." Magazine in hand, he'd already settled in. "But you could introduce me to your exquisite sister."

"Oh!" India looked at me. "Tavares, this is—"

"Yazmeen, the divine dancer," he supplied, lips curved in a sexy grin. "We've met."

Believe me when I tell you Sasha twirled around at that exit, snatching her head back so that both of my sisters stared at me like they'd been pimp slapped.

Ignoring them, I stared at that man and faked calmness. "Nice seeing you again, Tavares."

"The pleasure's completely mine. Most def."

That said, he sat and perused that magazine like his baritone hadn't tenderly licked my belly.

Sasha's positioning thumb and pinky finger alongside her head and mouthing "Call me" had my eyes rolling. India simply stood there waiting on the 4-1-1. Real focused on braiding, I offered none.

"You know we're going to talk, right?" she quietly advised.

"Wrong. Nothing to say. Move on."

For once, bossy big sister complied, leaving us to braid, chat, and interact with Aniyah who—crayons and coloring book in hand—had life goals of staying within the lines.

"So...you met while dancing?"

Glad for the neo soul streaming from speakers cushioning our conversation, I glanced over at Sir Sexy to make sure his attention was elsewhere. "You're not getting in my nonexistent business, India."

"Spill the tea already."

"Hush and braid." Her clap back was cut by my ringing cell phone that I gladly answered. "Hi, Mama."

"Yazzy, it's Daddy. I'm on your mother's phone because the boys dropped mine in the toilet. Uhh, Babycakes, we had a little accident."

My mommy hairs stood on end. "In addition to your phone taking a swim? What happened?" My father's telling me he'd allowed the boys to play basketball inside the house was so him. The man with seven grandsons was questionably crazy when it came to them. "Really, Daddy?"

"It's only that plastic set-up I bought for my M-n-Ms. And there's more than enough space in this big ol' game room. I didn't know the thing would fall over and bust Malcolm in the lip."

"Is he okay?" I held up a finger to silence my sister's concerned questions. "How bad is it?"

"The bleeding stopped, but it's a little swollen. I'm hoping he won't need stitches."

"I'm on my way."

"No need. I have antiseptic and thread. I'm only calling out of due diligence."

"Daddy, don't you even!" My father was known for acting like an armchair surgeon. "Where's Mama?"

"At the store getting ice cream and things."

"Can I speak to Malcolm, please?"

"Hi, Mommy." My busted lip baby sounded so pitiful.

"Hi, Malkie. What happened to my honey?"

"I did a dunk like Uncle Taj and the hoop fell and hit me. It hurt real bad, but I only cried a little, not a lot."

"You need me to come kiss it?"

"Yes." My firstborn added sniffles for effect.

"Tell G-Daddy I'm on my way. Is Uncle Taj still there?"

My sixteen-year-old brother got on the phone sounding like a grown man. "Whaddup, Yaz?"

"How bad is it?"

"Not too. Malkie's a soldier. Right, Twinny Twin?"

Hearing my son's brave response in the background, I felt better. "I'm leaving India's. Hide all needles and thread from your father."

That little nut cracked up. "For sure…if you hook me up with Kia."

A member of my troupe, Kia was one of my best dancers but had a nonstop mouth. "Boy, hook yourself up." Disconnecting, I filled my sister in. "If we wind up in the ER I'm revoking Daddy's grandfather license."

India laughed. "Go. See about our baby. Three braids and I'm finished." She extended a hug, while trying to slip a folded fifty in my hand.

I snatched my hand back. Accepting payment for Aniyah's hair would be like taking money from Tavares. "I'm good."

She stuffed the bill down my sports bra. "Yazzy, swallow that pride for another time. I appreciate you helping. If my five are at Mama and Daddy's doing anything they shouldn't, tell 'em I'm coming in swinging." With five sons aged five to thirteen, India was a consummate mom trying to talk her husband into child number six.

"Enjoy Jill. Little Miss Aniyah," I bent so we were eye-to-eye, "your braids are beautiful. You're no longer Princess of the Crooked Afro Puffs."

Giggling, she returned my high-five. "Thank you, Miss Yazzy. Now I have pretty braids like you."

"Yours are better than mine because you're cute."

Tweaking her nose and saying my goodbyes—looking and feeling like a scrub—I hurried for the door, wishing I didn't have to pass *him* in the process. Before I could open my mouth to offer some quick, slick farewell, he was standing. Intercepting. That man unfolding himself from his seat and straightening to his full height was like art in motion. Divine.

"May I walk you to your car?"

I had to step back from that smooth seduction-of-a-voice that could strip me butt naked in seconds. "Why?"

He chuckled as if humored at stating the obvious to the ignorant. "It's dark."

Preferring to take my chances with miscellaneous maniacs than have my treacherous hormones and I alone with His Lusciousness, I took off fast-walking and -talking. "I'll be fine. I hope you like Aniyah's hair. Good night." I was out the door before he could breathe again like Miss Braxton.

Really, Yaz? Get your life right.

Analyzing why one man left me uncommonly out-of-order and acting immature was a worthwhile pursuit. It wouldn't happen that night. I was too busy being dim. Bent on Tavares not sharing my air, I was half-way down the block before realizing my soccer mom, mini SUV was parked in the opposite direction.

Turning to retrace my steps, I nearly screamed, encountering a mountain. "*Tavares*! Are you part ninja or something?"

"Sorry for startling you," he apologized, *after* laughing.

"Can I help you with anything?"

He didn't miss a beat. "Why're you invested in running from me?"

Because you're fertile and I have Fallopian tubes.

He need not know my craziness, so I left that there and walked around it. "Nice glasses." I'd noticed them earlier but had kept the compliment. My off-timing was evident in his expression politely transmitting "disinterested in foolishness."

"Yeah...that right there, Miss Williams? Avoidance." I had to respect the man for being blunt. "That's sketchy and less than one hundred."

"Tavares—"

"I'll walk you to your car for your own safety's sake," he interrupted, done with my craziness. "Is that okay?"

Being man-less three years—and after marriage to the dumb-and-dim who wasn't demonstrative, just possessive—I'd obviously forgotten chivalry existed. "Yes."

Walking in silence, I felt his Black Man Magic with every step. It was insidious as smoke, and equally dangerous. While I respected his directness, it didn't feel good being called on the carpet for all the ditching and dodging. I needed the man to understand that being around him had me feeling deeply needy, like I could give him access to things better left under lock and key. And not just my body. Truthfully? That, too, was hollering. I wanted to back him onto a car hood and get to lap-straddling. Reaching my Honda CRV, I breathed with relief that I still had my virtue and my panties. "Thanks for being a gentleman."

"I do my best."

Unlocking my vehicle, I was caught off guard when he reached forward and opened my door for me. I didn't enter for standing there, staring.

"Is there a problem?"

"How'd you end up at India's?"

"You don't believe in coincidence?"

"Not where you're concerned. I'm just saying," I added when he laughed. "First, it was church. Now, here?"

That toothpaste smile was bright against the night. "And my being at LaVelle's party was also contrived so I could be heel-crushed by one particularly lovely lady, right?"

My smile was automatic. "Maybe. So...do you plan on satisfying my curiosity?"

"Only if you satisfy me."

I had instant images involving moaning, groaning, butt-naked booty and edible, lubricating jelly. Saying nothing, my eyebrow got to arching.

"I need to settle a double debt. One: per your sister, Sasha, I owe you for that introduction to her Essentials. Two: you stepped in and helped with my daughter's hair…but I sense that if I tried to pay you, you wouldn't accept. That's much for my conscience. So, let's level this. May I take you to dinner, Yazmeen?"

Baby Boy, may you say my name never ever again.

From his lips it was too sensuous—inviting, exciting.

"Thanks, but…" Floundering for a concrete objection, I stood in silence, prompting him to hold up his hands in surrender.

"No worries."

"Tavares, really. I'm not running from you. I'm running from me."

"Holla when you finish that jogging." Allowing me to settle into the driver's seat, he closed my door as I started the engine and lowered my window. "Good night, Miss Williams."

That was that. He turned and left, gifting me the backend of his magnificence.

Instead of being glad at getting what I wanted, I felt abandoned by potential and a good man.

Stop acting like a cowardly little lion cub.

I'd never been in-your-face feisty, just quietly confident and willing to take risks. But some contrarian streak had me ignoring the idea that these meet-ups with this man might've been God-intended.

Self had better sense and wasn't having it.

Yazmeen Renee, I will kick me in my own throat if you don't get him.

But dinner with Sir Sexy?

Is a meal with a man!

So self said when the man was beyond basic.

Talk yourself out of this attraction if you want. Don't go crying to God when His Fineness disappears.

"Tavares!"

At the door of India's shop, he stopped. As if debating whether or not the effort was worth the while, he took his time returning to where I sat feeling more nervous than necessary at his silence.

Taking a big breath, I went in. "I appreciate the dinner invitation. Unfortunately, it's not an option right now. However," I quickly added, seeing his unmasked disappointment, "coffee is."

Eyes on mine, he pulled a business card from his wallet and asked for a pen. Finding one, I handed it to him, our fingers touching and flooding what felt like infinite heat through me.

Those luscious lips lifting in that sexy, easy grin let me know he'd felt my flash of fire. He was polite enough not to comment, simply wrote a number and handed me his card.

"That's my private line. Call whenever." He returned my pen. "To answer your earlier curiosity, I was referred to Miss India by one of her clients: my cousin, Reina—who conveniently failed to mention you're related. So, no, I'm not stalking you, but I am direct when someone has my interest. That would be you. And for the record, I believe in divine providence, not coincidence." Propping his arms on my lowered window, he had the nerve to lean in, treating me to his clean, sexy fragrance. "You have my number. Whenever you're comfortable. Whenever convenient, coffee it is." Stepping back, he passed me what appeared to be a flier from beneath my windshield wiper that I'd overlooked. "*Buenas noches*, Yazmeen."

Feeling all warm and fuzzy about the belly, I waved before driving away thinking that after three years of no dudes, no dates, I owed self *something*.

Convincing myself coffee with a king was okay, I glanced at the event announcement removed from my windshield.

At a red light, I turned on the overhead light to better see what I recognized as Royal's ratchet chicken scratch on the back:

Dude's still interested in you. One time. $5K. Never again.

"What the heck!"

Lord forgive me for littering, but I tossed that foolery out the window and sped off.

It took the entire ride to my parents' doing mindfulness exercises to get my breathing back on track.

"You will not give yourself a heart attack."

Not behind a man ready to sell his ex for financial profit. I had no idea what new mess Royal had gotten himself into, but I was not the one to rescue him by dancing next-to-naked.

Pulling into my parents' driveway, I hurried inside unwilling to sit with the fact that I'd essentially married a pimp who was past desperate. Even so, I thought about that flier and the fact that it had been placed on my windshield while at India's.

A Friday night at my sister's salon was out of my ordinary. I'd never made Royal privy to the fact that I'd be there. Heading to the game room and my busted lip baby, I wondered if I had a stalker named Royal Jones while convincing myself there was no need for that tiny flicker of fear.

CHAPTER EIGHT
SLUT-A-RELLA, MUTT-A-RELLA
Tavares

You must be real thirsty.

More for Yazmeen than coffee. She had me braving a howling November wind whipping the rain sideways. Not to mention with Sasha's being located in one of downtown Sacramento's millennial hives, parking was a practice in patience.

Truth? I was willing to face a hurricane for a piece of that woman's day.

We'd touched bases during the week in a couple of conversations that were brief and always during work hours. She had my private line. What did I have? Her nine-to-five. She was cautious: I got that. One interaction with that Thug-a-Mug ex was enough to understand why men might've been on her "ish" list. He'd clearly screwed things up and had me paying the consequences. My challenge? Showing her I was worth her time and trust, because a brother needed a better kind of communication than what we'd experienced. There was only so much you could discuss when connecting with the woman you wanted to know when she was posted up at her job in a church office. You couldn't get deep. And you sure couldn't get sexy. Maybe it was God's roundabout way of keeping me on the up-and-up, instead of my old school trickery of working my way into Yazmeen's panties.

"Yeah...that," I acknowledged with a laugh, making yet another loop around the block, hoping a parking space opened up. When it did, I snagged it, situated the Kangol on my head, grabbed the umbrella and slipped on the jacket. Hustling up the walkway, I had a sudden appreciation for being a new creation in Christ and trying this "getting to know a woman" thing God's way for a change. I needed eyes wide open, to feel us out and ease into possibility. Not let my strong-arm personality run over things. Past randomness had taught me to move slowly, but this woman here? She had me wanting to go all in.

Indoors, I shook off the day's chill and appreciated the lobby's warmth. Wiping rain from my glasses, I scanned a wall-mounted directory in the remodeled, three-story Victorian housing a collective of Black-owned businesses.

Impressive.

The first floor housed a hair salon and boutique while the third was split between a massage therapist, custom-costume jewelry shop, and a graphic arts/web design outfit. Per the directory, Sasha's Essentials claimed space on the second floor along with an insurance broker, and travel agency.

"Wakanda forever for real."

Ignoring the elevator, I opted for the stairs to get that cardio in. Plus, my energy was on happy puppy-kind-of high and needed to be dialed back a bit.

Quit acting like a kid on a Disneyland trip.

Was I that pathetic?

Yeah, well, it had been a minute.

Not that I hadn't been attracted to women in the time since becoming born again. I had. But, my slightly A-type personality made me the kind of man who went all in. When I committed to something, I committed. There was no half-stepping. I didn't creep or sneak. Giving my life to the Lord, I gave Him one-hundred. I meant that thing. Guess I didn't fully realize that my living a Christ-centered life included celibacy. But studying God's Word, for me, it did. With me, a weaning process wouldn't work. I had to go cold turkey. Besides, I'd spent more than enough time bumping between random legs. My salvation meant much to me. I wanted to do right by my heavenly Father and His Word, and chose to live differently.

Scaling those stairs, I might've been hyped but, again, my sense was Yazmeen was nervous. Thus, my suggesting meeting at Sasha's before going elsewhere. Her sister's shop was familiar, neutral territory that could kick up her comfort. Plus, I needed a gift for *Abuela's* life celebration, and believed in patronizing minority-owned businesses. Meeting there was a win-win.

Finding Sasha's suite and walking in was like entering a sensory haven. The sound of trickling water features blended with background instrumentals playing softly. White orchids were situated about, adding a touch of elegance to a small space that was expertly arranged with built-in shelves, bins, and counters displaying hair and body products that scented the air with clean aromatics and sensuous scents reminiscent of Yazmeen.

"Nice."

Sasha showcased mad skills in creating an environment celebrating self-care. The shop wasn't large but, with a clear flare for presentation, the space had been maximized to display products to their full advantage. Simple packaging—color splashes categorizing items for hair, face, or body—conveyed sophisticated earthiness with cool color palettes.

"*Whaaat?* Wait! You actually stopped by?" Posted up behind the front counter, Sasha's bright greeting left me laughing.

"Ms. Sasha, I told you I would, right?"

Excusing herself from her customer, she hurried over. "Yes, but you're T-Alva Alvarez, and that's too big for my shop."

"Obviously, it's not," I countered, returning her brief hug.

"Welcome to the world of Sasha's Essentials. What do you think?' Grabbing my arm, she walked me about, hurrying on before I could speak. "We love old houses, so we tried to keep its integrity. The hardwood floors, crown molding, and vaulted ceiling are all part of the original design. But I had to knock out the front walls and replace them with glass."

"The landlord was obviously down with that."

"He had no choice. He's my husband," she replied, explaining that the house had been in her husband's family for three generations until her mother-in-law's sudden passing a few years back. "Dad didn't have it in him to stay here by himself, so Brandon—that's my husband—decided to turn it into a place of business. Whaddya think?"

"It's absolutely on point."

Her almond eyes narrowed with her smile very much like her sister's.

"Oops, I'm being rude to my customer. Make yourself comfortable while I finish helping her."

"Will do."

Clearly, Sasha was a savvy businesswoman. Looking around, I was impressed and wondered if this was the flagship or her only shop. Her set-up was far from shady or shoddy; if her product quality was as tight as her presentation, it might merit expansion.

While I was retired from the game, hustling and grinding hadn't retired me. My dad had drilled down into my psyche: "have your post-game hustle ready." Even prior to retiring, I had my next steps lined up before I left B-ball and it left me. Plus, growing up, I'd watched my father pursue multiple income streams. Pops was old school patriarchal in that he didn't want Moms working, but felt he alone should and could provide for his family. A multi-gifted manual laborer, Pops hustled hard to take care of us. And while she didn't "punch in," *Mami* made coin selling homemade sauces and candies at local swap meets on weekends. We weren't rich, but we usually had plenty. So, I knew from my parents' example not to sit on possibility, but had set that venture capitalist with a side hustle in real estate life up, before leaving the game. As a V.C., I was serious about finding and investing in quality minority-owned businesses, especially start-ups. Sasha's had my attention.

Sniffing a body butter sample, I scooped out a little. It was smooth, whipped. I sniffed it again, waiting on familiar notes of Yazmeen, forgetting about being a V.C. Missing those notes, I made a game of opening jars and hunting until noticing I'd trekked in rain. Seeing a glass bowl-topped washing station, I grabbed paper towels and got busy. One thing my mother drilled into her kids was "you mess it, you fix it."

"Tavares, I promise I'll be right with you and don't worry about that."

"Take your time, and I got this." Looking Sasha's way, I found her customer hardcore staring. I'd been good in the game, but never the world's greatest; and retirement had taken me out of over-rotation. Even so, at times folks reacted as if I was still a celebrity athlete. Sasha's customer apparently held such sentiment.

Dude, you need a crash course in IncogNegro 101.

If camouflage was my intent the black leather Kangol and eyeglasses weren't doing it. I guess going clean-faced and shaving the goatee and moustache off that morning was equally ineffective. Not to mention my leather, knee-length jacket had me looking like Shaft. Nodding in acknowledgment, I moved on, ignoring Fan Girl Female, conceding it was hard to make a six-foot-six-inch man inconspicuous.

Resuming my hunt for Yazmeen's scent, I tried something labeled citrus sage soufflé. It was good, but lacked her feminine sultriness.

That woman...

She was beautiful, sensuous, and saved: a combination I'd never experienced, but definitely craved. Was she relationship material? And was I—a man whose randomness never allowed for past commitments—ready for that sort of situation?

"Enjoy your purchase."

Hearing Sasha finishing up, I started in her direction only for her to be distracted by her ringing cell phone.

"Shoot! Tavares, I have to take this."

"No worries. Handle your business."

She hurried towards what must've been the stockroom, earbuds in, leaving me with my Fan Girl friend.

Posted up near the front counter, purchase in hand, she stared like I'd borrowed money and never gave it back. When ol' girl sashayed my way, leering not looking, I knew I was about to meet up with *something*.

"I know you." Her tone was too intimate for someone whose face didn't register.

I confess. My B-ball days were overrun with a plethora of sexual partners, but she wasn't one. I didn't appreciate being pressed unless it was a mutual attraction and consensus. This wasn't that. Still, chick was up on me like she'd flunked Personal Space-ology. She was easy enough on the eyes that I might've responded in a way that let sexual games have full play until we were butt-naked and bouncing in bed back in the day. But I wasn't attracted. Tail-chasing was no longer my game.

Stepping back, I put room where needed.

She wasn't having it and repositioned herself real close, intent on her end goal.

"Can I help you?" I appreciated strong females who went for theirs, but the aggressive space invader routine had my irritation up. Chick was bugging.

"*Yasss*, huntee, you can." Ol' girl got all whispery and kittenish, her fake, Snuffaluffagus eyelashes pumping like fans while pulling some promo postcard from her purse and pressing it against my abdomen. "Kryshelle and I used to kick it." Chick was so close I felt the silicone. "Was she lying...or are you a major beast in the bedroom?" Growling all Eartha Kitt-ish, girlfriend scraped her crooked hand down my thigh and up again. "Call me. I'll pump that beast and bring out the Tarzan....and you'll get a discount if you give me multiple orgasms."

What the!

I wasn't prone to going off in public, but if chick was a dude she might've got dusted.

Grabbing her runaway paw, I stepped away disgusted with females coming for me like I was a walking wallet and ever-ready erection.

Screw being a gentleman.

She merited a clap back. I had one, and lost it. Motion outside the wall of windows caught my peripheral vision and intercepted that action.

Damn!

My foulness needed forgiveness, but the woman I meant to spend my day with stood there taking the situation in and—based on her facial expression—misinterpreting it.

"Is that you? She's cute," Eartha Kitt Trick had the audacity to comment while switching her crooked hips towards the exit. "I don't discriminate and flow both ways, so you can bring her, too."

Feeling a need to disinfect myself, I went for the woman I wanted. She stood watching Fan Girl sashay away as if debating with herself whether to head back down the stairs or stay.

"Yazmeen." I escorted her indoors before she could play Flo Jo on me and hundred-yard dash in the opposite direction. We stood looking at each other, evaluating next steps. I spoke first, addressing the whackness. "I apologize that you encountered that, but trust that situation wasn't mine and holds no interest."

I had to give it to her: the woman had class. She didn't pop her neck or read me up one wall and down the next. But her stare was direct, peeping my soul for incriminating evidence until bending to retrieve what I'd obviously dropped. "I think this is yours."

Really?

A black lace G-string on red satin sheets sharing space with a phone number, the name Slut-a-Rella, approved payment methods, and a tagline, "I do real slutty things" decorated Fan Girl's postcard. I felt contaminated, like I needed penicillin and anti-crab cream. "Just wow. Yazmeen—"

"It's not my business."

"Getting to know you is mine, and I can't have foolery interfering." Shredding that mess, I dumped the pieces in the garbage bin. I liked my life and didn't play Russian Roulette with ejaculations-for-pay or the possibility of sexually transmitted diseases. I felt pressed to correct misperceptions and represent myself as a man disinterested in running game. "Yazmeen, you're my singular interest. I have zero need for Mutt-a-Rella antics."

"*Slut*-a-Rella," she corrected.

"Same difference." The deep breath I took nearly hurt my ribs. "So…can we push 'restart'?"

"We can."

Emboldened, I kissed her hand. "Good morning, Miss Williams."

"Good morning. You shaved off your goatee. I like." She reached as if to feel my hairless jaw, only to stop suddenly. "Is Sasha in the back?"

She moved in that direction, but I held onto her hand, urging her to face me again. "Are we good?"

"Yes." Her half-smile set me right with relief until she added, "For coffee and a chat. I know you offered to drive, but how about we meet there instead?"

Well, double damn!

Trust, I understood the need for spatial distance. Being close to this woman made me want to kiss and lick places I hadn't in five years of abstinence. I had only God to thank for restraint and self-discipline. But this situation felt like intentional distance and friction resulting from that foul female. It was fall-out from something I didn't solicit. "That's fine."

"I'll be back."

Watching the storeroom door close behind her, I felt on the opposite side of potential and possibility. The Taurus bull in me wasn't having it. I was following without thinking.

Give her a minute.

God and good sense put me on pause. There was no need to pound the door like a Neanderthal. I was fine with giving her time, but I didn't appreciate the idea that I'd been fouled and benched before our game began.

Lord, forgive me for real, but damn! Again.

CHAPTER NINE
NECK-PREGNANT
Yazmeen

T*hat wasn't your business, so shake the salt off.*
After my exes' devilment and disloyalty, I couldn't tolerate anything that looked like playerism. Not that Tavares and I were involved. But still.

Why're you acting pitiful and possessive?

That wasn't my nature and Tavares wasn't mine. Besides, throughout the week, hadn't me, myself, and I convinced Yazmeen we weren't interested beyond coffee?

Obviously, we'd done a poor job of lying.

Finding Sasha on the phone in the storeroom, I took a deep breath and put on some act right, reminding myself of a few things. One: I'd healed from the devastated condition Darrien and Royal left my heart in. Two: I was single and satisfied. Three: single, satisfied, saved and sanctified, I was blissfully celibate and disinterested in anything with Sir Sexy.

The liquid lies.

Nearing the store and finding him—my costar in recent hot and unholy dreams—shockwaves ripped through my body. Those waves fizzled and faded thanks to that thing between him and Super Boobies who—by the way—was vaguely familiar even if I couldn't determine how I knew her.

Sister was rubbing up on him with those surgical super twins holding up her chin.

Not one to hate on another woman, I reminded myself there was no need for saltiness. Tavares was barely beyond stranger status, and our limited encounters did not 'him my man' make. He could flirt and hook-up to his heart's content. Plus, I had no rights to be knee-deep in feelings, particularly after acting uncommonly skittish and confining us to coffee.

"Hey, Yazzy! Did you see my extra special customer?" Sasha nearly squealed, sounding too many shades of thrilled.

I played dim and dumb. "No. Who?"

"Either you're blind or buried. T-Alva Alvarez!"

"Oh…yeah, I saw him."

Chick laid a hand against my forehead like only fever could explain my ignorance. "Girl, get your pulse checked. You might be dead."

Laughing, I knocked her hand off my head.

"Unlike the last time I saw you in your Donkey Kong no-deodorant fit, you're looking cute like I trained you, Yaz. Where're you going?"

"Somewhere you can't."

"Whatever. Oh, wait! Your pre-holiday postcard promo idea was legit. I've been two, three customers deep all morning. It only slowed up an hour or so ago. Can you stay and help your favorite baby sister until my part-timer rolls in?"

"No, ma'am. I have plans."

"Such as?"

"Coffee with a friend."

"What friend?"

I took my time answering. "Tavares."

Sasha's eyes grew hyper big. Hurrying to the stockroom door, she pushed against it, making sure it was completely closed. "What is up with that? First, it was dancing—which you have yet to tell me about. Now, you're going out with Fine Almighty *alone*? Don't make me call Mama 'cause you know that woman'll enlist a chaperone."

I snorted, remembering how our mother religiously sent either of us on India's dates when big sis was a teen.

"For real! You know I will. So…are you giving up abstinence, and hitting him with that Williams Girl Big Booty Magic?" Tongue hanging out her mouth, she gyrated her prego self in a way that missed its sexy target.

"Mama had you because…?"

"She preferred perfection. And I'm just asking! I can't have my sexless sister going out for coffee and accidentally catching orgasms. Your makeup's beat, but take your coat off so I can make sure your fit is fiyah."

"Move, Your Ignorance." I waved her aside, knowing my wedge-heeled, baby blue leather boots, ankle-length denim skirt, silver statement jewelry and icy blue wrap-around sweater with angel sleeves were on point—all courtesy of my last thrift store trip.

Moving out of my way, baby sister swatted my behind as I passed. "Work that muscle booty, boo. I'm proud of you for getting back in the game before your coochie disintegrates."

Turning and rubbing her barely-there prego bump, I bent down and baby-talked. "Sweetie, I feel for you having to be born to one so mentally compromised and incompetent."

Wondering why God made younger siblings, I left that nut in the stockroom, laughing.

Sasha's shop was only so big. Everywhere I turned, Tavares was there consuming my air—that strong body, lush lips, and sexy scent impacting my equilibrium. His requesting my help in finding a gift for some unnamed woman had us sharing air and moving in tandem, forcing me to focus on the task at hand, not his effects on my heating flesh.

"What's her scent profile?"

Sniffing an open jar of sugar scrub, the look he gave me was quizzical, cute. "And that is...?"

"Does the recipient resonate florals?" I'd helped Sasha enough to know a scent profile pertained to the fragrant notes that complimented a person's molecular chemistry; *and* I preferred "recipient" to "your woman." He hadn't identified who we were shopping for. I told myself that business was his, and that I didn't care to know what other woman had his attention. Spending too much thought on it might have me tight in my feelings. "Is she woodsy and earthy? Sweet, bright? Or sensual and erotic? I mean *exotic*!"

Tickled by my tongue-tangle, he gave me that slow grin that put some melt in my nether region. "I'm not sure. May I smell you?"

Bending, gently inhaling beneath my ear, his nose brushed my sensitive skin.

Lord, my neck got pregnant.

His half-whispered, "Your profile is decadence," had me carrying triplets.

With Tavares the simplest acts felt intimate, sent my sexless cells into a tailspin. Shivering, I stepped back, avoiding a neck climax.

He immediately righted his stance. "Forgive me, I didn't mean to—"

I waved away my neck conception. Voice all choked, I sounded like Kermit. "Any idea what she'd prefer?"

"Your hair's different," he commented, versus answering my question.

"It is." I'd switched things up and had India incorporate burgundy highlights in the braids piled in a bun atop my head. The style was simple, but—per the warm look in his eyes—effective.

Doing his deep-stare-at-me thing that left my insides melting, he said something in Spanish. He could've called me a 'Nappy-headed, crack ho criminal' for all I cared. That Spanish sliding sexy off his tongue turned insults into ecstasy. He was quick in translating. "I like. It's elegant."

Thankfully the Muppet left my voice, leaving it semi-normal again. "Thanks, but back to my question. What profile suits your recipient?"

"What're you wearing?"

You can't have my scent for some Super Boobie chick!

"You think I'm wearing Sasha's Essentials because?"

"I quote, 'it's the only product worthy of your gorgeous skin.; I added the 'gorgeous'. So, what is it?"

"Mango Almond Spice," I supplied, inwardly quivering at his compliment.

"Duly noted. That's the scent I'll never give another woman."

Loading a shopping bag, he took my hand and headed to the front counter, undoubtedly blessing Sasha with her biggest, single purchase yet.

Girlfriend was all giddy arranging the plethora of items in a sizable gift basket. "Yazzy, test my men's body butters on Tavares while I finish this," that happy heffa had the nerve to suggest. "I've only tried them on my husband and would love your feedback, Tavares."

"I'm cool with it. Yazmeen?" The man had a way of wrapping my name in rhythm and incense.

Rolling up his sleeves and holding out his hands, he teased, "Come on, *chica*. Massage me."

I had instant thoughts of his long, strong, naked body face down on my bed, me straddling his back, massaging. And massaging. And him flipping things so that I was face down as he slowly licked a slow path down my spine and over my hyper sensitive behind.

Lucifer, you're a licking lie!

Needing to get my mind right, I made the mistake of noting the hugeness of his hands. I had to put my brain in chains to keep from wondering about other anatomical blessings. Touching definitely wasn't happening.

"How about this?" Grabbing sample jars from behind the counter, I filled them with the designated product, dropped the jars in a small bag and handed it to him. Minus all that rubbing.

Grinning like he knew something, he accepted the bag, took my hand and kissed it. Again. I swear those thick, luscious lips had me seeing chariots and cherubim. Obviously, I needed to fast forty days and forty nights. I'd be weak and hungry, but at least my temple would have some act right.

"Miss Yazmeen, looks like gentrification's swallowing the O.P."

Holed up in my favorite Black-owned tea shop in what used to be the 'hood, Tavares and I found a table in the most secluded corner we could. "Yep, Oak Park's victim of white bite."

Pulling out my chair, he waited until I was seated before placing his drink on the table and unzipping that buttery-soft leather jacket. I watched like it was a striptease, early Christmas gift from God to me. I'm just saying. His Fineness was fabulously fit and optically delicious in a salmon-colored, silky-soft looking long-sleeved T-shirt kissing that broad chest and loose jeans that pulled across his firm thighs when he sat beside me. And you wonder why I elected to drive.

The need to not be in close confines with his sexy kind aside, my salty response to that slut-a-mutt business was proof that the scars of infidelity don't heal easily. Despite therapy, daily affirmations and keeping my spirit clean, sometimes my wounds cracked and bled. I spent the drive time resituating my spirit and reminding myself all men didn't deserve judgment.

"White bite, huh?"

"Gentrification is vampire-like. It seemingly strikes at night."

"And sucks communities of color dry," he added to my analogy. "When rolling through I noticed white bite chewed up some Black businesses that used to be here."

"Which is why I love patronizing Black-owned. Like this tea shop." Jammed with folks escaping wet weather and sipping hot drinks, the shop's at-capacity crowd left minimal space so that we were crammed at L-angles, rather than face-to-face. Glancing about, appreciating the décor, my eyes locked onto the twenty-something, five-foot barista sister so busy staring at Tavares she could barely function.

Sis, trust, based on his shoe size, this man will snap you in half. Your precious uterus can't handle this.

Kicking that comical thought inside, I focused on His Fineness. "This isn't exactly next door to Sasha's, so thanks for making the drive."

He swallowed salted caramel macchiato before responding. "Not a problem. The O.P. is part of childhood memories."

"Really? How?" Plucking white chocolate shavings from my spicy hot chocolate, my finger smeared the cloud of whipped cream. Moaning at the deliciousness, I licked that digit like my mother never taught me about napkins.

Really, Yazmeen?

My lick-a-ration left him—mouth ajar—looking like he liked the way I cleaned cream.

I was so not a queen of seduction, nor was I trying to be. Simply? I was greedy.

Encouraging him to continue our conversation, I plopped my lickable hand in my lap and surrendered to the smooth flow of his baritone. His tales were sweet. He'd grown up in Philly, spending summers with maternal grandparents on the west coast—his maternal set in Vallejo, paternal in Sacramento, respectively.

"Every Saturday *Abuelo* loaded as many of us as he could into his truck and rolled to his "*Pequeño Rico*"—or "Little Puerto Rico" which was really Little Mexico in the Franklin & Twelfth district."

He had me laughing, calling his grandfather politically incorrect, piling his grands in the back of his pickup not caring about stereotypes or seatbelts.

"*Abuelo* had us looking all immigrant-ish. Only props missing were lawnmowers and leaf blowers."

That had my head back on a laugh. "You're *so* wrong for that!"

"'Ey, I *love* my culture and can speak on it."

"Hi!" Looking away from each other, we found Little Sister Barista at our table, grinning like she'd found gold. "How're your drinks?"

"Everything's good. Thanks."

His polite but tight response indicated his being accustomed to public interruptions, but not necessarily relishing them.

"I can't get you anything?"

"Yazmeen?"

"I'm fine."

"We're straight, but that gentleman over there might need assistance." He pointed out a patron frantically pulling laptop and papers away from the dangers of his spilled beverage.

Little Barista Girl had the nerve to roll her eyes and sigh. "I'll be back."

"No, not necessary. If we need anything, we know how to get it."

Watching her walk off, I grinned. "Fan girl follies?"

"Possibly, but I'm solely interested in you. Not interruptions."

Some little, unlicensed leprechaun did a happy dance somewhere between my heart and lap. "Back to where you left off…"

Soft music drifting through the shop's sound system, Sir Sexy shared those long-ago Saturday morning rituals. From *Pequeño Rico* to Martin Luther King Boulevard and Broadway, it was a cultural quest, connecting to community.

"Anybody whose head was raggedy wound up in a chair at Uncle Jed's Cut Hut. But the best part? That day ended with a stop at Flower's Fish Market for 'you buy, we fry.' Now…?"

We glanced at our fellow patrons: proof positive that Oak Park had become home to happy, white millennials.

"It's a new look, and Uncle Jed's, the Forty Acres Art Gallery, and a grip of other Black-owned businesses that used to be here have disappeared. That's why I got into real estate so we can keep a piece of this pie."

"It's like this country-wide. Folks who used to speed through, afraid of carjackings and drive-bys, are consuming underrepresented communities," I observed, ignoring how our occasional shifting had our knees, our thighs touching and stimulating sparks in places too private.

"And pushing *us* further beyond the margins," he remarked, sitting back. "I didn't mean to get us going on this track."

"It's fine." And it was. I enjoyed seeing various sides of him. He was obviously passionate about equality and opportunity. He had substance and was more than marvelous manliness and firm pecs for my fleshy fantasies. "What're you doing for the upcoming holiday? Does your family get together at your grandparents' for Thanksgiving?"

I offered condolences hearing his paternal grandfather passed a while ago. Since that time—and similar to mine—his family rotated holiday hosting.

"This year's at my aunt's in Land Park. She makes killer *mofongo*. That's all I need alongside my mother's *ponsit, lumpia,* and collard greens," he stated, explaining mofongo was a delicious-sounding Puerto Rican dish of fried, mashed plantains, garlic, and bacon, and that his mother was biracial: Filipino and African-American.

"I've never had *mofongo*, but I'm here for it."

"I'll make you some."

"You cook?"

"I have skills, but Moms is the master. I'm looking forward to getting fat this Thanksgiving. I'm serious," he added when I laughed. "I'ma be hitting that cardio hard between now and then 'cause a brother's going in."

"May I ask a potentially sensitive question?" When he nodded, I did. "You obviously identify as Black but being multi-ethnic, have you ever felt pressured to choose?"

"My parents never asked me to. America chose for me with its One Drop Rule."

"So society dictates how you embrace your cultures?"

"Let me explain another way." Arms on the table, he leaned towards me. "When Five-Oh pulls me over—and they have—all they see is a potential menace and some miscellaneous kind of Black man. They don't care which ancestor came from where. I do. I'm Filipino. I'm Puerto Rican. I'm African-American. All of that. And proud about it."

"Well, amen. And where'd you get your height and when'd you start playing basketball?"

"You just rolling in the business," he teased, laughing. "The height came from both sides. *Abuelo* was six-three. PaPa, my maternal grandfather's six-five."

I laughed at his recounting being a two-year old always running after his older brothers who were naturally athletic, and them picking him up so he could shoot baskets.

"I was six or so when my parents enrolled me in basketball camp just to burn up my excess energy."

"You were hyperactive?"

"Like you wouldn't believe," he responded almost in sync with my phone blasting that ex-monster march. "You're a Vader fan?"

Silencing my cell, I grinned. "Something like that. How's Aniyah liking her braids?"

He chuckled. "That girl caught a case of Willow Smith, whipping that hair all over the place. I think she thinks she's cute."

"She is."

"Thanks. I agree, but I try to keep that head from swelling. Are we good on time, or do you have a curfew?"

Darth interrupted again.

"Why don't you take that while I grab us a refill?"

If I could've afforded a new phone, I would've dropped mine in his water glass in a virtual, murder-free drowning. Instead, I reached across and held his arm when he stood. Turning my phone, I showed him the display. In my humble opinion, the "Ex-Monster" title wasn't overly bad. My replacing Royal's image with a photo of that saucer-eyed, knobby-headed, five-strands-of-hair-having hunchbacked "my precious"-coveting thing from *The Lord of the Rings* had His Fineness sitting down, falling out laughing.

"Really, Yazmeen?"

"What?" If anything, I owed Tolkien an apology. His problematic creature was cute in comparison.

"You're wrong for that."

"Am I? You've met him."

"Yeah…I have and no comment. Back to that curfew issue."

"We've only been here fifteen, twenty minutes. I'm good."

"Not that I'm minding, but we've been here over an hour."

Checking my phone, I was surprised to see time had flown. "Wow. Well, I'm grown enough not to have a curfew."

Sitting back and rubbing his chin, he gave me the once-over. "I don't know. You looking kind of young, Miss Williams. How grown are you?"

My eyebrow lifted. "If that's your way of asking my age, I'm thirty-two. Three-three on July tenth. And you, Mister Slick-n-Sly?"

He granted me that sexy grin. "Thirty-six on the fourth of May."

"Well, I wish you an advanced 'happy birthday.'"

"How about we work on my hearing that six months from now straight from your lips?"

"*A la* Marilyn Monroe or Jennifer Hudson?"

"Sweetheart, I'll take it any way you give it."

Leaving that too lush invitation on the table, I informed him the boys were spending the night with Godmommy Velle and Uncle Ronnie. With Aniyah being at his sister's, we could enjoy the rare gift of adult time.

"Cool. Let me get these refills. You killed that croissant. Want another?"

I declined, thoroughly enjoying this multi-layered man. He was intelligent, a good listener and communicator with a refreshing sense of humor. In his presence, I was completely relaxed.

I'm enjoying this.

Glancing around the shop, I appreciated that—other than Barista Boo—patrons had given us privacy versus acting ignorant over a celebrity. He'd autographed a napkin for a little girl with her grandparents, but that was that. His focus was us.

Dipping my finger in croissant remnants, I licked it, glad I'd taken a chance.

"I did ask if you wanted another one, right? Now, you gonna be all up in mine."

Laughing, I thanked him for the refill while eyeing his pastry as he sat. "I'm fine."

"I agree," he said, swirling the contents of his cup, eyes on me. "So...I've met Malik, but you have another son. He's why you had to leave your sister's salon early the other night."

Other than learning we were both parents and born-again, our phone conversations had been brief, non-revealing and more a matter of situating today's set-up. That was my preference at the time. Now? I realized how limiting that had been. Placing my cup on the table, I crossed my arms over my chest and leaned towards him. "You were ear-hustling?"

"'Ey, don't fault a brother for getting info anyway he can. It's Malcolm. Right? And how's his lip?"

Omitting his requiring three stitches and an ER visit, I smiled. "Malcolm and his lip are good. Thank you for remembering their names."

"You're welcome, and why wouldn't I?" he asked before sipping his drink.

"You'd be surprised by the responses I get when brothers find out I have twins."

When I tell you that man's eyes bugged and he choked trying to swallow without spitting macchiato at me, believe.

His turning red-faced and coughing so hard tears were leaking beneath his glasses had me out of my seat, patting his back like I was burping a giant baby. *"Are you okay?"*

He nodded despite wheezing like a two-ton champion chain smoker.

The mommy in me went into action. Ready to rush to the counter for water (since he'd drained his), I had to jump back when Little Sister Barista nearly knocked me over, playing EMT for the fine and choking.

"Sir, take this! Drink it." She was all command central, like mouth-to-mouth resuscitation and marriage were next.

"Thank you, sweetheart. We've got this." Taking the water glass, I gave it to Tavares and sat looking at her while slowly rubbing that broad back as if he needed me to help him breathe, and I was marking territory. Ignoring her side-eye, I focused on him. "Slow breaths."

It took a minute, but his color and respiration got themselves together.

"Better?"

When he said nothing, simply sat staring at me like I'd grown another booty, I prepared myself for that just-remembered-I-have-some-place-else-to-be ditch-and-dash.

"You have twins." It was a statement, not a question, that felt like some kind of challenge.

Getting my cell from my purse and pulling up a picture of the boys in class holding that Snickers-Snackers rodent thing, I handed it to him.

That man sat there shaking his head, staring at the twins' pic, as if stupefied. His words were so slow and low, I had to lean in to catch them.

"I'm one of God's hardheaded sons who does do-overs because of twisting things the way I want." Returning my phone, those whisky brown eyes relentlessly peered into mine. "So...I've learned to dial back and ask for confirming signs when it comes to matters of..." Abruptly, he rolled his shirtsleeve up and over that fit, firm right bicep. Angling his muscular arm in my direction, he displayed a tattoo of a name inked across two linked hearts and dates in a ribbon banner beneath.

Reading the name, I asked, "Who's Taia?"

"My twin sister."

"Are...you...*serious*? You have a twin?"

The semi-sad look that crossed his face tempered my exuberance.

He nodded. "Yes, but she died the day we were born."

Unable to imagine life without one of my sons or the heartbreak his family experienced, I squeezed his forearm, noticing the May fourth date tattooed in that ribbon banner, and that the year of birth and death were the same. "I'm so sorry you missed out on the blessing of living life with her." Heart hurting for him, I gently outlined his tattooed tribute.

"Thank you, but I've lived my whole life with Taia right here." He placed an oversized palm on his chest. "That twin bond is real. It's like she never left."

Completely understanding as a mother of multiples, I traced a finger over Taia's name only to realize my touching might've been unwanted. I pulled back, but he grabbed my hand.

"Keep going. That felt good."

"So you're opportunistic and milking my sympathies?"

"Maybe."

We both laughed.

"Like I said, I get it any way I can, Yazzy."

"You may not use my nickname." My legal name on his lips was already more than much. Derivatives might have me stripping, making my womb and all my insides available to whatever Tavares wanted.

He had the nerve to play pathetic. "You allowed Aniyah to."

"Aniyah's cute."

"I'm not?"

"Sir, you're eye candy gorgeous enough to melt a woman's panties off."

Trust me, brown girls blush.

Heat in my cheeks, I reached for his water, hoping he didn't have cooties. Draining what was left, I noticed his grin was satisfied but oddly shy. I found that unexpected bashfulness a sweet challenge to assumptions that men who looked like him were accustomed to flirtatiousness. Slut-a-Rella must've fulfilled his daily quotient.

"Tavares..." I couldn't even offer an apology for feeling like the Tourette's queen.

"'Ey." Reaching over, he stroked my hand. "I don't know about that melting action but, coming from you, the eye candy comment's a supreme compliment, Miss Yazzy Yaz."

"*Yazzy Yaz?*" I snickered, relieved at his not holding my loose lips against me. "That just earned you a five-minute silence, T-Alva Alvarez."

"Why you hating on my creativity? And what's wrong with 'Miss Yazzy Yaz?'"

"Nothing if I don't object to sounding like a grille-wearing, purple-wigged rapper chick swinging ten chains around my neck," I answered, liking the touch of his hand on mine.

His laugh was hearty, big, like the rest of him. "Miss Yazzy Yaz." He looked away as if visualizing an alter ego for me. "Naw, I can't see you spitting game on the mic despite your body being boss. You know your curves are straight *snatched* and banging, better than any video vixen's, right?"

Turning red in the face, he sat up straight and opened his mouth with what I presumed was an apology.

"It's okay, Tavares." Clearly, we shared a contagious case of blurt-a-rism.

"Actually, it's not. I can't have you thinking I'm not about nothing but your flesh."

"I don't, so can we move on?"

"We can. Tell me more about your dance career."

My studies had been long and the career portion somewhat successful but short-lived. "I retired when pregnant with my sons."

"Tell me one of its successes."

"I was a summer intern with the Alvin Ailey American Dance Theater. I didn't solo, but I was featured in a few performances." Sharing more on that amazing experience, I accepted his congratulatory fist bump.

"You're boss business, Miss Williams. So…care to share a less-than-success?"

His question had me shifting in my seat. "Maybe…in time."

"A brother has to earn your trust and prove himself to you?"

My, "Honey, yes, you got to work for this," had us both laughing until he switched it.

Voice low and sexy, he leaned towards me. "If I work it right, can I have all of you?" He sat back fast, looking shamefaced, apologetic. "I'm coming at you strong and wrong—"

"I'm fine, Tavares, so exhale and let it rest."

"No, for real…I meant no disrespect."

"None taken."

Silence copped a squat between us, along with that sexual heat that was behaving itself but so very present. Just when silence shifted uncomfortably, he sat forward, lasering me with those eyes smooth as brown whiskey.

"Listen…Yazmeen…can we keep it one-hundred?"

"Please."

"Getting to know you has me twisted."

A straight forward, uncomplicated person, I was nobody's seductive siren twisting men. That made me suspicious.

Just like that my mind flashed on the photos I'd found when internet surfing, featuring Sir Sexy with a plethora of women. Those pictures portrayed a suave, confident man who vibed off of female attention.

Could've been falsely fabricated for the public's benefit...

"May I ask another delicate question?" Feeling panicky, I didn't wait for permission. "Have you ever been...or *are* you attracted to men?"

Face scrunched like something stank, maybe my breath, he eyed me as if I was illegitimate. "No. Wait! *What?* Where'd that come from?"

Projecting from my painful past, I felt seizure-ready fearing his fumbling with me might've been because he preferred man-on-man contact. I didn't voice that, offering some lame "If I misunderstood" apology instead.

"You *truly* misunderstood. I'm all about the female and feminine." Un-scrunching his face, he quickly shook his head, choosing to let my insanity rest. "Anyhow...if I'm fouling out, coming at you out the side of my neck, it's because I'm new to this getting to know the whole woman concept."

I sipped my drink as he explained never being in a worthwhile relationship.

"Unfortunately, I was that rogue brother only wanting what a woman's body brought to bed. Now, that I'm living this life with the Lord?" He rubbed a hand over his head. "I'm committed to no randomness."

"Hashtag your past?"

"Exactly. Hashtag done with it. That's not to say I haven't gone out a few times here or there, but I keep that as clean as I can. What *I am* saying, Yazmeen, is you're the first woman I actually want to know beyond the physical. And that's not to say I'm not interested in you like that, because..." He took my hand, gently stroking it. "I am. Being around you hits every sexual note I know, and if you ever opened that part of yourself to me? Trust! I'd be calling on the Holy Spirit like, 'Man, Holy One, You gonna need to yoke me, choke me to keep me out them panties.' Okay...wait. I'm off my game and talking trash again."

If another man came at me that way, I'd want him to lick bricks and eat an asphalt sandwich. Instead, it took everything in me not to laugh at his self-frustration that was clearly evident. He was struggling with the same wild desire I felt for him that came up and out unrehearsed, when and how it wanted.

Oddly enough, there was something charming in this world-class athlete sitting, exhaling a streaming, aggravated breath as if—me, yard-sale queen, thrift-store-shopping, layaway-'til-payday Yazmeen—made him nervous. I wanted to do him like Malcolm and Malik, cuddle him up and rock him against my chest. "I get it, Tavares—"

"See...no. Let's try this one mo' again." Inhaling deeply, he offered heartfelt sincerity. "Point blank period? Who and what I'm interested in is the *whole* Yazmeen, particularly the one you don't let anyone else see."

Placing a hand atop his, I squeezed gently. "Thank you for your transparency. Like you, I'll take the compliments and discard the rest. And...I think we'd better go ahead and deal with all of this."

Since first suggesting coffee, I'd worked overtime convincing my-self that this man and I would stay firmly in the friend zone. But, look-ing into his seductive eyes, the honesty in me wouldn't let me sidestep blatant longing. I took a deep breath before confessing something I'd probably regret. "Grown folks' talk?"

"Mos' def."

"You're not the only one aggravated and discombobulated. There's a high, hot level of mutual attraction here." It was physical, sexual, and we both knew and felt it. "Doesn't mean you can come out of pocket with me, or me with you. But let's lay this on the table, dish the awk-wardness and own it...starting with friendship. Deal?"

"For real."

I held out my fist, pressing my knuckles to his.

After Royal's shenanigans and foolery, my life was devoted to rais-ing my sons. For the past three years, Malcolm and Malik had been my everything. Admittedly, I was anti-romance and kept all things male at arms' length—considered myself immune, if not impervious. But Tavares was a force I could no longer resist. "I'm unattached in every conceivable sense. And, honestly? I've had very little time for or interest in romance and nonsense. You?"

"Single dad, as you know. Never married. No side chicks, or friends with benefits."

"*Okayyy...*"

"Why you singing 'okay' like that's hard to believe, *Yazzy Yaz*?"

"It is! Maybe it's unfair and judgmental, but if you hadn't just told me you were done with randomness, I would've assumed a man as remarkable as yourself would have at *least* one, if not more, women."

He sat back, stroking a hand over his jaw. "Miss Williams, you're sexist and sinister. Dropping compliments and insults in one breath. All stealth bomber-ish."

I had to laugh. "Okay, fine. I'm wrong for assuming. But you're an *extremely* attractive, former pro athlete who had the spotlight on his life at one time. That right there put you in front of countless female fans," I rationalized, finishing off my cocoa. "I don't know what your on-court or pro-ball persona were like, but you're easy to talk to. You have a nice sense of humor and—"

"Per you, I'm the panty-melting, eye candy kind."

"To the tenth-degree times infinity."

"Umm, yeah, never had it phrased that way, but…no, I've never had a problem with the opposite sex. I'm not ignorant to the fact that in some matters my physicality might grant me unfair advantages." He shook his head. "I haven't cracked a mirror yet, so I'll take that as a positive. But as for all that other? I'm no better than another brother." He shrugged. "Whatever I am, I am. I don't credit myself. My parents presented the gene pool that did what it did."

Shifting my legs away from his, I crossed them and simply sat, studying him a moment. "Okay, last question, and I promise to be out your business. You said 'no side chicks or friends with benefits.' Does that mean you're…?"

"Celibate," he supplied when I didn't. "My commitment to it is the only thing keeping me from getting at you the way I really want to. For one: God would headlock me. Two: plain and simple? You're more than enough woman to keep my attention without sex in the picture. You have infinite value."

My grin was probably cheesy as cheddar. "Are you trying to make me like you?"

Something shimmered in me when he leaned forward, whispering in my ear, "Miss Yazmeen, you already do."

CHAPTER TEN
HANDS SOLO SINGLE
Tavares

ever be with someone who won't let you be yourself.
That was one of my father's favorite cautions. Of course, it was rendered in rapid-fire Spanish and—depending on the situation—decorated with a cuss word or three. But it came from the heart, most definitely.

Scanning notes before a presentation at a youth athletic symposium in Santa Monica, I flashed on that coffee date and the woman who'd assumed permanent residence in my head. No doubt, I'd been straight plain Tavares with zero excess. Genuinely kind-hearted with an easy, laid-back personality, she had a way of making me feel overly comfortable in my own skin. Her sincere interest in, not my public persona, but Tavares the man, had me for real on chill. The fact that she was easy to tease triggered my clown tendencies. When we weren't diving into deep topics, we were laughing. I'd vibed off her warmth, wit, and the fact that she'd abandoned her guard and was open. My one goal had been for Yazmeen to relax and let me into her world. She had, and now I wanted all in.

That woman's the whole package.

Sweet disposition. Calm spirit. Intelligent. Warm-hearted. Witty. Humble but unapologetic, like she loved herself and didn't care about popular opinions. Good conversationalist. Alluring. Natural and uncontrived. Born-again with a body that was straight banging and intoxicating.

I did what I could to focus beyond the physical, but we already know I caught a case of blurtitis and told all the wanting-her business. *I ain't never* acted that kind of babbling, bobble-headed fool. Even in my b-ball days, I was known for being calm under the pressures of the game. On and off the court, I was Rico Suavé. This woman parked my cool on the sidelines, left me acting fifteen versus thirty-five.

Truth?

I was accustomed to club chicks all about the turn up and wilding. This woman was sexy-cool. Classy. Dignified. That didn't keep her desirability from being explosive to me. It was. Truly. Had me stuck on the scandalous curve of her hips, those thick thighs, the roundness of her breasts perfectly fit for my lips. I wanted her sexually, absolutely. Learning that we were both born-again, committed Christian celibates, I knew intercourse wasn't happening. Just the same, her lushness had me, was its own kind of consuming. It wasn't that "get it and hit it," in your face type of vibe. Yazmeen's sensuality was powerful, dipped in endurance. It wouldn't make me come back for seconds. Her sexy would keep me, not let me walk away to begin with. She was that woman I had to see. Repeatedly.

Man, she got you going.

Apparently. The woman had me calling. Instant messaging. Getting in that communication as time permitted. I wasn't ready to admit she had my nose open so quickly, if at all. But she did. That left me tempering my take-over tendencies, questioning what she wanted, and moving prayerfully. But right then I needed my mind on my business, not Miss Voluptuous.

"Mister Alvarez, there's bottled water at the podium. The AV techs have your presentation cued and ready. I'll escort you in in just a minute. Can I do anything else for you?"

"Yes. Call me Tavares. Mister Alvarez is my dad," I told the young man assigned as my handler. Hoping he'd relax, I asked who he was and why he was there. I appreciated the respect my time in the game generated, but I was disinterested in some 'us versus them' reverence or distance. Part of my work with *Athletes & Academics* was bridging gaps and providing an inside look at baller life. Too many kids with hoops dreams were starry eyed over fame and money, and unready for the grinding. Escorted in on a standing ovation, I stayed true to me and kept it real while offering a holistic perspective. Grinding. Grueling practices. Beef with teammates. Not being drafted until after finishing my first year in college. Attending college during my off seasons to earn my undergraduate and MBA. As for money? I wouldn't have any without my parents taking over my finances that first year, and hiring a phenomenal financial manager whom I'd retained. This symposium, my speaking engagements, and *Athletes & Academics* was about giving back and, hopefully, helping other up-and-comings get a firm grip on handling success.

"Keep some act right. Live a good life. And don't forget to reach back and help another brother or sister," I concluded. "There's more than enough room for us all to come up. Thank you."

I left the stage to resounding applause, took pics, and signed autographs. All that. But only the youngster who'd played host to me got that private invite. "Email me some footage of your next game so I can see what you're working with."

Offering that one-armed-back-slap-bruh hug, he promised he would, waiting until he thought I was out of earshot before hollering and acting crazy like I'd just given him Christmas before Thanksgiving.

Grinning over his enthusiasm when climbing in the whip Lex sent, I bowed my head and thanked God for His goodness. "Father, I wouldn't be here without You, and *sure* couldn't do what I do. Thank You."

High on the happy that always came with positively connecting with young folks, I reached for my phone, ready to share that win. "Call Yazmeen."

What the...

Vocalizing that command felt natural, normal. As if she were my woman when she wasn't.

I cancelled the call.

Is that what you want?

Other than teen dating, I'd never had a substantive relationship. That didn't mean I'd ever experienced a lack of women. Whatever appeal I had exploded when I was drafted and went pro so that my pre-Jesus days were a series of females on rotation. That b-ball life made relationships unnecessary, overloading a young me with bedroom opportunities. Only God kept me from leaving a little Alvarez wherever I went, or contracting sexually transmitted diseases. Thankfully, my player ways were in the past, and I was all about that life with the Lord. That included keeping me in my pants. And while I'd *absolutely* connected with Yazmeen's sexual heat from day one, I was clear about her not being some miscellaneous female to get my rocks off. And if I even thought she was, that incident in the coffee house clipped that.

You'd be surprised by the responses I get when brothers find out I have twins.

That comment put that choke on my throat and had me tripping, wondering what God was up to.

It's like this. I'd messed up so much in my earlier years—with the liquor life, white lines, and flocks of females—that in some things I'd become overly cautious and was slow on the draw trying to keep myself moving in the right direction. God knew I wasn't rushing towards permanence or exactly thinking on marriage even if I wasn't opposed to it. Still, there was a prayer I'd prayed. Maybe it was a faith dare, or my crazy way of making sure God and I were on the same page.

Lord, You already know! I'm hardheaded and prone to miss it. So, when I'm blessed with the woman You really want me with, how 'bout giving Your boy a divine sign? Something straight crazy. Like let her have one brown eye, one hazel…or be the mother of twins, or triplets even.

Inwardly, I laughed at a prayer that was simple. Direct. Wild as heck. But I'd come too far for okey doke. I was done with "testing" women and all that foolishness. If and when I met the right one, my hardhead needed to know it. Enter, my crazy prayer that had me tossing thoughts.

Is Yazmeen for me?

I'd been dribbling on that notion this past week. We'd consistently communicated as much as two single parents can, trying to know each other better. I was liking what I learned. Granted, that calling her at work and instant messaging on social media was several shades of lame. But that's what her comfort level offered, so I accepted. Temporarily. We weren't in a place where relationship kinds of decisions needed to be made. Still, I knew she was a woman I couldn't play with. With Yazmeen, I'd have to come correct. My concern? Was I ready to be that man?

"What it do, short stack!"

"Whaddup, Southside Lex Ryde!" Slapping hands a good five times, I pulled my co-venture capitalist into a bruh hug. "Dude, you look like life."

From Chicago by way of Mississippi, Lex was a quiet, deep brown brother who made forty-three look goal-worthy. "Man, you know I keep this physique in case the NFL comes calling."

"Or, so Senaé doesn't pull your plate away."

He chuckled. "True."

"How's she doing?" I asked, sliding into our booth at the soul food joint he'd selected.

"She's four months, man! The belly's swelling." He extended his hands in front of his flat abs.

"Fault the father."

"Yeah, I *did* that," he bragged, bumping my fist, celebrating the divine goodness of God miraculously bringing he and his ex-wife together again—blessing them to conceive after a long ago miscarriage. "So, why're we here, Alvarez?"

"We'll get in it. Let a brother have some food first."

"Order innards and I'm outtie."

"Man, how you still hatin' on chittlins when you're from Mississippi?"

"How you dislike *El Pollo Loco* when you're from Puerto Rico?"

We fell out laughing.

"Dude, I'm from Philly, and starving. So, say nothing until some food's in front of me."

Over plates of southern goodness, I pitched *Sasha's Essentials*, my most recent V.C. interest.

Chewing intently, Lex studied me. "Sounds interesting, but brick and mortar ain't happening, kid."

"Which is why I'm proposing expanding her online ecommerce reach."

Sipping sweet tea, he nodded thoughtfully once I concluded my pitch. "How 'bout this, Alvarez? Get her proposal and business plan. Send me samples. Senaé'll try them. My boo is tactful, but brutally honest."

"Cool. But Sasha's launching a men's line, so you can try it, too. Now...about *Athletes & Academics*."

"Should've known *A&A* was the real dish," Lex griped, tossing his napkin on the table.

"Man, I'ma keep at it until you give in. Our board of directors needs you."

"First off, what's with the glasses and why'd you shave? You looking too smooth-faced. Like a fat-ass baby."

"Insults!" Elbows on the table, I leaned into his space. "You feeling pressed about this, bruh?"

"T-Alva, you're already in my pockets. Now, you want my time, too?"

"For true! Listen, Lex, these young cats wanting that b-ball life with dollar signs in their eyes can benefit from your perspective and experience. They need your dose of reality, and you know this. Life's more than the swish, how good you make a ball lick net, or how big a contract you get."

"I was NFL. Not NBA."

"Different sport. Same need. If necessary, I'm down for adding other sports to the program. Eventually."

He eyed me suspiciously. "You tryna trot me out so these cats see the gold ain't guaranteed? You want them eyeing my limping ass so they make sure they handle their business."

"You clowning." I had to laugh. Lex had manipulated that limp resulting from his accident into smoothness. "From my vantage point, you're a beautiful example of how someone rebounds *after* the game is gone."

Dyslexic, father murdered, abandoned by a mentally ill mother, Lex leveled up when drafted into the NFL two decades ago. That tragic motorcycle accident ending his career as well as his young marriage, he'd buried his pain in a bottle and briefly tangled with alcoholism. Which was how we met celebrating sobriety, at an Overcomers meeting—a Bible-based substance abuse recovery program.

"Ryde, you've survived more than most."

"My NFL days went sideways, Alvarez."

"Your resilience is precisely what these youngsters need to see! Come on, Lex. You're an award-winning businessman making *bank*. You did *that* after the jersey. ¿*Sí?*"

Pausing to order dessert, he watched me and slurped sweet tea. "T-Alva, you're full of ish…but I'm listening."

I went in on him, recounting what he already knew. Burn out, self-sabotage, substance abuse and other mess too often hammered down an athlete's potential and dreams. Looking at my own dumb past, I knew only grace kept me, and felt a responsibility to reach back and help someone else sidestep some foolery.

"What's in place?"

Encouraged by his interest, I updated him on *A&A's* non-profit status and receiving two sizable grants, with another grant application recently submitted. I'd already sunk a grip in the program, but the grants would supply salaries for the facilities director and part-time administrative assistant; as well as stipends for the two male, two female coaches on deck to teach drills and skills.

"You're including females in the program?"

"The game grinds on both sexes, and these young sisters need the benefits we're offering as well," I answered, needlessly outlining the benefits for him again.

Athletes & Academics was all about providing holistic services to up-and-coming high schoolers with hoop dreams. Designed to offer in-house services including scholarships, money management, counseling, and access to agents and sports management, the intent was to offer an intimate glimpse of the aspects of professional athleticism. Sports attorneys. A nutritionist. A public relations specialist. A sports clinician ready to school them on how to handle their bodies, avoid injuries and promote sustainability. It was all lined up and ready.

"And it's not about us just giving to them. *A&A* has a mandatory community service component so they know it's more than balling and banking."

"True that. T-Alva, that academic requirement of a 3.0 GPA or higher's gonna disqualify some cats."

"Which is why my nerd-professor brother-in-law's on the academics."

Participants needed consent forms signed by parent/guardians, homeroom teachers, and guidance counselors. Tutoring would be available as needed, and progress reports were mandatory.

"Man, my college professor brother-in-law, Milton, has seen too many college athletes lose scholarships for flunking classes. Then they wanna slide up on him asking for a passing grade when they didn't put the work in. If *A&A* does nothing, it better emphasize balance, integrity, and being about your business."

"So…" Dropping his fork on his plate, Lex leaned back. "You're talking a Motown move, like how Gordy took artists, polished them, taught them professionalism and kept them from being swallowed by the music industry. That's essentially what I see in this *A&A*."

"Basically!"

"You coulda said that in the first place. Wasting all these words and blowing smoke in my face."

"Lex, you a mess." I laughed knowing he got it. "We know a minute percentage of players with dreams end up pro hooping. They need to know what to do if they do or *don't* get in."

"Or have some bounce-back if they lose it. And you fo' sho betta know how to live—God forbid—after an injury…" His voice trailed off. "Man, you got me circling back on my own set-up."

"That's all you, bruh," I commented, digging into my untouched banana pudding. "You know *A&A's* legit and you have much to offer it."

"We'll see. No promises, but I know a couple of brothers with deep pockets who need some tax write-offs and might invest in a program like this. I'll make introductions." Scooping up peach cobbler, he stopped when interrupted by our waitress.

"You gentlemen need anything?"

"We're straight, sis. But he'll take the check," Lex replied, pointing at me.

Smiling, she handed over the bill before walking off with more switch in the hips than needed.

Lex shook his head and laughed. "Man, she serving you signals."

"That's you and that southern charm."

"Please! I got more hips at home than I can handle. Speaking of. Lemme run all this by Senaé. She might not wanna share me. Plus, the baby's coming."

"I absolutely respect that. Just know if you're in, we'll work everything to your convenience. You don't have to physically be at our quarterly board meetings. We'll teleconference you in. Make an in-person appearance with the kids however it fits."

"Smooth. I'll consider if you do me a solid."

"Speak on it," I encouraged, listening as Lex shared interests in expanding his transportation company to California's northern cities. "Man, consider me a client. And you're welcome to any connections I have. Let's do this."

Exchanging dap, he sat back, looked around. "T-Alva, Waitress Woman's still clocking your movements."

"Miss me with that."

"You gotta female situation I don't know about?"

Tossing cash on the table for our meals and tip, I stood, thinking on Yazmeen a moment. "I'm working on it."

"*What?* No more self-serve, party of one, Hands Solo Singles' club?"

"Huh?"

Grabbing the sugar dispenser, he put it on his lap and slid his grip up and down its length. "That."

"*You know what?* Pay for my lunch!" Snatching my money off the table, I walked off, leaving Lex in the rear, cracking up.

Posted in the back of the sedan Lex had arranged for my ride to the airport, I relaxed, thankful for a good symposium, and a productive lunch with a man I respected. Calling my parents, I checked on Nubs, asked about her day and advised I'd be there soon.

"Daddy, you said we can't keep secrets, so I gotta tell you something."

"Go ahead."

"I got in trouble in class today for talking when I was supposed to be working."

"Again, Nubs?"

"Yes…"

My daughter had fit into her new school too well, was already giving her teacher grief with the socializing.

Just like an Alvarez.

"Thanks for telling me. We'll deal with it when I get there."

"Okay. Don't forget I love you and you love me more."

Wrapping up our call, I laughed at her banking on love to mitigate punishment. "That girl…"

Leaning back, I rubbed tired eyes before scrolling email, glad for a notification that my contacts had been shipped and I could re-retire the glasses.

"Sweet," I remarked when further scrolling produced a confirmation of Yazmeen's delivery.

Seeing it, I grinned, hoping she enjoyed the gift basket of chocolate croissants, gourmet cocoa mix, and a floral bouquet I'd sent to her job. Respecting her privacy, I'd omitted a card to prevent putting folks in her business. Still, I hoped the gift triggered good thoughts of our time spent over coffee.

Launching social media, I noticed a post notification from her page. Visiting it, I was treated to a pic of a half-eaten croissant and mug of cocoa on her desk with the caption,

He feeds my greed.

Laughing, I scrolled comments filled with questions about the identity of "he." Her replies were cryptically comical, leaving my identity concealed.

Appreciating the privacy, I opened an unread private message from Yazmeen.

Thank u 4 being so thoughtful! I'm in greedy girl heaven.

And just like that I wanted to connect, to hear her voice and know what was new in her world, and to share my day with a woman caring enough to celebrate my wins.

"Call Yazmeen."

This time I didn't disconnect, but let that smart phone do what it did.

When she answered her work line, all professional yet inviting, her warm voice elicited a sensation that rolled through me, leaving me admitting,

This woman is mos' def getting in deep.

CHAPTER ELEVEN
TWO HEFFAS & SIX HOES
Yazmeen

Standing on the sidelines of the community center's gym—arms crossed over my chest—I watched my *Step-N-Style* kids fake-running. Every Saturday I started my troupe with warm-ups; and every Saturday they acted beat down and brand new.

"I refuse to ask you little people again. Put some life in those legs. *Get it in!*"

"Miss Yazmeen, you always got us running. We're here to dance, not die."

Acting all Debbie Allen-ish, I walked the gym's perimeter. "Quit complaining, Ms. Kia, and handle the business. Dance is *extremely* physical. It requires strong bodies and endurance."

"Yeah, but you ain't gotta have us up here acting like we some kinda cross-country Kenyans 'bout to run a marathon or something."

"Add two laps, everyone, and thank Kia for the privilege."

"Dang, Kia, you always popping off! Run the daggone laps and *shut up.*"

"Run without rudeness," I interjected, biting back a laugh as my troupe straggled two more again.

"Mommy, are we doing good?"

My troupe had designated my twins as mascots and took good care of them. Riding piggyback, courtesy of two of my strongest guys, Malcolm and Malik were getting in their quasi-exercise.

"Yes, baby, you are!"

"Come run with us, Mommy."

"Yeah, Miss Yazmeen. Try that running thing."

Needing to be a good example—and to burn the chocolate croissants I'd devoured at breakfast—I accepted Malcolm's invitation and ignored Kia's saltiness. When I passed Kia up and she tried to sprint, I had to show little chick I was made with grit, completing both laps before she did.

High-fiving my troupe as they came in, I laughed at their dramatic flops onto the gym floor—acting and sounding like geriatric candidates ready for a rest home.

"Come on, now. It wasn't all that bad."

"That's 'cause you only did two and not all seven laps, Miss Yazmeen. You just all kinda sadistic."

"That clap-back just earned *Step-N-Style* twenty sit-ups. Assume the position."

"Kia!"

Grinning, I got on the floor and did the reps with them, remembering a pre-twin time when my abs were cut and trim. Now? My Malcolm-and-Malik midsection wasn't flabby, but my eight-pack was on vacation. Coming up on that final sit-up, my eyes decided to focus on the basketball hoop on the opposite side of the gym. My mind did what it did, immediately swirling to a man I was falling in like with.

Unh-unh, not right now, Tavares.

Flat on my back, knees up, I needed those knees to stay together, not fall open thinking on Mister Orgasmic.

"Everyone good now?" Finishing the set, I hopped off the floor, feeling all Jezebel-esque. Cupping my ear, I leaned towards my crew. "Or do I hear more unnecessary comments?"

"No, ma'am!"

"Good. Please find your formation."

Ages thirteen to nineteen and twenty strong, my troupe were professional complainers. Some had formal training. Others were naturally gifted. Some came from stable environments, others from homes where trouble lived. But at rehearsals, we were equals. And to their credit, they were dedicated and knew how to deliver. Hustling up, they watched as I went through additional choreography for our newest routine which we wouldn't perform until our competition next spring. True, we'd been blessed with some phenomenal dancers, but I believed in advance preparation and allowing time to tighten and perfect as much as possible. Not wanting them to get tired with it, I'd only give it in pieces and parts, shelf it for a while, then come back to it—testing their muscle memory skills and teasing their enthusiasm. Crazy, maybe. But I had method in my madness.

"We're good, or does anyone need me to walk it through again?"

"We got this," someone bragged.

"Let's do it then."

Cueing the music, I put them through the new sequence multiple times before adding it into the existing choreography and running the whole routine from the beginning. Three run-throughs later, my kids—including the twins—were huffing, puffing, and sweating.

I loved that my sons enjoyed rhythm as much as me and, Mommy pride aside, they were both coordinated enough to follow along, but Malik actually moved like a little dancer lived inside.

My next generation dance baby, maybe?

My sons' paths in life were theirs to live. I'd never push myself on them. But if Malcolm or Malik ever showed an interest in the performing arts, I'd support that one-hundred.

Pausing the music, I praised my team.

"Now *that* was on point! But can I get one more again?" To my surprise, there were no complaints. They were in it. Invested. "Give me a little more energy on that last eight count. Especially when coming out of the turn and going into that stomp. In fact, double up on that."

Demonstrating the sequence and what I expected, I added stomps and flare at the end.

"*Dannnggg,* Miss Yazmeen. You krunking it!"

Laughing, I wiped the sweat beading up on my forehead and trying to send my hairline back to the motherland. Which was why I wore braids. My stuff could shrink and shrivel all it wanted and no one would know my nappy business. "I don't know about all that, but thanks."

"Naw, for real, Miss Yaz. You got mad skillz. You should dance with us at the competition."

"Instructors can't compete. Plus, it's all about you and what you do. Your families want to see the work *you've* put in, not me."

"They have those old folk sets at intermission."

"Really, Kia. Now I'm old folks. Let's go." Putting the music back on, I counted down and put us back in the mix where we belonged. They knew me enough to know this last set would be the hardest, with me expecting to see evidence of today's lesson.

At one point, I stepped out of the dance and watched them handle it, calling instructions and encouragement. I was cheesing like a clown when they came out on that double stomp perfectly synced with the dropping of bass notes. "Yassss, y'all! Turn what?"

"*Up!*"

Watching them clowning and congratulating themselves, I grabbed my water bottle, thankful for the opportunity to share the love of dance, and give back some of what I had.

"Okay, that's enough celebrating. Grab your water and cop a squat." As we all did, I voiced my observations, offered a few critiques before allowing their feedback on what they felt worked and what didn't. We didn't always agree, but their input was important to me. This was their investment of time and talent as much as mine. "Anything else?"

"Yeah, I got something."

Everyone groaned when Kia raised her hand.

"Hey, y'all! We honor every voice." I was serious about offering a safe and positive place where respect was upheld. "Go ahead, Kia."

"I don't like how you be on us, Miss Yazmeen, making us run and do all that hard-breathing. But I understand why you got us acting all athletic, and I appreciate you wanting us to do our best. And I like the fact that you don't just sit and tell us what to do, but you krunk it up with us. I think you're dope. That's it."

Kia's sentiments were met with melodramatic "ohhhs" and "awwws."

"Thank you, Miss Kia. I think you're dope, too." Her shy smile was sweet. I took my time looking at this group God had entrusted to me. We were all brown people. The majority African-American with a sprinkling of other cultures representing. "You...all of you...give the most every week." Hands over my chest, I bowed to them. "And I appreciate you for it. Yes, I work you hard, but there's a whole lot of love behind that."

"Glad you don't hate us. We'd be dead," one of my primary dancers quipped.

Laughter bouncing about, I hopped off the floor, stretching out my hands. "Get up and get in here." My troupe gathered in a circle formation as close as they could, our hands piled atop each other's. "What Kia said is true. I do want you to do your best. But more importantly, I believe in you. And others in our community do as well. So, good work. Have a good week. Stay safe, and don't do anything to crush your dreams. *Step-N-Style*...?"

"We'se wild!"

Yeah, bad grammar, but our spirits understood.

Bundling myself and the boys, we waited for everyone to be picked up, hop in their hoopties, or head home on foot before checking in with the facilities director to confirm class was finished.

"Don't forget we're closed next weekend for Thanksgiving, Miss Yazmeen."

"Thanks for the reminder, Mister Clarence, but sleeping in and doing nothing except reading a good book is already on my calendar."

High-fiving the twins, he offered them a snack-sized bag of their favorite cheese crackers like he did every week. Still, they looked at me for permission.

"Yes, you may."

Smiling like they'd won a food lottery, they accepted the snacks and said their thanks, before wishing Mister Clarence a "Happy Thanksgiving," holding each other's hands and practically skipping away. Except Malik's well-wishes came out 'Happy Thanks*living*.'

Sharing a humored look with the facilities coordinator, I waved and followed my babies. "Wait for me." They knew better than to exit by themselves, but that Mommy caution was automatic.

Catching up with them and taking their hands, our little trio pushed out into the November chill only to encounter Hurricane His Highness.

"Daddy!"

Children are the most forgiving creatures the Lord ever created. Despite Royal's fake and flaky ways, the boys raced across the sidewalk, their smiles bright like diamonds. I loved their pure adoration, but it hurt that it was directed to someone who didn't deserve it.

My ex egret knew my teaching schedule, so I wasn't alarmed by his appearance.

But that ride?

Double-parked in the space beside mine, Satan the Second stood leaned up against an obviously new acquisition: a pimped-out BMW with vanity plates announcing his ownership.

King Ryl.

My ex was good for fronting and flossing, but in this instance the vanity plate was legitimate. King Royal Jones was actually on his birth certificate.

"Any man needing all that excess on his name ain't about nothing to begin with."

I'd lived to regret not heeding my Gram's wisdom and warnings. But right then I was stuck on the fact that the uncircumcised amoeba I'd procreated with—who hadn't paid child support in many moons, and not long ago asked for help with airfare for Christmas—was rolling a luxury vehicle.

Picking up the twins, he was all smiles and deadbeat daddy kisses. "*Man!* Y'all getting big!" Tickling their stomachs, Royal left the boys laughing. "Whatchu been eating?"

"Mommy's mashed potatoes."

He turned his snake eyes on me. "Yeah, that's one thing your mama's good at: sizzling."

Malcolm and Malik started talking fast, finishing one another's sentences, trying to stuff months of living into minutes.

"...and we get to bring Mister Snackers home..."

"...'cause Mommy signed the," Malik paused, seeking reassurance from his brother, "*permission slip.*"

My beautiful babies high-fived each other.

"Oh, yeah, well that's good. Enjoy the goldfish."

"Daddy! You're not listening." Crossing his arms over his chest, Malik was indignant. "Mister Snackers is a hamster, not a fish!"

"Yeah? Cool. How 'bout we get y'all in your car seats and let me holla at your mom a minute?"

Unlocking my vehicle, I turned on the stereo for my children before standing there letting that November wind lower my temperature to less-than-boiling. I didn't move to help the leader of the heathen nation strap our sons in.

Let him do some parental duties for a whole two minutes.

"I'll be right back," he promised the twins, closing the door and unearthing his real reason for showing up. "Yo, Yaz, I need to use your garage a minute."

To know Royal was to feel as if perpetually trapped in an alternate universe. No 'hi'. No hug. (Not that I'd accept one without updating my vaccinations or immunizations). Just a request to use my garage as if a piece of paper or pen.

I couldn't respond for looking at him like he'd been hit by an extra case of stupid.

"Yo, Yaz, can we do this or what?" He had the same charming grin as our twins, except theirs' was cute and innocent. His was a sly, temporary mask at best.

"No, *we* cannot. Next..."

That cute boy grin vanished in that feeling-like-winter wind. "Why you tripping and acting all hard lately? Like we got beef instead of history? You need to boss up and help your baby daddy by letting me park my Beemer at your joint."

There were too many things wrong in that whole situation to respond, but in the whacked-out world of Royal Jones, idiocy made perfect sense.

Ignoring him, I stared at the new acquisition he'd put more care into than he did Malcolm or Malik. That ride was pristine. My reflection was gleaming.

It's so Royal.

When we first met, he'd presented himself as a together brother, but I'd learned the hard way that Royal was all about appearances. Eye-pleasing? Yes. Otherwise, he was straight empty calories and no nutrients, limited in substance. That overly-charming-when-I-wanna-be personality that first enticed me? A mere part of his hustler routine.

A pretend music producer-promoter, Royal wanted to live up to his name without the money to back it. When married, I'd learned how heavy-handed a spender he was, and knew better than to merge my bank accounts with his. With his zero-fiduciary finesse, I'd been the bill-paying spouse keeping us from being evicted or the utilities disconnected. Still, he'd tried to wear archaic man pants, behaving like he had a right to spend his and mine. Sad to say, time hadn't changed or matured him. Riding in, and wearing his income, Royal was still broke as a joke.

I can't believe I ever bought this okey doke.

Slowly moving around that car, I heard Royal gum-bumping, but I was so focused on his whip that not one word transmitted. Seeing that BMW all I saw was money my sons didn't benefit from. Pearlized, customized paint. Vanity plates. The smell of new leather despite the doors being closed, and windows rolled up. They represented what I'd struggled to provide. Food. Clothing. A safe place to live. But more than that, Royal's whip embodied what the twins deserved most: their father's time, love, and attention.

Some part of the Mommy in me must've snapped because when external sound registered, all I heard was Royal screaming.

"What the hell's wrong with you, Yazmeen!"

I jerked like coming up out of a dream only to see Hurricane His Highness coming for me.

"You know how much that paint cost me?"

Looking from Royal's twisted face to the car keys in my hand, I saw a flurry of pearl flakes decorating my brown girl skin. Eyes darting to the BMW, they widened seeing the long, deep scratch I'd just carved into it.

"Bitch, have you lost your whole mind again?"

True, I'd lost my mind once and he'd been the recipient of a me no one deserved to see. But now, like then, this man had been on the triggering end; and his calling me a name not on my birth certificate almost sent my good sense (like my cut abs) on vacation.

I probably looked like a cockatoo, head tilted sideways while approaching him. "No...not...how you will *ever*...refer to me...*never*."

True, Inez raised her daughters to be dignified; and by nature, I was tenderhearted. But, Daddy? That ex-military man taught us serious survival skills, including how to clock a man. At five-ten, two inches taller than me, Royal was built solidly. That did nothing to frighten me. Shameful or not, I'd hit a man once. Standing there staring at the very recipient of that right hook, both of us knew if backed into a corner, I'd do it again.

"Miss Yazmeen, everything okay out here?"

Squared up with Royal like I was ready to rumble, I saw Mister Clarence headed towards us in my peripheral vision. That, and the fact that my children were seated only mere feet away most likely watching, snatched me back to saved and sane.

I headed for my vehicle, leaving my former fraction-of-a-man looking at his ride like he wanted to commit ex-wife-icide.

"Do I need to call security?"

"Mister Clarence, I'm fine."

"I'm not moving until I see you drive off safely." A big, burly man in his early fifties, Mister Clarence was an O.G., the kind that didn't suffer fools lightly. Opening my door, he stood there sizing up my enemy.

There was no need. That petri dish specimen was squatted down, running his hands over his precious paint, possibly crying.

"Mommy, why doesn't Daddy like you?"

Leaving Royal inspecting his paint predicament, I waved at Mister Clarence before reversing, so caught off-guard by Malcolm's question that it took me a moment to respond. I knew better than to insult my sons' intelligence despite my never wanting them to experience the disconnect between their parents. Unfortunately, they had. Still, despite everything I'd gone through with Royal, I was "one of those women" who wouldn't tear down the man who'd help make my children. But I wasn't about to sugar-coat his foolishness.

"Malkie, Daddy and I used to be friends, but right now we're struggling."

"Do you think you'll be friends later...maybe next week?"

"Yeah, next week, by Thanks*living*."

The hopeful quiver in Malik's voice made my heart hurt so that I found myself pulling over to the side of the road. Shifting into Park, I repositioned myself to see my sons eye-to-eye, wishing I could singularly apologize for all the wrongs in their parents' worlds. "Malie, honey, I don't have the answer to that—"

"Mommy, just guess," Mister Old Soul Malcolm interrupted, wanting his straight-from-the-hip shot of 4-1-1.

"My best guess, Malkie? No."

Sometimes the boys used twin code—their own made up language only they understood and that sounded like Martian speak to me. But right then they did their twin telepathy on me—looking at each other, communicating silently until both nodded, agreeing.

"You and Daddy need a timeout," Mister Old Soul announced.

"Yeah, Mommy, like sometimes if Malkie and I aren't playing good and you make us separate for *two whole minutes*," Malik dramatically emphasized. "When your timer beeps, we play nice again. You and Daddy should try two-minute timeouts."

"Nice idea, Malie," I complimented, tickling my sons' knees, leaving them giggling.

Pulling back into traffic, I had one thought.

Lord, multiply those two minutes by infinity.

Thanks*living* week was comical with Royal's calls and texts demanding payment for paint damages. Finally suggesting he deduct the cost from that M.I.A. child support he owed me, I let that be that. Feeling like a ratchet hood rat for scratching up that car, I did, however, discuss it with First Lady. Her bottom-line conclusion? I was human. Out of order, but human, nevertheless.

Thanksgiving dinner at India's was so good I caught a food coma trying to eat everything within reach. Packing enough leftovers for my three-person family, I declined Mama's invitation to go Black Friday shopping that night, spending imaginary money. I did, however, leave the boys at Auntie India's for a cousin sleepover. That left me, myself, and Yazmeen going home to a *Living Single* marathon, unsolicited thoughts, and cold turkey and dressing.

Instant message him, Yazzy.

Eating a sliver of Sasha's pecan pie in bed, I laughed at my favorite character, Maxine Shaw Attorney at Law, to keep from dialing Tavares. Ten p.m. was too late for chitchat. Plus, it was a holiday: a time for family. I didn't want to be disruptive.

Yaz, you're full of sh—

Remote in hand, I increased the volume, drowning out my inner woman. We could disagree, but I wasn't about to tolerate her cussing me.

Three episodes in, I lost the battle to keep my eyes open. Turning off the T.V., I said a quick prayer, telling myself I'd read my Bible in the morning.

With toddler twins, indulgent, no-alarm-clock sleep was a rarity. That's all I wanted. But I swear Self and my subconscious were petty. Acting all vengeful over my not messaging Tavares, they took over my dreams, leaving them steamy.

I was booty-deep in some scandalous scene of Mister Luscious licking Thanksgiving giblet gravy from my belly button when my cell rang mid-morning.

Irritated by its interruption, I blindly reached for and silenced it, drifting back to sleep, trying to resume that dream and my being a baller's feast. Clearly, I was a dream master, picking up where we'd paused; but instead of gravy, it was cranberry sauce. That man was licking and lapping, blazing a trail south and about to treat my lady parts to that cranberry-covered mouth when I was snatched from lip bliss by a text chiming.

"Go away!" Growling, I snatched my phone off the nightstand and read a message I had no trouble interpreting.

Buenos días y hola, mi hermosa mariposa.

That Spanish had me rolling onto my back, rubbing my eyes. "Tavares?"

We'd been in constant contact the past few weeks, deepening our connection as well as our attraction. Those conversations, relegated to my time at the office or online, always opened with his standard greeting.

Hello, beautiful butterfly.

Now, he was texting?

"What the heck?"

Sitting up in bed, heart and thoughts racing, I came up with one culprit. No fool, I stored Tavares' number in my contacts before texting my disloyal insect.

Really, J! U gave T. my #?

Joy's emoji response was almost immediate, like she'd been expecting me.

Skip all that LOL, Joy! I so hate u.

She called. I refused to answer, keeping our text stream flowing. *U'r fired! Bye, boo.*

Whatever, Yaz. Got that fine a$$ man calling u @work & IM'ing like some outdated episode of Catfish, she responded before spilling the tea on Quinton's inviting Tavares to Thanksgiving dessert at LaVelle's mom's place, and her breaking best friend code and putting my number in his phone.

Warned him if he wants 2 get w/u he'd better go online and buy a life supply of patience. U can thank me l8r.

Tossing back the covers, I got out of bed earlier than intended, stomped to the bathroom, handled my business and headed downstairs for breakfast: leftover turkey and dressing. With extra giblet gravy.

Joy was still texting her two crooked cents.

U'r consenting, sex-needing adults. Explain the problem, 'cuz I don't get it. And it better not have anything 2 do w/that mind mess Rank A$$ Royal put u through.

My hesitation was simpler than that. My mouth wrote a check my behind couldn't cash with all that, "Let's lay this on the table, dish the awkwardness and own it."

Simple truth: I no longer trusted myself. And not just to keep from crawling in his bed and saying *bon voyage* to abstinence. But because—pathetic modes of communication aside—these past few weeks of getting to know Sir Sexy proved he was more man than I'd ever had. Kind. Perceptive. Respectful. Generous. That croissant basket had been the beginning. Every week since, some small gift arrived confirming his attentiveness to our conversations and the likes I randomly mentioned. I'd intentionally declined the invitation to his grandmother's celebration a few weeks back just to avoid witnessing his intimate self seen only by family. That would take me in too deep, and I could not, would not put myself in a position to have my heart stomped out of my chest by a man ever again. As smooth as he was, I was afraid he would be the one to do it, because he'd be the very man I let in. For my own sake, I *had* to keep Tavares "Peel Off My Panties Please" Alvarez at a manageable distance.

Popping my plate in the microwave, I decided to spell it out in a way my hot tail heffa of a bestie could comprehend. I started to, but several occurrences interrupted.

Tavares' still unanswered text pinged simultaneously with one from India informing me she was en route to get clean clothes for the twins before taking my two and her tribe of five to the movies. To avoid keeping her waiting, I trotted upstairs, making it midway before the doorbell rang.

"Dang."

That sent me *back* downstairs and accidentally stepping on abandoned Legos previously overlooked.

That there hurt made me lose my grip.

My phone fell. I sat on the stairs holding my foot, rocking and leaking real tears over Lego-induced pain I wouldn't wish on anyone but my ex. Pulling myself together, I hobbled to the door to find a flier featuring a shepherd and sheep, telling me I needed the Lord. Limping to the stairs, I agreed.

Snatching up my fallen phone, pain had me texting crazy but honestly.

Fine, J! I love Jesus & am all about pleasing Him, but Tavares' FINE behind has me wanting s-e-x!!! I'm SOOO OMG sexually attracted 2 that man. He has me hotter & hungrier than 2 heffas & 6 hoes. THAT'S the problem!

That there was truth my "monogamy ain't for me" best friend could fathom.

Heading up the stairs, eyes scoping for evil, lurking Legos, my phone rang. Seeing that newly stored contact, I slowly answered. "Tavares?"

That deep, delicious voice rumbled with humor and mischief. "Good morning, beautiful butterfly. So, I have you hungrier than how many heffas and hoes?"

Momentarily, I froze. Frantically snatching my phone from my ear, I stared at my text streams realizing that in my India's-calling, Saturday morning saints' front porch evangelizing, Lego-impaled, pain-induced delirium, I'd accidentally texted him instead of my bestie.

Stumbling into my room, I sank to my knees and pounded my

head on the carpet hoping to knock myself unconscious.

Just no! Jesus, send an angel escort 'cause I'm ready for my heavenly home.

"Yazmeen?"

I couldn't respond. I simply breathed.

"'Ey, Miss Yazzy Yaz?"

Slowly propping myself up, I sat on the floor, back against the bed. "Yes?"

His voice was soothing. "No need for embarrassment."

So said the man who hadn't just put all his nastiness on blast. I suddenly wanted an antidepressant, a colonoscopy. Something! "Ummm... Tavares...can I call you back?"

"No, ma'am, you can't. 'Cause you won't. So, let's move on. How was your holiday?"

Right then I really couldn't remember or care if I'd eaten raw turkey or Santa's dead reindeer. All I could see was that foul text message mocking me. "I think it was nice. Yours?"

"Good, but your text was better."

Reaching for a pillow, I propped it over my face and groaned as he repeatedly called my name. "How may I help you, Tavares?"

"That text already did." He was having way too much fun at my expense.

"Can we agree to *never* mention that text again?"

"We can *not* mention it. But I'm keeping it."

"Why?"

"That first text holds sentimental value. It's nice knowing you want me almost as much as I want you."

I sidestepped red heat rushing my body. "You simply want to use that text as extortion."

"For sure. And I'm about to make a withdrawal from the Bank of Blackmail. Go out with me."

"I heard a command, not a request."

"You have excellent hearing for a woman who's hornier than—"

"What time and where?"

CHAPTER TWELVE
GAME ON
Tavares

Five weeks of solo-parenting was enough to know not to sleep on opportunity. We'd first met a few days before Halloween, and it took until Thanksgiving to get where we'd gotten? (Which, by the way, wasn't far enough for me). I wasn't letting another holiday come and go without getting down this road to where we could be. Nubs was with my parents for the weekend, and Yazmeen's twins were hanging with Miss India. I was taking straight advantage of this adults-only prize presented on a Black Friday platter. Running Mister Bojangles down the beach and around these blocks, music bumping through my earphones, I schemed up sixty-eleven ways to keep Yazmeen to myself all day.

My mind scrolled typical date-day situations. Candy. Dinner. Roses. Wine. Vegas? L.A.? Jazz club, or a movie. Two boxes of condoms and warming jelly.

Man, you're bugging.

"Lord, forgive me."

Laughing at myself, Bo and I finished our last lap, made it to the house, and fell out. At least I did. Bo went for his water dish like he had good sense, finished up, and trotted into the den where I'd sprawled on the floor like a coma victim. Hunkered over me, Bo licked my face, panting funky canine fumes that could benefit from mint.

"Dude, your breath!"

He had the nerve to bark, acting offended before resuming that face-licking.

"Man, get a woman already."

His sudden whining as if he understood the dis, had me scratching behind his ears, laughing. "Yeah, I need a woman, too. But I'm working on it. That alright by you?"

Bojangles did his double bark, signaling agreement before poking his muzzle in my armpit and sniffing. Sitting back on his haunches, he had the nerve to angle his big head sideways with a look like,

"Fool, you better handle that."

Dragging my butt up off the floor, I headed for the shower. My dissing dog tagged along, posting up outside the bathroom door, true ride or die companion.

When I left the game, I'd normalized my life as best I could. Sometimes situations still called for traveling with security despite being out of the sports spotlight. Thankfully, this wasn't that. I couldn't have men in black, all menacing and having Yazmeen get ghost on me. I chose to roll alone. I was licensed to carry and, God forbid, if anything ever popped off, I was equipped to protect whatever needed protecting. Right then? I needed the woman I wanted to be on chill. Especially after our first quasi-disagreement.

Miss Independent had wanted to meet me wherever it was we were going. Being old school, I needed to know that at the end of the night she arrived home safely. With no one but me.

"Well, I'm new school and don't give my address to strange men."

"Oh, so now I'm strange, Yazzy Yaz? This from the woman of horny heffas and hoes."

She'd hung up on me, but my calling back found us both laughing. We fussed it out. I won. She agreed. Something as simple as her allowing me to pick her up from home was sweet victory, humbling.

She's trusting me.

Now, I had her with me, smelling edible and looking like every good thing this man could need. "So, where're we headed?" Acting the magnanimous male, I'd given her ladies' choice on how our daylight was spent. I already had nighttime planned.

"Rock climbing."

Holding her door open and cupping her elbow as she climbed in the Cayenne, I had to fix my face. An athlete who didn't fear exercise, I could think of endless physical ways for us to spend the day. Climbing rubber rocks wasn't one. "Say what?"

"Be open-minded, Tavares. Have you ever tried it?"

"No."

"Are you interested?"

"As we say *en Español*: no. Again."

"Because?"

"I let my life insurance lapse."

Her tossing her head back and laughing her slightly husky laugh that elicited a warm response somewhere near my abs, had me wanting to lean in and lick that neck. Taste that brown sugar chocolate. Refraining, I closed her door, telling myself to act the born-again gentleman.

Rolling down the freeway, I felt like millions, spending time with this woman. That tell-all text of hers obviously obliterated unnecessary shyness. She was absolutely open, conversing like a pro and pulling me deeper in.

We vibed. For real.

Earlier conversations had already revealed our shared appreciation for old school soul music, food, and family. I'd had enough of salad-eating females whose ideal kin was a tea-cup-sized dog pampered in a purse. I needed substance; and she was that.

Born in Virginia, she'd relocated often courtesy of her father's military career. After college graduation, she'd gone to New York seeking those dancing dreams, but left the Big Apple and became a west coast transplant after "the dance deal" that went bad.

"Is that deal disappointment why you gave up ballet?" I asked, signaling before changing lanes, following the directions she'd pulled up on my GPS.

"No. *That* situation was in my hip hop days. I opted out of ballet for modern and jazz years before."

"You didn't tell me the first time I asked, so I'm daring to again. Why'd you opt out?"

Toying with her seatbelt, she softly sighed before angling in my direction and offering a simple answer. "Black Girl Magic."

"Pardon?"

Patting her hips, she smiled without any trace of bitterness. "My physique wasn't conducive to lean, mean, European dominated dance aesthetics, and I got tired of being dismissed and denied because of *their* narrowness."

"Wow. Their loss. Do you miss it?"

"What? Thirteen years of fighting folks about *my* anatomy, and being told I had 'too much rhythm and too much body?'" She raised two fingers in a sideways peace sign.

"You threw up deuces."

"Absolutely. At least on ballet." She'd continued with other forms of dance and been blessed with numerous commercial successes and some "embarrassments."

"Such as?"

I could feel her staring at me with those clear, expressive eyes. "Let's just say I've performed with a variety of musical artists, and in venues church folks might find offensive."

Rubbing my chin, I posed, "For example?"

She paused to silence an incoming call. The ringtone told me it was Thug-a-Mug. Again. That made three times since I'd picked her up. If she hadn't already made their situation crystal clear, I might've questioned his insistence. But, having met dude, clearly love wasn't behind his persistence. "Do you need to get that?"

"I need to not."

"Fair enough. Back to the sketchy venues you danced in."

That had her laughing. "How about we just leave it at secular, and not the sanctuary? And, you can get that look off your face. I wasn't winding and grinding in strip clubs."

I wish.

Actually, I didn't. The thought of dudes rubbing dollar bills on her had my jaw twitching. Conversely, fantasizing a future featuring Yazmeen lap dancing for an audience of one, i.e., me, had me swimming in images of poles and edible panties. "Back to ballet. You're saying your physique pulled you out the game?"

Nodding, she explained how on multiple occasions dance instructors dared to insult her, saying her skills often surpassed others' chosen for lead roles, but that her physique was too "contrary." The critiques had been worse when studying ballet in Europe where her father was stationed. Repeatedly told to tuck her behind in, she'd often left class in tears. She was accused of being "lazy," and told she needed increased "abdominal and pelvic muscle control" to "offset her derrière."

"My mother believed in us knowing how to advocate and stand up for ourselves, but when Madame prescribed an eight-hundred-calorie-a-day diet and told me to 'stop eating too many parts of the pig,' my very elegant, genteel swan-of-a-mom marched her dignified self in that class and went gangsta kind of off!"

Humored, I glanced away from the road to see her smiling. "What did your mom say?"

"I can't recall every word verbatim, but I do remember, 'My child was born Black and female with parts some of you pale sisters pay a surgeon for. Take your last look at these "rotund assets" that haven't once prevented Yazmeen from flawlessly executing your pale dances

'cause that double derrière's about to *chassé* its roundness out of here!'
After that she told me if I ever started my own outfit to name it 'Ballet
& Booty Movement Inc.'"

I had to laugh. "I need to meet your mother."

"She'd like that."

Her statement was innocuous enough; still, I felt a little something
on it. My meeting India, Sasha, and even her cousin, Jamal, hadn't
been planned. Same with her meeting Reina. Our *choosing* to introduce
one another to family was different, decisive. Again, outside of high
school, introducing women to my family was something I didn't do. I
actually imagined myself doing that with Yazmeen.

Responding to the GPS instructions and heading for our exit, I
dared to ask. "Is that a possibility?"

Her voice was soft when answering. "We'll see..."

Stopped at the end of the off-ramp, I reached over and took her
hand. It was soft and small in mine. Raising her hand to my lips, I
gently kissed it. "We'll see," I agreed. "And for what it's worth...*all* your
Black Woman Magic is life to this Black man. Most definitely."

"Really, Miss Yazzy Yaz?" Opening her door and helping her from
the whip, I held her coat as she slipped into it.

"What?" She was grinning, looking all innocent.

"A book signing?" I suddenly preferred rock climbing. "So that's
what the Get Lit, Sis shirt is about?" I asked, eyeing the blinged-out,
long-sleeved tee she was rocking.

"Yep, the "lit" stands for literature. As in books. As in "welcome to
a book signing."

"You're bugging."

I loved the way she laughed. "I'm not. And stop looking like the
twins when we have broccoli."

"Malcolm and Malik have good sense!"

"We agreed that I choose our day activity. Correct?"

"I was delirious."

"Whining's not a good look." Grabbing my hand, she guided us
towards our destination. "You don't even know who the author is."

"Doesn't matter. I'll be asleep within five minutes."

Laughing, she stood aside, allowing me to open the door of Oak
Park's—and Sacramento's for that matter—premier, Black-owned
bookstore where an attractive, mature sister-woman with stylish, short-

cut hair was selling books in between dishing commands to teenaged staff.

"Hi, Mother Rose!"

Looking over her eyeglasses, she smiled, offering a warm and welcoming, "Oh, hey, Yazmeen! Those books you ordered for the twins came in. You here to pick them up, or are you staying for the book signing?"

"Both."

"Slick! You had an agenda in getting me here so you could get that purchase," I quietly teased, politely head-nodding at several patrons staring. We'd already discussed the issue of "fan'doration"—as Yazmeen called it. I didn't want her worrying about me jumping celebrity-ish, signing autographs and acting like the king of selfie nation. I'd assured her that, public or private, whenever we were together our time was *ours*.

Introduced to Mother Rose, I shook the store owner's hand only to learn that her son—a former NBA player who'd gone into politics and served a term as mayor—was often present at the store, supporting its various events when not busy with his soul food joint around the corner. Leaning over the counter, she got all secretive. "So, you shouldn't have any problems with folks in here acting like out-of-order fans. They're used to bigwigs."

Pulling my wallet from my jacket, that had me laughing.

"What're you doing?" Yazmeen grabbed my wrist.

Like an involuntary reflex, I'd handed Mother Rose my debit card, intending to pay for the boys' books.

Retrieving my card, Yazmeen slipped it back into my wallet. "Thank you, but I've got this. Take two steps back," she instructed when I objected.

I'd never had a woman decline a transaction from the Bank of Tavares, but the look on her face told me she wasn't playing. Stepping back as told, all I could say was, "Yes, ma'am."

That book signing turned out to be a gift only a caring woman would give. Afro-Latino and in his early seventies, the author was one of my late grandfather's favorites. Like *Abuelo*, he had that old school charm, edgy wit, and humorous anecdotes that had the audience hollering-laughing. His lapsing in and out of Spanish felt like home, as if having moments with my deceased grandfather once more.

Standing in line with the copy of his book that Yazmeen insisted on purchasing for me, I waited for an autograph like everyone else. When he asked for a selfie, I agreed seeing as how I wasn't the celebrity. I was the fan.

"That was nice. Thank you, Miss Yazzy Yaz." Back in the whip, we were rolling to eat before our evening activity.

"You're welcome. It was a long shot, but you'd shared so much about your grandfather that I took a chance, hoping you'd enjoy it. And when're you going to stop calling me that hood rat nickname?"

"Give me something to replace it with."

"How about Queen of the Skating Rink?"

As enticing as a dinner at a table in a secluded corner of a jazz club was, I'd gotten crazy in altering my original plans for our evening, and jokingly asked if she liked skating. Should've known the lady dancer did. Now, she was bragging prematurely. "You got to earn that 'Queen' thing."

"Oh, trust! If you don't want to get whipped, I suggest you bring your A-game."

Stopped at a red light, I gave her my full attention. "Girl, my game stays on A. I'm an athlete."

"You *used* to be," she teased.

"Woman, I *still* am. My skate action is Olympic-worthy."

When she tossed her head back on a laugh, I promised myself, one day soon, I was sucking that neck.

"You're saying you're fast, Tavares?"

"I'm fierce."

"Fine, Mister B-ball, you have speed. But this dancer has endurance. Can you hang with me?"

Taking her hand, I brought it to my lips, slowly kissing it. Didn't plan to put an extra dip in the tone, but words rolled out low and lazy, adding a little snap and electricity in the air quality. "Sweetheart, my endurance is life-size and legendary."

Immediately, I tensed, concerned my challenge had come across sexualized or suggestive. She surprised me when responding playfully, a little seductively.

Lacing our fingers together, she repositioned our arms atop the armrest, stroking mine gently. "Game on, baby boy. We'll see."

Put two competitive, physically fit people together and the game gets interesting. We tore up that rink like bets had been placed, and one of us needed to be paid. She pulled out all that dance finesse, trying to leave me looking weak and stressed. True, I didn't have her skills or grace, but I proved a point. T-Alva was no punk and went in with her a good hour-and-a-half before we took a break.

"Okay...so *who* needs this breather?" My hands on her hips as they'd been throughout the night, we exited the rink.

"Needing the restroom doesn't count as a breather or a break, Mister Alvarez," she retorted, turning and showing off those backwards skating skills.

"Why you tryna blame a weak bladder, Yazzy Yaz? Own up! I wore you out."

She was too busy laughing to be defensive. "Whatever, Tavares." Her suddenly stopping, brought our bodies together. "Just go to the bathroom, then meet me at the snack bar. And wash your hands when you're finished."

Her crack had a couple of folks nearby laughing as she rolled off.

With my weak IncogNegro routine, some in the place had recognized me and created a small buzz, unfortunately. I held to my resolve not to act Mister Celebrity. Kids were my exception. A small, elementary-aged group had hemmed me up asking for autographs when we first arrived. I'd been all apologetic only for Yazmeen to show her sportsmanship, playing camera woman and taking the selfies the youngsters requested. Other than that, folks had been respectful, snapping photos from a distance. That respect situation suddenly changed.

"Oh! My! Gawwwwd! Ain't you T-Alva?"

Sitting, waiting on Yazmeen, I looked up to see two, size zero-and-a-half sisters of the ratchet regime rolling in on me, looking like toothpicks on skates with olives for heads.

"Dannnnggg, son! Your ass is finer in person than on T.V. Oh, hell, yeah! Can we get a damn selfie widchu?"

Rubbing a hand over my mouth, I knew better than to get into that. Instead, I got myself up from that trap and headed towards the women's restroom. "Not tonight, ladies."

"What? Well, roll your stuck-up ass on off!"

I ignored the shade. Seeing Yazmeen exiting the ladies' room, those low-slung jeans and blinged-out tee kissing and hitting those commanding curves, I couldn't care about some birds yapping at my back.

"Oh, so that's how it is! You passing up all this fantasticness and dumbing down to get with her fat ass? And I don't mean *p-h-a-t*."

I stopped so fast, my neck almost cracked. I was ready to go bird hunting, but Yazmeen's grip on my arm snapped that.

Her voice was low, rational. "Don't bother."

"Hell naw! I can't get with insults," I snapped, watching Ratchet Thing One and Two skate off.

"Body-shamers have no hooks here. And who made you liable for other people's ignorance?"

I looked at her. She looked at me, letting her challenge-of-a-question soak in. Warm appreciation filled some part of me. I gradually grinned. "I see you and that real woman confidence, Yazzy Yaz."

"Glad you do, because I'm good with me." She lowered her voice. "I'm impressed sister-girl knew something about homophones and that 'fat' isn't 'phat.'"

"True that."

She bit her lip. "Was that catty and uncalled for?"

"Naw, boo. Errybody ain't hooked on phonics so color me impressed, too."

"Hashtag truth."

Grinning and fist-bumping, we rolled off.

I'd had the pleasure of her company virtually all day. It was after eleven p.m. and I still wasn't finished despite that skate-a-thon that had me needing Icy Hot. I wasn't ready to quit simply because I wanted to prolong my time in her presence. Prior to today, she'd been all turtle-ish on me, moving too slowly for my get-it-done personality. Living like I had in the past, we would have been in the bed already. For the first time since becoming sexually active, that wasn't my end goal. Rather, I wanted to know the whole woman. Returning our skates, I proposed going out for drinks, as in my coffee and her hot chocolate. I was still living that sober life; and she'd schooled me on her alcohol intolerance.

"I wish I could, but I'd probably be bad company," she admitted, yawning and easing her feet into her thigh-high, wine-colored, stiletto boots that were outrageously sexy.

"Hold the phone! You're admitting defeat on that," drawing air quotes I elevated my tone, "'dancers have more stamina than ballers' nonsense?"

"You had to mock my voice, Tavares?"

"No, but I enjoyed it."

"*Anyhow*! As Queen of the Rink the only thing I'm admitting is... you...got...*dusted*."

Shoes on, zipping my coat, I extended a hand, helping her stand in those boots that were bringing me love and happiness. "Woman, fall back on that."

"I will when you pay homage," she teased, one hand in mine, the other reaching for what was left of that licorice rope strung around her neck as we headed for the exit. Pushing back the cellophane wrap, she bit into it before stuffing the remainder in her coat pocket. "What?" she demanded when I laughed. "Skating is not complete without at least one roll around the rink with red rope licorice draping the neck."

"I guess. You enjoy yourself?"

Her response was interrupted by that Vader march. Her groan was animated. "Excuse me." Accidentally or not, she had her phone on speaker mode when connecting. "What, Royal?"

"*I been calling you all day!* Where you at? I'm parked in frontcho house, and you ain't here."

Her moving a few feet away didn't keep me from overhearing.

"You're at my home because?"

"I wanna see my sons."

"Not at nearly midnight you don't."

"I'm their father. I'll see them whenever, however I want. So, quit playing. Get my boys. And bring your ass home."

Only fools treat good women wrong!

Glad she gave him the disconnect, I didn't appreciate dude's tone or his coming at her like that. But it wasn't my place to speak on it or step in. I wasn't her man. Yet.

We 'bout to change that.

We'd been at this thing only a few weeks, but that was enough for me to know she was the woman I wanted. What I didn't want was dealings with her "ex monster," but it was what it was. We both came to the table with a past. She had a baby daddy. I had a baby mama. Both instigated drama. Still, she deserved better than that.

Her back to me, I watched the slow rise and fall of her shoulders. Her taking deliberate, calming breaths had me wanting to bust Thug-a-Mug upside his bowling ball head. Moving to where she was, I touched the small of her back. "You alright?"

"I am, and I apologize—"

"Like you told me: don't apologize for someone else's ignorance."

"True, but..." Her expression spoke the concern she couldn't. She was quiet a moment before doing what I hadn't expected. She gave me an out from whatever was growing between us. "Tavares, my whole heart values you, but you didn't sign on for baby daddy drama and ignorance. You're a wonderful man and if this is more than what you choose to deal with...I understand."

"Do you want me to back out of what we have?"

"No."

"Good, 'cause I'm not. I can't judge you. You have a Royal. I have a Kryshelle."

"Exes from hell?"

"Basically. I can't hold yours against you. Please don't hold mine against me."

"I wouldn't do that."

"Neither can I, Miss Yazzy Yaz."

Smiling, relieved, she accepted my hand, falling silent until reaching the exit. "Good God, it's freezing out here." She shivered as I held the door open on a California November night that was chilly, but clear. "At least it's not raining."

"Good thing for you, too, since *el azúcar se derrite bajo la lluvia.*"

"I told you I failed high school Spanish, twice. Right?"

"*Sí,* and that's pathetic."

"Whatever, *Señor* Alvarez. Slowly repeat what you said so I can try. Then translate, please."

I complied, playfully clutching my stomach and bending in fake pain at her pitiful attempts. "Yeah, no, don't. My ancestors can't take it."

She did that throw-her-head-back-and-laugh. "Fine! Just interpret what you said."

"Sugar melts in rain."

Her smile was like soft light in the night. "You're saying I'm sweet?"

"Most definitely."

Squeezing my hand, she was momentarily silent as we walked the parking lot. When she spoke, her voice was quiet. "Will you be okay driving back to the Bay? It's kinda late to be on the road."

"Glad for the concern, but Bo and I are bunking at my grandmother's."

I'd wanted to buy *Abeula* a place in the Bay Area to be closer to my dad and two of his siblings, but she refused letting go of the house she and *Abuelo* built in south Sacramento's Lemon Hill district.

"*Beau?*" The Cayenne was a few spaces ahead when she stopped, slightly wide-eyed, expression on the panicked side. "As in a French pronunciation and meaning?"

"As in short for Bojangles, that canine creature posted up at *Abuela's*, being spoiled like a ninety-pound baby. You good?"

She offered an embarrassed smile. "Must be my night for homophones."

Gripping the hand still in mine, I kept her by my side when she tried to move on. "Yazmeen, what's up?"

"I'm fine. So...I know you have at least one pic of the infamous Mister Bojangles. Right?"

Not understanding her tightening up in that Bo vs. beaux mix-up—and remembering her questioning if I'd ever been attracted to other dudes that day we had coffee—I watched her a moment before scrolling my pics. Finding one of Nubs hugging Bo, I handed over my phone.

"Ummm...that's a small horse. He's huge, but cute."

"Possibly." Moving us forward, I unlocked the Cayenne, opened her door and waited for her to climb in but she was occupied, closing the photos and looking for other apps on my phone. I already knew. She was after that inaugural text that put her lusting business on blast. "Oh, heck no!"

I went for her. She tried that fake right, then swivel left, turning and giving me her back while trying to keep that phone beyond my grasp. She must've forgotten who she was playing with.

Guess I forgot, too.

Yoking an arm about her waist—tryna get the phone she held hostage—I blocked that fake and wound up pressed against that *phat* yam mountain.

Don't let me lie. I'd been with a long, lean string of slim women sporting just enough to call a butt. That there built-up backyard? Lord, it was rich! Round. Real firm, it felt too good against my stuff, had me wanting a whole new kind of ride-and-grind.

"Move, Tavares!" She was wrestling, laughing, oblivious to my feeling fire in places best left dormant.

Keep the phone, boo. I wanna stay right here this kinda way with you.

Refocusing, I reminded myself the phone was my end goal. "Baby, gimme the phone and stop playing."

She went stiff, like I'd snatched her oxygen. Glancing over her shoulder at me, she slowly turned, staring.

"What?"

"Nothing...I just..." Might've been the night, but I swear her eyes got misty. She shrugged, dismissively. "It's been more than a minute since a man called me 'baby' with meaning or significance."

Pocketing my phone, her words felt heavy, yet hopeful. I wanted to touch her, to erase that look from her face that was a mix of longing and vulnerability. It had me speaking truth without procrastinating. "Would you snap on me for admitting I want you as my butterfly and my baby? Is that alright by you?"

Honoring her power to decide next steps, I didn't move.

"Yes."

That was all the green light I needed to lean down and get those lips. Trust, I wanted to go all in, especially after having felt the pure femininity of her form against me. But that phone call from Thug-a-Mug was cautionary: she'd already had too much of men running rough and bullying. That, plus the Power higher than me, had a brother taking his time and going easy.

Trailing a finger down her cheek, I watched her eyes flutter shut and her mouth part on a sigh as if she'd gone a long minute without a man's touch. And tenderness. That woke something in me, had me determined to give her what she deserved but might've been missing. A finger beneath her chin, tilting her face towards me, I licked my lips and went in. Slowly.

I made myself keep it brief, like an introduction, sweet. Yet, it held its own kind of heat. It was a simple kiss. A taste. No tongue. Brevity aside, its magnitude punched me in the gut. A trace of red licorice, she was exponential-percent woman. I kissed her lips as if able to taste who and what she was. Her smile. Her voice. The soft touch of her hands. The way this woman listened and looked at me as if *I* was a treasure.

As if I somehow made her world better, when all the while she was improving me, had me admitting what needed admitting: I was completely sprung. One-hundred.

CHAPTER THIRTEEN
MODERATION
Yazmeen

ord, them lips. And that there kiss! It was pure fiyah, certi-
fying the man as a master of seduction. I was in trouble and
knew it. How he took a simple kiss and made it so sweet, yet
filled with promising, tingling heat was titillating, literally. As in nip-
ple-bothering. Had me mentally quoting scriptures to avoid rubbing
against him to ease that swollen nipple situation. It wasn't just that I
hadn't kissed a living, breathing man in three years: that skill was real.
And the heat! Gentle. Teasing. Yet strong enough to make me crave
seconds. Thirds. How*ever* many, however long the man remained in
my world. Which was what I wanted. After his kiss—and that Black
Friday blurt-all-my-business text—I decided to be done with frontin'
and resistance. I unlocked my heart and slowly let him in.

Being so open again scared the cornbread and greens out of me.
My past track record didn't let trust come easily, but I wanted him
enough to try. He was strong yet gentle, and his stable dependability
made him risk-worthy. Yes, there were hiccups even in the honeymoon
phase of who and what we were becoming, but he made my every effort worthwhile.

As days, weeks passed with us evolving and building, din-
ing-and-dating, I loved having this incredible, genuinely warm-hearted
man as mine, exclusively. It was like fresh air and light growing with
someone who loved the Lord and, flaws and all, was committed to
godly living. Being born-again believers didn't make our relationship
perfect, but it was an invaluable bond.

It was interesting seeing two strong-willed people learning the art
of compromise. He was bullheaded and one-track when it came to
what he wanted, but I had the same tendencies. Still, he possessed
a sense of fairness, was accommodating and incredibly forgiving and
generous. Where our connected paths would lead, I couldn't predict.
That had me constantly on my knees, asking my heavenly Father in on

it. I poured out my heart to God. He knew my hurts, my hopes, and that I'd had enough man mess. I was serious about whatever Tavares and I became lining up with His divine will. Even if God kept us in the Cuddly Friend Club, I'd be okay with it.

The lies of your life!

Fine, alright! The man had me ditching thoughts of being dried up and celibate until the twins went to college. For the first time since before my babies were born, I was possibly, just maybe, craving romance and relationship. But I needed some 4-1-1 first.

"Tav, I have a question."

"I have an answer."

I laughed despite being tired after midnight. Thirty-two but acting sixteen was new for me. That's the effect His Fineness and our connection had on Yazmeen. Late-night phone calls after our children were in bed were our new normal. He had me acting all teenager-ish like I didn't have a job waiting on me come morning, laying up in my bed talking—sometimes—until one, two a.m. Sharing. Revealing. Delving. Giggling. The man had me giddy. Free. Open. Like I could show him who I really was and tell him anything. Nearly. There were buried parts of me that, just maybe one day, I'd unveil. Until then, I was blessed to have an intelligent, humorous, keep-birth-control-in-constant-supply kind of man in my life despite my crazy and ridiculous.

"So...that gift basket you bought at Sasha's? Who was it for?"

I loved his rumbling laughter even when my lunacy caused it.

"You been sitting on that question since last month? Why're you asking now, Yaz? You jelly?"

"I'm curious, not jealous. But should I be?"

He laughed again. "I'll let you decide. Hold up a minute..."

Grabbing my remote, I turned on the T.V. and channel surfed while he did whatever he was doing. Finding one of my old favorites, watching Lucy and Ethel making a colossal mess at the chocolate factory, I hollered, imagining me and my B.F.F. in those roles, making unrighteous mayhem.

My phone vibrated. Looking at the screen, I smiled, feeling as if I'd conjured her up. I clicked over. "Hey, J."

"Hey, Yaz, I expected voicemail. Why're you still up?"

"Talking to Mister Magic," I supplied, using the nickname bequeathed by my bestie. I'd told Joy about the "us" Tavares and I were becoming only after making her swear not to tell LaVelle, his number one fan girl. I loved Velle to life, but chick would have us walking down the aisle and pregnant with triplets in minutes. I needed to take this thing slowly without her excess excitability.

"Oh...well...get back to that conversation. We'll talk later."

"Honey, are you okay?" Her voice slightly off, I sat up in bed like a warrior ready to go in on whatever the disturbance.

She gave me some pitiful sounding reassurance versus a lie. "I'll be fine."

"Joy...sweetie—"

She cut in before I could extract the business. "Are the twins up to hanging out with their Titi Saturday?"

"You already know. They'd love it."

"Cool. Okay we'll chat before then. And side note, boo: I'm glad you and Mister Magic're making moves. Now hurry up with the *adiós* to abstinence so he can whip that wand on you. Love you, girl. Bye."

Her disconnecting before I could speak left me saying a quick breath prayer. Her sexualized quip aside, something wasn't right. Not knowing if what was going on had to do with Quinton, or that shady part-time job of hers and the crazy stalker-ish fan-man that came with it, I asked the Father for safety, protection, and resolution of the issue. Before I could breathe 'amen,' another call beeped in.

Jesus, it's too close to dawn for demons.

"Royal."

"My missing a few months has you filing for child support?!"

"Correct. Fourteen is more than a few, but who's counting? And just so you know, months in the life of your children might as well be years. They grow like weeds. They eat. They look for their missing daddy. I'd rather you step up and be a real part of their lives, but it's your choice. So far, you've chosen everything except them, so hopefully the courts'll help you get some act right. Nite nite."

I clicked back to Mister Magic and was greeted by snoring. "Tav?" I had to call him twice.

He came up from Slumberland grunting and moaning, 'Ey, sorry about that,' with some extra deep, snatched-from-sleep-bass that added to his sexy.

"Time to call it quits?"

"Yeah..." he mumbled after yawning. "You see the text?"

I'd ignored a ping that sounded while talking to my B.F.F. Opening it, I found a picture of a huge gathering of what had to be family. "Is this Clan Alvarez at your grandmother's celebration?"

"Yep. What's she holding?"

A tiny, elderly lady sat in the center, surrounded by her tribe, her smile beautifully bright. Tavares kissed one cheek, while another male kissed her other. On her lap? That overly large, gift basket loaded with Sasha's Essentials. "Your *Abuela* is adorable."

"She is. What's she holding, Yazmeen?"

"Nothing."

His laughter was drowsy, deep. "Yeah, alright, *Señorita Mariposa*." He yawned again. "I have an early conference call and you have the nine-to-five waiting on your sunshine so we'd better get off here. I think I might miss you this weekend."

He was flying to Seattle to handle real estate business and wouldn't return until Tuesday.

"Your missing me is a possibility, not a guarantee?"

"Yep. Kinda like your inability to see that basket."

I laughed. "Okay, last quick question. Why're you attracted to me?"

"Should I not be?"

"Based on the females I've seen you with in pics, I don't fit your profile." I listed the ways I differed from his prior cadre of women.

He was quiet before asking, "One: have you considered that the pics you've seen were what the press preferred? Two: do you think you're some boss body, chocolate-skinned experiment? Like I'm all about trophy chicks and not real women? I've been with women of many races and complexions and, yes, I often limited myself to a particular type, but that doesn't bastardize my interest in you. You're not my social science project, Yaz. Trust: this man is *ab-so-lutely* attracted by the skin you're in and loving the curves you serve. *Periodt!* We good?"

"Mmm-hmm."

"Sweet. *Buenas noches y dulces sueños*, baby."

"Good night and sweet dreams to you, too."

Proud of my limited Spanish interpretation skills, I plopped my phone on the nightstand and burrowed beneath the blanket, dispossessed of suspicious insecurities about his attraction to me and owning up to having had a hint of "jelly" when thinking that basket was for another female. Between that and that Slut-a-Rella chick, jealousy had been justified. That there should've told me something. Even before we decided to be "we," Mister Magic had proven himself a magician, putting me in my feelings and pulling me out of myself and into possibility.

I didn't tell the boys about going to Joy's to avoid days of, "Is it time to go to Titi's?" I kept that in my pocket, using it Saturday morning as incentive to finish their chores.

I'd offered to drop them off, but she preferred picking them up, citing something about needing to "get out the house." Seeing her slightly puffy eyes when she arrived, my red flag radar went on hyper drive. My fast-quipping, razor-edged best friend had been crying?

The boys swarming their Titi gave me the opportunity I needed to stand aside, trying to figure out what in her world had gone sideways. Me, myself, and I decided it was definitely Quinton. He was saved. Celibate. My girl was sexually liberal and liberated. She wasn't down for monogamy or waiting on orgasms until married. Thanks to the horrors of her parents' relationship, she'd shut down all opportunities and declined any inklings of l-o-v-e. But I knew my bestie, and watching her interacting with the twins, I was convinced her heart had started opening, something got chaotic, and now she was backpedaling. Still, I said nothing, instead holding on extra-long when hugging her.

"Okay, boo, you can let go now or I'ma start thinking you swinging both ways these days."

I released her even while saying a silent breath prayer. "Whatever, Crazy. What're you and the boys doing today?"

"What we always do," she answered, looking at the twins. "Baking…"

"Cookies!" all three yelled as only consummate cookie fans can.

"Titi, I want chocolate chip."

"No, Malkie, it's my turn to pick," Malik countered his twin. "I want peanut butter."

"What happened to oatmeal raisin? I thought that was your favorite," Joy posited.

"It is," Malik agreed, "but we like sobriety."

"Okay, we won't make alcoholic cookies."

"Did you mean 'variety,' Malie?" I asked, snickering at Joy's cookie quip.

"Yes, Miss Mommy Ma'am."

Both Joy and I snorted back laughs.

"How about we make peanut butter chocolate chip cookies so you're both happy?" my girl suggested.

After a quick, silent consultation, the twins agreed. "But we can't eat too many like last time, Titi. We came home with tummy aches," Malcolm reminded.

"Mommy says we have to 'do all things in mass-stir-bay-shun.'"

Like a reflex, Joy and I grabbed each other's arms, pinching skin to keep the other from falling out laughing.

I could barely talk. "Malik, baby, it's *moderation*. Where'd you hear that other word?"

"What, Mommy? Mass-stir-bay-shun?"

Nose red and eyes watering from the effort of not laughing, Joy covered her mouth and studied the ceiling, leaving me struggling to keep a straight face. "Yes, honey. That."

"GramGram. She was on the phone with her church lady friend—"

"And she said masturbation's a gift for lonely women," Malcolm finished. "Mommy, are you lonely? If so, put that on your Christmas list."

"Yeah!" Animated and excited, Malik got in his twin's face. "We could find a box—"

"And a bow—"

"And put it under the tree and when Mommy opens it on Christmas she'll have all the mass-stir-bay-shun she needs!"

"*I gotta pee!*" Joy took off for the bathroom, leaving me with my phonetically challenged babies.

"Umm...alrighty...I need you two to go upstairs and get your coats, please."

"Can we bring our coloring books and crayons?"

I nodded. "Put them in your backpacks along with anything else you want to take to Titi's. And, sweeties, add *that* word to the list."

Hurrying for the stairs, Malik commented, "Mommy's list of words we can't say is getting big."

When they'd cleared the stairs, I rushed into my family room and fell out on the sofa laughing so hard I barely heard Joy come in. When she plopped beside me, we looked at each other and fell out again.

"I love your grandmother," my girl wiped laughter-provoked tears from her face, "but the woman's a misguided mess."

"How many times have I reminded Grams that the boys're sponges soaking up everything they hear, and to be careful what she says around them?"

"Knowing your Grams, 'masturbation' *was* careful considering her other adjectives. And your grandmother's a church mother?"

"Church of God in Christ, boo! Front row sitting. Hankie on the knees. Peppermints in the purse. Tongue-talking. Water-walking. Satellite dish-sized hat *erry* Sunday."

"I don't know what kind of church juice she's drinking, but I'd sip some of it," Joy decided, emitting another round of chuckles. "Whew! I needed that laugh."

"Yeah…I noticed." Sobering quickly, I lowered my voice when asking, "Honey, what's going on? Really." Our calls and texts had been lean that week, and she had yet to tell me what had her so down that night she interrupted my call with Tavares. When she inhaled deeply, I knew it was something significant.

"Is that the chair?"

Glancing at my newest prize of an oversized armchair and ottoman in deep eggplant, I nodded. A lover of all things purple, I'd bartered with the seller at a community swap meet last week, offering the mother of a one-year-old two huge bags of the twins' gently used clothing and sixty dollars cash for the plush set that rounded out my family room decorated in shades of purple, ice blue, and ivory. "Yes."

"Yaz, you have a gift. Folks would think you'd spent a grip decorating this place when you barely spent hundreds. And I still love my oversized leather ottoman-slash-coffee table you helped me snag for pennies on the dollar. You should do something with that…like a side hustle helping folks decorate on a budget."

I appreciated the compliment and had actually started taking pics with the intent of blogging-slash-vlogging, but I wasn't feeling the stall tactic. "Joy…"

"Quinton left."

"What do you mean he left?"

My Joy, my beautifully wild and crazy bestie who never did monogamy and changed men like I did my underwear suddenly had wet eyes from holding back tears. "As in deuces. Peace. 'Kiss me where He split me.'"

"He went back to Philly?"

Joy nodded. "Bounced and bye-bye. I was feeling him. He was feeling me." She had an odd expression and her voice cracked when saying, "Unfortunately, we got in too deep, and fell out over something."

"Over what, Sweetie?" I wasn't prying. I was worried that her working nights as a companion at a gentlemen's club was backfiring. She kept her clothes on and didn't pole ride. That didn't make me comfortable about her working there. I had concerns for her safety that, unfortunately, proved valid when she'd recently started having trouble with this Randall Cummings clown who frequented the club. She'd made the mistake of getting with him once. Now, he was stalkerish, possessive, and had probably pulled some craziness that got between Joy and Quinton.

She confirmed my suspicions. "Cummings mailed pics of the two of us to Que's job."

"Pictures as in…"

"Me in bed with him."

Not believing the dumb stuff, my mouth fell open but Malcolm's hollering from the top of the stairs, "Mommy, we can't find the blue crayon!" interrupted my response.

"Or the yellow, or the green," Malik added.

"You had them yesterday. Look again, please."

Hearing the retreat of little feet, I zoned in on my bestie. "The man photographed you?"

"Yep."

"*Jesus!*" Every misgiving I'd had since she started working at that club started hollering. I had to breathe. Deeply. "Joy, that pop off between you and Cummings happened long before you and Quinton."

Her laugh was short, humorless. "Yaz, what does that matter to a man? Men never wanna see another man doing stuff with their woman."

Apparently, in the heat of things words were said that couldn't be retracted. Now, Quinton—whose job assignment in Sacramento had been temporary to begin with—was back on the east coast. And my beloved who'd never loved a man was broken.

"Oh, honey…" I grabbed her as that first tear fell. Gently rocking her side-to-side, we held each other as she cried. When she quieted, I did something she hated. I prayed.

I didn't bother wrestling over the ethics of Joy and Quinton's relationship, or the fact that he was a saved and sanctified celibate, and she was a highly sexual agnostic. I simply prayed from the heart, as her sister-friend.

"Father God, this is my girl, but You love her more than I ever could. She's hurting and I need You to take care of her. Please intervene in this situation as only You can. Allow Quinton to recognize and resist the seductive lies and devices of the enemy, and may he hear Your truth on the matter deep in his spirit. I imagine that he's hurting, too. So, I humbly ask You to mend both of their hearts and, if it's Your divine will, reunite them. In the meantime, grant them sweet peace. In Jesus' name, amen."

My 'amen' was single and solitary. Joy didn't echo it. But she squeezed me tightly, letting me know she'd felt prayer's power and appreciated it.

Releasing her, I wiped her wet face. "You sure you're up to twin torture today?" Someone's suddenly beating and banging on my door like they were part PoPo and I was a felonious pimp with multiple arrest warrants interrupted an answer. *What the?*

"Are you expecting company?" Joy cautiously asked as I headed for the door.

"No."

"Then don't answer," she practically whispered.

*"Royal! Open the f*** up!"*

That had me and my bestie looking at each other, curiously. Peeking out the peephole, I didn't recognize the two been-lifting-weights-on-lockdown-looking brothers on the opposite side.

On tiptoe, Joy approached like a barefoot Ninja Negress. Moving aside, I let her peep what I was seeing.

"Who is that?" she mouthed.

My shrugging and head-shaking had chick quietly but quickly retrieving her purse. Opening it, she showed me Ethel, snug as a lethal bug.

Ethel was my girl's .32 caliber pistol. The fact that she was rolling with it told me there was more to the whole Quinton-left-slash-Randall-Cummings story. But just then we couldn't get into it.

"Don't you dare!"

Ignoring my whisper-hiss, girlfriend started prepping that piece like she meant to shoot somebody when the burly dudes took to laying on my doorbell. Only Malik's reappearing at the top of the stairs put her on pause.

"Mommy, we found—"

My finger to my lips put my child on silent. I hated scaring my baby, but not knowing what I was dealing with, I gave him a hand signal I'd taught the twins. Being a single mother solely responsible for the safety of my sons, I'd implemented codes and signals that we practiced periodically, all designed for their wellbeing. Malik knew what that signal meant: hide. My baby took off without a second glance.

"Royal, time to pay up, mufu! Open this gottdamn door before I put my foot through it!"

"Can I help you?"

If I never thanked the Lord for my nosy neighbor, Missus Lawrence, I did then. A retired postal worker with five parakeets (including Solo, a bird with one wing), a three-legged ferret, and excess time on her hands, she had the neighborhood tea on everybody. The banging on my door had obviously triggered her busybody button.

The conversation was muffled, yet clear enough.

"We looking for the dude living here. Royal Jones. You seent him?"

"Don't nobody live there except a lady and two kids, and she sho' ain't gotta man. I don't never hear no bumping and humping. She don't even do it to herself. She one of them Jesus girls living without sex. You gots the wrong address."

Feeling like some Puritan schoolmarm from the 1800s, I praised God for Royal's absenteeism, and that he hadn't come around often enough for Missus Lawrence, the neighborhood note taker, to know his name, and that she hadn't given mine to my escape convict-looking callers.

"Yeah…aiight. If you see Royal, tell 'em Big Cain came to collect."

Jockeying Joy for the peephole, I got it in time to see two broad backs lumbering to a cherry red Chrysler 300 parked at the curb, both doors wide open. Those open doors scared me more than thug one and two had. Only hazardous and need-to-happen-in-a-hurry business was transacted like that.

Clearly, Royal had taken money from the wrong person, and now "Big Cain" wanted it back.

"Yaz, what was that?"

Heart beating fast, I admitted my ignorance. "All I know is Royal better keep his crap away from me and my children. And what's up with you and Ethel?"

We rarely kept anything from each other. Watching my girl struggle to say something but choosing to say nothing added to my worries. "Joy?"

"Let me go lock Ms. Gat in my glove compartment so the boys don't see her. I'll get their car seats while I'm at it," she offered, grabbing my keys off the entry table. "And you better get some battery-operated action so your neighbor can hear *something*. She obviously needs to know you're fu—"

"Hush!" I grabbed her arm. "Wait just in case those criminalized creatures haven't left."

"Yaz, I wish a fool would! I'm *so sick* of men right now, I don't even need a reason." Opening the front door, she walked out, talking loud. "*Please* come for me. Make my trigger finger happy."

"Lord..." Remembering my children were somewhere probably scared, I left that alone and hurried upstairs. "Malik...Malcolm...we won." Those were our "all is well" words, letting my sons know it was safe to reappear. They did, crawling from beneath Malik's bed. Kneeling, I opened my arms to them. They ran to me. Feeling their fear, I took my time holding them. "I apologize for scaring you, but you did good. I'm very proud of you."

"We're proud of you, too, Mommy. You're a big girl. You didn't cry."

Laughing, I kissed their heads.

"Why'd you make us hide?"

"Someone had the wrong address, Malie, and they didn't seem too safe. But we're good. Jesus has us. Okay?"

"Okay. Can we go to Titi's now and bake cookies?"

I loved my little people's resilience and one-track intent. "Put on your jackets and get your backpacks."

Task completed, hand-in-hand, we descended the stairs, finding Joy sitting on the bottom step.

"We're ready, Titi!"

"Good, 'cause I want some what?"

"Peanut butter chocolate chip cookies!" the boys screamed, grabbing their godmother's hands and pulling her towards the door.

"It's good out there?"

Joy nodded. "It's clear."

Even with her reassurance, I still scoped my street when we walked out. Thankfully, I saw nothing except Mister Swearinger watering his lawn while sporting a pink muscle shirt, one knee-length red sock, one calf-length sock in green, and a pair of orange and black Bermuda shorts with bunnies, looking like a confused Easter-Christmas-Halloween.

"Ummm...first of all it rained last night so there's no need to be watering the grass. Secondly, he's clearly not color-coordinated, but isn't he cold?"

Strapping the twins in, Joy's observation triggered my snickering. "He's sweet, so leave my neighbor alone," I defended, leaning into the back of Joy's SUV and giving my babies goodbye kisses. Wishing them fun, I reminded them to be good listeners and mind their manners before closing the door. "You ready to get worn out?"

Joy's laughter didn't reach her eyes. "I need this twin tornado to keep my mind off things. I might take them by Mama's. She's been asking about her surrogate grandchildren, and the *only* grands she'll ever get."

"So, you know what the Lord has planned?"

She snorted. "These eggs and ovaries are off limits."

Laughing, I hugged my girl. "If you need me, I'm here."

Nodding, she got in, drove off, leaving me waving at Mister Swearinger's fashion-challenged self.

"I can hang your Christmas lights and water your lawn when I finish here, Jasmine."

No longer bothering with that name thing after two years of correcting, I politely declined. The last time Mister Swearinger helped with anything, he ended up coming inside for coffee and fell asleep at my kitchen table, passing flatulent bombs smelling like rancid-corn-beef-and-cabbage, leaving me wanting fumigation and a breathing apparatus.

"Well, let me know if you change your mind. A nice young lady like you needs a mister to do these kinds of things."

Thanking him, I hurried indoors when Missus Lawrence's curtains moved. I wasn't in the mood for interrogation over Royal and the Big Cain Collection Crew.

Safely inside, I plopped onto my "new" purple chair, leaned back with a sigh, and watched a centipede shimmy up the wall like it was late for a bug convention.

For the next few minutes I did nothing except deep breathing exercises, re-centering self, determined not to be caught up by Royal's hood life.

When deep-breathing took me only so far, I grabbed my cell phone off the wooden steam trunk that served as a coffee table and launched my Bible app to Psalm 91. Reading aloud, it was—for me—a prayer. I personalized its promises not just for myself and my sons, but for my girl. She'd divulged some, but my spirit was vexed like she was holding cards behind her back. Knowing Joy would tell the rest when the time was right, I humbled myself to the Spirit and asked God to rescue Royal from his self-made mayhem. Not because I loved him, but because my sons did, and their contentment was important.

The peace Psalm 91 always produced for me was evident at the 'amen.' I felt calm despite whatever chaos the enemy intended. I wasn't even pressed over Mister Swearinger's comments.

True, I didn't have "a mister to do these kinds of things," like hang Christmas lights. Or cover and protect me from roughneck bullies. Or take out the garbage, pump gas in my SUV, and use his size sixteen shoe to squash centipedes. But my vacancy sign had been surrendered, and even if I didn't have a mister I had a man.

I miss him.

Risky to admit and crazy maybe, but I did. Single parents living in different cities, I was accustomed to our not seeing each other regularly—except for video-chatting. Since our skate date, we'd only been able to sneak in a quick lunch and one dinner. But his being out-of-state made distance feel exaggerated, had me checking our text stream for anything recent I might've missed.

Finding nothing, I reminded myself Sir Sexy was in Seattle making boss moves and handling business. Grabbing my can of cashews from atop the steam trunk and turning on the T.V., it struck me that I wasn't worried. For the first time since living through much male-generated disloyalty, I believed in a man. Maybe it was too soon to own it but, unless he showed me differently, I trusted Tavares.

CHAPTER FOURTEEN
SEXLESS IN SEATTLE
Tavares

Disliking prolonged hotel-living or holing up in rented spaces, I'd purchased bi-coastal properties for that road warrior life back in my game days. The New York joint I'd decided to keep, but that Seattle spread and I needed to part ways. The market was stable but not necessarily in a seller's favor. My profit margin might be slim, but my spirit felt pressed to handle the business.

"Amazing! You didn't butcher my document. Guess I can thank Ms. Yazmeen for that."

Reina's ongoing accusations that I rewrote versus edited documents sent for my review held a drip-drop of truth. "You saying Yaz has me off my game?"

"I'm saying she's taming your anal, uptight ways."

Rolling in the back of a sedan, appreciating the car service Reina had arranged, I scoped the calendar on my iPad. "She's smoothing me?" Scrutinizing the sedan I was riding in, it was nice enough but absent of those extra touches my bruh's company provided. I made a mental note to follow-up with Lex and encourage that northern Cal operation.

"Definitely!"

Eyeing next week's schedule, my responsive chuckle was deep but brief. "'Ey…whaddup with this six-forty-five a.m. meeting Wednesday morning?"

"That's the nature of the beast when your V.C. partner's an early riser. If I remember correctly, your instructions were to pin Lex down to his first available. It shouldn't be much of an issue since you're up before then on weekdays anyways."

"Yeah, *exercising*." My afternoon workout routine had switched to early mornings now that Nubs was with me. "My body's moving, but my brain's barely woke that early."

"Hit the coffee or an energy drink and be your best self Wednesday morning. It's a conference call, so no need to suit up or brush your teeth. You can bring all that stink."

"I'm always fresh."

"So you say."

"Whatever, Rae. Everything's in order for this ungodly morning meeting?"

Reina assured me she'd provided Lex with the Sasha Essential's data he'd requested. The deeper we looked, the more boss potential the business exhibited. But it could benefit from financial backing that would allow for expansion. Not wanting her to misinterpret my interest in Sasha's as some backdoor way of leveling up with her, I hadn't mentioned my interest to Yazmeen yet and chose not to until knowing if Lex was in.

"Mister Ryde has everything he needs, including samples."

"Cool. 'Ey, Rae, do me a solid and send Nub's new teacher something for Christmas."

"She's already on the list. Next?"

I was straight on Nubs and my family. Reina had mailed cards and edible gifts to business associates. That left my lady.

Yazmeen had pulled a swear-not-to-get-me-anything routine, citing some "I'm not with you for your money, *and* I can't reciprocate with anything in your price range" yang. I told her to park that nonsense. What we were building wasn't materialistic and I wasn't with her for tangible things she could or couldn't give. Didn't she get it that the cards she mailed, the tender-hearted affection she showed were priceless? But she got all animated like the issue caused her embarrassment, leaving me playing Mister Sensitive-to-her-feelings and capitulating. Sitting in the back of that sedan, wishing she was there with me, I had the sense that sooner than later she'd have me confessing what she gave was beyond money's ability. *She* suited and met all my needs. But that was strong talk that shouldn't come lightly.

"Yeah, one last one, Rae. Look for that language learning system I bought Nubs last year. Actually, grab two."

They were for the twins.

Yazmeen had met Aniyah, but not officially as my lady. And I definitely hadn't had that intro to Malik or Malcolm, but she'd told enough funny stories of Malik's tongue tangles, and her introducing a new word each week for me to think the colorful pint-size, laptop-like learning devices were suitable gifts. She hadn't mentioned my not dropping a little Christmas cheer on them, so I wasn't violating any promises.

Giving Reina Yazmeen's address, I zoned back in on my calendar.

I had a little down time until Christmas. After that? It was on and cracking.

The *Athletes & Academics* grand opening. An all-star charity game I was playing in. Promo spots to hype it. A trip to New York. And a day in family court to finalize full custody of my daughter. *"Man..."*

"What's wrong?"

"I'm good...just heavy hustling."

"You *have* been hitting it hard. Take a vacation."

"Why? So, you can take one, too?"

Reina's "Exactly!" had us laughing.

"We'll see," was all I'd commit to.

Telling my cousin I appreciated her, my disconnect coincided with my condo arrival where my realtor was waiting. Exiting the sedan and heading for the lobby, I was clear about my mission. Might've seemed strange or extreme, but hit by certain memories and realities, I had to handle this.

So, about Seattle. Or more precisely, that property. The idea to unload it had come and gone over the past year, but my spirit had been real pressed about it lately. I loved the piece. I liked the city. I simply no longer needed this part of my past. It wasn't just logistics—me living in the Bay, no longer traveling in the game. This transaction was about unloading a life.

It's like this. I bought that condo at the height of my sin-boy lifestyle. It symbolized my wilding. Way too much weed. Strippers. Pornography. Multiple women in a night, or at one time. Throwing back liquor like lemonade, and the occasional white line.

Some mornings I woke up not recognizing myself or my bed partner(s). And my dudes, my B-ball brothers and other cats I rolled with, knew my parties were popping and my Seattle joint was open to them. They could cop a squat any way they wanted. But, waking up one Sunday after a party that lasted all weekend, I walked in on a teammate in bed with his fiancée getting it with two dudes who looked like kids.

That mess had me physically sick. I'd been down for a lot of things, but never that.

I went off, clearing house and acting ten levels of ignorant.

The fiancée went into overdrive trying to dial me down and prove there was nothing illegal about the mess. Chick had their kiddie-looking sex partners pull out I.D.s to prove they were age of majority. Apparently, my teammate liked sidelining with guys who looked under-aged. Still, the visual was much, and I made them raise up. Finding folks sprawled here, there, everywhere—some in their own liquor-in-duced vomit and piss—I went room-to-room handing out verbal evictions. And that naked dude who was so drugged out he was painting his face with feces? Feeling like the owner of a high-end crack house, that helped seal the deal for me. I was done.

My teammate and his fiancée being arrested three weeks later for solicitation, sodomy and other illicit acts with minors merely reinforced my walk-away from wilding. The fact that it went down at a house party and the homeowner had been arrested as well, hit hard on me. That mess could've popped off at my place and I would've been caught up in it.

Taking the elevator, I had to thank God, *again*, for sparing me and showing me grace I didn't deserve. I'd gone cold turkey on wilding, gave my life to Him. Ready to sign whatever papers my realtor had brought with him, I was glad to unload this condo even if the return on my investment was narrow. Getting this monster-memory off my back was big.

With furnishings being built into the sale, I could've hired someone to pack the few personal belongings left behind, or donated them. Instead, something in me had a need to see. Maybe it was to measure how far I'd come, or to reinforce the fact that this was no longer me.

"Mister Alvarez, is everything to your specifications?"

Turning to look at my realtor's executive assistant, I wanted to laugh at her professionalism and formality when she'd been a part of this condo life—as in, in my bed—at least twice. But this was business not booty. Her boss was present, and she played her role to perfection.

Looking at her, I wanted to dismiss truth, but why lie? The woman was attractive. Tall. Slim with waist-length, jet black hair. Eurasian. And I was mystified. As to why I felt *nada*, zero stimuli. "It is."

"We bend over for our elite clientele." Her words were simple enough, but there was some double-talk in her tone that I chose to ignore.

"I appreciate the attention to detail."

An interior decorator had staged the place so that it looked magazine-ready, boosting its appeal and marketability. I'd been informed that my personals were boxed in a closet and would've been easy to ship but, again, my need to be here was real. "Let me check a few things and we're finished."

My realtor's suddenly ringing cellphone had him excusing himself with an apology, leaving me to do a slow walk through the place amid a mess of memories. Few were good. Most had the taint of stank.

My cell rang. The designated tune told me it was one of my parents. "*Hola*, parental person. Everything okay?"

"Daddy, it's me!"

"Hey, *Princesa*! What's cracking?"

"Nana's teaching me how to make *lumpia*, and she said I'm doing great!"

"Say what? Nubs, you and Nana are over there conspiring to make me fat."

Her giggle was effervescent. "Want me to save you some?"

"Only if they're good," I answered, slowly observing as much of the condo as I could from where I stood.

"I heard that Efren." My mother's soft voice filtered through, chiding but playful despite that middle name tag she reserved for discipline. Honoring both of their cultures, my siblings and I had Latin first names and Filipino second names. My parents decided to double up on me so that I had two middle tags: Joselito Efren meaning "May God increase" and "Doubly fruitful," respectively. To me they meant the same thing. But after Taia's death, it was their way of laying an extra blessing on me.

"Nubs, why you playing me and putting us in speaker mode so Nana can hear? *Hola, Mami.*"

"Don't '*hola, Mami*' me, Efren. The only kind of lumpia I know how to make is good."

Being biracial—African-American and Filipino—my mother had learned to burn from both sides of her heritage.

"True that."

My mother said something in Tagalog. I didn't understand.

We had a basic, rudimentary sense and could sometimes follow family conversations, but one of *Mami's* regrets was not fully immersing my siblings and me in our maternal grandmother's native language. "I know you just pulled a *Lola*."

My five-foot-two-inch Filipino grandmother, my *Lola*, was famous for putting extra speed on her Tagalog when upset with my six-foot-five African-American grandfather. When finished she'd swing back to English with an accented, 'I bet you wish you knew what I said.'"

My mother laughed. "I most certainly did. How's Seattle?"

"Cold and wet."

"Daddy, are you bringing me something back?"

"Yep. Tavares Alvarez."

"No, I meant something special."

Moms got a kick out of that.

"And can you bring something for my *Abuelita* so she can have a nice Christmas?"

"We'll see," I hemmed, appreciating the view offered by the wall-to-ceiling living room windows and trying not to spoil a surprise. Nubs had a daily ritual of talking to Kryshelle's mom after school and at bedtime; still, she missed her grandmother. What she didn't know was that I was headed to Los Angeles Monday morning. Petrified of flying, Miss Carmen had accepted my invitation to spend Christmas week with us. She had one request: I had to meet her at LAX and fly back to the Bay with her, most likely holding her hand as if God appointed me a guardian angel of airplanes.

Heading down the hall, I listened to Nubs rattle off a list of gift suggestions while stepping into what used to be my bedroom.

I didn't recognize it.

It wasn't merely that the decorator had swapped the decor for a brighter color palette. That room, that condo and all it represented, no longer resonated with or for me. Truthfully, it hadn't over the past few years and I questioned why I'd held onto the place.

Because it was familiar, and a prime piece of real estate? Or in case I slipped back into my playboy ways?

The sound of the bedroom door closing behind me had me turning. Seeing what I saw left me nearly stuttering. "'Ey...Nubs...I need to call you back."

"Okay, Daddy. Don't forget."

"I never do."

"Bye, son."

My daughter disconnected before I could respond to my mother, which was fine. My tongue was tied, seeing as how my realtor's executive assistant had locked the door and briefly leaned against it before unzipping her skirt while licking her lips.

"Yo. Whaddup with this?"

"It's okay. Carter's in the lobby on a call...dealing with an emergency." Her skirt hit the floor before she'd finished her sentence. "He respects a client's needs. Why do you think he headed downstairs instead of taking the call here?"

My voice was calm for a man unexpectedly in the presence of a nearly naked woman. "To handle his business. Which is the only thing we're doing."

Her laugh was indulgent. Like she was humoring some simpleton. "Exactly. I'm your business, so do me." She moved towards me, fingers unbuttoning her blouse with every step. "It's been too long, Tavares."

A woman who preferred being braless, by the time she reached me her get-up consisted of nothing but thong panties.

Jesus, yoke a brother please!

Slim in the hips, her bare breasts were small, pink-tipped. She stood in front of me, caressing herself until her nipples went rigid and were begging to be licked. When she slid a hand into her thong, I smelled a scent I hadn't whiffed in five years: the musk of a woman. It was a pungent invitation to what celibacy denied me. And it was there on a platter for the getting.

"Man…"

Smiling, pleased with her seductive abilities, she came at me, her hand lodged deep in her panties doing things that already had her breathing all shaky.

Her free hand was suddenly on my belt, trying to unleash the beast. "No foreplay. Just screw me."

I had to physically haul myself back from a perfect set-up for sin. Stepping out of her reach, I knew there was nothing to stop or block a brother. It was just me. A big, empty bed. An already wet woman. Choice. And opportunity.

The Devil was *slick*. And this woman was wild. When I didn't respond the way she wanted, she turned her back to me and bent over for her 'elite clientele'. Literally. Thong like a G-string.

Awww, hell!

Back in the day I would've slapped that, tapped that. Right then, I was stretched between doing right or ending five years of abstinence. Let me just say the pull for Team Fornication was real until a name exploded in my brain.

Joseph.

As in the dude of the coat with many colors. Little Homey in the Bible sold into slavery by his brothers who wound up in Potiphar's house only to be seduced by the Egyptian ruler's wife. The same one I read about last night. Yeah, him.

Instead of giving in and getting it when ol' girl tried to put that yum-yum on him, Joseph got ghost. Sure, he ended up in jail behind her false accusations; but God used that setup to eventually seat Joseph in power. Long story short, Little Homey ended up being second in command in Egypt and saving the Hebrew nation including his janky relatives who sold him there to begin with.

Crazy, yeah. But that's where my mind flipped.

I'd read and heard Joseph's story told and preached multiple times. But being there in that room with a prior sex partner ready to ride, I thanked the Spirit for redirecting me to that passage last night. He knew I'd need it, and it felt like I had Joseph, Jesus, and Heaven cheering for me.

Do *not* credit me! Credit Him. My Creator Almighty.

My legs might've been shaky, but I stepped back from temptation. "We're not doing this."

My definitive decline put her on the defensive.

"Seriously? You don't want to hit it?" Her sharp tone told me she was offended.

It took all the Jesus in me to pick that blouse up off the floor and hand it to her without giving into breasts and nonexistent booty. "Put this on. Please."

Slapping the blouse from my hands, she obviously wasn't feeling me. "What the hell's gotten into you, Tavares? You never turn down sex!"

Scripture drifted through my memory.

If any man be in Christ, he is a new creature...

Retrieving that blouse one more time, I draped it over her. "That old dude is dead."

No, I didn't jog like Joseph. But trust, I didn't waste daylight disappearing.

"Mister Alvarez, is everything okay?"

I must've exited that elevator like a hurricane hitting that lobby hard. My looking pressed had my realtor suddenly manifesting. "Is the listing active?"

"Yes, I submitted—"

"Accept the first offer."

"But—"

I didn't let him finish whatever okey doke comeback he had. "It's first offer...or I find another agent willing to work this the way I want it. And while you're at it, check your assistant."

Exiting with his 'yes, sir' at my back, I stormed out not caring about Seattle's drizzle misting me. Buttoning my coat and tightening my Kangol, I waved off my driver and headed who knew where, who cared. I needed to walk until my energy didn't feel erratic and my spirit was clear.

I wound up in Pike Place—Seattle's open-air market—trying not to think about what I'd bypassed. Truth? That clothes-less encounter left me wanting it. As in sex. But not with a woman whose last name I, shamefully, couldn't remember; and whose small pale breasts and slim hips were truly booted, overtaken by brown velvet and curves and swerves that couldn't quit. For the first time in my adult life, I wanted not just sex but intimacy. And I wanted it with Yazmeen. *Badly.*

Buying a sterling silver bracelet from an Erykah Badu-looking sister selling handmade jewelry, all I could think of was my woman. I wanted to touch her, taste her. Take my time filling her, pleasing her not because I had some reputation to keep, or to bloat some sexual prowess. As much as I wanted to be inside of her, I wanted to know what it felt like to be with a woman I genuinely cared for, go to sleep and wake up the next morning with her laying on my chest after I'd given her my best.

After returning to my hotel, I called hoping she would but wouldn't answer.

She did on the third ring.

"Hi, honey." Her voice was a smile, warm and silky.

"If I bought you a ticket to Seattle would you fly in tonight?"

"Pardon?"

I repeated my absurdity.

"Sweetie, are you okay?"

The fact that she'd come to know me enough to sense that something was off put the clamp on my crazy. I hated coming at her like that, but for some doofus-dumb reason I had a perverse need to know. "Would you, or wouldn't you?"

"Fly to Seattle? No."

"Good."

"Okay." She dragged the word out like a musical phrase. "I'm not

following this fly-in issue. Was it a rhetorical question? Or did you actually want me to?"

"Yes."

"Because?"

"I want to make love to you."

Prolonged silence parked between us until she quietly asked, "What happened?"

Telling hard truths is what makes this work?

You already know. That relationship thing was new territory for me, and silence was probably my best bet. If I had to talk it out, I could've called my boy, Quinton. Or even Lex. No woman wanted to hear about another female pressing up on her man. That Mutt-a-Rella mess that went down at Sasha's let me know Yazmeen was no exception to the I-don't-tolerate-thots plan. We were only a month or so in, and truth could shut down what we were building. Plus, I wasn't into all this being vulnerable stuff and looking like somebody's punk. I could've, maybe should've, kept it on my chest. But I couldn't shake a whacked out, *seriously eerie* sense that I needed to divulge what happened.

The risks involved had me saying a quick, silent but earnest prayer.

Turning off the T.V. offering background noise for company, I sprawled out on the sitting room sofa and went all in.

Her silence when I finished had me feeling seventy-eleven levels of ignorant.

Should've kept this ish to yourself.

"Yazmeen?" I had to call her twice before she responded.

"I'm here."

I didn't bank on the fact that her tone was neutral. That could've been the quiet before the storm. "Are you okay?"

"Where're you, and why'd you tell me any of this?"

I sat up squeezing the bridge of my nose, not missing the fact that she hadn't answered my question. "In my hotel room. *Alone.* And truthfully? I don't know…other than feeling some unprecedented need for next-level honesty and transparency. If I twisted that and good intentions went bad, forgive me."

I didn't want her hurt in my process of becoming a better man.

"No…I can appreciate the transparency…tomorrow maybe. But right now? I need you to know I'm not your fall-back chick."

"Meaning?"

"Real talk? One-hundred?"

"Yes, ma'am." Her deep inhalation let me know I was in for it.

"I'm not the one to alleviate another woman's giving you an erection."

That put us both on silent.

When she continued her voice was soft but intense. "I wasn't playing when I told you I'm celibate. As are you. But if I failed to articulate that I've no intention of having intercourse again except in marriage, lemme make that *real* clear. I don't. And I won't." She didn't say anything for a moment. "I'm not into *ménage à trois* so if I do remarry—and trust, that's a *colossal* 'if'—my man'll need to make sure he comes to bed *for me*. Not because some chick wound him up and my vagina's convenient."

I should've spent a grip of minutes reassuring her that she was all I honestly wanted; that she wasn't some substitute, secondary thirst. But after that, I couldn't say anything except, "Understood and duly noted."

"Been there. Done that. *Won't* repeat the process. So...no, Sweetie. I won't be boarding a plane to sex you in Seattle. Me, my abstinent assets and I will be staying celibate in Sacramento. You're on your own, boo."

For the first time since crap happened, I grinned while curious about her 'been there, done that' comment. I liked that she'd essentially dropped the mic about who she was and what she wasn't. I appreciated the fact that she wouldn't compromise and bow down to my carnal cravings, or make my issues hers. Her stance and integrity further boosted the act right in me. This woman didn't have just my hunger, but my absolute respect. Apologizing for unloading this mess on her, I told her as much.

"Honestly, Tavares, this isn't something I *want* to hear, but stuff happens. I'm glad it disturbed you, and that you think enough of our relationship and me to say something. As for respect, you earned a bigger slice of mine for walking away from Strip-a-Stank. What do you plan to do about the situation?"

The situation was serious, but that 'Strip-a-Stank' tag had me chuckling.

God knew if the shoe were on the other foot, I'd be swimming in claims of sexual harassment if not criminal charges. Pretty clear that no one wanted to hear about a former pro-baller's being on the opposite end of unwanted sexual advances—other than laying the matter out to her boss and choosing a different realtor—I'd decided to let it rest.

"Tav, may I ask you something?" She did when I consented. "Do you think this was your litmus test?"

That had me taking a deep breath. "Yeah, baby. I do."

"I do, too. The enemy was extreme with it, but I think Satan meant to destroy not just your integrity, but your moral standards and spiritual development. Hashtag you passed."

So, this was my first full-court skirmish with faithfulness and fidelity?

It had been insane, intense, and not something I wanted to deal with. I still wasn't sure how deep Yazmeen and I would get, but while we had what we had, this whole thing made me more determined to honor it. And us. And to earn her full trust. She had yet to tell me the down and dirty details of her divorce. Sometimes it felt as if she were holding something back about her ex, but I knew she had history that made letting another man in her life less than effortless. "Thank you."

"For?"

Noting the small box on the side table, I lifted the lid and toyed with that newly bought silver bracelet. It was for Yazmeen, but she was the gift. "Speaking your truth without cutting a brother in the process."

She laughed. "Let's just attribute that to cookies and counseling. So..." There was a playful lilt in her tone. "Have you had that shower yet, as in icy cold?"

"Oh, okay, *Mariposa*, you got jokes."

"I'm just saying."

Getting up from the sofa, I headed for my room, stripping as I went. "I'ma do you one better. Rain and all, I'm heading to the pool for a marathon swim." I didn't need a splash. Errrythang needed plunging.

Her laughter was musical, refreshing. It had me smiling, feeling like we'd crossed an invisible barrier. I had to thank the Father for the blessing of a woman of beauty and dignity who had a backbone I couldn't bend. Instead of cussing me out or getting ghost, she'd offered supportive partnership. Understanding. And trust.

Lord God, please don't ever let me mess that up.

CHAPTER FIFTEEN
HAPPY HOE-LIDAY
Yazmeen

B aby, let me have a little more of those sweet potatoes."
Seated beside our grandmother at Christmas dinner, my
baby brother Taj, had the privilege of providing Grams with
butler service.

"Add some of Yazzy's greens, and mac-n-cheese while you're at it.
And don't be stingy. I'm not eating for two like Sasha. I'm eating for
three. The Father, the Son, the Spirit, and me."

"That's four, technically," my father corrected, unnecessarily.

"And technically, no one asked you, Stu. Sit there and let that food
fill your ol' mannish mouth and stay out of grown folks' matters."

"Mama, you don't have any matters I can't get into."

"Son, either you're a fool or somebody lied to you."

Grams had us laughing as usual. She and Daddy—her youngest
and "favorite" child—could and probably would go rounds with their
banter, but it was always in fun and love.

Looking around my parents' crowded dining room, I had an "I'm
Grateful" moment.

My grandfather had passed last year, but everyone else important
to my inner circle and heart were still here. Grams. Daddy and Mama.
My siblings, two brothers-in-law, five nephews and Sasha's little bit on
the way. And my babies. My beautiful twins whose father had disappointed yet again.

I hadn't seen Royal since going Little Red Ratchet Hood on him
and keying his car, but he'd texted he'd be by at nine that morning with
the boys' Christmas presents. Knowing Royal's sense of time didn't
work like the rest of the world's, I didn't tell the boys when to expect
him. If at all. I was glad I hadn't because nine came and went without a call or his appearance. When one o'clock rolled around without a Swamp Monster sighting, I bundled up my sons, those greens,
and mac-n-cheese and headed to the bosom of my family. Here, I was

whole. Blessed. And wanting nothing.

Except maybe *him.*

The work week had been overly busy with Christmas pageantry, food donations, and other holiday outreach that was standard practice for our church's ministry. Not to mention last minute prep for the New Year's Eve Watch Service. All week I'd hustled as if a runaway slave who'd broken an arm and lost a leg. Thankfully, I'd have the next few days off. No work, Zumba, or *Step-N-Style.* But like I said, I missed Mister Magic; and his week hadn't been any lighter with work, his athletic program, and Aniyah's grandmother as a holiday houseguest. Thanks to life, our communication had been slim since that Stank-Ho-in-Seattle episode.

"Mommy, look! I spelled 'puddle.' P-O-O-D-L-E."

My box-headed brother laughed at Malcolm's misstep. "Yo, Twinny Twin, that's 'poodle,' not 'puddle.'"

"Oh...that's why there's a picture of a puppy," Malcolm conceded, jumping up from the 'Minion Table' where all persons under the age of eighteen had been banished. Hurrying to where I sat eating every fattening thing that fit on my plate, my first born leaned against me, happily displaying a colorful picture on his new "laptop" screen.

"Good try, baby." I planted a pot liquor kiss on his forehead knowing my greens were G-O-O-D! "Can you put your laptop somewhere safe while you eat?"

"Okay, Mommy."

"Hold up, nephew. What're you doing with a laptop?"

Sasha's husband, Brandon, was obviously humored by little people shenanigans.

"It's a Christmas gift from Mommy's friend."

"I got one, too," Malik chimed in around a mouthful of ham.

"Naw, man. Neither of you can have laptops."

"Why not?"

"You don't have jobs."

Malik's open-mouthed giggle treated us to the unsightly vision of half-chewed, mangled food.

"Sweetie, finish chewing."

Doing as I asked, he had a comeback. "We're too little to work, Uncle Brandon."

"Well, there you go. You don't need laptops. And you probably don't even have one, Malie. You just talking."

"I do, too!" Pushing away from the Minion Table, Malik took off for the family room.

"Auntie Yaz, your phone's ringing," my oldest nephew who'd been sent on a hot sauce mission advised, returning from the kitchen, that coveted bottle of liquid heat in hand.

Named after his father, he'd recently decided 'Kyle' was too "white bread" and opted on K.J. His mother, India, was convinced he was smelling himself courtesy of some "little heffa somewhere" who had his nose open.

"Thanks, K.J." Thinking it might be Royal, I excused myself from the table and headed to where my phone was charging in the kitchen. If my ex-ogre gave me cause to act up, I preferred to play the fool in private. Grabbing my phone, my whole face cracked hearing his ringtone, Fantasia's "Hood Boy." There was nothing 'hood about His Fineness, but the rhythm and beat reminded me of his swag-a-liciousness. "Merry Christmas!"

"*Feliz navidad, mi hermosa mariposa.* I know you're with your family, so I'm not trying to keep you. Just wanted to holler a happy holiday."

"*Gracias* and same to you! But, you're in trouble."

"Because?"

"The bracelet," I answered, lifting my wrist and admiring my new jewelry as if he could see it. Handmade sterling silver, linked squares featured delicate floral etchings so spot-on they looked real. "We agreed not to exchange Christmas gifts."

"Which is why the box had a 'do not open until January' note attached."

"And you trusted me with that? Hold on a moment." I hurried to the dining room, his laughter tickling me. "Twins, come here, please."

"Is it Daddy?" They both asked, seeing the phone in my hand. That put all the adults on silent, and had me trying hard not to hate a man who constantly disappointed them.

"No, sweeties, just come with me."

Taking them into the family room beyond the reach of any ear-hustling, I sat in my father's favorite chair. "It's Mister Tavares. You can tell him what you wanted to this morning."

When Royal left mere months into our make-believe marriage, I'd elected not to subject my, then as of yet unborn, sons to a series of "uncles." Having not dated since "divorcing," Tavares was a first for the twins. In the name of taking things slow, I hadn't intended to introduce them just yet. But coming in my bedroom last week and finding us video chatting, the boys' natural curiosity (a.k.a. nosiness) merited an explanation. At this point, they simply knew him as my "friend."

"Thank you for the learning laptops, Mister Tavares," Malik hollered as if His Fineness was hard of hearing.

"Yeah! They're super! We're gonna learn lots and be real smart soon."

Tavares' "Little Man, you both already are," coincided with the doorbell. Unfazed, the boys kept chattering, filling Mister Luscious in on the discoveries they'd already made until hearing a familiar voice calling their names.

"Daddy?"

Something about the way the twins stood there silently consulting each other instead of immediately racing away, struck me as odd. When the moment passed, they did their usual and tore out of there trying to be the first to reach pleasant-as-eating-raw-meat-Royal.

As for me, I ignored the arrival of their five-minute-father, knowing my family was monitoring all interactions. "Thanks again, Tav. That was very generous of you, and the boys love them."

"My pleasure. Hopefully the personalization on the cases'll cut down confusion on whose is whose."

"They do. And can I tell you I feel horrible for not dropping Aniyah's gift in the mail until yesterday?"

Ever have one of those relatives who routinely gave gifts after the fact? She would be me.

I still owed Taj a birthday present from October.

Being a strapped-for-cash single parent, I appreciated my family going Secret Savior (that's the sanctified version for folks too saved for Santa) these past few Christmases. My family was too big to try to buy everyone something and they had mercy on me. But the bedazzled ladybug purse I'd filled with a cute assortment of hair bows for Aniyah should've been in the mail.

"'Ey, Nubs doesn't even know it's coming, so she'll be excited when it gets here. And you didn't have to do that."

"Neither did you."

"I wanted to."

"Same here." I took a breath before broaching his other offered gift. "Tav..."

"I already know. You don't accept."

Bringing in a new year in New York and seeing some special showing of The Lion King on Broadway was a spectacular gift for the boys and I that I had to decline. "You are one of the most generous men I know, but we can't."

"Yaz, I was serious about nothing happening. You and the twins would've had your own room. And Nubs would've been there as well."

"I don't know about Aniyah, but the boys can sleep through a hurricane, so they're unfit chaperones leaving adults to all kind of inappropriate afterhours play."

His laughter was short-lived. "Are you declining because of my ignorant Seattle invite?"

"No..." True, Mister Magic upchucking his guts about that left me slightly salty and wanting to choke somebody. That Can-I-Ride-Your-Pole-Realtor-Ho nonsense had me flashing in my feelings, courtesy of past multiple incidents of infidelity. Trust, I'd had more than enough of side chick, any-hint-of-an-affair foolishness. I gave His Fineness points for stepping away from shady games and disclosing what he had. In a crazy way, it took our relationship to a different, deeper dimension and intimacy level that I wasn't necessarily ready for. "I appreciate you thinking of us."

"However..."

I sensed his disappointment, but had to stay true to me. "It's too soon for family trips." We weren't ready to be the Black Brady Bunch.

"Understood, but again, there was no intent to get at you. You've been hustling hard. I just thought you could use a getaway. So...anyhow...enjoy the rest of your holiday."

"You do the same. And give your family my regards." Apparently, Mister Magic had shared our relationship with those closest to him. Me? Still hesitant, I hadn't broached the subject with my Williams clan.

"Will do. Later, baby."

Disconnecting, I had a second-guessing moment. A good man wanted to gift me with blessings and I was declining? Part of me was certain I'd done the right thing. I was disinterested in compromising my Christian walk, or doing anything suspect. Kids or not, where there was a will there was a way. The enemy would love nothing better than to have me and Mister Magic butt-naked in a hotel room fornicating and sexing night into day. So, I stood...okay *hid* behind godly propriety.

Why?

I needed camouflage. Distance.

From what?

The fact that I was falling too dang fast.

Intentionally, I was pumping my brakes and spending more time in scripture-reading and prayer. Committed to avoiding a repeat of my past, I needed God to lead me in this dating thing. Pocketing my phone, I reassured myself of the rightness of my not going to New York and headed to the dining room expecting to see Swamp Monster's rancid rump.

He wasn't there. Neither were the twins. "Where're the boys?"

Grams snorted. "In the living room with that jackleg marble-head. Don't worry. Your sisters are in there monitoring. Now…mind you, we don't care for him, and he don't care for us, but that thing you married could pretend he had some hometraining and pop his ol' mangled mug in here even if it's nothing more than to holler, "Merry Christmas, nappy-headed niggas.""

That had Taj and my brothers-in-law hollering-laughing, Daddy shaking his head, and Mama humming.

"Grams!"

"Yazzy, baby, don't 'Grams' me. Go'n in there and give that fool my seasons greetings. Tell 'im I said, 'Happy *Hoe*-liday sorry motherfu—"

"Mama!"

"Hmph! Daughter-in-law, you must've put something besides your foot in these candied yams 'cause I'm going in for thirds. Taj do the honors."

Hurrying towards the front of the house, hoping my sisters hadn't cut Royal yet, I rounded the corner and did a quick stop at what I saw.

It wasn't just the fuzzy-fluffy green jacket he wore that had him looking like Oscar the Grouch mated with a Grinch, but the new roughrider Royal was rolling with. He and Sydney—the thing we separated over—were obviously on strug. Again.

At least this one doesn't look like a man.

"Why I gotta chase you all around town just to see my kids, Yaz?" Other than that Grouch-a-Grinch get-up, the Christmas spirit had clearly missed him.

"'Cause dogs chase balls and yours are lost," Sasha mumbled.

Royal rolled evil eyes in my baby sister's direction. "You might wanna say nothing, with your knocked-up—"

I stepped in. "Here we are, so just enjoy your sons, Royal, without unnecessary clap back."

"Oh, you tryna strong up now that you riding that basketball nigga's dic—"

India interrupted before he could finish. "Malcolm and Malik, come with auntie."

"My kids ain't moving until they open my presents."

My babies were already on the floor digging into recycled gift bags, ignoring or unable to read the "Happy Birthday" and "Get Well Soon" decorating the outside of them. Yanking out wadded up newspaper substituting for tissue paper, they dug in, pulling out presents that had them stalling.

Hear me when I say we were in unified disbelief at my sons being the confused recipients of mismatched girls' socks, footed baby PJs, tubes of antibiotic ointment, realistic-looking toy guns, eyeglass repair kits, vape pens and oven mitts.

My sisters' simultaneous *"Unh-unh!"* and *"What the?"* were the only sounds for several seconds.

Me? I was frozen by the foolery.

"The vape pens were freebies. Treat 'em like a personal anti-nicotine campaign or something. But all the rest? Bargain General had a sale," that test tube specimen proudly commented.

That totally defrosted me. Functioning again, I snatched that madness off the living room floor. Stuffing it back in those bags, something dropped from the wadded-up fake newspaper-tissue paper and hit my foot.

Malcolm picked it up. "Mommy, what's this?"

"My bad. That must've slipped out my pocket." Royal leaned down, retrieving the rolled joint resting in the palm of our son's hand.

My sisters went into action, grabbing my children like Laurence Fishburne did when the mayor slapped Miss Sophia in *The Color Purple.*

They knew.

This fool could play all day on my nerves if he had to. But exposing my children to idiocy or messing with their wellbeing, sense of safety, or dignity was *nobody's* option.

I was in his face without realizing it, my voice so low and throat so tight it hurt to grit, *"Get. Out."*

"You better step back! I didn't come for you. I came for Christmas with my kids."

"And you better step the hell out of here." Profanity was a novelty for me, not something I did. But I was done with okey doke and nig-gardliness. With my heels on, we were eye-to-eye and our past already indicated I wasn't an easy win. I pointed in his roughrider's direction. "Take It with you and kick bricks! And do *not* come back until you buy your ass a lifetime supply of act right."

Royal had his crooked finger in my face. "Girl, I already told you to back back. Do it quick before I put my foot up—"

"I *know* you ain't pressing up on my sister like you cray cray!"

It suddenly got way real with my baby brother busting into the living room ready to clock a fool. My father and brothers-in-law were close behind him.

Taj might've been the baby but when it came to his big sisters, he was protective. I literally had to snatch that boy back.

"Naw, Yaz! I'm sick of this fool." He jerked free of me.

"Whatchu wanna do, son?" Royal challenged, squaring up on Taj.

"Dear God." My mother's voice came from the rear of my family that had formed like the mafia.

Brandon, my "NFL all day" lawyer of a brother-in-law built like a linebacker, repositioned me behind him. Next thing I knew, all four of my menfolk stood between me and my babies' daddy like a wall of Black Man Authority. Appreciation and a sense of security flashed through me, but I didn't have time to relish it. This was *not* the picture I wanted to paint for anyone's Christmas. I tried diffusing the situation, but no one was listening.

"Jones, my daughter asked you to leave. I suggest you do so. *Immediately.*"

Daddy was in his early sixties with the firm fitness of a man in his forties. He was hard muscle and military discipline, and didn't take nonsense. He didn't sell wolf tickets: any threat from him was as good as a promise and Royal knew it.

To the "idjit's" credit, he backed down after a short-lived show of resistance.

"Yeah. Whatever. We ain't done with this, Yazmeen. Oh, yeah, serve her, her gift," he instructed his roughrider of the moment. When Roughie didn't move fast enough, Royal snatched the envelope and handed it over himself.

Daddy intercepted it, standing his ground until The Grinch and his gargoyle left. "You alright, Babycakes?"

Disturbed beyond words, I nodded as my father handed me Royal's "gift." My mother was immediately there, stroking my back. My sisters had already removed my sons, giving me a moment with my parents. Thanking Taj and my brothers-in-law, I waited until they'd left before turning back to them.

"Daddy, Mama, I'm *so done* with him." My father's arms felt like sanctuary when wrapping me in them. "How'd I get mixed up with him in the first place?"

Mama's quiet, "You were running, honey," was poignantly accurate.

So, the pitiful story goes something like this. Girl was engaged to her high school sweetheart. Both were serious about serving God and made a pact to save themselves for each other and marriage until after college. She earned her undergrad degree; he went to medical school on the opposite side of the country. She kept their pact. He cashed it in, coming home one summer introducing his very pregnant, fellow med student. They married. *She* was left to pick up her life from the litter of bitter, broken dreams.

That was Darrien Jackson's devilment and she would be me.

My first love's betrayal broke me wide open and left me accepting an invitation to perform in a video shoot in the Bahamas.

Angry, devastated, I poured all my emotions into that performance. When that was a wrap, I lost my professionalism and panties to Mister Wannabe Music Producer who'd been sniffing around me. Thanks to untold drinks too many, I woke up the next morning having given him my virginity. He gave me pregnancy. A missed period later, I was officially entangled with a man I didn't love and barely liked. Exchanging crooked vows of matrimony in Pastor's office, I'd run from disappointment and raced into disaster with that criminal creature now known as my ex.

Moral of my story?

One: drink not multiple Raspberry Cosmopolitans and countless shots of alcohol when you can't tolerate a sip. Two: drink not in the presence of a man you know is bad for you because, inevitably, liquor will paint him so he's looking and smelling like everything you've missed.

Never again with liquor love. Been there. Done that. Have the stretch-marks and unpaid bills to show for it.

"Babycakes, it's time to stop square dancing with the Devil. By now you ought to be real tired trying to negotiate an amicable existence between you two. Do what's legally necessary to protect yourself and my grandsons. Get that court ordered child support and, if necessary, scheduled visitations."

My voice was no bigger than it was when a child getting some of Daddy's discipline. "Yes, sir."

Kissing my cheek, my mother spoke quietly. "We'll step out so you can open your envelope."

I grabbed my parents' hands. "It's okay. Stay. Please."

Opening that mess, I was so glad they did. Otherwise, I might've hit the floor and cracked my crazy head.

Withdrawing an officious-looking document and seeing my name listed as a defendant, I wanted to scream and swing on something.

My ex had filed for sole custody of our twins?

Royal had struck again. Or as he'd written on the envelope, *Merry X-Mas, beeyotch.*

"Yaz, you didn't sign a Waiver of Service of Summons and Complaint."

It would make sense later, but right then my lawyer-of-a-brother-in-law, Brandon, might as well have been speaking my bad Spanish.

My nerves were so shot, I was physically shaking and not exactly comprehending that a disinterested and neutral party should've served the papers, not my ex-underbelly. Now, when he filed proof of service it would, essentially, be defective. That didn't nullify the transaction, but it gave me options.

I could ignore Royal's mangled mess and not appear in court; or, I could appear and contest being improperly served.

There was no hot way in Hades I wouldn't show for anything pertaining to my children. Trust! Me, myself, and the whole Yazmeen would be there, not only contesting but also filing for sole custody with multiple forms of evidence confirming the sperm donor's absenteeism and lack of financial support. Like all the voicemail messages and texts he didn't know I'd kept.

"Do you think Royal will lawyer-up?"

Brandon had actually laughed at Taj's question.

"He can if he wants, but Yaz will have the representation of an attorney with an impeccable record. As in yours truly. That is, if you want it."

Assured that Brandon's offer didn't pose a conflict of interest, I immediately accepted. That combined with my family surrounding and laying hands on me and praying divine protection as I held my babies, kept me from losing it on the ledge. Still, that night I put the twins in my bed.

I needed my sons safe. Close.

God, I'm terrified of losing them.

My traumatized mind lost some sensibility and raced from A-to-Z, imagining worst-case scenarios. All I could see was Royal and his wifey thing, Sydney, getting custody and rolling in luxury cars while raising my sons on a steady diet of government cheese, Bargain General potted meat, powdered milk and Kool-Aid. They'd be constipated and not color-coordinated, going to church every five years on Easter only, wearing mismatched shoes, girls' socks, oven mitt hats and fuzzy green-Grinch jackets.

"Hood Boy" sounding softly on my phone snatched me from my ridiculousness. Grabbing my phone, I so wanted to accept the call and comfort on the opposite end. Instead, I hesitated.

Already close to tears, the simple sound of his voice would have me upchucking every bitterness. As much as I wanted and needed to spill the tea and my tears, his holiday happiness didn't deserve to be diminished. I had no desire to be that baby mama shrouded in drama.

I sent the call to voicemail, shut down Sacramento Family Law Court's website, and launched my Bible app instead.

Isaiah 54:17 was all over me.

Gently rubbing my babies' heads, I prayed it aloud.

"No weapon formed against me or my babies shall prosper... and every tongue that shall rise against me in judgment, shall be condemned...this is my heritage as a servant of God and my vindication comes from Him."

I wanted vindication, and Royal dealt with. By God. The courts. I even considered Joy's gangsta-genius cousin, LaVelle's big brother, Day-Day. Joy swore he had a crush on me and I was desperate enough to use it to my advantage, and have him roll up on Royal, all Al Capone'ish.

That's when my still, small (still sane) voice had the nerve to ask,

You want your children fatherless?

"They already are."

Of course, 2 Corinthians 10:4 came calling, reminding me that my weapons weren't carnal, but mighty in Christ.

"Lord, do You understand my plight?"

Royal was petty, but this was lethal. He knew our sons were my world and wanted to destroy me by taking them. Didn't that deserve a bullet? Or a beatdown?

Relax and let Me have this.

That's how I drifted to sleep, cuddling my sons, soothed by the Holy Spirit.

Joy picked the boys up the next day. I didn't want them out of my sight, but I wasn't in the best head space. I needed quiet time to pray and center myself again.

"I'm not even playing about that silver bullet. You want Ethel loaded? You got it."

I was tempted, but the verse I'd read the night before about our weapons not being those of the natural helped me decline. I hugged my girl, and stood there waving until she and the boys were out of sight, praying God would prevent our separation.

I took a bubble bath, ignored another call from Mister Magic, meditated and listened to ambient music. Warming up leftover Christmas ham and sides that evening, I was finally in a place of relative peace. Until my phone rang and hearing my bestie's mother, Miss Lucretia, screaming, *"Joy's in the ER,"* on the opposite end.

CHAPTER SIXTEEN
CRASHING
Tavares

My parents were in hog heaven thanks to my oldest sister, Gabriela's, grand idea of a family sleepover. For the first time in years, my parents would have all five of their children and fourteen grandkids under their roof for Christmas and, courtesy of Bree, they went crazy with it.

"Stop bellyaching, Efren. You know you enjoy it!"

Bree—Gabriela, the oldest girl—was only seven years older than yours truly, but forever the other mother I didn't need. Since a kid, *Mami's* second-in-command had been bossy. But she was on point. My fussing about not being able to hear or see the T.V., or that I had to pounce as soon as food appeared if I wanted to eat was simply me filling that role as baby of the family.

Don't let me lie. I loved the throwback feeling of loud, crowded, and crazy. Christmas Eve we were camped out in my parents' bonus room in sleeping bags, or piled two to a bed like back in the day in our small house in Philly. Twenty-plus folks sleeping over for Christmas was dizzy fun until Bree lost her whole sanity.

"Miss me with that ugliness!"

Don't ask how, but big sis had the *exact* sweaters we wore in a Christmas pic when I was five replicated in adult sizes.

"Put it on or else, Efren!"

It took Gabriela, my sis Julianna (who insisted on the Spanish pro-nunciation, "Hoo-liana"), and brother, Rico, to get me. Big brother Juan sat digging some old black and white movie unfazed by our usual foolery. A couple of nieces and nephews turned on *me*, the fun uncle, and joined the enemy so that I lost the war and ended up sporting some abomination of a green and red thing with literal flashing lights and Rudolph in 3-D. By the time Bree finished dressing us she had me and my siblings looking like Christmas clowns.

As if we weren't already a sizzling mess, big sis's inspiration caught another case of ignorant, demanding we assume the same positions as in the original pic. Guess she didn't account for the fact that that photo had me seated on her lap thirty years ago.

"That's what you get!" I thoroughly enjoyed plopping my six-foot-six, two-hundred-forty-some pounds on Bree's narrow knees. The timed camera caught the five of us crazily laughing for posterity.

That was my holiday. Parents. Siblings. Rugrats: Nubs, nieces and nephews. Bojangles running around being spoiled with food not on his canine diet. Miss Carmen completely at home, sucking up the whackery of clan Alvarez as we retired *Papi's* Fred Sanford truck that he insisted was a classic, and treated he and *Mami* to brand new his and hers Benzes that I could've paid for solo, but my siblings insisted they pitch in on.

"You bought them the house, Efren. Let us help on this."

I did. My parents were ecstatic.

Armed with enough holiday food to eat all week, I enjoyed a few days off with Nubs doing our thing. My only dark shadows were Kryshelle's emailed request for five-figure "Christmas cash" without bothering to ask about our child, and a failure to connect with Yazmeen.

True, holidays were all about family; but the fact that our Christmas conversation was the only one that week was concerning. I'd recently put two invitations on her plate that might've come across as stank. That whole Seattle set-up and situation certainly did. But the NY trip? Absolutely innocent with zero sex agenda. I knew the Taurus bull in me could come on strong, and sometimes wrong. Being in a first relationship had me, maybe, doing the most. Perhaps, I'd pushed too hard, leaving her no option but to backpedal.

Why you tripping over a female not phoning?

Facts?

She was all feminine, but nobody's miscellaneous female. She was... my woman. My boo. For true. Yazmeen had spoiled me with daily texts and nightly talks. I might've been breaking man code acting all sensitive, but her sudden withdrawal had me craving. Praying. She was completely meaningful to me, and her sudden absence had me feeling whipped, like I was catching feelings.

Man, sounds like you're slipping up and falling...

"Miss me with that." I muttered, sinking a two-point warm-up shot, not tryna hear nothing heavy like love.

"Damn, look at T-Alva!"

"Man, he's getting fat doing nothing since retirement except scratching that ass."

I laughed at the lies of my B-ball brothers walking onto the court, ready for our charity game practice. "Dude, you getting me mixed up with your mirror." I was serious about keeping fit after the fact, and was still solid.

Finished with the hand-slapping, bruh hugs and trash-talk, we huddled up, listening to our team coach before stretching, drilling, and running the court. I didn't miss the game, but admittedly it felt good doing something as natural as breathing.

"We 'bout to *kill* this charity game," our coach crowed, pleased with our heat. We were grinding, and we were good. But by the time practice ended, I was winded from showing those knuckleheads I'd been doing more than "eating chittlins and *menudo* and watching reality T.V." since retiring the jersey.

I gave it another day before getting all quasi-detective. I hit her social media accounts, looking for clues that could explain my woman's absence.

I came up with *nada*. Nothing. Her social media hadn't had a hit since before Christmas. Calling her office, I learned she was out for the week. Knowing that hadn't been her plan kicked up the worry. I'd already left enough texts and voicemail messages to qualify as stalker-ish. Instead of leaving more, I got on my knees and prayed, feeling like something was real strong and wrong.

Finished praying, I called my ever-faithful admin.

"'Ey, Rae, I need you to do something for me."

My cousin's living in Sacramento was suddenly a huge blessing.

"What, *primo*?"

Truth! Before I could ask her to do a drive-by and check on Yaz-meen, an incoming call beeped. Seeing "Mariposa" flash on my screen, I leaned back and breathed a "Thank You, Lord," before exiting the conversation with my cousin and clicking over. "Woman, I swear I was rolling to SacTown if I didn't hear from you by tomorrow."

"Tavares..." Her voice, all choked up, set off alarms and cut my clowning.

"What's going on?" I waited, giving her time to speak, only to hear what sounded like muffled crying. That had me tensing. "Yaz? Come on, baby, talk to me."

She made an effort to sound like her normal self. "I'm okay."

"No, you're not. Where're you?"

"At home."

"I'll be there in a few."

"Tav, no…that's a ninety-minute drive."

"I'll be there in sixty." I was already up finding car keys. Heading down the hall to get Nubs rolling, I remembered Miss Carmen was still here and could watch her while I was gone. "I'm on my way."

"No, baby, listen. I stopped by my house long enough to shower and change. I'm headed back out as soon as I finish." Her voice was heavy with exhaustion. "Forgive me for being M.I.A…but, I'm okay."

I didn't buy that lame reassurance the first or second time. Hunkering down on the end of my bed, I sat saying nothing for a moment. "Look, Yazmeen, I'm not trying to be in your business, but I'm concerned. Are you dealing with family? Malcolm and Malik?"

That's when she broke on me.

I felt useless hearing the woman I cared for sobbing knowing there was *nada* I could do.

Her voice was a fraction of itself when she quieted. "It's the boys. It's my best friend. It's so much."

"You feel like talking about it?"

Her words erupted like she'd been holding herself together by a thin thread.

Hearing the ish the ex-monster pulled at Christmas had me wanting to unlock my glock and put on my clown suit and act a fool. What kind of idiot did that? "I wish you didn't have to deal with any of this."

"Ditto, but I do, so…" Her sigh was soft and slow. "We'll be alright."

"How can I help?"

"Your listening's enough."

"Cool, but I mean in actual, tactical terms." It was good hearing her brother-in-law was providing legal representation, but I was ready to assist, however, if she allowed it. "What do you need?"

"I don't know, Tav…" Her exhale felt heavy. "I don't like dropping this on you. I'll handle my issues like I always do and—"

"Yazzy."

"Yes?"

"No offense meant, baby, and I'm not trying to undermine you, but no need to be Strong Black Woman on my watch. Take the cape off."

Her voice was small, soft. "Honestly, Tav? I'm tired. Of my ex. Of the situation my bestie's dealing with. With being on my own and raising not one, but two male children who need from their father what I can't give them. I'm a fighter, but right now? My managing to survive and do my best in raising my sons and still walk around semi-sane with my hair combed and matching shoes on doesn't mean I'm fierce. What if I just want to check out of that Strong Black Woman mystique and be vulnerable and cared for? Or have a man rub *my* feet, or cook dinner for me? Does that make me weak or anti-feminist?"

"No, it makes you real."

We sat, saying nothing until she offered an apology I didn't need.

"Sorry for dumping on you."

"Last time I looked we were in a relationship. Isn't unloading part of that?"

"It is, Tav, but..." Her voice trailed to silence.

"Today it's you. Tomorrow it could be me. I'm no pro at this, but my understanding is that our being together includes the good and the nasty. So, if you need to fall on me, fall Yazmeen. I'm man enough to hold you up. I'm imperfect, but I promise I got you."

"Stop trying to make me ugly cry."

I laughed. "You could never be that." I grinned when she snorted.

"If we were to video-chat right now you'd see reality and lose that fantasy."

"Yeah...alright. Anyhow. Day. Night. Doesn't matter. I'm here. Whatever you need. Clear?"

"Yes. I should get off of here and finish up so I can get back to..."

Her abrupt silence wasn't lost on me. My woman still had something she was holding. I figured it involved Joy since she'd mentioned some of what she was dealing with had to do with her best friend. I hadn't talked to my boy Quinton in a minute; but last I knew those two were headed to something solid. Hoping no ish had come to mess with that, I quietly waited for Yazmeen to say whatever she needed to. Telling myself not to push, I let her lead.

She switched up on me. "I don't know if I'll make the charity game with all that's going on, but I'll do my best."

I wanted her there, but understood if circumstances prevented it. "Sounds good. I'ma let you go handle your business. But I can do something real quick?"

"Yes. What?"

"Pray." It was the first time we'd prayed together since becoming a couple. It felt real. Right.

Taking the lead, I kept it simple but direct when asking the Heavenly Father's wisdom, intervention, and divine protection for my woman, her sons, and healing in the unspoken situation of her beloved. I prayed God's peace and serenity through all the processes; and that He would be her fortress and strength. With the "amen" and her whispered "thank you," it felt like something had shifted significantly. For Yazmeen. For me. We sat in the aftermath that resonated heaven's quiet contentment and peace.

"Yazmeen...I think prayer is something we should do together on a regular."

"I agree, and I'd like that. You're a very special man, and I appreciate you."

"Likewise, beautiful. You're beyond appreciated, baby. I lo—"

Nubs knocking on the door and barging in kept whatever I was about to say from happening.

"Daddy, *Abuelita* says it's time to eat." Hand on her hips, she had the nerve to ask, "Are you on the phone with Miss Yazmeen?"

"Why?"

Hopping onto my lap, she was semi-indignant. "You said the next time you talked to her I could say 'thank you' for my ladybug purse and hair bows."

I put an earbud in her ear. "Hurry up and say it, Big Bossy." She did. So loudly I had to drastically lower my phone volume. "Really, Nubs? Why you so extra always?"

She and Yazmeen laughed before my daughter launched into not just 'thank you', but 'what did you get for Christmas?' and a bucket of other questions I had to run interference on so my lady could get to her business. "Nubs, save some of this for next time."

"Okay. Tell Malik and Malcolm I said 'hi'!" With that, my daughter jumped up, pulling my arm. "Come on, Daddy. Time for dinner."

"I'm coming. Go wash your hands."

She ran into my bathroom as if she didn't have one of her own.

"I would apologize, but you're the mother of people under the age of five. So, you get it."

It was good to hear her laughter again. "She's still adorable, and I do. As much as I love hearing your voice, I need to get going. Thank you, sweetie."

"For?"

"Being you. Good night."

Echoing the sentiment, I disconnected and sat rubbing my head, feeling like I'd come too close to crashing over a cliff.

What was that?

What had I been about to say before Hurricane Nubs blew in? Had *those* three words really been that close to my lips?

"Naw...not even."

Truth? I deeply cared for and about this woman. But we hadn't been together long enough for them there type of feelings.

Must've been the situation. Relief at finally hearing from her again. Yazmeen's distress. My sense of helplessness. All of that had played on my heart and had me nearly blurting those words.

Heading for my bathroom where Nubs was slinging soap and singing, I told myself it was simply the moment. That reassurance was obviously weak because I couldn't shake the notion. It was like I'd drank some kind of double cocktail of peace and panic.

Dude, you're tripping.

No, I was honest.

Looking at it and calling it what it was, I saw that I was panicked at falling, but peaceful when realizing I already fell.

I wasn't sure when it happened. But it had.

That simple truth had me real shook. I. Was. In. Love?

Nubs chose hanging with her cousins at my sister Julianna's versus peeping her old man play the charity game. I didn't mind. Family was everything, and she deserved to get as much in as she could before heading back to school when we returned from New York. Plus, it was a good distraction from her missing Miss Carmen who'd flown back to L.A. with my brother Juan and family.

I was grateful the females in Clan Alvarez had always been there for my daughter. With an incubator-egg-donator like Kryshelle, Nubs deserved all the mother love she could get. That mother ministry was even more important now that Nubs was with me on the daily. Miss Carmen might've been too soft-hearted for my taste when it came to Kryshelle, but she was my daughter's grandmother and a good woman whom I respected. We'd never had beef and her Christmas visit was good proof that that hadn't changed.

Neither had my game.

Being gone from the grind didn't keep T-Alva from showing up in that charity gig like he'd put five on it. Wasn't nothing lazy or shady about me. My assists and rebounds were off the hook; my swish was still hot. And I wasn't soaring solo. My b-ball brothers—on both sides of the court—put some heat on it. The hustle was real with all that drilling and skilling we put in. But in the end, my teammates and I had to bow to the opposition's six-point win. It was a sold-out crowd and the charity would benefit, so everything was everything. Of course, the trash talk was thick, but that didn't keep us from dapping and hugging up at the end. But those weren't the hugs holding my interest. Hustling up a shower and a change of clothes put me in position to get that plush and lush.

"My baby is a balling *beast!*"

Suited in a soft pink fit and smelling like strawberries and cream, Yazmeen had me wanting to lick some things. Her exuberance left me blushing, realizing how much I'd lacked. True, I'd had females sit courtside or in a private box. But this was genuine. Without strings attached, like afterparties, liquor, drugs, or booty. She was strictly there for me.

I held onto her like a man who hadn't eaten in weeks. And I hadn't thanks to the holidays and that SacTown-to-Bay Area commuter relationship thing. I wanted the lips, but seeing my parents in my peripheral vision and knowing Carlos and Perla Alvarez missed nothing, I kissed her cheek. "You had a good time?"

"Absolutely." Her smile was reassuring as sunshine, reminding me that God miraculously intervened.

Respecting the fact that Yazmeen held her best friend's confidence, I still didn't have a play-by-play of Joy's situation. Whatever had popped off, heaven clearly stepped in and brought a dynamic resolve. The very thing that had Yazmeen so twisted days ago had turned, one hundred. Might've had something to do with Quinton's flying in and being with Joy again. All I knew, the issue was settled and my lady had transformed back into that light, bright butterfly who first caught my eye.

"I would've paid attention to you during your career had I known you had mad skills."

That had me laughing for real. "Yeah, you missed out on magic."

Kissing her hand, we joined the small entourage of my parents, Joy, and Quinton.

When my boy texted that he was flying in from Philly for a quick minute, I extended that game invitation to he and his lady. With Nubs, my parents, and I headed to the Big Apple late that night on a red eye, I meant to milk every minute I could and stay in Yazmeen's presence until the last possible moment. With a reservation for six, we headed to dinner at Sausalito's trendy, *La Promenade*.

Any concerns I might've had about my parents meeting *mi mariposa* like 'who-dis-chick-tryna-be-in-the-midst' proved unfounded. *Mami* intentionally sat next to her, throwing off that seating symmetry of man-woman-man, not just to be in the business, but because she genuinely liked Yaz. Apparently, whatever time they'd spent at the game was enough for my mother to know I hadn't been selling wolf tickets when telling her about Yazmeen. And Pops? He did his usual look-and-listen routine, scoping her out until catching my eye and winking. If I didn't know what that meant, my father made sure to tell me when my parents exited.

Citing a need to get home and finish packing for our trip, they dished out hugs and love—kissing Yazmeen, embracing Joy, and treating Que like the fourth son he was.

"Come to California again without stopping in to visit and see what happens," *Mami* playfully threatened. "I bet you'd stop by if I was making peach cobbler or *ponsit*."

"Miss Perla, you already know this!"

Laughing, *Mami* wrapped an arm around my father's with a final 'good night.' Excusing myself from the table, I walked them out, anchoring my mother on her other side.

Giving the valet his ticket, we waited on *Papi's* new Benz.

"Thanks for coming."

"Efren, have we ever missed a local game you played? Tonight wasn't the time to start."

"I still appreciate it. So...any thoughts?"

"On?" Three inches shorter, my father stood looking blank-faced at me.

"*Papi*, quit playing."

They both laughed.

"She's *very* lovely, son."

That earned my mother an extra tight hug. "I agree. *Papi?*"

Old dude had the nerve to twist up his mouth and shrug, which prompted a playful swat from his wife. "Carlos, do right."

The consummate clown, my dad grinned before jabbing a thumb towards the restaurant behind us. "That woman right there?" He grew serious. "She's the real deal. I suggest you do right by that one, son." From Carlos Alvarez, that was sermon, benediction and an I'll-beat-you-down-if-you-don't.

"She'll only get my best."

He gave a thumbs-up and helped my mother into his Benz the valet delivered before confirming what time the car service I'd scheduled for the airport would pick them up. Waving, I turned back towards the restaurant only to be hit by a strange sensation that had me asking myself a question.

Is she the one?

That had me stalling, more shook than those three words that had almost slipped from my lips.

It was too soon for 'the one' conversations and all that went with it. Like long-term relationships. Marriage. At least, in my opinion.

So, son, you can't level up?

That voice that I'd come to know as the Holy Spirit had me chuckling. God didn't talk to me in King James 'thees' and 'thous.' When He got in my grille, He spoke my language.

"No, Sir, I didn't say that."

I love you, son, but don't think I'll stand by and let you play with my daughter until you're done.

"Abba Father, why You going in on me? I'm just saying I'm not ready."

I waited, but God obviously had said His piece. Shaking my head free of wild notions, I walked up on Que, Joy, and *Mariposa* digging into dessert and laughing. In typical Yazmeen-laugh fashion, her head was tossed back on that luscious neck. Que's noticing me and nodding my way had her turning in my direction with a pure smile that made my abs tighten. This woman was as in to me as I was in my feelings about her. Reclaiming my seat and her hand, I couldn't dismiss a sense of supreme satisfaction resulting from her nearness. I might've sat there swimming in it if the mood hadn't shifted to serious, if my boy didn't kiss Joy's hand, exchange a look with her that screamed 'I'm in love,' before clearing his throat and announcing,

"We're pregnant."

Outdoor heat lamps combating the night chill, we walked the promenade holding onto each other, trying to slow down time. I had a red eye to catch, but we needed those final moments. Que and Joy had walked the opposite direction. Yazmeen had been subdued since their announcement, and I was interested in its impact. "'Ey."

"Hmmm?"

"You okay?"

Looking up at me, she spilled her feelings. "My apologies if I'm being bad company...but I'm concerned for my girl. Quinton's a good man and I celebrate this beautiful life they're bringing into the world, but Joy's been through enough and I don't want her hurt, or to see her single parenting because things didn't work."

True, that announcement wasn't what I expected. Since accepting the Lord as Savior, Que had been about that Christian living. In fact, watching his transformation and holding conversations about salvation is what led me to the Lord. Bruh's upholding his abstinence all these years with that silver ring thing—a token reminder of his celibacy—had been inspiring. So, he'd slipped? That didn't negate all the good he was. Noticing he was a little tense after the reveal, as if unsure how I'd respond, I'd pulled him in for a hug, telling him, "It's all good, and God's got you." He'd clapped me back and relaxed. I was in no position to judge.

"I've known Que practically all of my life and one thing I can say about my bruh is he's dedicated. When he's in, he's in and will go all out loving and protecting his woman," I assured, flashing on the time we'd had to keep him from wasting the fools who'd sexually violated his college sweetheart who, unfortunately—because of the trauma, and mental illness—took her own life. "Is my boy perfect? Nope. Neither am I. But my dude's in love with your girl. He's solid. Her heart's in good hands."

"It better be. If not, I'm coming for both of you."

"Baby, you can't come for me over someone else's relationship."

Her "Watch me" left me laughing.

She took a deep breath before admitting, "I'm probably just projecting. Honestly? I like Quinton. More importantly, my girl loves him. On another note, have you heard from Kryshelle?"

Snorting, I brought her up on Chick's latest and greatest.

I wasn't one of those parents buying presents and claiming they came from the absentee other. Nubs was too smart for that, plus it was what it was. My daughter had had to do without a Christmas gift from her mom. Still dodging the law for child endangerment charges, Chick was too busy emailing dumb-a$$ requests to consider Nubs. "Ask what she wanted."

"I'm afraid to."

"I'ma tell you." Yazmeen bit her lower lip to keep from laughing at Kryshelle's wanting twenty-five grand for her newest get-rich-quick-so-I-can-snort-it shenanigan: a drive-through coffee-slash-tattoo-stand featuring decaffeinated-only, homegrown, organic java. "I guess you roll up, stick an arm out the window and get a one-minute half-a-tat while sipping calm, Compton coffee." I did what I did with all of Kryshelle's emailed, texted nonsense: saved it in the "K-Krazy" file in case it was ever needed as evidence of her foolery. Hashtag receipts. I had them.

"*Whew!*" Swiping laughter-induced tears, her words were breathy. "That's extra!"

Stopping, I turned her towards me. "Let's segue to something pleasant."

Her voice was gentle and her eyes warm when asking, "Such as?"

"You. Me. Us." Stroking a finger against the smoothness of her cheek, I wrapped an arm about her waist and pulled her against me. Her body was firm, athletic from years of dance; but there was no mistaking the lushness of her real woman curves and femininity. Holding her was the aphrodisiac I wanted but didn't need. "I missed you."

Leaning down with a kiss and catching her mirrored response with my lips, I breathed it in. She tasted like the mint chocolate dessert she'd eaten, and felt like everything I wanted. Tonight. The next day and maybe always.

Whoa...no...

Refusing to overthink things, I deepened that kiss, parting her lips with my tongue to taste more of what I wanted. I needed to back back, but my woman was luscious. She was my drug. I was addicted. When she wrapped her arms about my neck, I moved in until the soft firmness of her breasts met my chest. Her moan was immediate, the sultry sound my personal stimulant.

Unfortunately for me, my body was quick in responding. I questioned the intelligence of earlier eating a side of oysters when my stuff starting twitching. My spirit was like 'reel it in, Big Beast,' but beast was happy. Definitely hardening. Mariposa's kissing me like I satisfied her own hungry needs had that downtown blood rushing.

If there was a bed nearby, we'd be bumping and banging.

That choked my chain, but the Pit Bull in me still wanted what it wanted. Thankfully, she pushed away, breaking our connection.

"Okay...wait." Her breathing was accelerated. "I *will* come to my saved and sanctified senses and keep T-Alva from messing with my thrift store virginity."

"What?"

"Recycled and repurposed. Second-hand. As in celibacy."

I couldn't laugh. Absence and abstinence had me sweating. Had me standing there flashing, thankful for that winter air to aid my cooling process. But her candor felt good. I wasn't the only one thirsting after what we knew was off-limits.

Alvarez, get your life. You cannot have this woman unless she's your wife.

That backed down the beast.

Refusing to revert to old habits and treat Yazmeen like booty business, I got my goods under control before stepping to her again, careful to keep some physical distance down below.

I opened my arms. She stepped in, shivering. "This Bay breeze is tryna freeze some things I need."

Removing my coat and wrapping her in it, I smiled as she lay her head against my chest, sighing like the good place she wanted to be was inside of me. As if just now hearing the instrumentals flowing from the promenade's outdoor speakers, she began to instinctively sway to the slow beats. Her arms around my waist, I wound up moving in sync. Slow dancing in the moonlight was sweet, had zero to do with booty. The simple intimacy plunged me deeper into that crashing-over-the-cliff feeling I wanted to avoid but was experiencing. "I need to say something."

Her head against my chest, her voice was muffled. "Yes?"

I wasn't ready. Maybe I wasn't all the way right. But only God had perfect timing.

Remembering what my boy had been through kicked up the courage. Quinton had loved after loss and was about to be a father. For a born-again, unmarried Christian, his situation wasn't ideal, but he was man enough to own up and do right by love. I admired that, and refused to do less. The thought of not standing up or losing her, of doing life without Yazmeen, calmed all need to rationalize what was happening. Shook or not, I'd always been dare devilish and she was worth every risk.

Resting my jaw against her head, I said what I said before talking myself out of a confession.

"I'm in love with you."

Her head jerked up, and she stiffened, her mouth moving without words like she couldn't find them.

"You don't have to say anything, baby, but yeah...I am." Tilting her chin, I kissed her. Slowly. Deeply. Praying she'd taste the power and truth of every good thing I was feeling.

CHAPTER SEVENTEEN
THE RIGHT WRISTS
Yazmeen

uttery and fluttery.

B That's how I walked around for days after Mister Magic laid it on me. Not just the lips, the kiss that had me rebuking I-Need-To-Be-Naked imps, but his love gift.

Too shocked to respond, I was grateful he'd granted me the out of silence. I needed that and time to let his reveal situate itself in my soul, my spirit. Lord knew my body was vibrating and burning with it. Days later, I was still negotiating what his admission meant for us, for me precisely.

I mean, I knew the man was good to and for me. But I'd messed up so much in romance that I couldn't be guided by feelings. I'd fallen into past traps, and couldn't go that way again. That's why I'd created my She Needs lists. I needed to be clear about what I wanted, what worked for my life and for my sons' benefit, and what didn't. The morning after his love admission, I pulled out my journal and consulted my list. I'd dedicated a page to "If I Ever Find Love For Real." It outlined traits and characteristics I considered essential to any future relationship. A man might not possess everything, but I needed it to keep me straight, focused.

My "must-haves" tick marks proved His Fineness embodied what was on that page.

Kind. Compassionate. Considerate. Caring. Humorous. Intelligent. Gentle. Good with children. Strong. Determined. Non-egotistical. Realistic, but optimistic. Respectful. Respectable. Protective. Goal-oriented. A gentleman. Masculine. A leader. Good listener. Good communicator. Solvent. Attractive in my eyes. Educated. Family-oriented. Born-again believer. Sexy.

He even hit some bonuses.

Good credit. Bank account in the black. Wholly heterosexual; no down low. Lives on his own; not with parents. Chews with his mouth closed.

Doesn't mine for gold in his nose. Has a Bible and opens it. Says 'shrimp' not 'skrimp'; 'library' not 'liberry.' Smells good. Deodorant is his friend. Uses Chapstick, lotion, or some other dry-and-ashy repellant. Speaks in complete, grammatically-correct sentences. Taller than me, even in my six-inches.

"Mommy, we can't find Mister Snackers."

Putting a load of laundry in the washing machine, Malcolm's announcement had me snatching out my earbuds, interrupting my India.Arie music fest and forgetting about my list. *"What?"* I could pet a tarantula. Snakes didn't bother me. But palm-sized, furry-with-four-legged rodent things? I'd sell my townhouse in a hot minute if one ever took up residence. *"How'd he escape his cage?"*

The twins stood at the laundry room entry looking guilty of Liberate a Rat Today campaigns.

Malcolm decided to be Mister Spokesperson. "We didn't mean to, Mommy, we just wanted to hold him."

"Yeah, and make sure he was happy," Malik added, taking his brother's hand like *they* needed emotional support instead of me.

I'd repeatedly postponed their weekend with their class pet-thing. Feeling bad about their Christmas fiasco with their dad, I'd finally stopped procrastinating and submitted the signed 'vermission' slip letting that gerbil-hamster-thing enter my living space for the weekend. But it had been with clear instructions. Snickers-Snackers was to remain in his happy habitat at *all* times, even in a case of fire.

"Lord, Jesus..." Starting the wash cycle, I leaned against the machine, head in my hand, wondering if the boys and I could move in next door with the know-all-the-business Wilona of our neighborhood, Missus Lawrence. "Okay...go upstairs and close your bedroom door so he doesn't get out."

When Malik came and wrapped his arms about my hips, looking wet-eyed and apologetic, I knew I wouldn't like whatever came next.

"We brought his cage downstairs so he could see the rest of where we live. We think he likes purple—"

"That's why we showed him your new chair," Malcolm finished. Not one to be left out, he walked over, adding his hug to my hips. "And we wanted to see who was softer, your chair or Mister Snackers. We didn't mean to let him get lost and crawl down in it. Now we can't find him."

The tears of twins. They were double-crying. Trying to distract me from the fact that we were about to be homeless thanks to a rogue rodent that had burrowed into my new favorite swap meet find, my oversized purple chair that now needed to be burned.

I started to call Joy to bring Ethel over in case I needed to shoot something only to remember she was in Philly meeting Quinton's family. By the way, that mess that had His Fineness worried and me M.I.A. around Christmas? In a nutshell, my girl wound up in the hospital thanks to that crazy stalker patron I didn't trust. She'd been drugged. There was initial concern of sexual assault. Thank God that proved false. But bloodwork led to her finding out she and Quinton were pregnant. Now, she was in Philly, freezing her behind off all in the name of love. And, as if that wasn't overturn-the-world enough, hear me when I say my girl got saved! As in "Jesus, I love You; be the Lord of my life again." That part there! Her bowing before the Father was everything to me. But that's her testimony, not mine, to tell. Her absence left me dialing my baby brother.

Thankfully, Taj was just leaving basketball practice. A newly licensed teen, he took every opportunity to get behind the wheel of my parents' cars and was too happy to roll my way. He found my fear hilarious.

"Just hurry up and get your narrow behind over here."

Exiting the laundry room with the twins in tow, I scurried us past the family room and into the kitchen. "Have a seat." I waited while they did. "Honeys, we had an agreement which you broke so, unfortunately, there will be consequences."

"Like what, Mommy?"

"Your laptops are on timeout for the rest of the day, Malik."

"But, Mommy, I wanted to show Mister Tavares the new words I can spell!"

"Oh, Lord..." Having a rodent on the rampage gave me momentary amnesia. We were expecting company: Aniyah and Tav. My recent blubbering about wanting a man to cook for me and rub my feet had him offering to drive up and prove his culinary skills after his Big Apple trip and the grand opening of the center for his *Athletes & Academics*—which the twins and I attended, and was absolutely fantastic. Today was that day, and I was a hot mess from *Step-N-Style* practice. Having just tossed my outerwear in the washer, I looked like I was auditioning for a Messy Mama commercial with my braids in a lopsided bun, wearing nothing except a sports bra and dance shorts that were so short and close-fitting my mother called them 'pretend panties'. I needed to shower and change and, per the microwave clock, I had a two-hour window before our guests arrived. That was time enough to get my look on lock and, hopefully, find that claw-footed terrorizer.

"Okay, let's compromise. If we find Mister Snackers before company arrives, I'll reconsider your punishment. *But*," I cautioned at their cheering, "you still get one."

Our ten-minute search-and-rescue mission failed. Yes, Snickers-Snackers exited my chair only to run into the living room beneath the sofa that was flush with the wall. Not that I wanted to catch him before baby brother got there, but still. I laid on my stomach, big behind in the air, using a flashlight to daze that thing and keep him from coming for me. I never let my children answer the door, but when the bell rang—knowing it was Taj—I allowed it while keeping a vigilant flashlight eye on the critter creature backed against the wall as if it were scared of me.

"Twins, open the door for your uncle."

They did. And trust when I tell you my life got lost hearing the boys yell, *"Mister Tavares!"*

"What the...?"

I was on the floor, butt up, dressed like a scrub and maybe less than hyper fresh after an hour of dance. I got up from there with the quickness. Turning and seeing Tav at the entrance, the look on his face told me it wasn't fast enough. Arms filled with grocery bags, he stood there, slowly roving the mess that was Yazmeen and obviously liking something based on the heat in those eyes the color of whiskey. That's when I realized, for all intents and purposes, I was basically in bra and panties, and had just had my double-butt in the air in a possibly sexual position some men preferred.

"Miss Yazzy!"

Aniyah's running at me provided a perfect cover. Literally. Hugging her, I used that baby to hide my near-naked realities. "Hey, Princess of the Crooked Afro Puffs." Although India remained her braider, it was our ongoing joke. "You're early."

"Goody. That means I can stay longer."

"Malcolm, Malik, you wanna show me where to put these?"

Still staring at me, Mr. Luscious let the twins pull him towards the kitchen to deposit the bags. That was my opportunity to make a break for it and run upstairs, but Aniyah had my hand and was chattering.

"Honey, I'm really interested in hearing more about Mister Bojangles being a bad boy and eating your new goldfish, but I need to go upstairs real quick."

"Okay, I'll be here when you get back."

"Me, too."

Looking up, I found Tav—still sporting that hot stare—devouring me visually. Grabbing sofa pillows, I covered what needed covering, breathing hard and feeling in danger of climaxing just by the way he was watching me.

"Miss Yazzy, do you have a pet?"

"What?"

Following where Aniyah pointed, I saw Snicker-Snackers inching along the baseboard.

"Mister Snackers!" Malcolm's running towards that thing and hollering excitedly had it redirecting its route and running full speed towards me.

"*Wooooowoooooowoooooo!*" I was running, too.

Unaware I had those kinds of hops, I was Swan Lake *jeté*'ing and airborne, flying like a half-court, three-points ball. I landed on target: Tavares' arms. I had that man choked about the throat, my limbs squeezing the heck out of him like he was Gerbil King and all fuzzy things were his obedient minions.

The kids took off chasing a guest pet. I stayed right where I was, in Tav's face, my every limb wrapped about him in an iron grip. He probably couldn't breathe, but such were the sacrifices of loving me.

"Babe..."

"*Mmm-mmm!* I'm not moving until they catch that thing."

The Lord must've heard his unspoken plea for oxygen because momentarily we heard, "Mommy, Aniyah caught him!"

"Your pet's cute, Ms. Yazzy."

"He's not our pet. He's our school maggot," Malik provided.

"Mascot," Malcolm corrected.

"He's still cute. Huh, Miss Yazzy? Look!"

"No, I'm good, sweetie. Put it in the cage, please. Twins, take it upstairs."

"Can we show Aniyah our room?"

"Yes. Do." They'd have my permission to play with matches and gasoline while eating unlimited cookies and ice cream and beignets butt-naked on the roof in the rain provided they got that thing away from me.

Impatiently, I waited as they disappeared upstairs before loosening my death grip on Mister Magic. That's when I realized that either I *really* had hops, or I'd scampered higher up his frame in my effort to escape. My legs about his shoulders, my bare belly was in his face. All he had to do was stick out his tongue and he'd taste that navel piercing I'd gotten after the boys were born, Royal chose Sydney, and I needed to reinvent my womanhood and my sexy.

Unfortunately for me he did.

His lips against my stomach were feather-soft. But his tongue slowly tracing my navel piercing combined with the friction from his recently regrown goatee had me Mount Vesuvius-ish.

"Tavares…" My voice was all choked from slobbering at the back of my throat. "Stop. And put me…down…please." I needed his too talented tongue to make its way back into his mouth.

He complied, lowering me to my feet but grabbing my hand when I tried to make a great escape. Holding me firmly against him, he purred in my ear, "Your body's amazing."

"I need," was barely out of my mouth when he granted me a kiss saved, abstinent folks had no business sharing, particularly in my quasi-nakedness.

I cannot lie. His strong hands felt way too wonderful slowly skimming my body, his firm, hungry touch doing things to me that hadn't been done in ages, if ever. His hitting all my right places with precise pleasure-producing pressure told me he knew his way around a woman's body. Feeling like I was sitting butt-naked on a sidewalk in August, my stuff got to burning and boiling.

I really meant to pull away, but his broad hands traveling down my spine had me forgetting my whole alphabet, squirming, and arching my back. Feeling the hard pulse of his own below-the-belt responsiveness, I was deep under his spell until his hands passed my waist, palmed my hips, and gripped my dense derrière.

"Unh-unh." Breaking that kiss and all his mystical, physical magic, I removed his hands from my rear end. I was breathing like a convention of asthmatics, but I managed. "Just no…"

"Not now?"

"Not never." Every woman's EZs were unique. My behind was a minefield of erogenous zones that made my backyard *way* sensitive. Just trigger-loaded. His touching me there was a guaranteed path to my giving the kids that ice cream and gasoline and really letting them play on that roof until we finished climaxing and shuddering "Why're you early? I didn't expect you for another two hours. Did we get our times mixed up?" I was breathing hard and babbling.

"Maybe," was all he said, too busy filling his eyes with my scandalousness and palming my waist to make a fuller sentence.

"Make yourself comfortable. I'll be back." Grabbing the sofa pillows I'd dropped, I used them like Eve getting a garden memo, subject line: you're naked, Trollop. Refusing to look back, I rushed upstairs out of eyesight, but within earshot of his lust-heavy,

"Damnnn..."

A cold shower later—dressed in the most loose-fitting, unsexy lounge pants and baggy t-shirt I could find—yours truly got on her knees and breathed a short prayer to the God of celibacy and rebuked booty-wanting behavior before descending the stairs to find His Fineness in the kitchen with the kids.

My space seemed smaller trying to contain him.

I was proud of the townhouse I'd purchased with my dance-days earnings. Still, after visiting *La Casa Alvarez* when taking the kids to some indoor pizza/amusement spot near Tiburon a few weeks back, I'd been concerned about the humbleness of my home when hosting him.

A lover of all things oceanic, his backyard facing the Pacific had been simply amazing, as was his home. Soaring ceilings. Travertine tile. Large living areas with—unlike my yard sale finds—furniture that matched. Beautiful cultural art. Oversized bathrooms that made me want to bathe somebody, especially him. An office and home gym. A gourmet kitchen that Mister Magic swore he regularly cooked in. A media room boasting several arcade games, a massive aquarium featuring brightly-colored tropical fish, and home theater—his home had it. State-of-the art and luxurious, the place could've come across as cold and model-perfect but for the fact that it was well-loved and lived in, exuding the warmth and spirit of its residents.

Introduced to the menacing-as-a-marshmallow Mister Bojangles and accepting Aniyah's invitation to a future tea party in her princess-perfect bedroom, I'd accompanied her father through two guestrooms and into his master suite complete with sitting area, and fireplaces in each. Displaying awesome architecture and design, that space held traces of his signature scent, reeked his manliness and had my head swimming with thoughts of being spread-eagle and butt-naked thanks to that sumptuousness custom-made, baller-sized bed of his. Fingering its luxurious linens, I'd wanted to bounce my behind on that mattress and test its sturdiness.

I bet he sleeps naked. I wish I had a nanny cam.

"Yaz..."

Looking up, his expression had been a blend of soft heat and humor, as if privy to my lusty looniness. When he came towards me, I'd backed away, deciding his bedroom was a dangerous place for two folks calling themselves celibate and saved. Complimenting his taste, I'd suggested we get the kids and head for the pizza arcade, thankful for three little underaged chaperones unknowingly keeping their parents from getting it in a place perfect for fornicating.

That arcade hosting a pizza buffet was essentially an indoor amusement park housed in a huge, renovated warehouse featuring carnival-like rides, miniature zip lines, arcade games, ball pits, trampoline-styled floors, inflatables, rock-climbing, race cars, and seemingly endless opportunities for kids to run ragged as parent-chaperones sat on the sidelines winded and wondering when we'd get a nap in. That place was Aniyah and the twins' new favorite crave.

"Mommy, look! We're helping Mister Tavares." Malcolm's excitement brought me back to the present. Wearing the miniature chef jackets from their Titi Joy, the twins were at the table massacring bell peppers with their plastic chef knives.

"Good job. Aniyah, would you like an apron?"

"Yes, please."

"I'll take one, too."

Glancing at Mister Magic, I found him scoping my outfit and chuckling. "Any looser, Yaz, you'd get lost."

Sticking my tongue out at him, my heart did a little flip seeing the naturalness of his actions, as if the humbleness of my space was of no consequence as I double-wrapped an apron around Aniyah's waist before finding one for him.

He refused to take it. "I want the same service you gave Nubs."

"Stop playing and put it on yourself, Tav."

"You see my hands are busy, right?"

I complied only because he was seasoning raw chicken and I didn't want salmonella skipping through my kitchen. Having to maneuver that apron around him had me reliving what went down in my living room, and its effects on us both. I hurried up securing that apron so I could move to a safer zone.

"Thanks, baby."

"*De nada.*"

"I know what that means! We started Spanish last week and it means 'you're welcome.'"

"Nice, Malik!"

My baby glowed at praise from His Fineness.

"Mister Tavares, why do you call Mommy 'baby'? That's not her name."

"Malcolm, it's a term of erection...I mean *affection*."

My blurtiritis left Tavares laughing so hard he had to walk away from his chicken.

"Forget you, Tav," I mumbled, distracted by the sound of my front door opening.

"Yo! What it do? Where y'all?" my little brother hollered. My siblings had keys in case of emergencies.

"Oh, Lord, I forgot about this nut." Hurrying from the kitchen, I intercepted him. "What happened to being here forty minutes ago?"

"I'm good, big sis. Thanks for asking. You still got a rodent situation?"

"No. And where've you been?"

"A brother's got business and you at the end of it. I was talking to Kia. Why's it smelling good when you can't cook?"

The nut took off before I could inform him I had company. Right behind him when Taj stepped into the kitchen, I bumped into his back when he stopped abruptly. "Whoa, Yaz, whatchu doing with a dude 'round my nephews?"

"Hi, Uncle Taj!" the boys sang as Tavares stopped seasoning duty, washed his hands and turned in our direction.

"Hey, Twi— *WHAT! THE! WOO!*" Taj stood there, mouth open, bugged-eyed, looking double-dumb. "Wait. Wait. Wait. I got the wrong address." The nut actually ran out of the house and returned. "*Naw!* This ain't *even* happening! I do *not* see the one and only, my all-time fave, T-Alva Alvarez cooking in my sister's kitchen!"

"You do. Now, go home," I instructed. "Your services are no longer needed, plus there's not enough food for you."

"Yaz, babe, that's cold."

Hand on his heart, Taj did a perfect Redd Foxx "I'm Coming, Elizabeth" stagger back. "*Babe?*"

"Don't worry, Uncle Taj. Mister Tavares knows Mommy's real name. 'Babe' is just a term of erection," Malik assured.

"Yeah...okay...Twinny Twin." Taj was all distracted trying to take my new mystery man in.

Okay, so my family kind of, sort of, was vaguely aware that I was seeing someone. I'd simply never gotten around to telling them who exactly. Sasha and India had their suspicions, but I didn't confirm them, granting His Fineness and me time to grow our relationship without outside speculation, influence, or opinions. In a way, I *was* hiding him. Not out of embarrassment, but protectiveness. With his celebrity status, we'd be public soon enough. And, yes, I'd met his parents, and we'd lunched with his two older sisters when he'd returned from New York, but other than that, we'd kept family on the outskirts. Okay, I had. According to Tav, Clan Alvarez knew all about me. Glancing at him, I caught a look on his face indicating he didn't exactly appreciate my secretiveness. Thankfully, Taj's ridonculousness prevented any kick-back.

My bubble-headed brother was all animated and extra, pointing back and forth between us. "You? Are with *her?* Why?"

"I beg your pardon!"

Laughing, Tavares kissed my cheek. "Because your sister's everything."

"Yeah...naw...I guess...maybe, but... Naw... You serious? Y'*all legit?*"

Tavares confirmed it.

Head down, hands in the air, Taj was moaning and backing up like sisters at my parents' church when touched by the Holy Spirit. His dropping to his knees and pounding the floor—confirming he didn't have good sense—left the kids laughing.

I ignored him. "Aniyah, this is my brother, Taj."

"'Ey, Short Stack," Taj briefly greeted before resuming his antics, wrapping his arms around my legs and fake crying.

"Taj, get up!"

He did only to push me out of Tav's arms. Laying his head on *my man's* chest, that fan boy fool hugged Mister Magic. "Yo, as your fan *número uno*, I'm feeling this. If my sis don't work out, you and me gotta keep our bromance."

Taught to cook by his mother and grandmothers—women who fed large families daily—Tavares made enough black beans and chicken, fried plantains, and *Arroz con Gandules* (the best peas and rice I'd ever tasted) to feed the twins and me all week. Good thing he did seeing as how—thanks to Taj texting my business—folks last name Williams suddenly decided to "pop in" trying to see up close and personal if the man I was dating was real. Even my "NFL all day" brothers-in-law suddenly had a love of basketball and a case of "I need to see." Within minutes of meeting His Fineness and his food, them Williams folks fell under his charm. Even Grams—wearing some bling tee warning "Hell is Hot! Don't be a Thot!"—approved of him. After, of course, examining his wrists.

"Tamales, come sit so we can talk."

My multiple apologies for Grams' intentional mispronunciation were apparently unwarranted. Maybe it was the soft spot he had for grandmothers (or the feebleminded), but Tavares found it hilarious.

"Yes, ma'am?"

Grams went in on him, digging down in his personal business until satisfied she knew enough to decide he was "worth my grandbaby's time." Then she went in on the wrists. "Let me see them."

He looked at me for a clue as to what was happening. With Grams, only God knew.

She was poking and prodding and examining like a graduate of somebody's medical school.

Sitting back in a wheelchair—which she didn't need—she announced, "Yazzy, he's got the right wrists, baby. Unlike that switch-hitter you had, he's all man. He loves vaginas, and vajayjays love him."

"Grams!!!"

That had Taj literally on the floor crying-laughing, Tavares ruby-faced and choking, me blushing and mortified, and Daddy wheeling his mother onto my small back patio and locking the door behind him.

"Isn't vajayjay anatomically correct?" Out of her unneeded wheelchair, Grams stood at the backdoor hollering. "I could've followed my first mind and said p-u-s—"

Closing the vertical blinds, Daddy walked away, mumbling about hiring a priest for an exorcism. Such was His Fineness' introduction to

The Wonderful World of Williams.

Three hours later, I'd managed to evict all persons who didn't reside at my address. Except Taj and his bestie, James, also known as 'Snook.' Snook's being there was fine, but I'd had to take their phones to prevent them inviting their entire basketball team over. Either Tavares genuinely liked the bubble-heads or was merely earning jewels in heaven by being indulgent and entertaining their nonstop questions, conversations, or requests for tips on how to better their shots and up their game. Yes, I was glad he'd connected with my clan and they with him, but I also wanted some alone time with His Fineness. As much alone time as being chaperoned by Aniyah and the twins allowed.

I'd already grabbed their hoodies and distributed them. Still, Taj and Snook were posted up in my kitchen watching Tavares and I wash the dinner dishes, blabbering about basketball sixty-miles a minute. "Okay, already, Taj! Sweetie, you've been going in on *my* company for the past hour. Don't you and Snook have something else to get into on a Saturday night?"

"Naw, we good."

The brickhead didn't get it. "How about hitting up Kia's phone, or going home or, let's say, finding something outside of these four walls?"

"What? Wait. You jelly, Yazzy, 'cause I got T-Alva's attention? Don't be mad at me. Up your game, girl. Starting with that fit. You look like you wearing a blanket. All baggy and ish."

Snook found that particularly funny. Tavares' biting back a laugh earned him a look.

"Do me a favor, Taj." I was finished with sharing my space with musty-armed teenagers sitting there doing nothing except defiling the air. "Be useful and take out the garbage."

Then disappear like your deodorant did.

"Yeah, okay. I will. Lemme peep this first," Taj bartered when the phone I'd returned to him pinged.

Taking the clean dishes Tavares handed me, I placed them in the cabinet, ignoring his, "Look at my baby acting all jelly. You want me all to yourself, boo?" His leaning down kissing and nibbling the side of my neck almost got him handcuffed, stripped and frisked. "Do I need to make it up to you?"

The tingling sensation flowing from where his lips graced my neck down to places that were suddenly warm and wanting to be fed, left me purring, "You just did."

"Whoa! What the?"

Taj hollering all extra snagged our attention.

"Yaz! T-Alva! Y'all peep this yet?"

"What, it do? Let me see." Snook's big head was leaning over Taj's shoulder looking at the phone then, mouth open, in our direction.

"I swear! This nigga here!"

"Not in my house, Taj Williams." Glancing at the kids seated on the floor eating popcorn, engrossed by an animated movie in the adjacent family room, I was relieved to see they were oblivious to my brother using unacceptable language. Last thing I needed was Malik walking around talking about, 'Hi, n****s.'

"Whaddup?" Tavares walked over to see what had Taj boisterous and bothered. Seeing a plethora of unpleasant emotions cross Tav's face as he read let me know it was serious.

My eyes on Tav, I took the phone when my brother handed it to me. What I saw and read had me frozen, temporarily incapable of feeling.

Yo, Taj, this your sis? asked a text, followed by a hyperlink to a post featuring two photos of me and Tavares. One from the skating rink. The other from his recent charity game. The photos were innocent. It was the long, rambling, rancid post that left me seeing twenty-fifty shades of crimson.

The title caption 'When Ex-Beeyotch Goes Baller' was followed by a stream of disgusting falsehoods I couldn't stomach:

4 y'all who wanted 2 know...this is what got me ghosted. This ish here broke the marriage. What I gave wasn't good enough. Beeyotch all about that coin & the come-up.

Trying to hit where it hurt, the nonsense continued with lies straight from Lucifer. They were sharp, bitter—publicly blasting, frying me on social media, and I couldn't do a thing except breathe and scroll through Royal's twisted wickedness that finally ended with,

Now she talking that full custody ying yang. Tryna leave me with nothing? Ain't happening. Plus, she still owe me coin on Purrrfect. She gonna pay that. Trust. Even if she gotta get that pay from this athlete nigga here tryna raise my sons when he need 2 focus on that lil girl I hear might not be his bio kid 'cause he might be shooting blanks and ish. Ex-Beeyotch all about the bank. Baller Boy betta watch his coins. #ruthless.

Royal's rant was horrifying enough, but I added torment to torture by briefly scrolling the comments that were equally vicious, crucifying me as a disloyal, money-hungry 'ho from hell' who deserved—and I quote—"whatever disease she gets from that basketball d***."

Stunned senseless, I couldn't think. Speak. Nothing. Had I been alone, I might've screamed. Peed. Cut something. But I couldn't wild out the way I wanted. I had company. Looking up and handing Taj his phone, part of my company was missing. I'd been so snatched by my ex-slug's white-hot lies that I hadn't even heard him leave.

"Yazzy, you okay?"

"No, Taj, I'm pissed!" Hurrying from the kitchen, I found Tavares at the front door helping Aniyah into her jacket, the twins standing there looking like they were losing a best friend.

"We were having fun."

"Yeah, we don't want you to go," Malcolm finished his twin's sentiments.

"Maybe you can come to my house and we can play a really, *really* long time," Aniyah offered, hugging the twins.

"Can we, Mister Tavares?"

"Sure," he answered, squatting and fist-bumping them.

"Tavares—"

He cut me off as if words from me were unwanted. "Nubs, tell Miss Yazmeen and the boys 'good night.'"

Hugging Aniyah when she wrapped her arms around me, I kissed her cheek and thanked her for visiting. Waving, she joined her father who'd already opened the door and was waiting on the front steps.

"Twinny Twins, come help Snook and me eat this ice cream."

Glancing over my shoulder, I appreciated my little brother having an adult moment, knowing I needed to talk to Tavares without my sons being present. When the boys took off, I grabbed a jacket from the entryway closet and stepped outdoors, mildly wounded at Tavares' hustling Aniyah into his vehicle as if far away from me was where and what he needed to be.

Returning Aniyah's wave as her father closed her door, I stood arms across my chest feeling anything but warm. "Tav...we should talk." He stiffened when I laid a hand on his arm.

"Naw, we're good." Leaving me on the sidewalk, he moved to the driver's side.

I proceeded as if he hadn't spoken. "I can't atone for my ex's insanity, and I *hate* that you were dragged into—"

"I'm man enough to handle ish, but what you or your ex won't do is drag my daughter into your mess. Good night, Miss Williams."

Feeling suddenly and excessively cold, I watched him drive away.

My heart hurt. For him. For Aniyah who—whether the biological pot shot was true or not—didn't deserve to be publicly humiliated, scrutinized, or the subject of my ex's evilness. But I hurt for myself as well. Had I finally opened myself and been blessed with a good man only to lose him to a pack of vile, vicious lies?

Exhaling, I tilted my head towards the dark winter sky, daring myself not to cry.

CHAPTER EIGHTEEN
PROBLEMS WITH PATERNITY
Tavares

I wanted a drink.

For the first time in five years, I *needed* a sip with some kick, that burn-the-back-of-the-throat, inebriation process. Liquid hypnosis. Something suitable to deadly thoughts and plots that would land me in a jail cell and leave Nubs parentless if I acted on them. Thankfully, for sobriety's sake, my house was liquor-less; and Holy Spirit had better sense than me.

Your daughter's in the backseat.

That caution interfered with my pulling up to a store like I intended and buying that liquid sidekick that would've done nothing except inflame a situation that was already stupid.

Remembering times I'd actually twisted caps and tossed some back despite being behind the wheel, Holy Spirit's caution was legit. It kept me moving towards Tiburon. Sober. Almost sane.

Livid ain't even a description. I was glad I didn't know where dude lived, and that the glock was at home, not in the glove compartment. My mindset might've necessitated his hearse and my living my not best life in an orange jumpsuit courtesy of California.

Did dude really come for my kid?

He had. And like I already said, I was man enough for ish and clap-back. But as long as I was living, *no one* came for Aniyah Chanel Alvarez.

A glance in the rearview mirror confirmed Nubs was conked out from playing with the twins. It was good they got along and that she liked them. Unfortunately, I had contrary feelings towards their parents. Their father was a straight up, ass-backwards idiot who deserved a bloody beat-down or a short life instead of the breath being wasted on him. But their mother...

You already know you're headed down a wrong road.

Maybe. But right then and there I didn't care. Her ex-clown had that rage rolling.

Be angry and sin not.

"Really, Lord? I'm not tryna hear all that."

You obviously need to.

Signaling a lane change, I moved left and set the cruise control, jaw grinding like I was trying to crack stones. But the Father was right. My old nature was flaring in my face, and I was letting it. I'd never been violent, just bullheaded and easily triggered. I grew up in Philly and knew how to scrap in the streets, and had a few confrontations and altercations in my teens. But I'd stepped away from all of that. Didn't mean I didn't have blood kin who lived outside the law who'd readily roll on dude if asked to. I hate to admit, but I was nearly there, ready to handle that ex; but I wasn't ready for Yazmeen.

The sane part of my brain was hollering, telling me she had *nada* to do with dude's acid, that she wanted no part of it or him and that she'd suffered at the center of his rant. She wasn't coming for my coin like he claimed, and she sure didn't cosign that stunt questioning my paternity. But my state of mind was flipped, twisted, and I transferred blame instead of acting like a grown a$$ man and correctly dealing with my feelings.

"I swore Kryshelle would be the last woman to play me."

She's not Kryshelle. She's Yazmeen. The woman you say you love.

Rubbing a hand over my head, I readjusted myself in my seat, seeking the physical comfort my inner self was missing. Needing additional aid, I flipped the music to smooth, instrumental jazz to massage my mind and help get my thoughts right, seeing as how I didn't have liquor's benefit. Or my old trickery relief of banging it out in sex. My phone contacts were free of booty set-up situations. But, trust, if I wanted that ill na-na I knew how to get it.

"Dude, you're *tripping*."

I had to dial it back, but something a former coach drilled into our team flared up.

Don't get caught in the games some females like to play. You will get slayed.

Had I been played by Yazmeen? Was I the only one feeling them there feelings?

I was the knuckleheaded one to admit I loved her out loud. She had yet to return the sentiment. I'd put her out there to my family while she'd clearly kept me her secret.

If I weighed the evidence, it seemed she was hedging bets and straddling the fence. Maybe she had come to slay and play.

The SUV's system announcing an incoming call from 'Zalo interfered with that thinking. "Whaddup, Cousin?"

"'Vares, it's hanging and happening. You need me to handle something?"

My Uncle Julio's youngest, Gonzalo, was straight gangster and had a prison record and tattooed tears beneath one eye to prove it. That's why, in my initial rage stage, I'd called looking for him. Now, his readiness to handle business actually had me grinning.

And inhaling, exhaling. "I did, but it's done."

"For real, Cousin! You iced somebody?" he fired off in Spanish. "I'ma 'bout to be proud of you for walking on the dark side?"

I chuckled. "Naw, Cuz. It's not like that. I'm backing up a bit so I can get my head straight."

"What had you going?"

Maybe I told him on the down-low hope that he'd still go in and handle that business. But I told him.

"What the fu—"

Snatching my phone, I deactivated its connection to the Cayenne's sound system before Nubs could get a language lesson she didn't need, even in her sleep.

"'Vares, you serious?"

"Look it up for yourself." I told him how and where to access the post. I was silent while he surfed the net. His ending with a truckload of cuss words in our grandparents' native language let me know he'd found it.

"I got this."

"Naw, 'Zalo, my lawyer's on it. Let her handle that cease and desist."

My violent as a mufu cousin took some convincing, but I got him to back down on planting Yazmeen's ex ten feet beneath *Abuela's* herb garden.

"I'll mummify his ass in the toolshed. Give *Abuelita's* weed some fertilizer that don't quit."

That had me laughing for real.

My grandmother swore she grew herbs for medicinal and cooking purposes, but we'd known since we were kids that she grew marijuana in the toolshed we were banned from entering. "Yeah, naw, 'Zalo. Stay free. I ain't tryna visit you in jail again."

"You ain't gotta visit. Just put that money on my books."

We laughed, joked, and talked a little more until hanging up, wishing each other peace and love.

Thought I had love, but...

"Aiight, Alvarez, enough punking up with the pity party."

That idiot's actions were no reason to question my woman's authenticity or sincerity. In the few months we'd been together she'd shown integrity, loyalty. I knew enough about her to know she didn't want anything monetary. She fussed whenever I gifted her something, and seemed embarrassed when accepting, citing an inability to reciprocate on like terms. I wasn't interested in what her wallet could or couldn't afford. I wanted Yazmeen. And, yeah, I knew she wanted only me.

"Doesn't mean she's not hesitating."

Now, that she was. Taking her time like she was making sure everything was everything instead of diving off the deep end and joining this love fest that had me open.

Merging from I-80 to the 580 that would take Clan Alvarez that final stretch, I reminded myself I was new to this and nobody's love genius. I did, however, have expectations. I expected my woman to have my back, like I had hers. I'd always step up for her; I needed her to do the same for me. No, we weren't running at the same pace. We had individual histories that made us stop and look both ways. But she was extra on that caution tip. I knew this. And I had questions. Mainly, was she all in?

Athletes & Academics was up and running like boss business. The coaching staff, the kids enrolled were hot for it. I watched every session those first few weeks, got on the court and ran drills with them, and even hosted "Courtside Chats" where I chilled with the enrollees and just straight-talked B-ball. There were strong opportunities presented for athletic improvement and basic citizenship, as well as good bonding moments. In short, the program was proving a success. As for those venture capital moves, Lex and I had our sights locked on two minority-owned businesses that were small, but had mad potential if afforded better advantages. We were positioned to do that, and were even in preliminary discussions with Sasha about upping her online, ecommerce presence and helping her Essentials go national, and ideally, global. In short, my business life was on lock. The personal side?

It could benefit from some time and attention.

Since that social media mess two weeks back, Yazmeen and I had barely talked. Our communication had been sketchy at best due, large-ly in part, to me and my stubbornness. Granted, my calendar was tighter than tight, but that had never stopped our prior connections. Truth? I hadn't made much effort. Because?

"Mister T., you have a visitor."

The college intern/receptionist's voice crackling through the walkie talkie clipped to the waistband of my warm-up pants had me hurriedly lowering the volume on the device so as not to interfere with a coach's courtside chat with our *A&A* kids. Vacating my sideline seat, I headed for the front office, abandoning my former line of thinking and stop-ping short when seeing the lusciousness waiting on me.

"I hope I'm not interrupting."

Seeing her—coat across an arm, wearing killer heels and a wrap around dress handling those honeyed curves—it took a moment for me to say anything. "Yazmeen?"

She misinterpreted my surprise for disinterest. "I should've called—"

I didn't let her finish. "Is the conference room open?" Grabbing her hand, I headed down the hallway with the receptionist calling out that it was scheduled for a meeting in twenty minutes. Entering the room, I closed the door behind us, not caring who had to wait for the space. Right then, I needed time to simply take her in. Everything she was, everything I saw and felt, I wanted. Her scent. Her whole self. She was the goodness I'd been wanting and missing.

"What're you doing here?" I knew she was supposed to attend some women's ministry thing in Richmond, but her being at our sports com-plex in San Rafael was the surprise I needed in my life. "Shouldn't you be at your brunch?"

My tone housed some residual roughness it didn't need and she didn't deserve.

"I left early hoping we..." Eyeing the hardness of my jaw, she pivot-ed towards the exit. "Forgive me for intruding."

I pushed the door closed that she opened. When she turned look-ing as if wanting me to hear something only her heart could articulate, I steered us towards the conference room table. Sitting on it, I pulled her between my legs and held her hands.

We stayed that way in a silence that was its own language, our eyes locked, reluctant to say anything.

She was first to speak. "I was taught to never repent for someone else's errors, but if that's what we need in order to heal then I'm sorry Royal did what he did, and that he is who he is. He was unnecessarily malicious and vicious, but he doesn't reflect or represent me in any—"

Cradling her face, I kissed her into silence, letting that kiss communicate for me. Primarily, the fact that I missed the bond I'd built with my baby, that I needed it like I needed all of her. Not just those lips and her kiss that I wanted more of but forced myself to pull back from in order to address what we were dealing with. "Baby, we've already talked it out, and I told you I know that woman he wrote wasn't you."

"Yet you've spent the last two weeks low-key treating me like I'm guilty of something."

That had me by the ear like an old-school teacher dealing with a class cut-up. Yes, I was bullheaded, but one thing *I'd* been taught was the power of forgiveness. Still, she was right: I'd been uncommunicative and distant, low-key punishing her for crimes she didn't commit. Because?

"You're wounded."

Her statement caught me off guard. I flinched. But there was truth. I'd been in my feelings because I'd failed to protect my daughter. And to some degree, in my mind, Yazmeen.

But you can, and need to trust her. With everything.

"Have you eaten?"

She gave me a look like I was practicing intentional avoidance before answering that her mind had been too on us to enjoy her brunch.

Her hand in mine, I exited the conference room, telling Miss Receptionist I was headed out and wouldn't be back that afternoon.

She simply wanted a hot sandwich. Granted, she loaded it with practically every available topping. Regardless, her simple wants reminded me that she differed from that lobster-chateaubriand-Cristal-demanding baller boo I was accustomed to.

Rolling up on the secluded lakefront community I'd stumbled on a while back, we sat at an outdoor table eating in companionable silence until she broached the uncomfortable subject.

"So…was I correct in my assessment?"

"Which was?"

She paused to pass a napkin over her lips. "Your being not merely angry, but hurt by that social media madness. Am I that woman, the one in this relationship for your money not for you?"

I inhaled long and hard as if needing a second wind before going in. "I was a lot of things, Yaz, but yeah, my feelings being banged up was in there, too. And I absolutely know you're not coming for the coin. But you gotta admit it was much."

"It was. But you pulled away and punished me for someone else's ignorance." Her attempts to neutralize her tone and expression failed. Clearly, *she* was wounded. "Still, the parent part of me understands. You needed to protect Aniyah."

Appreciating her insightfulness, I took her hand and kissed it before lacing our fingers and staring at the lake as if it held the solutions to life's challenges. Seduced by its placid surface, I launched a voyage of sharing what I hadn't with anyone except family. And Quinton. "I was multi-level pissed. When someone comes for my daughter, I'm not having it. So, yeah, unfortunately you got some clap-back mainly because I was bent behind my failing to keep my child out of someone's mouth."

"You can't blame yourself," she softly consoled. "You had no control over that."

"True. But that whole piece? It cut. Deep, baby. Mainly because... there was some truth to it. Aniyah Chanel Alvarez is my daughter to the bone. All day, every day. That girl is so much like me, it's scary. But," I had to deeply inhale again, "she's mine in every way except biologically."

In her stunned silence, I told the tale. Meeting Kryshelle at a strip club. Sexing the weekend away. Being too drugged and drunk to remember if condoms came into play. Going our separate ways. Shortly thereafter giving my life to the Lord only to learn I was about to be a baby daddy. Falling in love with Nubs the moment she was born, but stipulating that paternity test that came back 99.89% positive.

"I don't understand how there's any question as to whether or not Aniyah's yours with test results like that."

Redirecting my attention away from the lake, I looked into eyes filled with confusion and compassion. "Those results weren't real. They were tampered with."

I hated digging in that mess, but wanting no secrets between us, I spilled the business.

Kryshelle fooled with two other dudes besides me in a five-day period, including a lab tech who wasn't her boo, but a repeat sex partner. Dude was freaky for being way too interested in the fact that she'd been with me. Freaky, and full of foolery. Kryshelle and Mister Lab Tech, who obviously had access to the process, schemed up some lavish ish involving tampering with DNA and documents so that yours truly provided a positive match and was listed as my baby's bio dad.

Like I said, I loved my daughter from the time she took her first breath so taking care of her wasn't a stretch. I did what I did. Flew back and forth to L.A. on a regular. There for every milestone. Family photos. The works. I did what daddies do. Including set up an account for all of her expenses. The only catch? Kryshelle couldn't touch a cent. Clothes. Food. Daycare. Whatever for Nubs and Miss Carmen. It all came from that account. But after making a money mistake with her once, I'd refused to fund Kryshelle's drug habits and wilding. Real clear she wouldn't get what she wanted and not the least interested in mothering, she terminated her legal rights and left Nubs to be raised by Miss Carmen and me.

"When you helped with Aniyah's braids, did you notice a scar on her scalp?"

She had.

"That happened a month or so after Nubs' third birthday. She was with me one weekend. We were at a family function in L.A. Kids were running around. Playing. Having a good time. There was a *piñata*. My teenage nephew was acting crazy swinging the *piñata* stick, practicing. He was teasing the younger ones trying to get it from him. And just like that. Out of nowhere. Bam! Nubs walked into his swing." Clear memories had me reliving my daughter being hit in the head. Her staggering back. Falling to the ground. Blood everywhere. Her shaking and convulsing.

The nightmare must've replayed on my face. Had my woman rubbing my arm, gently. Speaking quietly. "We can postpone this discussion."

"I'm good." Getting myself together, I picked up where I'd left off. That seemingly endless ambulance ride. Nubs being rushed into ER. Doctors. MRI. Brain swelling. Talk of major surgery. Blood work. Internal bleeding. Possibility of seizures. Threat of epilepsy. "Kryshelle shows up, hopped on dope and acting for an Oscar. Crying. Snotting. Blaming me and calling me all kinds of unfit fathers." My trying to calm her down simply escalated issues. She was cussing. Screaming. Getting violent. I threatened to involve hospital security. "That's when chick went in with the 'You wanna put me out? If she needs blood for this operation, who's gonna give it to her? Huh? Me! That's who. Not you! I'm her mother. You ain't even blood, Tavares. *You're nothin' but her fake father!*" Exhaling noisily, I paused before concluding, "Yeah... that happened."

Elbows on the table, hands clasped, I leaned my chin on them and stared straight ahead seeing nothing. Soothed by the gentle pressure of her slowly rubbing circles across my back, I powered through the rest. Kryshelle's being put out preventing me from hurting a woman. My family keeping me focused. The miracle blessing of reduced brain swelling; and Nubs needing only minor surgery, a short hospitalization and observation followed by pediatric occupational therapy. A God-sent full recovery. When my daughter was back home with her grandmother, I went to work on that 'fake father' situation and discovered Mister Lab Tech Lover's falsifying footwork. He was fired. Kryshelle acted human for a whole ten seconds and apologized for her part... before asking for a new car.

"Fortunately for her, paternity fraud isn't a crime in California or I would've had her on lock."

"It may not be illegal, but it's morally repulsive. Why would anyone do something so cruel?"

"*Dinero.* Cheese. Cash money. They thought I'd set Kryshelle up, like I was paying for the privileged use of her womb. I should've been stupid enough to give a druggie money for my daughter? So, Nubs could go without while she and ol' dude lived off the Bank of Tavares?" I sucked my teeth like *Papi* did when disgusted. "I made that clear while she was pregnant. Wasn't happening. Guess she thought I was B.S.'ing."

We fell quiet after that, lost in thought until she asked, "Does Aniyah know?"

Slowly, I nodded. "I wanted to wait until she was older, but she had a family history project in school a few months ago and asked question after nonstop question even after the project was finished, to the point I felt I needed to tell her. Plus, Nubs doesn't have internet access, but some kids her age do. This whole issue is hushed, but folks have a way of finding out what they want. I wasn't risking someone disclosing information when that's my responsibility."

"What was her response?"

"I quote," I cleared my throat, "'I live in your heart. You live in mine. That makes you my whole daddy, and me your whole daughter.'"

"Out of the mouths of babes." The smile Nubs' words brought her suddenly faded. "Her mother terminated parental rights. What about her…biological father?"

I snorted. "He was Kryshelle's dude number-three-in-five-days-of-sexing. And very married. Trust, he didn't hesitate signing that silence agreement and terminating rights so he could fade to black and keep wifey from knowing he'd impregnated someone else. *Again*. As for Lab Tech Lover, unfortunately, I hear dude died of Leukemia. So…it is what it is."

She sat thoughtfully before asking, "Do you ever worry about Kryshelle saying anything?"

"That's another reason why I told Nubs in case her mom decided to pop-off. At this point, now that Nubs knows, I really don't care other than protecting my daughter from folks tryna make mess out of it. But back to Kryshelle saying anything? Not happening."

"Because?"

I shrugged. "Let's just say I know where Kryshelle's "bodies are buried." Yeah…so…" I'd legally adopted my daughter and now had full custody. "That's my child. I'm her daddy and would die for her in a heartbeat."

She studied me a while before reaching for her half-empty chip bag. Slamming a chip in her mouth, she fussed. "I don't understand evil people who mess over children."

I grinned. "Baby, you chomping down on those chips like you got beef with them."

She frowned at me before laughing. "Speaking of evil." Pulling her cell from her coat pocket, she launched an app and scrolled until finding what she wanted. "I figured it out."

"Figured what out?"

Her expression turned sheepish. "After Royal's rancidness, I read every article I could on you. Not one questioned your parentage."

With the exception of a Father's Day spread, I'd vigilantly, intentionally kept Nubs out of the limelight. So, news heads didn't know.

"I couldn't put my finger on his source. Until seeing this."

Leaning over her shoulder, I peeped a post of her ex hugged up with that Slut-A-Rella chick we'd encountered at Sasha's.

"Now, I know why she looked familiar."

"That's not Sydney, right?" I wasn't sure if she didn't completely trust me yet or was protecting her ex. I knew about that shady first fiancé but was still clueless on some of the details of her marriage. She had, however, shared enough for me to know adultery had been at the core.

"*Sydney?*" She laughed loudly. "Not unless *Miss* Thang got a... Never mind. Royal's family's down south, and I've never met any of them. But this is his god sister." She pointed out the caption as proof. "We never met face-to-face, but I remember Royal video-chatting with her when I was pregnant. I was in my first trimester and having horrible morning sickness, and was too busy trying to get to the toilet to pay close attention. But, that's her."

Crap!

Kryshelle obviously said enough of something to Slut-a-Mutt, chick-she-used-to-kick-it-with that ol' girl found worth repeating to Yaz's ex, even if it was twisted. "Well, now we know."

"You're alright with it?" she asked, rubbing my arm as if diffusing any steam.

"It'll get handled."

She leaned away, stared up at me. "You're kind of scary sounding all The Godfather, or Tony Soprano or something."

I grinned. "Naw, it's not like that, baby. It's all good." I kissed her temple. "But are we? I walked out of your house that night because I know how I get. I didn't want the kids seeing or hearing anything inappropriate, and there was Taj and his friend. I couldn't have your family watching me going 5150. And, yes, I've been a cut-up these past few weeks with the low-key penalizing. Forgive me, please." I pushed a loose braid behind her ear. "I need to know that you're still all in."

She held my gaze before stroking my goatee. "I'm not going anywhere, sweetie...and thanks for confiding in me." She stretched upward into a kiss that infused her sentiments with depth and deliciousness.

Her pulling away too prematurely for me, had my hands at her waist, bringing her tightly against me until—the way that kiss was going—I was concerned about overheating. I broke it off, whistling. "Let's get up before we get into something."

On my feet, I extended a hand to help her stand.

"We're outside. Essentially in a public space. Nothing's going to happen," she assured, accepting my assistance.

"I'm making zero promises."

"You do outdoors sex, Tav?" she teased, going into mom mode and grabbing the garbage from our meal.

Taking the crumpled debris from her, I shot it in a nearby trash can before sliding an arm about her. "If you want to know, you'll need to marry me." That stopped her cold. "Girl, close your mouth and let's go."

Her throwing her head back on a laugh had me fulfilling a promise. Leaning down, I sucked that silky neck. Her surprised gasp slowly melted into a deep moan that confirmed what I knew when licking that navel piercing: my woman was *highly* responsive.

My relentless sucking had her body doing this subtle undulation, gyration business that had Beast bothered by, not just her sensual moving, but the audible proof of her pleasure. She had me on hype and, pressing against her, I made her aware she had me hard.

She pushed away from me, voice thick and husky. "You will *not* be giving me hickeys."

We both knew a hickey wasn't the worry. She was afraid of exploding.

The thought of bringing her sexual satisfaction left me wanting to lay her on that table, sucking that neck and grinding against that perfect place between her legs until she orgasmed.

Lord, help me!

"I have a question," I grit, fighting contrary thoughts of wanting her naked in my bed, wet, writhing, moaning and groaning.

"I have an answer."

Needing distance from what we'd unleashed, we headed for the parking lot, both with bothered breathing. "It's the last time I wanna discuss that post, but what did your ex-monster mean about you owing him coin for *Purrrfect*?"

She sighed noisily. "Remember asking about my commercial embarrassments, and my saying I've danced in venues church folks might find offensive?" She continued when I nodded. "It's not so much venue as choreography. You're obviously familiar with Pantha's *Purrrfect*."

A multi-platinum rap artist, Pantha celebrated Black power, exotic beauty, and utilized utopic scenery. But that *Purrrfect* video? Classic!

It featured some *mega* built sister dancing in a Bahamas rainforest wearing a full-face mask and sporting nothing but head-to-toe black and gold body paint better and badder than any costume ever created. Highly skilled abilities aside, she'd delivered pure, erotic dance that was sex on sight. Babygirl was responsible for wet dreams, erections and fantasies. I needed to readjust my pants at the mere memories. "Yeah… what about it?"

Appearing embarrassed, she raised her hand. "She was me."

"Who was you?" Aiming my key fob, I unlocked the Cayenne.

Head cocked sideways, she waited for my dimness to disappear. *"Unh-unh! Bae, you lying!"*

"I'm not. Royal's still under the impression that because we met on set, got married and had kids, he was entitled to the earnings from that video and the side gigs it generated for me. Thus, the coin comment."

I heard what I heard while suspended in the fact she was Pantha's Miss Purrrfect. Idiotically, I walked a circle around her, scoping her physique like I didn't already know it was lethal, or that she didn't have mad dance ability. *"For real?* That wasn't *you,* boo?"

Rocking back on her legs, she crossed her arms beneath her breasts. "Whatever, Tav."

She walked off, leaving me stuck and staring as she removed her coat and tossed it on the back seat before glancing over her shoulder at me. A devious grin lifting those sultry lips—her back to me—she perfectly executed a complex, highly sensuous move from the video's routine.

"Awww, shi—"

Watching her seat herself and shut her door like she was too boss to be bothered, I thanked God for letting me fall in love with that class-act video vixen. Grinning and crushing like an infatuated teen, I headed for the whip praying *I* didn't explode in her company.

CHAPTER NINETEEN
EX-MONSTER MOVE
Yazmeen

I disliked discord and appreciated being back on track with Mister Magic. Days after that lakeside chat, he remained apologetic for lapsing into sullen silence and ghosting me behind that social media idiocy. After Royal and Darrien, I had little tolerance for out-of-order men so my stepping to him versus dashing the opposite direction was huge for me. Thank God for acts of forgiveness, maturity, and therapy. Growth kept me from being outtie. Our dealing with each other like sane, valuable humans highlighted the fact that I'd never had that with a man. Thankful we'd worked through the issue, I came away with a greater appreciation for him and our grown folks' relationship.

"You're getting ridiculous." Readjusting my headset, I leaned into the gentle fragrance of the frenzy of flowers overtaking my desk, unable to dismantle my crazy girl grin. The weekly deliveries to my place of business had become so customary that the delivery guy and I were on a first-name basis. But this over-the-top arrangement of lilies, peonies, roses and some exotic bloom I couldn't name was extraordinary. "They're beyond gorgeous, sweetie, and I so appreciate it. *But*! I'ma need you to not buy out the florist and save a flower for someone else."

"'Ey, it's what I do 'cause I love you."

My heart did its usual dip-and-dance over priceless words from luscious lips. I soared whenever he said them. Despite my having yet to vocalize that sentiment to him, I breathed them, lived them, was so afraid to speak it. And, still, he showed me love in a myriad of ways. Everyday.

I've been blessed with something and someone beyond my imagination.

I wasn't a sister so bent and burned by a brother that I deemed all men as dogs. But hurt had flatlined my romantic dreams and expectations. Loving Tavares and being loved by him breathed life into my hopes and reversed my jadedness. The depth of our relationship was new territory for me. We prayed together. Communicated honestly, openly. Listened. Laughed. Our discussions were light, deep. They varied. Differing in temperament, we didn't always agree. He was chill, but passionate and driven. I was mellow, but strong-willed. We were stubborn and far from perfect but were committed to offering our best selves. Our challenges were real: residential distance. Our socio-economic disparities. Our limited time together due to life obligations and single-parenting. Our having children meant limited adult-only opportunities, forcing us to focus on not just our interactions, but their quality. At times the kids had skirmishes. Aniyah was accustomed to being "the only"; and Malcolm and Malik were Team Twin. Helping them negotiate disagreements actually strengthened our unity, reinforcing our commitment to our team. We were all about that respect and harmony. I needed him. He needed me.

"When I figure out what I did to deserve you, I'm bottling and selling that to single women and banking millions."

He laughed. "Do your thing, Mamacita. Speaking of...how's your money this month?"

So, remember how the boys' daycare costs went up? Add to that an increase on my automobile insurance premium, thanks to my ex-idiot filing a comprehensive claim for my keying his car. He was smart enough not to admit it was flat out vandalism to make sure the repair costs would be covered; but that "questionable intention" piece on my part impacted my rates. As if that wasn't enough, that trip to the emergency room for Malcolm's busted lip while in G-Daddy's care? The services were covered by my medical insurance except the deductible on which I was still making payments. Things had been so tight the last few months that I felt like wearing overalls and singing The Blues while strumming a "geetar" and eating corn pone and fried coon.

His Fineness became privy to my problems after I'd turned down an invitation to see Lalah Hathaway at a jazz club at Jack London Square last weekend.

Because? I needed to reserve gasoline until payday.

I rearranged facts as best I could without straight lying. Not buying my bull, he'd finally wrangled the truth from me.

That there? Humiliating.

Who wants to tell their deep-bank baller boo, "I'm broke and can't roll with you?"

"*Mariposa*, my parents raised five kids on side-hustles and one paycheck. I didn't grow up with bank," had been his "consoling" comeback.

"So baby, trust, I understand, and I'm here to help however needed."

Nope. Not happening.

My pride wouldn't let him do his magic and make my money mishaps disappear. My sense of independence already went on strug behind his filling up my gas tank whenever we were together, or his never letting me treat when dining out. And after Royal's social media liarization, I was doubly determined to stay out Tav's wallet. But trust, I didn't fuss too much when he arranged car service so that I was there to see Miss Lalah live with him.

"Thanks for asking, Mister Overprotective, but my money's marvelous," I playfully retorted, finalizing database entries for a report First Lady needed next week.

He said something in Spanish for which I had zero comprehension. "Come again?"

"I said your stubbornness is epic, *Mariposa*, and that I don't believe that money comment."

"Wow, sweetie, so now I'm untrue?"

"No, but funny how you latched onto that while dismissing that part about your mule-headedness."

"Stop taking away my Friday high, Tavares."

We shared a laugh.

"Yeah, aiight, Miss Yazzy Yaz. We're still on for next weekend?"

The kids had roped us into taking them to that pizza arcade twenty minutes from Tavares. Again.

"We are."

"Try to stay in the game this time."

Tearing it up on the skating rink was one thing. Running behind three high-energy little people in some gigantic kiddie wonderland had whipped my behind and left me limping. But Mister Magic? He'd hung tough with Aniyah and the twins in the ball pits, climbing rubber rocks, zip-lining, or whacking them with foam poles in their quest to knock each other over. Learning that he was a big kid at heart endeared him even more to me. I still gave him grief. "Some of us are mature, while others are childish and can effortlessly do all that juvenile jumping."

He snorted big time. "If mature means geriatric, you were that."

"You're dismissed."

"You started it. Anyhow...you and your crew don't get too turnt up tonight."

"Huh? We rock that church girl vibe."

"Church girls wild out at bachelorette shenanigans just like the best of 'em."

"We're simply helping Joy pack." My girl, who'd spent the majority of her life anti-all-things-Christ, had not only accepted Jesus as Lord but returned from Philly and meeting Quinton's family flaunting a huge engagement ring. My heart was beyond thrilled for them, even though that meant her moving back east, in April, in a few weeks. After that? Their Caribbean wedding! As maid of honor and with the boys being ring bearers, I'd scrape the barrel, play credit card games, or dance on a downtown street corner with a hat collecting change to finance our trip if necessary. But there was no way we wouldn't be there. "Well, we *are* going out to dinner first—"

"I *knew* y'all were posting up in a club! I hope you get some diseased-looking, five-hundred-pound stripper dude wanting to grind his dirty draws on you."

Thank God most staff had left to jumpstart the weekend because I actually screamed, laughing. "Get off my phone and stop impacting my professionalism."

"Love, you impact my everything."

The downward roll of his baritone dipping into sensuous tones caused some stomach tingling.

Four months into our relationship and I still wondered if and when the butterflies would lessen, if he'd ever stop stimulating me with the simplest comments, or if I'd ever cease wanting him. Because trust, I did, and was holding onto abstinence by prayer and a KY-Jelly-kind-of-slippery thread.

After our lakeside lust the day he'd confided about Aniyah, we'd left sexually bothered and needing to dip our booties in ice water. The deeper our relationship grew, the stronger the sexual pull. Of necessity, we established parameters. Crazy maybe, but we'd been bluntly honest about what we could, or couldn't tolerate physically. It wasn't about being sanctimonious, but avoiding triggers that could lead to us "accidentally" falling into bed butt-naked, or finding ways to satisfy ourselves without penetration.

All I can get is a kiss? I can't touch nothing? Breasts, thighs, hips, this Grade-A sonic behind—all off limits? If I hold your hand will you climax?

Mister Magic's exaggerated teasing highlighted the restrictiveness of our way-to-stay-out-of-bed agreement. Our sexual attraction was well established. Going forward, I preferred shifting our focus and energies to the non-flesh related aspects of our relationship. Realizing another brother might've ghosted me, my appreciation for him increased.

"Honestly, sweetie, I need to go, but thank you."

"For?"

"Honoring us. Not compromising me." A man of standards, he didn't bend to his wants, never pressured me to step outside myself and give him what he might've needed sexually. His desiring me the way he did helped heal something in me. I said what I said before vulnerability interfered. "And for helping me believe in my femininity again."

He was quiet before softly stating, "*Mariposa*, next time you stand in front of a mirror thank yourself, not me. Your femininity is unquestionable. That's all you, baby."

"Okay, you're tryna make me cry so I'm not cute for my diseased-looking stripper dude."

That had him chuckling. "Enjoy your evening, baby."

"You, too."

Disconnecting, I tried lifting that floral mountain. Unable to move my oversized bouquet, I snapped off a bloom and tucked it into my braid bun before digging my keys from my tote bag. Light reflected from my diamond and ruby bracelet in the process—my birthstone, Valentine's gift from Mr. Magic.

I had sincere appreciation for beautiful things, but single-mothering forced my frugality. Tavares' generosity was often hard to accept but, powering down my computer and straightening up so all would be in order come Monday, I elected to embrace the blessings.

Lord, thank You for a beautiful man!

Keys and tote in hand, I headed down the hall to say 'good night' to First Lady and Pastor debriefing after counseling a couple in crisis. "Don't stay too late, and get some rest this weekend."

"Yes, Miss Mommy Ma'am."

I cracked up at their using the twins' sometimes label for me.

A smile was still gracing my face when climbing into my pint-size SUV.

It was Friday. My bills were paid. My sons were spending the evening with my parents. I had fresh flowers, a fine man, and was about to spend time with my girls. I felt blessed.

Now, let's get to this obese stripper fest.

"Who chose this place?" Joy questioned, stank-eyeing an odorous and outdated interior featuring faded carpet, pleather seats, mismatched tables, a staticky sound system, and faulty-flickering lighting resulting in some 1920s juke joint deep in the Delta effect. The only things missing were Moms Mabley and Prohibition.

"I did." Candace—our girl who we swore was narcoleptic and known to fall asleep at concerts—sounded defensive. "I thought you'd appreciate it being Half-Price-Appetizer-Night."

Poking a chicken wing with her knife, Joy commented, "I'd appreciate food that didn't look like it's growing lice." Wrinkling her nose, she asked, "What's the name of this place again?"

"A Touch of Pizazz."

"Smells like a touch of ass."

I couldn't swallow my drink at Joy's comeback.

"Dang, Yaz!"

I tried apologizing to Candace for showering her with a ginger ale bath, but was too busy hollering-laughing.

Handing her a wad of napkins that clearly came from the Chinese restaurant down the street, LaVelle helped Candace mop her face and neck.

"Which of you lucky ladies are we treating to the next dance?"

Glancing behind me, my laughter dried up. I didn't understand anything. Not the brother's lavender and orangesicle checkered suit—the pants of which were tucked into mid-ankle, white patent leather boots. Or the bald on top, remnant of hair circling his head ear-to-ear flowing down his back in beaded extensions *a la* Rick James-slash-Patrice Rushen. But his ventriloquist dummy sporting an identical outfit rendered me completely confused.

Velle's *"Jesus,"* perfectly coincided with Joy's, "Who let you loose?"

Candace and I were stunned mute.

"So...who wants to dance?" Pastel Man's dummy demanded.

Velle was quick with, "I'm married."

"I'm engaged, pregnant, and hormonal so you don't want none of this," Joy added.

"I'm in a relationship and my man's extremely jealous." My last tidbit was untrue, but Pastel Man and Company didn't need to know that.

We looked at Candace.

"I'm a lesbian," she lied.

"So, am I," Pastel Man's dummy replied.

"Oh God, I gotta pee!" Joy headed for the bathroom, laughing uproariously, leaving us to gently let down Pastel Man and his inanimate buddy.

"Okay, but if any of your situations change while you're here, we'll be in the kitchen."

We somehow managed to keep it together until he'd gone, but when he did we were done.

"I can't breathe!" I laughed so hard *I* nearly peed. "What was that?"

"Crazy on a cracker," Velle offered. "And why the kitchen? Whew! I ain't never in life."

"He was sweet," Candace insisted. "Maybe the doll's a support animal alternative."

"Maybe being penis-less has you overly sympathetic."

"Velle!"

"What, Yaz? We know Candace just lost her man to a vagina drive-by."

"Another woman's not why we broke up," Candace objected, looking more sleepy than sad over her year-long relationship that recently ended. "He called me boring."

"And that's better than his being nookie-napped by an intruder vajayjay?"

"LaVelle, *really?*"

"My bad, Yaz. I forgot we can't talk about sex in your presence. Speaking of, did you get that vibrator like I suggested?"

"You're so filter-less."

"Maybe, but I get to go home to a husband and orgasms. Did you buy it or not, Yaz?"

"I'm thinking that's zero your business."

"That means you're still living without that silicone dic—"

"Don't you do it!" I warned.

"Listen here, chick, I'm trying to help you—"

"How?" Candace interrupted. "By being in her grill about it?"

"Take a nap, Candace, I was talking to Yaz. Listen, girlie, my goal in getting you a fake *phallus*," she hyper-corrected, "is to help keep you holy, less horny, and Tavares from tapping that yam."

I rolled my eyes and sipped my drink saying nothing.

"Honey, trust. I've been where you are. Ronnie and I did that saved and semi-celibate thing when dating, so I understand. *Completely.*"

"What the heck is semi-celibate?" I challenged, eyeing but afraid to try the cauliflower and hummus dip looking like wet cement in a misshapen bowl atop our table.

"Don't *nobody* better go to that bathroom unless you have life insurance," Joy cautioned, returning from the restroom and sliding onto her seat. "I swear we need to get out of here, but back to Velle's ignorant self first. Being semi-celibate is as wrong as being partially pregnant. Either you is or you ain't."

"And you are, thanks to your birth control faileration," I teased with a wink.

"Yaz, I'm pregnant because my boo busted my diaphragm. Hashtag blessed penile problems other men wish they had."

That had us howling.

"I cannot with you two," I sobered enough to breathe.

"And it *cannot* be easy loving an Afro-Cuban divine specimen like Tavares without constantly needing sex."

"Afro-Puerto Rican," I wasted breath correcting.

"Same difference." Velle was relentless. "Yaz, if I was you, I'd be seeing penises *errywhere*. Cucumbers. Bananas. Eggplants. Avocadoes. Monkey wrenches."

"Did she say 'avocadoes?'" Joy asked Candace.

"And monkey wrenches?" Candace asked back.

"I did. The point being: Yaz is inundated with penile images."

"I'm not."

Sick chick had the nerve to reach over and pat my hand. "You are, and there's nothing wrong with that. It's called Baader-Meinhof Phenomenon or "frequency illusion." You know how you click an ad on Facebook, don't buy whatever it is, but all of a sudden that item keeps popping up on your feed or your email banner over and over again."

"It's called 'retargeting', stupid," Joy stated. "Advertisers have apps in place to do that."

"Cousin, gestate silently. Yaz, talk to me. Are you or aren't you trapped in Penis City? You probably can't walk through a bakery and see baguettes or breadsticks without thinking what you could do with them."

"And you wonder why we didn't tell your crackhead self about Yaz and Tavares being together to begin with," Joy quipped, rubbing her baby bump.

"Remind me not of your egregious sins for which I am still forgiving you. Anyhoo. Yaz. Back to you. If I were dating some *finnn-nnnnnnnnne bruthaaa…*" She had to inhale after holding the words unnecessarily long, "I'd be in a constant state of arousal and needing A/C in my panties."

"Velle, sweetie, let me know when your good sense gets out of prison."

"Whatever, Yaz." Laughing, she scanned our surroundings. "This place feels like diarrhea and depression."

"It's so not lit and not the way I want to spend one of my last weekends as a bachelorette. Remind me, Candace, why we let you pick?"

Candace was impervious to Joy's insults. Girlfriend was already nodding, head bobbing.

"Lord, you can't take a narcoleptic nowhere."

Joy's quip left us laughing.

"For real, though, if this place doesn't get out the pacemaker zone and pick up, I'm going home and play with my husband's," Velle paused to look pointedly at me, "monkey wrench. Ooo, wait, Yaz, I got a workaround so your relationship with Tavares stays sexless. Get you a little side sinner to blow out your back." She wiggled her eyebrows. "You know DayDay would gladly do that."

LaVelle swore her computer genius, lovable thug of a brother, Day-Day, had a crush on me.

My clap-back was prevented by Darth's March that had me throwing my head back and growling, "Lord, just *not*."

After that Christmas gift foolishness and his filing for custody, I'd made it crystal clear to Royal that we had zero to discuss unless it involved the twins. He was free to contact the boys at my parents' during the day if he wanted to speak with them, but he was to call my phone never in life again. Sadly, per my mother, he'd called the boys once since the beginning of the year. What's sadder than that? Royal's failure to show up for his sons no longer bothered Malik and Malcolm.

Since that Christmas craziness, I'd noticed the steady, steep decline in their interest. They'd gone from daily inquiries as to when they'd see their father to absolute silence as if Royal didn't exist. When I questioned them about it, they offered heartbreaking responses.

"We don't want to be around Daddy any more."

"He's scary."

"And mean. You know how he doesn't like you, Mommy? Well, he doesn't like us, too."

"Malik, honey, why would you think that?"

"The Christmas presents. You said when we love somebody, we should give good gifts."

"Yeah," Malcolm chimed in. "Daddy gave us things that can hurt us. Like cigarettes and guns."

"And we don't wear glasses and we don't need tiny tools to fix them." Malik pouted, lips poked out, arms across his chest. "He doesn't even know us."

"So that makes him a stranger. And since he acts mean to you and wants us to have guns, then that makes Daddy a stranger danger. We can't be around him until he's nice again."

My heart was a little crushed for my sons, but for once I didn't try to dissuade them or gloss over their father's actions. Unfortunately for him, he'd escalated his misbehavior far too often in their presence. Christmas, a time that should've held childhood bliss, was the end for them. They'd been hurt and scared and were left without desire to be with him. I'd vowed never to be that mother who kept her children from their father, but their feelings as well as their observations deserved respect, validation. With our custody hearing a week away, I prayed its outcome wouldn't be to my sons' detriment, putting them in the care of a man they'd come to fear.

"Yaz, are you answering that?" Joy asked, looking slightly excited as if ready to rumble with Royal. "When you do, use the FaceTime option so he can see Ethel's at the party."

"You brought your gat?" Velle asked.

"Honey, yes." Eyeing our environment, she added, "Aren't you glad?"

"I need you to not." Shaking my head, I reluctantly took the call. "Yes?"

The answer on the opposite end put my blood on chill. Obviously, it was accidental, as if Royal had bumped into something, or his phone did a "butt dial" because, based on agonizing screams, clearly, he hadn't intended to call me.

"Yaz, what's wrong?"

Glancing at Velle, I shook my head while engaging the speaker mode.

Even above the noise of the club, we heard what sounded like fists meeting flesh and someone's obvious, extreme distress.

God knows I'd never loved my sons' father. And despite vengeful fantasies, I didn't relish what sounded like excruciating physical pain being inflicted on him.

"Big Cain?" Joy's articulating my thoughts made the possibility seem like reality.

Royal's ish had finally caught up with him?

"Who's Big Cane? Or is that some phallic obsession?"

"Velle, hush!" I couldn't take her ridiculousness right then.

Our silence amplified the disturbing sounds on the opposite end.

The continued, escalating violence had me feeling physically sick. "Royal!" I hollered his name as if he'd somehow hear me above the racket and ruckus when I heard him cussing and calling another individual every name except the one God and parents gave.

"Royal, baby, I'm sorry. I messed up. Please...don't!"

"Yaz...that's..."

Staring at Joy, I nodded. "Sydney."

My heart hurt at the horror of hearing someone, even Sydney, being viciously assaulted.

"Lord forgive me, but *aww-hell-to-the-nigga-no*! Let's go." My bestie and her baby bump eased off the chair. "Any man who lays hands on the feminine deserves whatever clap-back he gets—"

Velle butted in. "I agree, but technically Sydney..." Her voice trailed off as if even she realized the inhumane direction she was spinning. "Yaz...did Royal ever put his hands on you?"

"No." But had he been capable of violence? I didn't know because I'd married a stranger.

"Candace! Wake up so we can go," Joy commanded.

"What? Where're we going?" she sputtered.

"We're rolling up on a wifey-beating troll."

Grabbing my purse, I hurried to catch up with my girl. "No, ma'am, not happening."

Eluding my attempts to snatch her car keys, Joy kept walking.

"Joy Matthews, I cannot with you! I'll call 9-1-1, but your pregnant behind's not going anywhere."

"Yaz, you already know."

I did. Her father's violent death and her own childhood abuse had left my girl with a serious aversion to assaults and violence. I also knew Royal was high on her "spit" list after all the mess I'd experienced with him. She'd like nothing better than to deal him some payback. In college we'd dealt some Black Girl justice on trifling Negroes once or twice. But we'd matured since then and no longer did ride-by revenge. Right?

"Yes, sweetie, I know. But squash any itch 'cause we're not doing this. Ehhh!" I put my hand in her face when she tried to object. "No, ma'am. I cannot have Quinton coming for me if something happens to you or this baby. *And*," I continued when she interrupted again, "my godchild will *not* be born behind bars, sporting cornrows and baby tats 'cause his or her mama went cray cray."

I thought I'd won when she handed me her keys. Instead, she exited the club, aiming for the parking lot.

"You drive. I don't know where we're going."

I was ready to fuss her out only to see Candace and Velle climbing into the back of Joy's vehicle looking like I'd better hurry up or get left.

"Yaz, we're waiting."

"Shut up, Joy," I mumbled, wondering when I'd been cast in a backyard remake of *Set It Off* while reluctantly hopping in the driver's seat, thinking this ranked high on the Dumbest Things I've Ever Done list.

I wasn't hyper-versed in criminology, and felt like a first-class fool rolling up to Royal's without headlights. "Velle, this is dumb."

"The element of surprise is everything, per DayDay."

With his extensive prison record, her brother was quotable and would know. Still, I was highly uncomfortable when pulling onto Royal's street and barely missing a cherry red Chrysler 300 flying in the opposite direction.

"Wait! Weren't those the same fools who came looking for him at your place?"

Nodding at my B.F.F., the night was getting freakier by the second. I would've turned around and went home if I had good sense. Obviously, I didn't. Instead, I parked at the curb and got out as if God anointed me lead of Ratchet Rescue Teams.

We must've looked ridiculous, four intelligent sistas—one packing and pregnant—rolling up on Royal's apartment complex engaged in some vengeance mission. I had to push Velle's head away from ear-hustling the door just to knock on it. Thankfully, the only sound we heard coming from within was music. No more struggle or violence. Still, hearing the door being unlocked, I tensed not knowing what condition we'd find Sydney in.

"May I help you?"

The short, pale, twenty-something-ish blond with a Midwest accent caught us off-guard.

"Oh...sorry to disturb you, but we're here for Royal."

"That's really someone's name? I keep getting their mail, and thought it was a misprint. They must not've changed their address with the post office. Is Royal Jones a he or she?"

"It's a sub-human species."

I would've elbowed Joy, but didn't want to jab her in her baby belly.

"Okay...well, like I told the guys looking for him or her last week—and who keep driving the neighborhood in that red Chrysler like they want to catch them—I live here. Royal doesn't."

That had me peeking over her shoulder at the apartment's interior, noting the complete change of atmosphere and furniture wiping out evidence of my ex-quadruped. Disliking my nosy scrutiny, she pulled the door closed a bit.

"Sorry for being intrusive, but do you mind my asking how long you've lived here?"

Eyeing me warily, she provided a vague, "Since sometime before Christmas." Grabbing a rubber band-bound stack of mail, she extended it. "Do you want to take Royal's mail?"

I declined the privilege until hearing, "Oh, and do you know Yazmeen Williams Jones?"

I'd never used Royal's last name when married, still she would've been me. "Yes."

"Can you tell her she's got mail, too?"

"We'll take it," Joy advised, snatching the envelope before Miss Midwest could object.

Thanking her, I grabbed Joy and rerouted us to the car, Candace and LaVelle bringing up the rear. Seated inside, I used a key to slice open a letter notifying me that "my" Victoria's Secret account had been closed and sent to collections behind a nearly three-thousand dollar balance "I'd" failed to pay. Not only was there such a gross disconnect between me and my sons' dad that I didn't know he'd moved months ago, but his she-thing had falsely opened accounts in my name.

CHAPTER TWENTY
CONVICT CALLS
Tavares

When it came to the ex, I minimized my comments. No woman wanted to hear the person she'd loved or let in was perfect for target practice. Speaking on his issues wouldn't do a thing except highlight her regret of bad choices. But that Secret Squirrel relocation and opening accounts in her name? It was in keeping with his character, in my opinion. But, again, I said nothing, only offered a supportive shoulder and assistance when my love vented her frustration and took corrective measures. I couldn't compensate for his actions, but the more the fool acted a cut-up, the more determined I was to show Yazmeen real love.

"Daddy, I found one!"

"Let's see."

Nubs came running across the sand with Bojangles, the ever-faithful canine companion. "See! It's a whole, unbroken one." She proudly held a perfectly formed seashell.

"Naw, *mi hija*, you got that in the mail, came down here, and hid it last night while I was asleep so you could pretend to find it."

That had her giggling hysterically. "No, I didn't, Daddy. I found it on the beach." Handing me her prize find, she leaned against me where I sat on the sand. "I think Jesus washed it up here for me."

"I agree." Not that Miss Carmen hadn't patterned good living, but Nubs' immersion in our church's children's ministry and growing love of all things Jesus was one of the best blessings coming from our residing together. Holding her seashell to the light of a warm, spring sun, I nodded, liking its color striations. "That's pretty boss, Nubs."

"Thanks." She held out her hand. When I faked a throwing motion, she screamed. *"Daddy!"*

Her panicked disbelief left me snickering. *"Mi hija,* I didn't throw your ol' raggedy rock."

"It's not a rock!" Taking it from my hand, she carefully placed her precious find in her plastic pail before narrowing her eyes at me. "Daddy, that was mean."

I toppled over when she jumped me.

Our antics had Bojangles barking and getting in on it. It was two against one and I wound up on my stomach.

"Say you're sorry." Big Bossy was commanding, but I was declining. "Nope."

"Daddy, say it!"

"It." That set off more roughhousing, Bojangles' barking, and me hollering laughing for real. Flat on my stomach eating sand with Nubs sprawled on my back, arms choking my neck, she elicited a winded promise of better behavior that I had no intention of keeping. "Alright! You win. Get off my back before you break it." I did a push-up that sent my child sliding off with a laugh.

"Daddy, do that again," she commanded, resituating herself on my back.

I gave her ten. "Alright, Nubs, I'm done."

Grabbing her pail and shovel, she took off running with Bojangles for the shoreline intent on new finds.

She knew the rules, still I cautioned, "Stay where I can see you."

"Okay."

I loved seeing my daughter unquestionably happy and enjoying life like a child should. Knowing I'd stepped up and offered her the best I had felt good. Did that mean single-parenting was easy?

Hardly.

Our daddy-daughter living situation had unique challenges, but I wouldn't trade seeing my daughter on the daily. She had school, a schedule, and the right to stability. Too much alike for our own good, we occasionally bumped heads. She was part lawyer and wanted to negotiate too much for me. But she'd been taught to be respectful and knew when I dropped that bass enough was enough. Thankfully I had a full-time housekeeper who kept the joint on point, still Nubs was responsible for making her own bed. My house wasn't a 'them and us' atmosphere. Sometimes my housekeeper cooked. When she didn't, I did. If Nubs was sick, I was the one spooning medicine. That all-in nature of mine had me mostly acing my Mister Mom routine even if it meant delaying my needs. I couldn't do like I used to—hop a plane, jump in the whip and ride whenever, however without consideration for Nubs and her needs. We got in some hoops occasionally, but all that hanging with my boys was largely in my past, as was nightlife and clubbing. Even so, I was content—blessed with a beautiful daughter, what I wanted in life, particularly an incredible woman.

And spasms in my back.

"That girl." Nubs jumping me obviously had something out of whack. Launching a series of stretches, I kept an eye on her, appreciating that she was still childish enough to roughhouse with.

Except when Mariposa's in the pic.

I grinned, thinking on how Nubs liked to switch up with my woman. With 'Miss Yazzy' she was all things girlie. Polishing nails. Tea parties. Giggling. Yazmeen's efforts at building a relationship with Nubs were priceless, offering a femininity connection that I couldn't. Aniyah's being crazy about Yazmeen was a benefit and blessing I didn't take lightly. Still, I teased Yaz that she was dating me for my daughter.

Me? The twins are just as goofy over you,

True. Malcolm, Malik, and I had that twin thing going. When Yazmeen was posted up with Nubs? I had two inescapable sidekicks with endless conversation and questions. Despite my explanations, they still didn't get that my twin, Taia, could be in heaven while I was on earth. That kind of separation was implausible to them.

We won't let you be lonely, Mister Tavares. You can be our other twin.

They were good kids, and I enjoyed them.

I didn't take that for granted.

I knew couples with children from prior relationships, some who'd split because their kids never felt that new fit. Some stayed together, but lived a little hell when blending their families wasn't a smooth success. Neither Yazmeen nor I was down with faking happy family, or pretending we were some solidified unit versus dating, bonding, and becoming. But the fact that we'd bonded with each other's children, and those children with us was something we often visited in our joint, nightly prayers.

"Daddy, I found another one! Oh, oh, never mind. It's broken." Nubs threw the damaged shell towards the surf as if she couldn't be pressed.

"Nubs, there's nothing wrong with less than perfect."

"This shell isn't good for my goals."

Shaking my head and stretching out my back, I laughed as my cell vibrated in my hoodie pocket. Glancing at the screen, my father's mug popped up. "Whaddup, Carlos Alvarez?"

"Hola, mi hijo! ¿Dónde estás?"

"Out back with Nubs. Where're you?"

"At your front door."

"Come on back. Grab a beach chair from the patio on your way down."

"Si señor."

I cracked up at his overemphasis, sounding like some *gringo* tourist playing at Spanish.

Getting in a few more stretches, I eventually eased onto my feet. "Nubs, your grandfather's here."

"Where?"

"Right here."

"Abuelito!"

Big Bossy *and* Bojangles took off running. Reaching my father, she hopped into his arms, doing their ritual nose rubbing and raspberry kisses with Nubs talking two miles a minute about her beach discoveries.

Grabbing his beach chair, I peeped the oversized shopping bag my father had dropped alongside it. "What's this?"

"I have the kitchen to myself since your mama's in Jersey. What did I make?"

"Chicharónnes!" Nubs and I were happy and harmonizing.

"Yeah, baby." I'd already opened one of the four gallon-sized Ziploc bags.

"Daddy, save me some."

"Maybe." Carrying the chair and my loot to my spot on the beach, I let them get their grandparent-grandkid time in and went to munching.

In fried pig skin bliss, I watched Nubs drag my dad up and down the beach, chasing gulls, and digging for shells. That girl had him going.

"Alright, Nubs, let your *Abuelito* take a break."

"I don't think he needs one."

"Yeah, *mi niña*." He chuckled. "I do."

"When your break's over you have to finish playing with me. Deal?"

"Done." They fist-bumped before my dad walked over to settle in his beach chair. *"Aye, Dios mío.* If I could bottle my granddaughter's energy, I'd be a trillionaire."

"Definitely. What has you way over here?" My parents only lived twenty minutes away. I teased. "You missing Perla Louise?"

Papi was grinning. "Yeah, I guess. Your mama's been visiting your Aunt Imelda the same time every year since you kids got grown. You think I'd be used to it." Grabbing a handful of *chicharónnes*, he admitted, "But, I'm not," before stuffing his mouth. "These are pretty good, huh?"

"Always. But you did something different."

"You noticed that little dried ancho chile powder in the seasoning! Gives it a little heat...and the slightest hint of something sweet. Speaking of sweet heat, how's my future daughter-in-law, Miss Yazmeen?"

I laughed.

"*Mi hijo*, you see something funny in facts? You saying your young lady isn't sweet? Or that she ain't fiery enough to keep your behind in line? *Or,*" he paused, looking at me like he saw something, "you wanna sit here claiming you haven't given thought to the possibility of making her your missus?"

"Alright, old man."

My dad popped the back of my head. "Don't 'old man' me in a serious discussion," he spewed in rapid fire Spanish.

"Dang, *Papi.*" Drawing my legs up to my chest, I rested my arms on my knees and studied the ocean a moment. "We haven't been together but a few months—"

"How long did I know your mother before marrying her?" My parents' whirlwind romance saw them meeting on Christmas and married on Valentine's. "So, don't give me that. Next."

"*Papi*, can I finish what I was saying?"

"Go ahead."

"I haven't made definitive moves, so don't say nothing to *Mami,* but," I rubbed a hand over my head, "I've been thinking about that ring thing. Just *thinking.*"

Grunting, Pops stared at me until catching enough of whatever he was seeing. "You finished with your ho'ing?"

"Really, Carlos?"

He chuckled. "Son, a good marriage requires more than usual B.S. If you didn't know, let me school you: Miss Yazmeen ain't having it. She's the kind of woman who'll pull something better from you that you might not be used to giving, or might not've known you had. I'm schooled in what I'm talking 'cause your mother was like that."

"You were wilding when you met *Mami?*"

A born-again Charismatic Catholic, he looked semi-embarrassed when semi-admitting, "Let's just say before your mother, I bought into that sow your wild oats, 'Latin men are the world's lovers' okey doke. But when I came sniffing around Perla? *Shoooot*, she made it real plain it was monogamy or the highway. I had to decide if I wanted a good woman to carry my name, or just some good-timing." Extending an arm, he made a crude gesture for impact.

"*Sí, Papi*, I get it."

"Good. Now, what about that 'ring thing?'"

"Nubs, you're throwing rocks at seagulls because...?"

"They're messing with my shell-hunting."

"Their pooping on your head would be a whole lot worse, so quit it," *Papi* warned, curtailing her antics. "Back to you, *mi hijo*."

My parents knew I'd accepted Christ but weren't necessarily versed in my celibacy. That was a private, intimate choice and not a-topic-to-discuss-at-the-dinner-table-while-we're-eating. In fact, I'd shared that with two individuals only: Quinton and Yazmeen. But sitting there with the man who raised me, I confided in him, even while experiencing what I'll call an epiphany.

It was like Holy Spirit took me on a lightning-flash trip of the past five years.

Essentially, I'd been in boot camp. This walk with the Lord—learning to pray, studying His Word, changing from the inside out and becoming a better me, and celibacy—it had been training, conditioning, reorienting my whole self for holy living. Camp Celibate had been absolutely aggressive and far from easy, but necessary in disciplining my spirit, soul, *and* body. But this boot camp was bigger than me. The entire process was proof I could be committed to something beyond the game and getting paid. That commitment to God and self was the same level of lifetime real I could offer a woman. It hit me that God had divinely orchestrated a turn-around in me *for me*, but the overflow benefit was that it made me fit for Yazmeen?

"Deep."

"*¿Qué, mi hijo?*"

"Nothing. Like I was saying, I've been off that wilding track five years at least."

"Look at my youngest acting grown-up." *Papi* snatched me in a headlock before sitting back, chest poked out. "So, where do we go from here?"

Arms folded beneath my head, I stretched out on my back. "I need something real. Consistent. Solid."

"Are you saying you don't have that?" he asked in Spanish.

In his native language, I answered back. "I'm saying the opposite, as in I have that and more than I asked God for."

"That's good, son." He switched to English. "Forever's nothing to play with so give it thought and prayer, *but...*" he stalled for effect, "don't sleep on what could lead to permanent. Aniyah Chanel, you ready for more seashell hunting?"

"*Sí!*"

"Good, 'cause I'm coming." And just like that, my father was finished.

After all that beaching, cooking was not the business. I copped out and ordered pizza when Aniyah invited my father to stay for dinner.

It was good having quiet time with my old man. Relatively speaking, that is. Nubs being her usual over-the-top self, quiet came after she was in bed. That left me and *Papi* watching a game and chilling until the "itis" kicked in. Declining an invite to stay in the guest room, he headed home citing an inability to sleep somewhere other than his own bed with Perla Louise. My reminding him *Mami* was in Jersey had Pops spouting in Spanish,

"So what? I can sniff her pillow and get her scent."

Yep. Pops was still whipped.

Showering and hopping in bed, I was half-asleep after getting that text from *Papi* that he'd made it home safely, when the cell rang. Half-conscious, I grabbed it without a caller-I.D. check. "Yeah..."

Half-hearing something about a correctional facility, I accepted the charges thinking my cousin, Gonzalo, had gotten himself in again. The voice I heard wasn't expected.

"Tavares, I'ma need you to get me outta here."

"What...the?" Kicking back covers, I sat *all* the way up. "Kryshelle?"

"Yeah, I don't have phone privileges this late, but I worked out some things. I'm clean, and off that stuff. But I need out. These four walls are driving me cray! How soon can you make my exit happen?"

My mouth was on mute. Too pissed to speak, I let her do the talking.

"Tavares? You still there? Can you call your lawyer? Pull some strings for me. I shouldn't be up in here with all this. It's not like I killed somebody." Kryshelle's rapid babbling had me thinking she *was* on 'that stuff.' That or scared 'it'-less. "It was just some money-making."

The charges? Add to child endangerment, six-figure credit card fraud and identification theft.

"I didn't keep *all* that money to myself! There were a couple of other players in on it. So…can you help?"

My tone was rough, gritty. And sarcastic. "Aniyah's good, thanks for asking."

"Why ask? She's with you, which means she's fine."

"Bye, Kryshelle. I can't."

"*Wait!* I know I'm not always on point, but can you at least put a little on my books so I can get what I need and not have to play anybody's wifey? I *promise* it'll be the last time you have to help me money-wise." When I didn't respond, she tried it. "Fine! You can't come through? I'll do whatever…including sell the truth about your relationship to Aniyah to any interested news sources."

My laugh was dry, humorless. "Do what you do."

Disconnecting, I slid onto my back and stared at the ceiling, wanting to punch something.

Kryshelle's threats didn't faze me. It was that other piece: her lack of maternal instinct. Blessed with Carlos and Perla as I'd been, I didn't get Kryshelle's parental disinterest and was determined to keep Nubs unaffected by it.

Fooling with this freak makes me appreciate Yazmeen.

Comparisons might've been unfair but dealing with someone like Kryshelle had me focusing on the fact that God Himself had blessed me with a good woman who happened to be an excellent mother as well. I wasn't mom shopping, but the woman I loved had to appreciate children. And she did.

But that ring thing?

My mind bounced back to the conversation with my father and the ongoing one I'd been entertaining lately. With Yazmeen, I was ready for next. But did 'next' constitute marriage?

My argument was brevity: had we been together long enough to justify that line of thinking? Time aside, I was a man who knew what he knew. I rarely needed to stack pros against cons in decision-making. I typically followed heart and head. Didn't mean every choice was a success. Failures? I learned from them. Consequently, I approached choices with clarity and confidence. But this was huge and had zero room for my typical bullheaded antics. Still, I couldn't shake a sudden decision.

I choose Yazmeen. For life. As wife.

"Dang…"

I said it. Admitted it. Owned it. And felt daggone good about it. Kryshelle's aggravation was suddenly nonexistent. If anything, I thanked her for providing that last pivotal push.

Snatching up my phone, I started to call Yazmeen.

To what? Tell her "I've decided you're the woman I'm marrying?"

I'd never proposed before, but I doubted a woman wanted it that way.

Dismissing my craziness, I slid out of bed and onto my knees to seek the Father's face in making this love with Yazmeen a situation built for eternity.

CHAPTER TWENTY-ONE
PAPARAZZI & PAIN
Yazmeen

G od has not given me a spirit of fear, but of love, power, and a sound mind.

In the family court foyer waiting for my case to be called, my soul had that verse on loop. Rather than cave into the worries of 'what if,' I silently recited 2 Timothy 1:7 over and again.

"You alright, sis?"

Seated beside me, perusing documents, my brother-in-law Brandon was a godsend. Our consultations in preparation, as well as his presence, were beyond appreciated. Silently chanting God's Word like a member of a purified pep squad, I merely nodded.

"Good. All I need you to do is stay calm. Don't let him bait you. No reacting to anything contradictory or inflammatory. Just relax. Let me represent you. And keep positive thoughts."

Philippians 4:8 flooded my spirit like reinforcement.

Whatever is true, noble, right, pure, lovely, admirable, excellent, or praiseworthy, think on such things.

Despite this necessary court appearance, blessings in my life were certainties.

Sasha's baby was due soon, this June. And she'd recently acquired a silent partner who was catapulting her Essentials to boss levels.

We were two weeks away from Joy and Quinton's tropical island wedding.

Step-N-Style was hyped about a summer camp being hosted in Harlem by one of the nation's African-American premier dance companies next year. The only catch was the two-thousand-dollars-per-student cost, fifty-percent of which was due when applying by the July deadline. We were brainstorming fundraising ideas to keep them from missing out on such an incredible opportunity.

My incredible Sir Sexy had become a main part of my heart. Despite my not speaking those words into the atmosphere, I was so deeply, done in love with him. I thought I knew love with Darrien, Mister Med School, who'd stomped my heart and left me ripe for rebounding with Royal. Hindsight showed my Darrien episode as a comfortable crush. There'd never been much heat, which was probably why I'd maintained my virginity. Had Darrien been Tavares? We already know. Yours truly would've conducted herself like Tribe Heffas-n-Hoes.

"You okay?" Brandon questioned my suddenly laughing.

Assuring him I was, I decided on a restroom run. "I'll be right back."

Scrutinizing documents, Brandon mumbled, "Sounds good."

Finished handling my business, I stood at the sink soaping my hands and meeting my mirrored reflection. I'd been taught to love myself but, truthfully, my sense of worth had endured a beat-down thanks to my Royal rebound and bargain basement marriage. Therapy, positive affirmations, and being kind to me had helped restore my loving the woman Yazmeen.

Staring at myself, I gave humble compliments.

"Girl, you're rocking this second-hand suit."

Brand name and ivory, it paired well with the blood red blouse sitting like silk against my Brown Girl complexion. Pairing that second-hand suit with the ruby and diamond bracelet from His Fineness was so me. Unique. Miss Frugality stared out of gentle, almond eyes while rocking switched-up braids featuring bronze highlights. In my heels, I was pushing six-feet. Statuesque. I was simply me. Yet complex. A woman blessed beyond herself and her faults. I couldn't allow my ex to ever again stomp on that.

He wants my children...

Immediately, I stopped the thought. I'd done too much to get myself to a place of calm. Including, scouring my bathroom for any overlooked antidepressants I could find last night.

I'd been so nervous over what could happen in court today that, when finding a hidden bottle with one overlooked pill, I'd popped it dry. Before I could swallow Joy called, checking on me. Just like the Holy Spirit crashing my pity party. Confessing my fears, I wound up spitting that pill in the toilet as my B.F.F. dialed LaVelle so they could pray me off the ledge.

My sons' godmothers were crazy as sin, but those two divas pressed that prayer in. LaVelle was in Dallas on a layover, and Joy in Philly where she'd moved in preparation to start her new life with Quinton, but when they finished calling on heaven and naming Satan every kind of lie, I knew everything would be alright. Didn't mean I didn't have to swat fear from my mind. I did. Every time the enemy tried it, I let God's Word take care of me. And I'd taken extra care with the twins.

Their father had long ago stopped picking them up from daycare, but I'd made sure to update their records, indicating they no longer had permission to leave the premises with him, and that I was to be immediately informed if he ever popped up. Not that he would harm them, but with the custody issue at hand, I took no chances.

Trust in the Lord with all thine heart, and lean not unto thine own understanding.

"Amen." I'd executed due diligence to the best of my ability, now I had to do like the Proverbs instructed and trust that the court's decision wouldn't cause detriment.

Inhaling several cleansing breaths, I discarded my used paper towel while double-checking my lipstick.

Father God, I thank You in advance for ensuring that the outcome of all things for my sons and me are stamped and sealed by Your perfect will. Amen.

Retrieving my purse from the vanity, I turned towards the door only to stop at what came in.

Sydney.

Dressed to the nines, ready for the runway versus court, Royal and his *haute couture* Cousin It obviously poured their coins into what hung in their closets. Or maybe that fit was courtesy of my credit. The weave was wonderful, and the makeup was beat but heavy, as if hiding something. Particularly beneath the right eye otherwise shielded by designer sunglasses. Scoping me like I bought brand-less, two-for-one sneakers from supermarket bins—and I did, *once*, and it wasn't a sin—Royal's "wife" smirked when practically sneering,

"Yazmeen."

Only a good God kept me from cussing.

If I had a stun gun, I'd zap you in your malformed account-opening kidneys.

I squashed the ugly thought, my mind suddenly filled with Royal's accidental dial and the sounds of assault that led to me and my girls riding like the save-a-thieving-heffa calvary.

I wanted to reveal that I'd been privy to what happened and suggest intervention. But I'd read somewhere that victims of domestic abuse often denied the incidences even happened, as well as sometimes protected their violator. Sydney and I were far from confidantes, and nowhere near friends. Between us was that inherent contempt that occurred when two people have simultaneously shared a man. Still, I was willing to take a chance. "Sydney...?"

"Hurry up already. I have better things to do than share space with you."

And just like that Sydney's snap cut my compassion in half. I was ready to leave, but the God in me pressed me to speak. "Your thievery aside, you should never be made to feel unsafe...with anyone. Even Royal." I tried going at it delicately; but Sydney wasn't feeling me.

I was looked up, down, and sideways like I stank.

"You had your turn with my man because I wanted it that way. But don't get it twisted. You and your services—including your bad credit and ability to speak to me—are no longer needed."

Sashaying narrow hips into an empty stall, Sydney left me standing there as if that weave was too wonderful to be seen by me.

Turning towards the exit, I chose not to act unsaved. Besides my misused credit, our only common bond was infidelity and the dissolution of marriage. Sydney had a right to dislike me. It was complicated. And I hated admitting it. But, technically? I'd been the other woman.

Making as dignified an exit as I could from the ladies' room found me running smack dab into Royal, waiting in the hallway for his she-thing. Remembering Brandon's counsel against engaging the enemy, I ignored him. Of course, that was too much like right for a wrong man.

He stepped in front of me. "'Ey, Yaz, you look good. Since we're here, how 'bout I holla at you a minute?"

Can I 'holla' back with a butcher knife without doing twenty-five-to-life?

He countered my attempt to move past him, stepping in my path. Again.

"Yo, Yaz. Let's squash all this and do right by our kids. We're their parents, so let's work things out like mature adults."

Too stunned to speak, I wondered what psycho-surgeon I needed to thank for performing Royal's lobotomy.

"So...peep this. I'll go in there and drop this case. You keep the kids. I'll sign whatever's necessary giving you sole custody. *If* you do something for me."

With Royal there was always too much smoke and okey doke. You could never come off your guard thinking he offered anything without strings. Saying nothing, I stood there too curious about his latest to leave.

"I got three, four video producers lined up. Two are solo projects, the others would be group things. The music's hot, and the chore-ography ain't nothing for you. Then there's a couple of roles in some films this dude's setting aside if you want them. You wouldn't be the main star or nothing, but it's a start. You'd have major screen time and enough lines to make big bank—"

"And your role in all of this?"

The grin on his face told me he mistook my misguided curiosity for genuine interest. "I'll be your agent. We'll negotiate fair terms. And... yeah, well, so you know...the roles are X-rated and require skin, but you oughta be alright with that after *Purrrfect*. And the way filmmak-ing is today, penetration's unnecessary unless that's what you're feeling. They know how to angle those cameras to make it look like you really getting it in and not just simulating."

This half-dead dog wants to pimp me in skin flicks?

That had me so nauseous, I might've run back into the restroom to vomit had it not been occupied by his bobble-headed "better half." Instead, I took off walking, hoping to make it back to my brother-in-law without snatching off my pump and smashing the heel in Royal's forehead.

He had the nerve to grab my arm, but threw his hands up in sur-render when I yanked free.

"Yo, I ain't tryna offend. I'm just saying. Miss Purrrfect still has a cult following and these industry folks are willing and ready to pay—"

"Who's Big Cain?"

Royal was street-tough and not easily punked, but hear me when I tell you his whole face cracked and caved. *"What do you know about Cain?"*

My eyes got tight. "Are your children and I in any danger?"

Cursing, he raked a hand over his face. "No. I'm about caught up on my payments." He ripped another expletive. "Come on, Yaz, baby. One film."

His begging ended when Sydney exited the restroom.

I left that foolery and, instead of giving him the finger, I mentally wished him the blessing of jumping hopscotch butt-naked on the freeway during rush hour traffic with cars without brakes in the carpool lane.

He'd offered to rearrange his day, including several important meetings.

I'd convinced him not to, assuring him I'd be okay. "Just pray for us."

He had right there on the phone last night, moving my heart with his intercession and care. "No worries, *Mariposa*, God will bring you and the twins out victoriously."

I never wanted to subject a man to my ex's consistent clown act, which had factored into my choosing not to date. I didn't like dumping on Tav, and never wanted him to feel misused or as if I was leaning too much on him when I could just as easily stand. While the subject of Royal was never right, it was nice knowing Tavares "got it." It wasn't that I didn't trust him. I simply hated the idea of being framed as a Baby Mama with Much Drama. Laughing at Kryshelle's crackhead comics was one thing. Her issues were fueled by drug addiction. Royal's were straight evil ignorance and I sometimes felt that highlighted my choosing-a-right-man inabilities. But believe me those reservations melted away that day.

Feeling his signature warmth the moment he walked in—I gripped the arms of my chair to keep from running to him. Turning and seeing Sir Sexy taking a seat, my whole heart caught a case of over-the-top happiness. When our gazes connected, I was so moved by his being there, that I couldn't do a thing except mouth 'thank you.'

Putting two fingers across his heart, I understood his motion to mean, 'I got you.'

Feeling Royal's staring from his seat on the opposite side of the aisle, I refused to even glimpse his hater aid. What I shared with Tavares was none of his concern and, to quote Sydney, his services, his whole self, were no longer needed.

Thankfully, a door opened and the presiding officiant—Judge J. Renee Powells—entered, handled preliminaries and started the proceedings. Our having the same middle name felt like a good omen.

As the one who'd filed the motion, my ex-Muppet was addressed first. He sounded like he had good sense until that, "Your Honor, I can't afford legal fees so I'm Pro Perm."

I looked at Brandon.

"*In Propria Persona*, or *Pro Per* not 'perm,'" he whispered, "meaning he's representing himself. When one party has legal counsel and the other doesn't, that can cause the judge to lean in the unrepresented person's favor. But don't worry. Judge Powells," he nodded towards the dignified, regal-looking African-American justice, "is extremely fair and unbiased. And her B.S. radar's flawless."

It was that, *and* on point, questioning Royal's assertions that—apparently to her—sounded and smelled like boo from the back end.

Trust, he tried it, that whole character assassination yang.

According to Mister Malignant, I was promiscuous, vindictive, financially irresponsible; psychologically imbalanced, dependent on therapy and sleeping pills; a poor-credit-having, self-righteous Holy Roller working a dead-end job, who turned our sons against him. He called me everything *except* unfit, and demanded full physical custody and child support payments.

Judge Powells' demeanor was clarifying not accusatory when turning to me with a line of questions stemming from Royal's statements. Her dignified air intact, it was almost as if she was humored by his antics. For some reason, that helped me relax and respond openly, honestly.

"And as for your seeking and obtaining care from a mental health professional, I commend you, Miss Williams. That is too often taboo in our African-American community." I swear I heard her murmur, "God knows we need it," before turning to Brandon.

As agreed, I remained silent as my barrister brother-in-law expertly did what he did.

Having never seen him in action, I was impressed by Brandon's professional execution. Not only did he present written declarations from the twins' pediatrician, their daycare director, and children's church administrator attesting to the fact that Malcolm and Malik were healthy, well-mannered, well-loved and -cared for little boys, he'd also obtained declarations regarding my character from Zumba students, my employer, and the director of the community center where I taught *Step-N-Style*. Mister Clarence provided a declaration, not only of my character, but Royal's volatile response in the parking lot when I'd keyed his car.

"I object, Your Honor, to all this unsolicited ish. It's two-faced and had I known I could've brought in some declarations, I would have.

Plus, how she gonna bring up my behavior in response to her vandalizing my whip?"

"Knowledge of your ability to submit supporting documents, sir, is one of the benefits of doing your homework prior to appearing before a court when opting out of legal counsel. Have a seat, Mister Jones."

"Miss Williams, is it true you vandalized Mister Jones' property?"

Tavares' clearing his throat was his suppressing a laugh.

Brandon nodded, indicating I should respond. I did. Without excusing my actions.

Judge Powells' reprimand was preceded by a cough and clearing of the throat that made me wonder if *she* was laughing. Reprimand delivered and received, Brandon continued, presenting proof of Royal's history of absenteeism, emotional withdrawal, and failure to co-parent our children. Emails. Text records. Voicemail messages. Photos of *those* Christmas gifts. The accounting I was glad I'd kept, showing Royal's erratic financial support and contributions. Records of my employment and banking statements that more than substantiated my position as the sole provider for the twins. A log from daycare showing Royal hadn't picked up the boys in over a year. Unlike Royal, Brandon's approach wasn't vicious. He simply delivered indisputable evidence.

"Your Honor, I also believe it's important to note that there's a pending case regarding Mister and Missus Jones illegally establishing merchant accounts in Miss Williams' name—"

"We'll leave that for criminal court, Mr. Calloway. Anything else?"

"Yes, Your Honor, please note that Mister Jones has changed residences four times in the past year."

I was aware of his recent relocation thanks to that drive-by. But four times? Again, he hadn't been present enough in the boys' lives lately for me to know.

"What's my address got to do with this?"

Brandon continued as if uninterrupted. "Unfortunately, there's also a history of unemployment and domestic violence—"

"What the hell, Yazmeen!" Royal was on his feet, hollering. "I never touched you."

Judge Powells' gavel made a crashing sound. "Sir, you will not conduct yourself in this manner in *my* courtroom. Sit down. Any further outbursts or interruptions will see you removed."

Order restored, Brandon presented police reports substantiating a series of domestic battery that had led to Royal's multiple arrests. The most recent incident being the prior week. Thus, Sydney's extra heavy layer of makeup hiding injuries.

"Judge Powells, all that ain't got nothing to do with this and is irreverent—"

"Irrelevant," she corrected. "And actually, Mister Jones, it does. When deciding such cases, the court must do what is in the best interest of the children, including ensuring their safety in a nurturing, warm environment."

"Listen, Judge Judy, my joint ain't cold. I keeps utilities. And as for that other ish, just like any other couple, wifey and I disagree sometimes. It's normal."

I nearly felt heat rolling off Judge Powells in the ensuing silence.

Her rich, well-metered voice was low and controlled. "Any person who believes that the physical violation of another is 'normal' is anything but."

"Ain't that about a bitch," Royal mumbled in response.

"Mister Jones, do you have a comment?"

"Listen, lady, I'm just saying. If wifey and me got beef, that ain't nobody's business."

Readjusting her eyeglasses, she skimmed the documents before her. "Three arrests in the past year. Four incidents of law enforcement responding to domestic abuse calls at your residence. An additional one occurring in public. I'd say it's the taxpayers' business. Two hospitalizations." She glanced up at Sydney who sat in the back. "Missus Jones, I would be remiss as an officer of the court if I failed to inform you that there are resources designed to aid persons in your situation—"

"Ain't no situation. Let's stay on point and deal with this ish with my kids."

Judge Powells raised an eyebrow. "Nothing would delight me better, Mister Jones, so, yes, let's. When did you last time spend time with your children?"

"Christmas."

"Four months ago?"

"I've been busy."

"Have you made any attempts to, if not share space with them physically, perhaps call or utilize technology such as video chatting?"

"Like I said, I'm busy hustling tryna make things happen."

"Yet, you want your sons full-time? And if that were to occur, who would be the primary care provider? Yourself? Your wife?"

He shrugged. "We'll hire somebody."

"I've gone through the documents, Mister Jones, and see inconsistent evidence of earnings. You'll hire somebody with what resources? Do you have pay stubs or proof of income you'd like the court to consider?"

He was quiet before proudly advising, "I'm in the music industry and an entrepreneur."

"Entrepreneurs keep financial records, sir—"

"Yo, listen! I'm done with this. The bottom line is Black boys need to be raised by men. Not women who'll make them weak sissies, or have them all up in their ho'ing. I'm the only one who can raise my boys into men. How about you concentrate on that fact?"

Neatly arranging the documents before her, Judge Powells folded her hands on top of them, staring Royal down before stating, "In an attempt at fairness to both sides, it is my standard practice to enlist a mediator in the hopes of arriving at an amicable solution. However, what I've witnessed and what has been presented to me today—in documented form, as well as your own behavior, Mister Jones—necessitates a deviation. I believe mediation would fail, sir, as it requires willingness to negotiate, the ability to hear and not just be heard, consideration for others and the ability to modify one's wants for the greater good, and integrity to abide by the outcome. You, sir, possess none of these necessary traits or skills. Thus, we will forego mediation. I will be entering a judgment today."

Removing eyeglasses, she pinched the bridge of her nose before replacing them and exhaling.

"Under normal circumstances, a mediator would also arrange to speak with the children regarding their relationship with both parents. That, however, could prove challenging in light of the fact that your presence in your children's lives of late has been inconsistent, if not nonexistent." She proceeded despite Royal's mumbling and grumbling. "As an aside, please be mindful that gender neither guarantees nor prohibits a loving, dedicated person from parenting effectively. That said... Mister Jones, as an advocate for your sons, I conclude that you are and would be an inappropriate custodial guardian. You lack the necessary maturity and stability to raise a child into an upstanding, law-abiding, contributory citizen. I will not subject your sons to inappropriate living conditions, or make them witness to ongoing domestic violence so that such behavior becomes normalized for them. Or scar their psyches so that they're predisposed to repeating and perpetuating that deadly cycle in adulthood—"

"Ain't nobody dead!"

For the first time since the proceedings started, Judge Powells displayed full irritation.

Abruptly turning away from Royal, she ignored him and gave me her attention.

"Miss Williams, you better thank Heaven you got out when you did. As stated, I am foregoing the need for mediation. Your counsel excellently represented you today, and it is without reservation that this court awards you legal, physical custody of Malik Amal and Malcolm Amir Jones as well as child support payments, including those in arrears."

"Aww, *hell* naw! This ain't even happening."

"It's happened. Baliff, be kind enough to relieve my courtroom of this man's presence."

She waited until the Royal removal was completed before continuing.

"Miss Williams, please know that while you've been awarded custody, Mister Jones may seek visitation. For the welfare of your children, I'd request supervised visitations only. Even if there's no current risk of him physically hurting your children, I fear Mister Jones could, perhaps, assault his wife in their presence. If at any time you or your sons feel at risk, you would do well to consider filing a restraining order. Good day and good success, Miss Williams."

I tried not to gloat, but that God-be-praised smile was cracking my face as I thanked Judge Powells before she exited. What the devil meant for evil, Abba Father turned upside down and around for my good.

My actual input during the proceedings had been minimal, reminded me of a song my parents' congregation liked to sing.

Victory, victory shall be mine...if I hold my peace and let the Lord fight my battles...victory shall me mine.

Throwing my arms around Brandon, my feet did a happy dance. "*Thank You!*"

"It's nothing, sis. You gave me good ammunition."

"No, you're brilliant! When invoicing me your fees—"

"We're good. Let's go." He stood, buttoning his suit jacket and ignoring my protests as he turned, extending a hand to the one who'd just walked up behind me. I let them do their Black man hand dance before wrapping my arms around Tavares. His embrace was safe, delicious.

"Thank you, sweetie, for being here and being you."

Kissing my cheek, he reminded me, "Baby, always believe when I say I got you."

My hand in his, we followed Brandon up the aisle as my brother-in-law informed me of what to expect next only to exit the courthouse and enter media mayhem. I'm sure in his career, Tavares had encountered far worse, but that petite paparazzi parade of reporters waiting outdoors had my whole body frozen.

"What the?"

Brandon's voice fizzled beneath a sudden onslaught of cameras and microphones thrust in our faces.

"Mister Alvarez, is it true you're here to establish paternity of Miss Williams' children?"

"Miss Williams, were you indeed having an illicit affair with Mister Alvarez during your marriage?"

"Was Royal Jones threatened with physical harm and other reprisals as a result of seeking custody?"

"T-Alva, a source alleges that your sports mentoring program is an auction block for you to scout and sell the talents of up and coming athletes to unscrupulous agents. Care to address that?"

Mister Magic and I'd discussed the possibility of paparazzi during the course of our relationship; and thanks to having shared the stage with notable entertainers as a dancer, I'd witnessed the tiniest taste of celebrity frenzy. But I wasn't ready for this. Not for the hurled questions. The falsehoods and accusations, the multiple bodies blocking our path. It had me disoriented.

"Say nothing," Brandon quietly hissed, going into lawyer mode and informing the press, "We have no comments."

My brother-in-law on one side, Tavares on the other, I felt myself being quickly propelled in an alternate direction.

"I know you didn't inform anyone, so how'd they know you were here?" Brandon was clearly ticked. "And what's with the twisted questions?"

"We both know who's responsible," Tavares growled, clutching my hand as Brandon hustled us far from prying eyes, back into the courthouse, down a corridor, and out a side door smack dab into the culprit.

Posted up at the end of a narrow walkway leading to the parking garage, Royal and Sydney were knee-deep in a heated argument until Sir Sexy's stalking towards them caught their attention.

"Tavares!"

He ignored Brandon and me.

It was scary, that mask of pure evil claiming my ex's face when he grinned. "You coming for me, Refried Beans? Let's do this." He postured up, ready.

Thankfully, Brandon physically intervened, positioning himself between Tavares and his target. "Come on, T., let's not."

"Naw, let's," Royal incited. "Whatchu mad about? Huh?"

"You pinged the press?"

"Nigga, whatchu talking?"

Tavares lunging had Sydney screaming, "He didn't call them. I did!"

That reduced the testosterone barely a bit.

"You bent 'cause the press is up in your stuff?" Royal chortled like he was kin to Charles Manson. "Good! Now you know how I felt with y'all playing me like a fool in that courtroom. But you got nothing to be bent about. You got it all, mufu! My kids. You got my ex so churched-upped and twisted she won't dance." He leered at me. "But I bet she dancing that phat ass and making you cum hard with those mad moves, huh?"

Funny how enemies can sync in war. Sydney and I called our men simultaneously when they both moved within striking distance.

Royal's "Get your ass to the car, Syd," countered Mister Magic's bulldog silence.

Wrapping an arm around his, I urged him away from conflict. "Baby, let's go." I'd gotten him to take a step back, but Dim Dumb Dinosaur keep spewing venom. Egging the mess on, he kept going. And going.

Sick of his idiocy, I found myself yelling. "Royal! *SHUT! UP!*

"Aww, *hell naw*, bitch! You been coming out your neck since you started sucking his rich dick."

Only Sydney's yanking him out of arm's reach saved Royal from Tavares' swing.

Royal's laugh sounded satanic. "Yeah, alright, Enchilada Sauce. I'ma forgive you for swinging on me if you thank me next time you digging deep in that puss—"

Brandon whirled on Royal. "Man, back that up! Sydney, get him out of here *now*."

Struggling in the process, Sydney had the good sense to do as asked.

"Yeah, that's right." Being dragged away or not, Royal had to get his last licks in. "Remember and recognize! I was the first nigga in that virgin. I drilled down in that wet-and-ready. *I busted that open!*"

It took Brandon and me to restrain Tavares physically.

Holding tight for life, we didn't let go until they'd gone.

"I'm good." The raw, guttural tone of his voice proved he was anything but. *"I'm good!"*

Slowly, we released him. The quiet enveloping us was thick, intense—trapping us in motionlessness. Silence had me jumping when Tavares suddenly gripped my hand and took off marching.

I was taking two steps to every one of his. "Sweetie, please slow down."

He dialed it back a fraction.

"I suggest we stay focused on the positive," Brandon counseled as we marched through that parking garage in tandem. "You won majorly today, sis. Don't let this imbecilic crap mess with that."

My heart was drumming from all the vileness we'd just experienced as well as my trying to keep pace with Tavares. "I know, Brandon." My voice was breathless. "Again, I can't thank you enough for everything. This other piece?" I had to inhale. "It is what it is."

"Why're you excusing him?"

I stalled, feeling some serious flames rolling off Tav towards me. "Pardon?"

"'This other piece? It is what it is?' Call it by its name, baby. Your ex is an ass."

"I know this—"

"Then stop letting him disrespect you like that."

I stopped dead in my tracks, forcing him to do the same. "'Let him?' Is something here my fault, Tav?"

"I'm just saying, *Mariposa*. He's in your face like he is because you allow it. You've never checked him. What's he got over you that makes you go blind to all his ish?"

There was a cyclone of emotions in those whiskey brown eyes. Care and concern were clearly there, but from my vantage point, controlled anger was at the forefront. That soured every note of today's victory more than Royal's ridiculousness ever could. "What would you like me to do, Tavares? Take a page from your book and swing on him?"

"Sis." Brandon's caution was gone in the wind.

I told myself to dial back, but felt under attack, as if I were at fault and today's court case was a result of my failure to adequately protect myself or my sons. I felt suddenly tense, exhausted, as if wearing the weight of every mistake I'd ever made. "You hit him? He sues you. Is acting a monkey worth that to you?"

"To see him flat on his ass? Yes."

I exhaled irritably. "Honey, I'm not a man and can't go in on Royal the way you think I should, but I've done the best with what I've had."

"I don't dispute that."

Seeing Brandon take several discrete steps back, I lowered my voice, realizing this conversation had become a lovers' spat. Perhaps it was the stress and anxiety I'd carried over this court case, or all the years I'd dealt with Royal's ignorance, but I felt intense heat coursing dangerously through me. "So, you're disputing how I handle my business. Our conflict resolution will differ simply because we have different temperaments and tactics. Don't judge me by what, in your opinion, is or isn't appropriate. You're a man. I'm not. Your money can solve your problems. Mine can't."

"Really, *Mariposa*. That's where we are?"

"Where we are, Tavares, is I don't appreciate you coming for me."

"Sweetheart, I'm not coming—"

"You are." I moved away when he touched my arm.

"All I'm saying is, as your man, I will stand up and not let your fool disrespect you."

"*My* fool?"

"Dude was talking all up under your clothes—"

"Is that what this is? The fact that he's been somewhere you haven't?" I should've stopped at his lowering his head and loudly, slowly exhaling, but something in me was cracked, crumbling. Had years of Royal's misuse come to this: a square-off between men over who had or hadn't accessed what was between *my* legs? That evoked an abject sense of powerlessness, and I couldn't draw my words back. "Do you really think I enjoyed hearing him talk about having been in me? If you didn't know it before, if Malik and Malcolm weren't proof enough, he has been. Still, no woman's intimate history deserves to be paraded around just so men can go at it!"

When he reached for me, I jerked backwards. "Please don't. Bottomline, I'm not you. I'll handle my affairs however I—"

"Are you filing a restraining order?"

"Why're you questioning that?"

"Case in point. You're not. You'll give him a pass. Like you did child support. Even if it means you're unprotected?"

"I never jeopardize my sons or myself. I'll do whatever I need to, but my way. Not yours!"

"I'm dictating?"

"Yes," I insisted. "Again, I could manipulate my situations better, too, if I had your bank, but I don't. I *cannot* control Royal like you have Kryshelle and anybody else you want silent or subdued."

"You might wanna back up a bit, Yaz. This conversation's going left."

God knew, *I knew* I was barking up a bad tree, but something in me was rolling downhill and wilding. "I'm backing up nothing. I'm sick of men wanting to bully, boss, and control me."

Say nothing, Yazmeen.

My inner woman, the one with good sense was yelling. I wasn't listening.

"And please don't think I'm ignorant enough to believe your money didn't shut that paternity situation down. But, I'm not that win. You cannot buy me."

"Okay, sis, come on." Brandon's stepping between Tavares and me let me know I'd gotten loud, stepped outside myself.

Every mantra or conflict resolution skill learned in therapy disappeared on angry wings. I was a raw Yazmeen I hadn't seen in years. "I'm worth more than your money!"

"Sis, take a breath. Don't let Royal's clownery skew things. You *know* T-Alva's good people. And *he* knows he can't buy you. Whatever he does, including how he's put up capital for Sasha's expansion, it's out of love for you. Nothing less..."

Brandon's sudden change in expression conveyed he'd said too much. I stared him down before honing in on Tavares.

"You're Sasha's investor?"

Dead silence was my only answer.

"Is that what wealthy men do? When you don't give them everything they want, they buy the people around you?"

"Alright, baby, stop. Clearly, we can't touch this right now—"

"*Clearly* you haven't and clearly you won't touch this, hit it or be 'digging deep' in it," I gritted. "If that's what all the largess is about—

getting the one who hasn't spread her legs yet—move on, baby boy. We're finished."

I heard Brandon's cautioning tone but was too far gone.

"I'm not your happy ho and sexing me will cost you more than money!" Frantically snatching the jeweled bracelet from my wrist, I flung it at him. "Memo to Mister Alvarez: I'm not for sale. My family's not for sale. Your money might be magic, but it's not needed here. And if I haven't checked Royal the way *you* think I should…maybe that's because *he is* my children's biological father. My situation's not yours."

If that multi-level parking garage had crashed on us right then, it would've hurt less than the pain and irreversible damage I'd just inflicted.

I saw it, felt it, practically tasted its raw ripping—desecrating and demolishing the honor, trust and love we'd painstakingly built. My spirit ached. Something in me caved. Yet, possessed by overwhelming inertia, I could move nothing. Not even my mouth to speak infinite apologies.

My capacity had been reduced to viewing the nightmarish avalanche of hurt and devastation crashing over his face only to be swiftly replaced by a stone-cold wall of self-protectiveness. His taking several steps backwards while facing me, screamed that he'd put himself beyond my reach.

"My God. *Tavares…*"

His turning and stoically walking away was like hot daggers—stabbing, cutting so deep that somewhere inside I was bleeding, wailing over the unthinkable things I'd said, and what I knew to be the termination of our relationship.

Afraid to move, as if the slightest motion would reduce me to dust, I barely breathed, terrorized of collapsing into the dark pool of nothingness suddenly waiting for me. Something kept me upright. Maybe it was my brother-in-law's arms. Maybe it was foolish pride. But the moment Tavares rounded a corner in the parking garage and disappeared from sight, my entire broken self screamed from the inside.

CHAPTER TWENTY-TWO
SNATCHED
Tavares

My game face had always been good. On the court, I could front and fake out the finest. That skill served me well in the days following the breakdown and dissolution that transpired between me and Yazmeen. I kept it moving.

My life stayed on lock. Real estate and venture capital funding. *Athletes & Academics.* Everything that had to do with business stayed on task and on target. If anything, I went in deeper, driving successes that took the spotlight off the fact that my personal arena was wrecked. I kept my head down and did what I did. Only the women important to me saw past the okey doke and came poking and prodding at ish that was already killing.

Mami was all, "Efren, you don't sound right, son. I'm coming over and making some meals you and Aniyah can freeze and eat throughout the week."

I assured her everything was everything, but she still came, cooking all my faves, sitting and watching me eat to make sure I 'didn't waste away,' believing in the power of food to heal anything. A lack of appetite had never been an issue for me. Trust, I ate. But that didn't throw *Mami* off. She got her rosary and went to praying.

Reina was just as bad with her constant, "Cousin, you sure you're okay?"

Even Nubs got on my case. "Daddy, you don't look like yourself."

"Who do I look like?"

"A very, very sad man."

Add to that the fact that I felt the need to deny her frequent requests to video chat Malik and Malcolm or get with them for playdates. Nubs semi-accepted my lame excuses until frustrated and blurting, "Daddy, if you and Miss Yazmeen are mad at each other, does that mean I can't be friends with the twins?"

I was so done with female scrutiny and philosophizing that I nearly ran aboard that plane to Quinton's bachelor party in Philly, hosted early to accommodate those unable to attend his destination wedding.

"Whatchu mean ain't no strippers? Man, I left *The Golden Girls* marathon and The Shopping Channel for this? I coulda stayed home and got the same satisfaction."

Que's cousin, Nate, had us going.

"'Ey, man, my wife-to-be made it real clear I'd be soloing on our honeymoon if we got carried away tonight."

"Well, shoot. Get the dollar bills out and make it rain 'cause I'ma 'bout to strip for y'all."

Cranking up the music, Nate got to gyrating and acting his usual fool. When he unbuttoned and removed his clothes showcasing a Little Mermaid t-shirt and some Lion King draws, I was dead! Done.

Where he got that mess in grown-man size was anyone's guess. All I know is that fool had me laughing so hard I probably squirted piss.

Three hours in when we called it a wrap, I could still glance at Nate and fall out.

"It's good to see you looking better than that half-dead dude who walked in the door when you got here."

"Who?"

"You!"

"Que, you're bugging."

"No, I'm saying what I saw," Que clapped back, steering through the streets of Philly at dark thirty in the morning. "I've known you since first grade, so think before you lie to me. Are you saying everything's straight?"

"I'm saying you need to quit staring in my grill and watch these here streets. It's April, dawg. Why's it snowing?" Staring out the passenger side window at snow flurries drifting against the dark night had me remembering long ago winters when Philly was home. Its sense of familiarity was soothing.

"Man, I thought you knew Mother Nature's a woman and does what she wants."

We both laughed.

"Yeah, I guess. How're you feeling about getting hitched? You ready? Need anything?"

Old School R&B bumping through the stereo, Que glanced at me. "Everything's straight, T., but I appreciate you asking. All I know is I'm ready to make those marriage moves. And you know what I mean," he added, flashing that silver ring we'd both received when attending a singles' conference promoting godly living through purity and celibacy a few years back. Where mine was was anyone's guess.

"You burning, bruh?"

"Like a mufu."

We cracked up.

"That aside, I cannot complain about a thing. I'm ready for that wife life, and I praise God Joy and the baby are both thriving."

I caught the steel in my boy's tone on that piece.

That situation this past December that had Yazmeen spinning? It had involved Joy's hospitalization due to some unhinged, stalking dude. Shortly thereafter is when she and Que found out they were pregnant, and they'd had concerns about the baby's welfare. It was good hearing those concerns were unfounded.

"All I'm saying is dude needs to thank the devil he's already breathed his last, or somebody would be posting a brother's bail."

My boy wasn't bumping his gums. He'd served time for going in on one of the dudes who'd gang raped his college sweetheart. Saved and sanctified now or not, Que was half-Haitian, and that Haitian half was *cray-zay*.

"So, Joy's at your condo and you're at your parents 'til after 'I Do?'"

"Might sound ignorant seeing as how we're pregnant. But that's how we had to do this and maintain some righteous living. Separate residences until marriage. No creeping when we're supposed to be sleeping."

That left me chuckling. "Trust, I hear you. Ready for daddy duty?"

"Man, I'm skeered."

"You clowning."

Que chuckled before spilling what was on his chest. "I look at my dad, my older brothers...at you and what you do for Aniyah on the daily, and I'm pretty much intimidated."

"Bwoi, it's hard, real talk. But you'll find out who you are as a father and do you, Que. You've always been all-in, never less than one hundred. Trust. You won't give your child less than your best. And it's all worth it. That love? That satisfaction of knowing your child is good? Man, you can't trade it."

"Yeah...I'm in love with my rugrat and haven't even met him or her yet, so understand I have zero regrets about us being pregnant. What twists me is the fact that I didn't honor God or Joy, and stepped out of line in the process."

Saying nothing, I let my boy speak his piece.

"I can't even lie and say the enemy trapped me. Grown men's talk?"

"Always."

"I wanted my woman. I'd been three years celibate and could've kept myself in my pants. Instead, love…okay, and some lust…had me shook and all kinds of greedy."

"And needy?"

He held out a fist for bumping.

"I was supposed to be leading by example as the saved one in the relationship. Which, by the way, was out of line in the first place. I know God's Word says don't be unequally yoked, but I wanted what I wanted and misused what the Lord told me to my advantage."

"Which was?"

"That Joy was my one. My big head and me were like, 'Well, shoot, let's set this party off early!' Wrong way. For real. I should've manned up and not played games with my flesh and tarnishing my Christian witness."

I sat a moment digesting what Que said before offering, "Man, believers don't get everything right just because we're in relationship with Christ. We gotta walk this saved life step-by-step just like the next man. We might be filled with the Holy Spirit, but we're still human. Sometimes we miss the mark. We slip. You slipped. But you're back on track and honoring your woman and your relationship with the Father. You made corrective steps. And I bet you gained wisdom in the process."

"Mos' def'."

"Then reach out and help another brother avoid some pitfalls when you can. But right now? Go'n and get that life with your wife without condemnation. Point blank period."

He was quiet before uttering, "Amen, preacher. You hungry? Those little chicken wings and things from that bachelor party set-up ain't holding me. You want a burger?"

"Dude, you know I can always eat."

Cranking up the stereo, we rolled until finding a fast food joint. Ordering, we posted up in the drive-through line.

"So…I hope you don't think you sidetracked me, T."

"What?"

"Boy, quit playing." He lowered the stereo volume. "What's going on with you and Yazmeen?"

"Joy didn't say anything?"

"T-Alva, you already know women get all sister-circle protective. She said we needed to add y'all to our prayer list. That was it. Then you come in tonight looking half-dead. Only thing I know to drain a brother down like that is beefing with his woman. So, what's up?"

Looking at the night, I toyed with telling Que everything. Trusting my boy wasn't an issue. We'd been ride-or-die since always, seeing each other at our best and our worst. Even so, I was disinterested in punking up. Dudes didn't sit around leaning on each other's shoulders the way women did. We weren't into that vulnerable ish. But truth not fiction? My insides were tore up, straight broken.

"T.?"

Nodding towards the car moving out of line ahead of us, I suggested, "Let's get this food first."

I wound up having to give the window cashier an autograph, but it was all good as Que and I drove off, scarfing food that had nothing to do with fitness.

"Man, you better ease up on that second burger if you plan to fit that tuxedo in the Caribbean."

"Boy, miss me with that and envy these abs." A few inches shorter, Que was heavier but built like a brick. Solid. "I keep it tight and right for my woman. So...dish it, Alvarez."

Chomping on onion rings, I went in. It took more than a minute. When I finished, we were at my hotel's roundabout entry and Que was speechless.

"Yeah, that," I mumbled, slurping what was left of a strawberry shake, feeling as if none of this was real. Not this conversation, or the elephant posted up on my chest, or that I'd finally loved only to lose.

"Dude, that's much," Que eventually managed.

"Yep."

"But so is the way you love this woman." He was silent before adding, "I'm not minimizing what went down, but Yazmeen's good people. You have moves to make—"

"Naw, I'm good. We're done. Hashtag period."

"Man, please. Squash the foolery."

"You're not hearing me, Que. Our relationship, whatever it was, is *terminada*. Finished."

He was quiet a moment. "T., do me something: just listen. Every relationship gets tested. Question is: can it be mended? I mean, all the ish aside, Yazmeen is the only woman you've ever opened yourself to, and the only one to ever have you tangled and tied. I peeped y'all that night we went to dinner after the game. Clearly, she loves you."

My bwoi was so on a roll that I didn't bother to admit she'd never said "it," those three words that could've confirmed us. My jaw getting rock-hard, letting Que know I was shutting down on this convo, did nothing to curtail his insistence.

"I'm just saying, there's no such thing as perfect. Sometimes things are said or done that lead to regrets even in love. But what about forgiveness? What about taking a step back before making irreversible decisions?"

"What about not acting like you don't see what you see and being alright with accepting that it is what it is?" I challenged.

He got quiet. "But that's my point: you're *not* alright, man. You're twisted. Trust, I've been there and I get it. Joy and I fell out a minute," he confided, "but in my case I had to man-up and admit where I was wrong, and that what I wanted with her was worth fighting for even when she said *she* was done." He laughed abruptly. "Did I tell you about the time she cold-cocked me?"

Wrong or right, that had me snickering.

"I said something way out of line," Que confessed. "Next thing I knew, stars and birds and things had my head swirling."

"Man, you're a mess."

"I'm serious. I wasn't feeling that slap then, but I don't know. Something about her coming at me like that? I might like a little slap-and-whack in kinky, married sex."

We fell out laughing.

"Have you talked to her?" he questioned when we'd sobered.

I hadn't accepted her numerous calls or texts.

"Okay. Let's pray this through," Que suggested, placing a hand on my shoulder.

"Heavenly Father" was barely out his mouth when his cell rang. Anita Baker's "My Joy" signaled it was his fiancée. Que didn't answer initially, and continued praying. The ringing stopped only to start again. "Excuse me, Lord, but I may need to get this. Hey, baby."

Seated in the passenger's seat, I could hear Joy screaming. Crying?

"Bae, hold up! I can't understand what you're saying."

Something got tight in me, hoping there was nothing wrong with their baby.

"Yeah, T.'s here." He sat staring at me. *"What the?"* His leaning back and slapping a hand on his head had me praying. "Baby, hold on." Activating speaker mode, he continued. "I'm on speaker and like I said, T.'s here."

"Tavares, you gotta get to Yaz!"

That was not what I expected. "What's going on, Joy?"

"Royal took the twins!"

When conveying our break-up to Quinton, I'd been so in my story that I hadn't paid attention to the increased snow flurries. It wasn't until trying to get a flight that I learned planes had been grounded due to, what in my opinion was, a minor snowfall that should've affected nothing.

TSA didn't see it my way. I was stuck in Philly and not flying home.

"Yazmeen?" The only thing I heard on the opposite end were her strained efforts at breathing. "I'll be there as soon as I can. In the meantime, what do you need from me?"

"Nothing. Just sit with me."

The sounds of her brokenness had me wanting to fatally wound the man causing her misery. "I'm here, baby. If you never believed a word I've ever said, believe me now. We *will* get the boys back."

I understood none of it. Not Royal showing up at the boys' daycare, or a return substitute provider filling in for the woman who was out sick, remembering him from back in his half-sane days and not bothering to check for any possible update in records before releasing the twins to him. The fact that it went down hours ago and I was just now finding out added weight to an already impossibly heavy situation.

Whenever away from home, I was hyper diligent about keeping my phone charged to maintain connection with Nubs. How I'd let the battery drain was a mystery. Plugging it in, I'd found countless missed calls from Yazmeen. Joy's turning off her own cell while attending some culinary class earlier and not remembering to boot it up until minutes before calling Que had left us all late to what transpired. Now, I was grounded three-thousand miles away, at the weather's mercy.

"I...need...my...babies..."

Her voice ending in body-wracking sobs had me wishing I had wings.

Father God, please stop this snow. I need to be home in Cali.

"Your babies need you, too, *Mariposa*," I gently reminded when her sobs quieted. "Stay focused."

"He snatched my sons! Would he hurt them? Would he do something—"

"Yazmeen, stop. That's not helping."

"Why're you?"

"Why am I what?"

"Helping after every nasty thing I said after my custody hearing. *I'm so, so sorry.* And embarrassed. And ashamed by my behavior and every vile thing I said. But most of all for hurting you."

"Right now, that's irrelevant. In case you didn't know, I like your kids."

"I overheard the boys the other day saying they wished their daddy was as nice as Aniyah's...and that they love you. I screwed up. I *never* should've been with Royal." The unsteadiness of her voice indicated her tears were flowing again. "My babies are paying the penalty for my stupidity and sins."

My tone was soft, intentionally. "Last time I checked God was a god of forgiveness and mercy; so, let's not do the beat-up-on-Yaz dance."

She said nothing, but it was as if I felt her spiraling descent. She was weighted, sinking beneath the darkness of what was happening.

"*Mariposa*, stay with me."

"I'm here. But if my babies don't come home, I won't be. I can't be on this earth without them."

That sent what felt like knife strikes across my skin. I'd never known her to be fatalistic. Her optimism and positivity were two of the qualities that drew me. But this situation was past heavy.

Lord, I can't solve this. But You can.

That simple prayer had me remembering Psalm 91: the chapter she turned to at night before bed.

Launching my Bible app, I pulled it up. It was all I had to give. I read it. Slowly. Quietly. Letting God's Word soothe as it wanted and willed. Taking particular care with the last three verses, I emphasized, personalized and paraphrased as if God was speaking:

"Because the twins love Me, I will rescue them. I will protect them. Because Yazmeen calls on Me, I'm answering. I Am is with her and her family even in trouble. I will deliver the twins and honor them. With long life I will satisfy Malik and Malcolm and show them My salvation..."

Call me crazy, but I practically felt her sigh of relief when finished reading.

We sat silently embracing God's comfort and perfect peace.

"Thank you." Her words were whispered, but her voice was stronger. Clear.

I didn't respond for hearing someone needing her attention on the other end.

"Tavares, I have to go. One of the officers needs to speak to me."

"Handle your business, baby. When this weather cooperates, I'll be there."

Disconnecting, I stood at the window of my hotel room, feeling as cold as the snow steadily drifting and blanketing the city. Its whiteness was suddenly irritating.

"I'm done with this."

If I had to take Amtrak, a private car, *something*, I was getting back to Cali. The situation had me stretched. I needed to do something. Anything besides sitting up in a hotel while the woman I loved was home hurting.

That parking garage conversation might've ended us, but it didn't terminate what I felt for her, which was love. Love had me tight inside. All I wanted was to ride. Strapped up. Ready for this situation, if not someone, to die.

Son, you're out of line.

I heard the Holy Spirit inside. Still, memories of Kryshelle abducting Nubs for a night had me seething. That had been an incident of stupidity and neglect that—with God's grace—resolved without detriment. This here? Completely different. It felt volatile. Damn dangerous.

You think I can't handle this?

Tossing my phone on the bed, I perched on its edge knowing better than to tell God He couldn't.

Confidence in Him didn't squash the Pit Bull in me from wanting to strap up and hit those SacTown streets. Law enforcement was doing what it did, but the ex's residence was unknown, leaving dude in the wind. With the twins. Add to that the fact that his and wifey's cell phones were disconnected, and not even his family could say how to find him.

Sitting idly by went against every instinct I had. Maybe I was wrong for getting in the business, but I'd put Gonzalo and my grip of sub-law-living cousins on standby. If the law didn't do it quick enough for Yazmeen, for me, all fam needed was a call. Might've been crazy, but sometimes you needed criminals to find criminals. I'd given the caveat not to kill simply because I didn't need the blood of Yazmeen's ex on anyone's hands. But short of murder—sorry, not sorry—if we found him before Five-Oh did, I sincerely didn't care what happened.

CHAPTER TWENTY-THREE
DEALS & DEMONS
Yazmeen

I'd been awake thirty-odd hours. I couldn't sleep. Couldn't eat. Only at my mother's insistence I managed to drink something. But thoughts of what could be happening to my children, or that I'd never see them again, had me regurgitating. I was depleted mentally, emotionally. Yet, I refused to close my eyes in my delayed vigilance, as if sleep deprivation could cure my negligence.

Should've taken care of that custody thing from jump.

Never should've married or had sex with him.

Could've prevented all of this by giving him what he wanted and dancing or doing those skin flicks.

Countless "shoulda, woulda, couldas" sat on my heart and head like boulders and concrete. Whenever their weight shifted, raw guilt and horrific fear set in. While Royal had never physically hit me as he had Sydney, this emotional abuse was debilitating.

Doubting that sleep would provide a reprieve, I lay curled up on my bed, my head on my mother's chest, welcoming insomnia and wishing my stomach would stop rumbling and simply accept its emptiness as just punishment.

"Honey, you need to eat something."

The motion of my mother's hand stroking my head was metronomic. As if keeping time. A heartbeat. Its steadiness somehow helped me. "I only need my babies."

My mother's sigh was pregnant with sorrow and her own regret at being seven minutes late to pick up the twins.

I'm always there at two on the dot picking my grandsons up from daycare, but that accident slowed down traffic. Yazzy, baby, I promise I was only late by seven minutes!

For Mama those minutes were the make or break that constituted a world of difference. Like I wouldn't sleep, Mama wouldn't accept that Royal had snatched my sons shortly before one—an hour before her typical pick-up time. In the scheme of things, her being tardy was of no consequence. Just as that substitute daycare provider's tearful apologies were nothing to me. That woman had failed to follow protocol. Just because she'd subbed before and remembered Royal from back in the day, how did she not think to check records to see he was no longer authorized to remove the boys from the premises, or that there had been a custody dispute? She'd failed my sons, massively.

Same as you for even being with him...

Rolling onto my back, I stared at the ceiling, tired of cyclical rebukes and regrets that got me nowhere. Exhausted, I pushed into an upright position.

"You need something, baby?"

"Just the bathroom." I eased off my bed and away from my mother's warmth, feeling eighty-plus instead of thirty-two.

I was slow doing my business and wound up sitting there wishing the world would end. That Jesus would just come back and snatch me up so I could escape feeling as if my heart was lifeless, anchored to the bottom of an ocean.

Finished, I washed my hands and stood staring at the crushed woman in my mirror who looked already dead.

Just do it. No sense in being here.

I scoured the medicine cabinet for anything that could prove fatal when taken in mass quantity.

And who will raise your sons when you leave?

I didn't want to die. I just wanted the pain to end. But visions of my babies living life with Royal, or asking why I didn't fight for them stopped suicidal seductions.

Girl, you better woman up and go rogue if you need to. It's wartime, boo.

The fighter in me wasn't having that lay down and play dead routine. She was speaking. Demanding. And I was answering.

Closing the medicine cabinet, I walked down the hall to my sons' room. Standing in the doorway, I had an odd sensation that prevented me from entering. It was as if I needed to mentally enshrine the room exactly as it was and hold that in my memory.

Shaking off morbidity, I stepped inside, touching surfaces, straightening shoes and picking up discarded clothing. Taking both of their pillows, I lay on the floor, hugging them and inhaling little boy scents.

"Abba Father, I'm an imperfect person, but one thing no one can call me on is loving my children. They're everything to me. Would You, in Your sovereign majesty, please bring them home safely? Even if it's necessary to sacrifice me in exchange for them."

My death on the cross was sacrifice enough for all.

The Lord's speaking calmed the enemy's ugly lies that my children were being laid on an altar to atone for their parents' ignorance. Soothed, I lay there a while longer, more at peace but still sleepless.

Go take a bath.

My nerves and underarms could certainly benefit.

Returning pillows to their places, I headed out only to stop at the door. Looking up, I marked the spot on the doorjamb that Pastor and First Lady had touched with blessed oil. They'd arrived after law enforcement and my family, offering consolation and walking throughout my home, praying. At the time I'd been focused on answering and re-answering the officers' questions and telling them everything I could but now in the silent aftermath, it was if I could feel the power of their spiritual warfare and intercession. Somehow, despite what was happening, I managed to give God thanks for the essence of His presence.

Reentering my room, apparently my mother had intuited my needs. She was in my bathroom, pouring fragrant salts beneath running water. She looked up, hearing my entry. "I thought a hot bath might help you relax."

Saying nothing, I walked to her and fell on her chest, crying tears I didn't know I still had. I so appreciated that she didn't offer false platitudes. She simply held me as if I was still *her* baby.

"Enjoy your bath," she encouraged when my tears abated. "I'm going downstairs to check on your father." Pausing at the door, she looked back. "You're stronger than you think, Yazmeen. Remember that."

Removing my phone from my pocket, I placed it on the vanity, undressed and eased into the tub, dreaming a multitude of ways to maim, blind, murder, cut, and castrate the man I'd married.

I. Hate. Him.

Clearly, the loathing was reciprocated. There was no more effective way to show his whole disgust for me than taking my children.

He never even wanted them.

He'd offered to pay for an abortion in one breath, and was proposing marriage in the next. My life felt so inside out at the time that, in my confused state of mind, I'd accepted. Everything about that situation had been far from right, but when Sydney entered the picture stuff got stupider.

"Stop it, Yaz. Focus on your sons. Send them good thoughts."

Malcolm. Malik. Can you feel me? Wherever you are, so is my spirit. I won't leave you. And I won't stop looking. I promise, Mommy'll find you.

Clean, but not necessarily calm, I wrapped a towel about my body and stepped into my bedroom to find India and Sasha seated on my bed watching mindless television as a distraction.

"Hey, Yazzy. You hungry? You want anything?"

"No."

"You sure? You haven't eaten since yesterday. You need to—"

"What I need, India, is Royal in hell or a jail cell and my children home with me. If eating can do that, bring me a fork and my whole entire kitchen and let's make it happen."

My sisters said nothing, but I could feel their concerned gazes as I turned away, slipping into panties and an oversized t-shirt. Sure enough, when I faced them, they were watching, worried. "What?"

Shifting over, Sasha patted the empty space available between them. "Sit with us."

Feeling like I should be actively doing anything that could possibly help recover my sons, I hesitated.

"Yazzy."

My baby sister's soft summons had me relenting, joining them on my queen-size bed.

"Here. Mama made us bring this up."

"What is it?" I asked, peering into the large mug India extended.

"Some of Grams' "tea" that's one-fourth tea and three-quarters brandy."

"I pass."

Grimacing after one sip, India set the mug on the nightstand before getting comfortable on a mound of pillows and snuggling her forehead against mine. "It's going to be alright."

"When?"

"Honey, I can't timestamp it. Just know God's at work and in the midst."

"Big sis, all five of your sons are present and accounted for." There was no malice in my voice, just facts. "And Sasha," I turned to face my pregnant baby sister. "Yours definitely isn't missing like mine are."

Like my mother, my sisters didn't attempt empty-calorie comfort. Instead, Sasha took my hand and placed it on her belly as India wrapped an arm around me from behind, offering what consolation they had.

Rubbing Sasha's belly, cocooned between them, exhaustion was winning and I was losing the fight to keep my eyes open.

"Didn't nobody invite me to the sibling set."

"Boy, hush! Don't you see she's asleep?"

India's scolding our brother pulled me back to full consciousness. "Hey, Taj. When'd you get here?"

"Ten minutes ago. This was on the porch." Handing me a small, padded mailer, he climbed on the bed, forcing himself between Sasha and me, which had her fussing.

"Dang, Taj, you're here because?"

"'Cause I'm the real baby up in this sibling piece."

Ignoring their fussing, I opened the envelope addressed to no one. Inside was a burner phone. I held it up, not minding that with sibling number four my bed was severely overcrowded. "What is this?"

"You might need to tell the officers about it. It seems shady, Yazzy."

"I will," I assured India, powering up the phone that proved new, with no contacts or activity other than a missed call from an unknown number. My radar went up. "Taj, how do I redial an unknown number?"

"Star sixty-nine that bitc—"

Sasha hit him in the back of the head. "Cuss again and I *will* tell your parents."

"Here. Lemme see it." Taking the phone, my brother did what he did, winding up with a failed attempt. "Okay, fifty-seven it." He tried again. Hearing ringing on the other end, Taj handed me the phone, looking triumphant.

"I see you got the phone."

Sitting straight up, I nearly dropped it hearing Royal's drunken slurring on the opposite end.

My siblings tossed questions like bullets at my darting off the bed and into my bathroom, locking the door behind me to ensure I didn't miss one word the demon sea creature said.

"Knowing you, the PoPo's probably tapped your cell and tracing calls, acting like I'm some kind of criminal just 'cause I'm with my sons. So, we're using these burners to handle ish. I don't want cops involved."

My heart was hammering, but I was, otherwise, dry-eyed and oddly calm. "What *do* you want?"

"Don't ask questions! Just own that you did this."

I was willing to do or say whatever it took to get my sons back. "I own my part—"

"You own it all! You trapped me with kids. You broke up me and Syd. You did the most, Yazmeen." His liquor-laced slur was thickening.

I'd known him to drink beer, wine, a little Hennessey or Courvoisier occasionally; but I'd never experienced this inebriated being.

"You had me looking bad in court, came for my coin, and got Syd dealing with all your fake account foolery when you know I got real money worries. But you don't know nothing 'bout money being funny after rolling with Mister Chimichanga, huh?"

"Royal, do you need something?"

"Hell, yeah! I need you to know what it's like to do without what you want. I need you to feel deprived for once. You feeling that way yet without the kids?"

"I am."

"Good. You don't deserve them."

"You're right. I don't. They're God's gift—"

"Yeah, but I'm the one who busted a nut and put 'em here. Listen, unlike you, I got real issues. The IRS in one ear. Collection agencies in the other." His volume was getting progressively lower as if liquor was lulling him to sleep. "I can't get no music acts to promote with me after Cain's scrilla went missing. These wypippo wanna repo my ride. A brother can't catch a break for all y'all tryna beat him down. So that's whatchu gonna do for me, Miss *Yazzzzz*MEAN. Get that break I need."

"May I speak to the boys?"

"No! *Concentrate...*" he hiccupped, "on *my* needs. Your basketball boy's 'bout to help me level up, *royally*."

I immediately knew where he was headed. "Not happening."

"You wanna see the twins? Do what you need to. Get 'im on the phone."

Sitting on the tub's edge, I rubbed my temples, trying to mitigate the headache coming on strong. "Tavares and I aren't together anymore."

"Don't matter. That nigga's wide open for you. He'll come through."

"Let's find another solution—"

"*You ain't understanding, are you?* I got your whole life right here! So, we gonna do this my way, or you *won't* see the twins again. Call him."

"You want what you want? *Let me speak to my sons!*"

"Quit getting loud. Hold on."

Seconds passed with responsive shuffling on Royal's end. I was tense until hearing,

"*Mommy, I wanna come home, please.*"

Malcolm's teary plea broke me.

Bending at the waist and gritting my teeth, inside I was screaming, wailing. God held me together externally. "You will, baby. I promise. Where's your brother?" I could barely breathe.

"Right...here." Malik's broken breathing reflected his crying. "We don't like... this stranger danger daddy."

Trying not to upset my children, I muted myself and inhaled hard to regain composure. "Do you know where you are?"

"Girl, skip that." Royal was back. "You ready to dial them digits?"

Beyond my last breath, I will never forget or be able to repay Tavares.

My frantically placed call found him rock-strong, fielding that demon's evil demands like a boss. Only the cold steel in his voice let me know he was beyond livid. Still, he held it steady. "What time? What location?"

"I'll let you know. When I do, Yazmeen's dropping off."

"She's not going anywhere you are."

"Y'all still bumping your gums like I'm the one needing what you got. I got two little boys here that say you need me more than I need you. So, again, she's the drop-off."

Tavares and I were mutually silent until he questioned, "One-hundred Gs is all you want?"

"What? You scared I might get in them panties when she comes through?"

Tavares' "I doubt you could manage" struck me oddly. "I'm talking about the money. Your sons are only worth one-hundred-thousand to you?"

"You right. Make it two. One for each twin."

"That's it? Mufu, you're a cheap thrill."

"Tavares—"

Royal overrode my caution. "Oh, you smoking! Go'n and add another fifty as compensation for banging my baby mama. And make sure it comes like I said. Small units. Untraceable. No Five-Oh. *At all.* I get this? Yaz can have the kids back."

"Done. But be real clear. You hurt the twins or Yazmeen? Caps are popping in your—"

Royal clicked off before Tavares finished, leaving us in the quiet aftermath of his absolute vileness. I had to inhale-exhale, slowly, repeatedly before I could speak. "Tavares, I don't want you used like this."

"Understand. The money means nothing to me, Yazmeen. I can get that back. I can't get what we..." He stopped, breathing deeply and falling silent.

Taking my time, I prayed he felt my sincerity. "You never should've been pulled into this. I have no words and no way to thank you. It'll take a lifetime, but I will repay—"

"You still don't get it. That ignorant bastard can have whatever the hell he wants as long as the boys get home safely. I make moves for what I love. Including emptying the bank if necessary. Are we clear?"

"Yes."

We fell silent.

When he spoke his frustration was evident. "This snow has everything backed up."

"At least it's stopped and they're letting some flights out now."

"Yeah, but I can't get on anything earlier than a red eye. That might not get me there in time. I need you safe—"

"I'll be fine."

"I don't trust him. Point. Blank. Periodt. So, I'ma handle some things on my end."

"Meaning?"

"If I don't get there before he calls, the money and an escort will."

"You heard his demands that I do this delivery alone?" I tried and failed to keep panic from my tone.

His voice was soothing, gentle, yet insistent. "I'd never do *anything* to jeopardize the twins. But I can't have you out there in those streets by yourself." I'd barely opened my mouth in protest when his, *"Yazmeen, please!"* cut me off. "He wants bank? He can have that! What *he* can't do is further harm you, Malik, or Malcolm. Yes, I understand the risks." He took a calming breath. "Just trust me and let me work on this."

My family was nearly hysterical, tossing questions like Molotov cocktails and threatening to call the officers on the case as I moved silently as if hearing nothing. I was fully focused on dressing, being prepared when Satan's seed called with instructions. I understood my family's concerns as well as Tavares', but I couldn't sit waiting for the law to find Royal when I now had a direct line to him. Whatever went down between us did.

Lord, just keep my babies safe through it all and I'm good.

Bombarded by family—LaVelle on a layover in Albuquerque, and Joy who kept calling—and needing a quiet place, I exited, opting on the tight confines of my garage. I appreciated the concern, but I needed a moment for me. Sitting in the middle of the backseat of my SUV, eyes closed and head back, I laid hands on the twin's car seats. As if in touching them, was touching my children.

Crazy, but the thought of them having been transported without the safety of their booster seats was enough to set me off again until that burner rang. "Yes?"

"Since you been acting all bossed up and wanting to have it your way, we gonna do this exchange at Burger King. I'll let you know which one and when. You and that cash come alone. No PoPo."

His abrupt disconnect had me practicing meditative breaths before calling someone I never knew I'd need.

"Yeah, speak."

"DayDay, it's Yazmeen."

"My baby mama in my next life's calling! Girl, whaddup?"

I'd never been afraid of Royal. But after Sydney's domestic abuse, and the despicable and inexcusable way he was endangering our sons, I couldn't afford to play games. The fact that he was essentially selling them to pay his debt was something God could forgive if He wanted. But I was done. "I need a gun."

Only Joy would think a firing range was the perfect place for Girls' Night. But she had. Willing to try something new, I'd agreed and gone. Now—not that I remembered anything I'd learned last year—I was glad about that fact.

"Baby Mama, you're no criminal. Let me take this."

Had this been the Wild West of the 1800s, DayDay would've been an outlaw bandit. He was a brilliant, analytical techno geek with an

N.W.A. "eff the police, anti-establishment" streak. He'd done two pris-on terms, and nothing much fazed him except family. Loving to out-maneuver others at their own game, nothing would've pleased him more than rolling up on my ex unannounced and "dropping him at point-blank range." I prayed the matter ended without violence, but my desperation said whatever it took to end the nightmare was justified on my end. That didn't include pulling others into it.

It took a lot of persuasive arguing to get DayDay on Team Yaz-meen, but I managed. Facing my stubbornness, he capitulated, offering an abbreviated tutorial that ended with, "Just aim for the mufu's balls. If you miss, they weren't big enough to begin with."

That's how an unregistered, untraceable, fully-loaded firearm with backup ammunition came to be in my possession when Royal called. "Be at the Burger King at Florin and Greenhaven in one hour."

Dropping the burner phone in my purse, I barely thanked Day-Day. I was too busy running to my SUV while calling Tavares on my cell only to reach voicemail. In a rush, I left details, praying he'd call back immediately.

I was half-way down the block when some dark car came up from behind. Veering left, it sped by on the wrong side of the residential street until screeching to a stop, perpendicularly in front of me. Brak-ing hard, I barely avoided a collision as two tall, shady-looking men jumped out of the car and rushed at me.

Hear me when I say a sense of danger choked my whole throat. That had me reaching for my purse and that new equalizer, courtesy of DayDay.

God, I don't want to, but I will hurt somebody.

"Miss Yazmeen!"

That was the only thing that stopped me from defensively aiming.

The sun had set, but there was enough light left to see clearly. Star-ing at the driver, something about him was familiar, but I couldn't place his identity.

Had my door been unlocked, he would've opened it. Instead, locked out, he spoke through my raised window. "I'm 'Zalo. 'Vares' cousin. Not tryna scare you, but we've been tailing you, and will until he gets in."

I suddenly remembered him from that picture of Miss *Abuela's* Cel-ebration of Life festivities. He'd been kissing her cheek, and Tavares the other.

"Hood Boy" sounded on my cell as if he'd been summoned.

He didn't waste oxygen on greetings. "There should be two dudes with you. 'Zalo and Ali—or Gonzalo and Alejandro. Both are fam—"

"Royal just called."

"The cash is coming." Even as he spoke, another car rolled up.

Alejandro trotted to the driver's side to hold a conversation I couldn't hear. When he looked up and nodded, Gonzalo advised, "Tell 'Vares it's all good."

Lowering my window, I did.

"*Mariposa*, the flight already boarded and I'll have to disconnect in a sec. Gonzalo's going with you."

"He's not—"

"He is. Your ex just ramped up this situation. Do you know Big Cain?"

"Yes...no." Quickly, I explained the men who'd come looking for Royal. "Why does that matter?"

"Trust me and ride with 'Zalo—"

The line went dead. Or he'd switched to airplane mode? Either way, he was no longer on the other end.

"Miss Yazmeen, 'Vares is fam, so you getting that same loyalty. We're down for whatever. We'll get your boys, but you gotta come with us. *Now*."

My thoughts were spinning in countless directions. How had Gonzalo followed me without my noticing, and why this ride-or-die 'hood posse? Would Royal take the money and give me my sons despite my not arriving alone? Or would he exact some penalty my heart couldn't manage? And why was Big Cain even mentioned?

I suddenly wanted to be home folding laundry. Cleaning bathtubs. Toilets. Impaling myself on Legos and sweeping up Cheerios. All those mundane irritants or must-do's that symbolized normal. Not living neck-deep in a nightmare.

My nerves were dangling on dental floss, but I was clear on my course of action. "He'll be expecting me in my SUV, not some car full of men. I'm the one who needs to do this." Something in my tone must've conveyed to Gonzalo my seriousness. Studying me a moment, he hurried to the "money mobile," returning with a black case. Unlocking my doors, I watched him place it on the front passenger seat.

"Miss Yazmeen, on the real. You need to get out of this whip and come with me."

"You have seconds to get in your own ride and follow if you choose, Gonzalo, but I'm leaving."

Driving off before he'd completely closed the door, I didn't wait to see who was or wasn't complying.

Royal was a no-show.

Sitting in that fast food parking lot, I nearly left my right mind waiting for that devil seed to bring my babies. Excruciating seconds turned into minutes, and I hated him more with each tick-tock of the clock.

Gonzalo and crew were trying to make moves, calling who they knew and orchestrating what I wasn't privy to. But, bottom line, we were at Royal's mercy.

I ranted. Raved. Cried. Prayed.

Ninety horrific minutes after the agreed upon time he—relishing his control—phoned with new instructions for a park on the other side of town. "I don't need witnesses. It's dark. No one else'll be out. There's one of those industrial-sized dumpsters. Put the cash by it. Roll back a minute...and the twins'll be there."

I was being played with, but my sole option was doing as instructed.

Conveying the change in location to Tav's crew, I made them vow nothing physical would jump off, endangering my sons. They agreed to hold back until my babies were safely in my care. Whether or not I believed them was another story, but I did what I had to.

Following Royal's directions landed us at some funky-looking strip of a park occupied by despair and dusty-looking BBQ pits leaning on their last legs.

Royal's pearl Beemer seemingly came out of nowhere. When the driver's door opened, Sydney appeared, not him. Before Cousin It could snatch that black case, I was driving across the lot, speeding, doing my best to block an exit.

Only good sense had me leave that gun beneath the seat. Flinging my door open, I was running. *"Malik!"*

Seeing my baby being put out that Beemer was the sweetest sight ever.

He was screaming, crying hysterically, running towards me.

Snatching him up, I hugged him with all the life I had.

"I want Malcolm, Mommy!"

Cold, piercing fear shot through me. *"Where is he?"*

Expecting him to emerge, I froze seeing Royal's Beemer reversing so wildly that it pitched over one of those concrete parking space marker, bump things. That slowed it only temporarily.

"Malcolm!"

I heard feet pounding and another vehicle rolling up behind me, but—Malik in arms—I was too busy running after Sydney to process everything. *"Where's Malcolm?"*

Before speeding away, Sydney's tear-streaked face and words were terrifyingly clear. "Big Cain has him!"

CHAPTER TWENTY-FOUR
TALK TO ME
Tavares

S talking off the plane, texts communicating Malik was home safely kept me from acting ape crazy. But, exiting Sacramento Metro into the night—and seeing 'Zalo and Ali rolling up to the curb—the fury I'd suppressed while airborne reignited.

I was tight-jawed, ninety degrees above angry. I'd never been gangster, but raised in Philly's streets I knew how to scrap-and-come-strapped. I wasn't about that bloodshed, or interfering with law enforcement. But ish had escalated. And I'd lied to Yazmeen. I didn't like the twins. I loved them. Taking the gat Ali handed me, I was clear that whatever it took to get Malcolm home, I was in. "How do we get with Cain?"

At the wheel, 'Zalo shrugged. "That's like getting in the U.S. Mint. Ain't happening…however, I did a bid with one of his boys and had his back when we were inside. So, give him a minute to work on it."

Per my cousins, Big Cain—a Miami-based music impresario I'd heard of—was Lucious Lyon, Suge Knight, and Don Corleone in one. Formidable. Untouchable. Not playing games with a breed called Royal, he'd sent his crew to collect that debt. They wouldn't back off without Cain's instructions or cash in hand.

Thanks to criminal underground connections, 'Zalo knew Yaz's ex owed Cain seventy-Gs. His demanding four-plus times that much from me was plain greed.

Years ago when faced with a family emergency, I'd learned to keep stacks of cash on hand. As my admin assistant, Reina had access to it. Her being able to facilitate those drop-off funds during my flight proved that in-home safe was a godsend.

"What kind of sorry mufu ransoms his kids to pay his debts?" Ali demanded.

"This one," I replied, wishing up five minutes with Yazmeen's ex and a lead pipe. "So, Cain's dudes're sitting on Malcolm because?"

When Zalo and Ali exchanged glances, I knew nothing good was next.

"They're not."

In the backseat, I leaned forward, not liking what I was hearing. "What's going on, 'Zalo?"

"When Cain's boys went in to collect, dude and wifey used the twins to skid out the back."

"'Used?' As in protection to keep from getting popped?"

"Yep. That," he confirmed, explaining that those two freaks had literally carried the boys like human shields to keep Cain's crew from firing. "Ish went sideways and, intentional or not, dude went one way. Wifey went the other. Both with a twin. That's why wifey showed at the drop-off spot with only one of them before grabbing the stacks and bouncing. Fam trailed the whip thinking wifey was headed back to hand in that cash. Chick got on I-80 driving like hell towards the Bay. Fam lost wifey in traffic and that's that."

"And ol' dude's still in the wind, holding the other son as protection," Ali concluded.

Choked by the same violent anger I'd experienced when Nubs went missing, everything in front of me turned red. Leaning back in my seat, I closed my eyes to the rage waiting to sink me. Not because of the funds, but the fact that Malcolm was being used like some sacrificial lamb. "Wifey has his car. So, what's he rolling in?"

"Most likely hers: a yellow C-Class Mercedes."

Disgusted, I said nothing while calming myself enough to call. It was after two a.m. Still, she answered on the first ring.

"Tavares?" Her voice was hoarse with fatigue.

"I'm in Sacto."

"Thank God," she whispered. "Hold on..."

Hearing her attempts to calm Malik, it was obvious she held him. Even across the phone I felt his pain when hearing him.

"Mommy...I...want...my...brother." His words were spaced on broken breaths, as if reflecting their physical separation. Having lost Taia at birth, my whole self went out to him.

Soothing, quieting Malik, she returned to me. "I'm here."

"How's he doing? Would my talking to him help?"

"He's actually asleep, but keeps jerking half-awake...asking," she exhaled, "for...Malcolm."

God!

My thoughts were interrupted by 'Zalo's phone ringing. My cousin's quick hand signals had my pulse racing. I disconnected with promises to be there ASAP. "What's happening?"

"We got him!"

Parked at the back of some sorry, seedy two-story motel on a desolate strip, that yellow Mercedes couldn't be hidden. Not knowing if ex-monster was strapped or not, I climbed out of Gonzalo's whip praying: for Malcolm's safety and that whatever we were about to get into in these streets wouldn't leave my daughter fatherless.

A red 300 rolling up had me tensing.

"That's Smokes."

Pausing long enough for Gonzalo to bruh hug the driver, the passenger, and make intros, I headed for the front office, intent on getting management's assistance versus us "busting heads and kicking in doors" like my cousins suggested. But that office was locked, leaving me and the night manager conversing through a bulletproof window that—based on the bullet-like hits that hadn't fully penetrated—was effective.

"Nope, nobody registered tonight with a kid, but if—"

Gunfire kept him from finishing. Dousing the lights, he hit the ground.

I took off running.

Rounding that corner to the parking lot, I nearly dropped seeing the shooter aiming a gun at Cain's crew.

"I won't ask again. Where the hell is my son?"

"Yazmeen!"

Ignoring my scream, the guttural growl in her voice sent chills through me.

I approached cautiously.

I'd never known her to be violent, but the stakes were ridiculous enough to push the most peaceful person over the edge. *"Mariposa…"*

Set on her end goal, she refused to look at me, but my focus was on her when hearing 'Zalo's "Yo, y'all, don't even" directed to Cain's men who'd obviously reached for the heat they were packing.

The volatility was suddenly on ten.

Angry over that shot-out front tire, Smokes hollered, "All we know is your ex is holed up in here some—"

Her firing, knocking out the 300's back tire as if that answer was unacceptable, had Cain's dudes cussing as the Chrysler leaned left on its rims.

"Yazmeen...baby...look at me." I moved towards her. Slowly. I positioned myself in front of her, keeping her from hurting someone or being hurt in return. "Malcolm's here. Somewhere. We're not leaving without him." I slowly reached out a hand, needing this situation finished. "*Mariposa*, give me the gun."

Silently, she stared at me with fiery eyes that were almost scary. Engaging the gun's safety, she didn't hand it to me. Instead, she walked away, hollering. "*Malcolm! It's Mommy!*"

Banging on doors, she yelled Malcolm's name, repeatedly. Occupants didn't respond, or slammed doors, or cussed over the disturbance, but she was beyond caring. There was a fierceness in her I'd never seen. It was crazy dangerous, but it had us in action, mirroring her activities.

I moved alongside her, focused on finding Malcolm but wanting to protect her as we walked the back of that property without success. Midway, she stopped, bent over.

"*Where's my baby?*"

That just about broke me. Pulling her upright, I held on as she cried. When her tears eased, I reached for that gun, asking her to relinquish it to me.

"Mmm-mmm." She backed away, shaking her head, calling again. "*Malcolm, it's Mommy...we won!*"

Recognizing that as the safe code she used with the twins, I found myself hollering it in between praying.

Heavenly Father, You see even hidden things. Show us Malcolm's whereabouts, please.

"'Vares! Right here!"

Seeing Gonzalo and Ali leaning over the second-floor railing at the far end, we took off running. Cain's dudes were running towards us from the opposite end as we mounted the stairs, but all I could register was Malcolm, inside a locked hotel room, pounding against the window, crying.

Forget a key. We tore that door halfway off its hinges. Busting in, I grabbed Malcolm and handed him to Yazmeen while we checked every conceivable hiding place.

"It's clear."

The only evidence of the ex was a burner phone and the son he'd abandoned.

Fatigue and relief hitting me, my adrenalin sagged, nearly crashed; but I held it together for Yazmeen. On her knees, she was bawling, hugging, kissing her child repeatedly. I stood over her, protectively, giving them the time they needed, until helping her up when she stood with him.

"Mister Tavares!" One arm clutching his mother's neck, he reached for me with the other.

"Hey, Twinster." Kissing his forehead, I embraced them both, praising God for the miracle of Malcolm.

If the motel's residents called Five-Oh, we didn't know. I'd paid for the busted door, arranged for Smokes' vehicle to be towed and law enforcement still hadn't showed which was fine considering our criminal contingent's aversion to all things PoPo. Yazmeen's contacting the officers assigned to the case, had our crew vacating, taking her gun with them. But Smokes made sure we knew, "Little dude was always safe in this. Cain ain't no kid killer. But Royal?" He let the implied threat dangle in air.

Not caring about that, I focused on Yazmeen who held up like a boss when interrogated by law enforcement.

Arriving on the scene, they impounded that yellow Mercedes, collected evidence that had my blood chilling: four one-way plane tickets to Georgia and fake I.D.s for the ex and wifey. They'd planned to leave Cali with the twins and my money? A warrant had been issued for dude's arrest. Now, he was a flight risk. And I was tired as hell but cooperated when we were taken downtown and subjected to further questioning. I refused a recorded statement without my lawyer present when officers slipped some yang about my possibly facing obstruction of justice charges for interference by providing ransom money. They backed down, but I didn't relax until the ish was a wrap and Yazmeen and I exited to find our transportation waiting: her father and Taj.

Their wrapping her and Malcolm in hugs and love was a beautiful sight, but that night was one I chose to never relive, and prayed I'd forget.

Seated in the back with Yazmeen and Malcolm, I thanked God for his unending goodness before mentally going in on that whole gangster geek DayDay piece. Desperate, she'd gone back to him *after* he'd fitted her with a gat, letting him do what he did, tricking that burner phone with some Double-O-Seven, burner-to-burner tracking ish that connected to the ex's like some 'hood genius GPS. That's how she wound up at that motel, followed—without her knowledge—by Day-Day himself who'd, seeing she was okay with our crew, parked across the street "in case another nigga was needed."

DayDay was next level and if I ever needed an undercover gangster genius he'd be the whole list.

Looking out at the dark, I felt Yazmeen's hand cover mine. Malcolm between us, she leaned her head on my shoulder, leaving me with an ill-defined feeling. Not that I hadn't embraced her repeatedly, but there was something different in my sitting in the back of that car holding Yazmeen. I felt intimacy. That crazy ordeal bonded us in a different way. Even so, there was some elusive separation preventing a seamless fit. That didn't keep my whole self from burning with the truth that my arms were the haven she needed; and that I was where I was supposed to be, doing what I should be doing—covering, protecting. I felt destiny.

By the time we entered her home crowded by welcoming, celebrating family, Yazmeen was weaving on her feet, nearly delirious from more than two-and-a-half days without sleep.

Trust when I tell you Malik—asleep on the sofa in his grandmother's arms—bounced up the moment we walked in, screaming, running for his twin. Jumping up and down, he was hugging, yelling, "See, MoMo! I told you Jesus said He was bringing Malkie home."

Only God.

Guiding Yazmeen onto that plus-size purple chair, I stepped back, allowing India to cover she and the twins with a blanket. Watching them cuddle up, I smiled for the first time in God knew how long.

"Tav...thank...you." Like Malik, she was virtually talking in her sleep. Kissing her temple, I followed Yazmeen's parents to her front door, praising God the insanity had ended.

"This family can never repay you for your part in our grandsons' return."

I accepted Mister Williams' firm handshake and sentiment. But when Missus Williams stepped onto the porch, her words left me in disbelief.

She squeezed my hands while saying nothing. When she managed to speak, emotion had her choked up. "I know things aren't right between you and my daughter. But please don't give up on her. She loves you like nobody's business."

Returning Missus Williams' embrace, I found it ironic that, twice now, someone felt the need to highlight a love Yazmeen had yet to own or admit. I accepted her family's heartfelt appreciation, but I was disinterested in thanks and a broken relationship. I wanted my woman.

Son, trust the process.

Climbing into 'Zalo's whip, I thanked my cousin, amazed that he and Smokes doing time together had proven a blessing in disguise, helping to recover an innocent child caught up by his father's life of lies. Gonazalo. DayDay. Smokes. Not that I was about that life, but they gave me a whole new appreciation for criminal-on-criminal connections.

That was the last thought I had before being shaken awake in my parents' driveway.

Stretching and exiting 'Zalo's whip, I headed for the house needing my daughter's loving hugs and innocence.

Two weeks later and a world away in the Caribbean, everything that transpired felt like a finale of some dark, deadly 50 Cents drama produced for T.V. Except the aftermath was too raw, real.

Despite their pediatrician's examinations resulting in a clean bill of health, Yazmeen had to temporarily withdraw the boys from daycare. Traumatized by their ordeal, they were afraid to be away from their mother and wouldn't let her leave when attempting to drop them off those first few mornings. Subdued and withdrawn, they had nightmares and refused to sleep unless in her bed. Decreased appetites, crankiness, and occasional bedwetting aside, they heavily relied on twin code—their safe language that excluded a potentially dangerous world. I caught snatches of their real selves whenever Nubs video-chatted. Oddly enough, they didn't withdraw from me, as if I had some special twin pass allowing my entry. Still, I fully supported their mother's enlisting a child therapist, and resuming her own counseling with First Lady. The horrors required help in the healing.

Pulling my suit and Nubs' dress from my leather garment bag, I hung them in the hotel closet, not wishing away the time it took to heal, but wondering if Yazmeen and I would ever be right again.

I was there for her and had her unquestionable gratitude. The past two weeks had been all about her tending to the twins' needs, and rightly so. There'd been neither time nor opportunity to confront the rift and the wreck of our relationship. Honestly? That mess that went down that day of her child custody case had been the blow-up, not the beginning. The elusive, unwanted entity we had yet to deal with had always hidden itself between us.

"Daddy, I still get to dress in the room with the ladies, right? Auntie Joy invited me."

"Yes, ma'am."

Nubs squealed and did a little dance. With Que's nieces already in the role, the soon-to-be newlyweds had made Nubs an honorary flower girl. Joy had added to her excitement by inviting Nubs to dress in the "ladies' suite" with the bridal party. Now Miss Grown was going through her travel bag yanking out shoes and socks and whatever else she needed.

"'Ey, slow down before you rip something."

"I don't get to walk down the aisle with Malcolm and Malik, right?"

They were slated as ring bearers, with two of Que's nephews on standby should—in light of everything—the process prove overwhelming. "Right, but you'll have your own special seat up front behind Mama 'Cretia." Joy's mother had immediately taken to Nubs, adopting her like she had the twins, as a surrogate grandchild. "Do you remember what to do if the boys look scared?" I squatted in front of her when she nodded. "What?"

She demonstrated. "I say their names real quiet and wave so they see me. Then I smile and say 'You can do it!' I'ma add two thumbs-up so they know I'm proud of them."

"That, ladies and gentlemen, is Aniyah Chanel...what?"

"Alvarez," she yelled, running to a wall-mounted mirror. "Daddy, you like my hair? It's almost like Miss Yazmeen's. At least the front is. And it's not dry or crooked."

India's intricately flat-twisting the crown ended in an explosion of an afro puff on top that had been two-strand twisted and released. My daughter standing in the mirror shaking her well-moisturized and non-crooked natural curls had me laughing. "Your hair's on fleek."

"What's that mean?"

"It means repack your bag, and let's go if you want to be an honorary anything."

Maybe it was the tropical scenery of St. Thomas. The scents of bougainvillea, jasmine, and that wide, rolling ocean. Or the romance of the occasion. It was all of that but, unquestionably and invariably

Yazmeen. Posted up as one of two best men at the back of the aisle waiting for the maid of honor, I was floored as she approached me.

Daggone amazing in a one-shoulder, persimmon orange, floor-length dress kissing those crazy curves with sexy, sophisticated elegance, clearly she'd succumbed to that island magic. She was care-free, floaty. The distance to me wasn't much, yet enough to experience a surreal moment imagining her walking an aisle as my wifey-to-be.

Whoa...wait. Not happening.

Our disconnect dictating internal distance, I extended an elbow, wrapping her hand about my arm and headed up the aisle for my bwoi's nuptials.

The service was succinct, lovely. I think. I wasn't one hundred, seeing as how my focus continuously drifted to Yazmeen, and hers to me. That magnetic attraction between us remained undeniably deep. Unfortunately, it continuously collided with that invisible entity I could only call distrust, or hidden things claiming too much space, pressing me farther away from the woman I craved and wanted with my everything.

Anchoring my attention on the ceremony, I heard the minister's, "A union built on anything less than pure trust and absolute honesty is one that will shrivel and most certainly fail."

Shaking off the cold creeping down my spine, I kept my eyes on Que and Joy feeling as if the man of God had just pronounced a benediction for me and Yazmeen.

My dude was lit with love. Pictures and posing. Kissing whenever forks were clanked against glasses. Dining and dancing. Through all the typical reception shenanigans, it was evident Que and Joy had it: a love destined for everlasting.

I was pleased for them. Still, some internal thing had me squirming and yearning just from being around Yazmeen.

Throughout the ceremony and reception, she was never far from physical reach. Her fragrance was a tempting mist, her presence and essence triggered me. But that distance thing?

I'm done with this!

We needed a private conversation, and if necessary, confrontation. Whatever it took to resolve our mess and find our way back to us. Determined to let things rip however they wanted, I pushed away from the table ready to get in it when Nubs ran up.

"Daddy, dance with me."

Nubs being Nubs, it was a command, not an invitation. Dragging me onto the floor, that girl's wild gyrating had me wanting to buy her a crate of rhythm.

"Oh, oh, I need to use the bathroom," she decided halfway through a "Single Ladies" throwback. A group of sisters, including the woman I needed, was reenacting the video's routine and had the guests cheering. "Hurry up, Daddy."

My semi-distraction—watching Yazmeen—clearly interfered with my daughter's bladder needs.

By the time Nubs finished her business, a slow jam was playing when we reentered. I couldn't tell you the song if my life depended on it. All I recall is some dude, hands at her waist despite her trying to move away, grinding on Yazmeen and wanting me to catch a case.

My whole life got tight seeing another man touching her as if he had rights.

Ready to wreck mess, I was stalking across that dance floor when Que appeared out of nowhere. A halting hand flat against my chest, he spoke so only I could hear. "Don't do it, T."

That yanked my chain. Never would I disrespect my bwoi, his bride, or their celebration by making a ratchet scene. Even if I wanted to clown, I couldn't. Hadn't our relationship slipped into category "undefined," if not finished? Yazmeen was, essentially, a free agent. I had to accept that despite wanting to snatch dancing dude's crossed eyes out the back of his sanctified preacher's pack-of-hot-dogs-having neck.

"Take a walk. Cool off," Que advised.

I nodded. Still, I was stuck staring across the way at Yazmeen who'd stopped dancing the moment she saw me. Hot Dog Neck tried that hand-on-her-waist-pull-her-back-to-the-dance routine, but she was out of reach, moving towards me. With every step she took I felt heat.

For all our disconnect, the fire hadn't faded. But for the first time, for me heat wasn't everything.

Pulling away from her gaze, I headed to the children's zone where Nubs and the twins were laughing and playing with other little folks. Quickly communicating with Que's teenaged cousins assigned to kiddie care, I exited needing space, air.

Thankful the reception was held at our hotel versus elsewhere on the island, I headed for my room floored by the fact that sexual attraction alone was no longer enough.

I want love.

"Tavares..."

Damn!

Needing her to not come for me, I might've kept it moving except something in her voice had me stalling. Turning and watching her approach, I tried not to get caught. By beauty. By sexy. Or her alluring clash of power and vulnerability.

"Give me a minute," I cautioned, wanting to escape being aggravated by her femininity—that warmth and fragrance I found effortlessly seductive when she stopped all up on me.

"Can we talk when that minute's finished?"

"Naw, baby, let's not."

"Yes, baby, let's," she countered, hands cradling my jaw, lifting on tiptoe until our mouths practically met. She whispered on unsteady breath. "You deserved these words so long ago. I love you, Tav."

Her kiss was butterfly soft. Some stubbornness in me wanted to resist, but those lips weren't having it. She poured her whole self into it until, what started as delicate, wound up on ten. Pumping the brakes on what was on its way to quasi-erotic, she slowly released me. We were both breathing erratically.

"Please." Lacing her fingers with mine and leading us to her room, she didn't wait for my reply. An emboldened Yazmeen, baby girl knew she had me. But I couldn't help flipping it a bit once her room door was opened.

Standing aside and allowing my entrance, she turned, closed the door, and was caught off guard when I backed her up against it. That was it. I didn't touch. I didn't kiss. I let my eyes do what they did, silently conveying every hunger I had while slowly taking her in, top to bottom and up again. Palms anchoring that door on either side of her, I leaned in, jaw next to her chin. Traveled down her neck. Without my mouth touching her skin. Inhaling and gently exhaling in those places I knew were sensitive. Letting her feel nothing except soft streams of breath until her breasts did this rapid rise and fall against my chest, articulating her sexual responsiveness.

"My minute's finished." My mouth near her ear had her shivering. "Talk to me, *Mariposa*. Tell me everything."

CHAPTER TWENTY-FIVE
MIRROR ME
Yazmeen

We couldn't remain in that room. Not with fire, desire, and a bed constructed of sturdy-looking wood. Truths were necessary. Not fornication and overdue orgasms.

Relocating onto the enclosed lanai, I offered to call room service, but he was disinterested in food, delay, or avoidance. The twins shocking me with their wanting to stay and play—and Mama 'Cretia and Mimi 'Velle assuring me they had an eye on them and they'd be okay—left me without excuse for a conversation long delayed.

Get with it, Yazmeen, if you don't want to lose this man you say you need.

He already knew some things. Like my growing up a "good little church girl" dedicated to saving herself until marriage to my high school sweetheart, Darrien, who chose getting his freak on, impregnating and marrying a fellow med student. And that my heart being a whole hot, broken mess had me drinking and winding up in Royal's bed while in the Bahamas shooting *Purrrfect*. Plus, my coming home de-virgin-ized and pregnant.

Tight jawed and unwilling to even say Royal's name, his voice was quiet but no nonsense. "Dude was a rebound situation. I get that. What I'm not getting is the secretiveness still attached to it," he commented, removing his tuxedo jacket and draping it over the back of his chair.

Taking a deep breath wasn't enough. I sipped bottled water and called on Jesus, knowing the truth was a risk I had to take. "Royal and Sydney were married when I got with him."

He processed that before asking, "Did you know that at the time?"

I answered honestly. "I didn't."

"When and how'd you find out?"

Seated across from each other, I forced myself not to look away. I was done with shame. "After 'I Do'...when I was five months pregnant. Sydney showed up out of the blue *with* their marriage license. Royal couldn't deny it."

That pushed Tavares back in his chair. "Hold up. You're saying dude was simultaneously married to *both* of you? As in he's a bigamist?"

"Yes."

"*Aww, shiii—*" Stopping abruptly, he rubbed a hand over his goatee and down his chest before sitting wide-legged and sliding lower in his chair. Quietly he questioned, "How'd you handle that?"

Ticking each act off with a finger, I reminisced. "I went ballistic. Threw things. Punched him in the jaw. Went crazy-lady-in-movies and tried cracking a vase against his head but missed. Put him out. Dissolved the union. Tried filing for alimony, but seeing as how we were never legal that didn't go so well. I could've pressed criminal charges, but," I shrugged, "I was mortified and just wanted the whole thing done with ASAP without dragging my pregnant self through legal processes. I had some vindictive moments after the twins were born and didn't allow him to see them, but I didn't press bigamy charges because I didn't want to be responsible for taking my children's father away from them. Now? I'd *love* to see him on lockdown and could kick my own behind for having acted that kind of ignorant."

His silence allowed me to continue.

"When you confronted me about putting up with his stuff, I was resentful, but you were right. *I have* repeatedly excused Royal's behavior and not thoroughly checked him because…"

He softly finished when I didn't, "You blame yourself."

"I do…*I did*," I corrected, refusing familiar tears, disgusted at how I'd allowed Royal to use my embarrassment and guilt as control mechanisms. "That entire situation was scandalous, but I took any subsequent fallout as some sort of holy retribution. Any mess I went through behind him? It was payback and punishment for getting drunk and having sex outside of marriage, then mocking the holiness of matrimony by exchanging five cent vows with a virtual stranger. So, I dealt with it."

His touch was gentle when he leaned forward and laid a hand on my knee. "You know those were the enemy's lies, right? He's an accuser and comes to condemn and harass; while, the Lord convicts our hearts and forgives."

Covering his hand with mine, I admitted, "Knowing versus living can be challenging when you think you deserve whatever you get."

"True that."

Looking away from his intense stare, I leaned my head back, admiring brilliant stars beautifying the tropical night. "Royal and I were never in love. We barely knew each other outside of my dancing with industry celebrities."

"Why'd you marry him?"

It was hard, yet cathartic telling the man I loved the secrets I'd told no one outside of immediate family, my "bestest," and First Lady. The compassion and care in his touch allowed me to go even deeper with him than I had with them.

"Shame. Embarrassment. Compensating for my actions."

My parents weren't the type to pressure us, but at the time I was their only unwed daughter, and both my sisters had experienced success. Sasha with her Essentials, and India as a hair care specialist. Me? My dance career had started off promising but stalled; my fiancé had left me for another woman. I felt like a failure and disappointment, and wasn't only devastated, but angry at God and heaven.

"I was a twenty-eight-year-old virgin. I'd kept myself. Followed His Word. And that's all I had to show for it? Broken dreams and a cheating ex-fiancé?"

Twenty-eight was too old for stupid; still, when the original dancer slated for Pantha's *Purrrfect* fell through and I received that call within days of my breakup with Darrien, I jumped at escapism and spent that island weekend sexing in a hurricane of hurt and rebellion.

"I remember flying home after the video and falling on my knees. Crying. Repenting." I whispered my worries: separation from Christ. Sexually transmitted diseases. Pregnancy. When that final fear became a confirmed reality, I reached out to Royal. "I was floored when he suggested marriage...*after* suggesting abortion." Which wasn't a moral option for me. Single-parenting was intimidating. I wanted my children to grow up in an intact, two-parent home. Hesitations and reservations aside, I accepted that whack proposal versus questioning his switchery and motives. All in the name of mitigating the stain of being an unwed, pregnant Christian.

That there won every award for dumbest of the dumb things I'd ever done. Trying to right my wrongs, I'd been determined to make things work even though we weren't in like or love.

Royal relocated to Sacramento from southern Cal and moved into my apartment. Working on his music producer dreams, he traveled extensively.

"Might sound crazy, but I actually didn't mind his traveling."

Truthfully, I wasn't ready for that overnight add-water-and-mix marriage, preferred my independence, and quickly found out my baby daddy wasn't a man I'd even want to befriend.

"I was close to five months pregnant when he was away one weekend promoting a concert. I get home from thrifting for baby things, walk into the apartment and some random chick's cooking in my kitchen."

"Sydney?"

I actually laughed. "Mmm-hmm. If I had popcorn, I'd serve you some and have you sit back for the rest of this ratchetness."

Unlike my ignorance, Sydney knew about the marriage and my existence. All that travel Royal did? I later found out it was primarily to see Sydney. So in love with him, Sydney was willing to do whatever, including communal, polygamous living.

"You're serious?"

"I am." Tucking my legs beneath me, I stretched a kink from my back before continuing. "I put Sydney out my kitchen. Had the locks changed. Called and cussed Royal sideways. He gets back from his trip two days later, key doesn't work, and he sees I'm not playing. Hell hit the fan." I had to ignore Tavares' leaning towards me, brows knitted, looking worried, just to keep it together when saying, "We got into it—"

"At five months pregnant."

My voice was barely audible. "He never touched me. I was the one swinging. But..."

When I fell silent, he pulled my chair forward, centering me between his legs. His lifting my chin forced my focus onto him. "I'm your safe place, baby. Talk to me."

"Royal used me. Sydney wanted kids, but couldn't have any. So, they..."

I wasn't aware of the tears until he wiped them from my cheeks. "Take a breath, *Mariposa*. You got this."

I inhaled slowly. "When they saw I wasn't okay with being their baby-maker, or us living some sister wives, three-legged marriage together, Royal offered me surrogate money. Like I was Rent-a-Womb or something." I let the air gush out of me while looking into those beautiful brown eyes and articulating past pain. "When I refused, he claimed he never wanted children. He never even wanted me sexually."

"What did he want?"

"My pregnancy to prove his masculinity."

"Meaning?"

"Tav, Royal's gay, and Sydney's a man."

That whole Royal experience? It was all about him struggling with his sexual identity, not accepting himself, and not wanting to come out to his family. He was hardcore. Street. He struggled to reconcile that with his homosexuality. His denial contributed to multiple separations from Sydney and dating transgender while searching for clarification. Broken and tossed aside, I was the perfect pawn for his misuse-erization.

"In a sense, I guess we used each other," I conceded, hating memories of his subsequent rejection. "I was rebounding. He was fighting." Once married, Royal showed subzero interest in sexual relations with me. Pregnancy hormones had my body out of sync. Between that and extreme morning sickness, sex wasn't primary on my plate. Even so, I was confused, internalizing and misinterpreting his disinterest as an indicator of my sexual inability. "I was an inexperienced virgin when we hooked up. His sexual dissatisfaction? He had me believing it was *all* me...and that had I been," I drew air quotes, 'female enough,' I might've 'cured' him of his same-sex wants."

Looking at me in disbelief, Tavares cussed. "He actually said that?"

"Yep," I confirmed, thankful—in hindsight—that we'd discontinued sex. After everything went down, I was petrified enough that I might've exposed myself to some STD that weekend of repeat copulation and conception. Royal claimed he never practiced unprotected sex. The condom broke. We conceived. (Despite his claims, I still tested regularly. Thank the Lord, my sexual bill of health was and is clean).

"Can I ask a question without sounding insensitive: how'd all of this affect you...sexually?"

His question was an arrow in a bullseye.

"My femininity took a hit. He had me questioning who I was as a woman. I didn't feel desirable. I even questioned my own orientation, thinking something non-hetero must've been present for a gay man to get with me."

"Baby, that was his deceitfulness, not your identity."

"I know, sweetie, but you asked. And that's what happened. Not to mention..." I had to swallow "...I was so messed up and needing affirmation, I got with a college friend a couple of times after everything happened. We did some…things…but for some reason I couldn't let him penetrate me. As far as actual intercourse, Royal was the only one. So…that, my love, is my sad, sorry story," I said, checking my phone when it pinged. We'd earlier texted Velle to check on Aniyah and the boys. She responded, assuring us they were having a ball. Opening a music app, I launched my smooth groove playlist before placing my phone on a side table and facing Tavares, wishing I could read his thoughts.

I'm not sure what I expected when a long silence evaporated, but his taking my hands and kissing them wasn't it. "That's all I wanted, *Mariposa*, for you to finally trust me enough to tell me what I already knew."

"Huh?"

"Sydney's Adams apple, boo. The hands. The feet. I peeped all that the day of your custody hearing."

Stunned, I remembered that three-way call when Royal had taken the twins and his taunting Tav about our getting together physically when I delivered that ransom money.

I doubt you could manage.

Tav's response at the time seemed strange. Now, I got it. "You knew."

I sighed, realizing I'd barricaded myself, unnecessarily so, and nearly lost a good man. All behind fear, embarrassment. Embracing shamelessness, I threw out the rest. "Another reason Royal repeatedly pressured me to dance professionally? Operation money for Sydney. Yes, that," I confirmed, making scissor motions with my fingers when he looked down at his lap. His horrified expression and squirming in his seat had me grinning.

"Why does that roadkill think you're his private ATM?"

"Roadkill Royal!" I straight up laughed. "He marches to the beat of his own demented drum. And as I said before, he's delusional in thinking I owe him."

A breeze drifted in, fanning the loose end of a wavy braid piled atop my head across my face. When Tavares reached to push it aside, I took *his* hand and kissed it. "Thank you for listening, and for all you've done for my sons. The bracelets…" My children's abduction terrorized me. I had recurring nightmares, but was doing my best not to smother them with hyper overprotectiveness. With Royal still out there somewhere, daily I prayed, asking protection and grace. The boy-themed bracelets containing microchip locators gifted by His Fineness helped in the aftermath. "I have no words for the wonder that you are. And I'm beyond sorry for withholding myself from you."

"I acknowledge what you're saying, but I don't need gratitude." His voice held no malice. Yet, my conscience was pricked. "I knew you didn't trust me with all of you, and that I couldn't force that or fix whatever it was you'd gone through."

Squeezing his hand, I knew my concealing myself had hurt him. I was the first woman he'd opened his whole self to, and I'd withheld me, sitting on my deepest truths as if I couldn't trust his steadfastness.

"I'll always appreciate you for opening me to this love thing, Mariposa. I hope I gave you my best, and that you enjoyed what we had because I did. *Sin arrepentimientos.* No regrets."

Untucking my legs from beneath me, I sat up straight, preparing myself for whatever was next. My heart was pounding, afraid he'd had enough. "But?"

"But we're not doing this hidden heart, hidden part thing. I don't need to be all in your everyday business. You're a grown woman. But do you remember my saying I want to know the Yazmeen you don't let people see?"

I did.

"That's all I'm asking."

Sitting, staring into his eyes, the slow jam serenading us from my music app caught my attention. First hearing it a few days following our big blow-up, I'd switched songs midway because something in the melody felt haunting, profound. Glancing at my phone, a shiver ran through me seeing the title. "Not Ready." Self-protective and snared by my past, I *hadn't* been ready for Tavares. Or for full love and absolute living. But the temporary loss of my children tossed my heart completely open. I was no longer interested in self-preservation keeping me from this man. A changed woman, I dared to ask, "Where do we go from here?"

His voice was gentle. "You have me, Yazmeen. I can't go back to my old okey doke of wanting a woman's body, not her soul." His suddenly asking if I'd forgiven myself shook me.

"I have. Finally."

"Can you give me your everything?"

"Sweetie, I *need* you to have me. Completely. I remember not wanting to live without my sons. Well, I don't want a world without my boo." Leaning into him, I cupped his jaw, my thumbs massaging his goatee. "I love touching you."

"Then go'n and touch me like you love me, Miss Yazzy Yaz."

"I really do," I murmured against his lips, "love you."

I couldn't kiss him enough. Trust, I tried. Needing the taste and feel of his tongue, I opened his mouth with mine. His hands at my waist, moving to my hips, had me warming and easing into him. I actually lurched forward when he disconnected and stood, abruptly.

"What?"

Extending a hand, he pulled me to my feet. "Let's get busy."

"Boo, we're not getting in that bed," I joked, as he led me indoors.

"Baby, I won't necessarily need a bed when I finally get to do what I want to you."

Using one of Grams' words, I called him 'fresh.'

He laughed, before sobering and repositioning me in front of him where we'd stopped opposite a wall mirror.

"What're we doing?"

"I'm curious if you know the Yazmeen I see?"

"Really, baby?"

"Humor me." Positioned behind me, he laced our fingers. "Yazmeen Renee Williams, meet my beautiful butterfly." Releasing one of my hands, he trailed a finger up and down my spine. "She's exquisite. Gorgeous. Loving. Feminine. Hecka sexy."

I shivered as his broad hand skimmed up my arm and across the skin bared by my dress, as his lips brushed the back of my neck.

"She's God-fearing. Virtuous. Sensuous. She exceeds my needs."

His lips against my throat were wreaking havoc on my nerve endings. "Tavares..."

I tried turning. He clamped a hold on my waist, kept me forward-facing.

"Can I continue?"

Nodding, my eyes started tearing.

"I love her strength. Her spirit. Her mind. Her genuineness." His touch was tender as his knuckles grazed my cheek. "Physically? She's devastating. Every part of her has me sprung. My only issue? I can't have her the way I want. Not without being her husband."

"And if you were?" I barely breathed, entranced by his touch and lush litany.

Gripping my hips, he pressed his firm, anatomical response against me. "I'd give her *everything*. Slowly. Deeply. Until she felt me in the center of her whole self and screamed, cried, was...*absolutely*...satisfied."

Lips against my shoulder, his hardness at my behind, that man had me needing to wring out my panties. "And once she was?" I husked.

"We'd repeat. However. Whatever. Wherever she wanted." Sucking my throat, he had me moaning. "Roadkill lied, *Mariposa*." He paused to breathe against my ear. "You're more than enough woman."

Call me useless, because I was. My only ability was reclining against the strength of his chest, leaving him to some kind of sensual wickedness.

Do not ask precisely what he did. All I know is his hands were on my hips, gripping my thong through my dress. He pulled, gently tightening the fabric, causing the crotch to create friction against the hot jewel between my legs while his mouth possessed my neck. Sucking. Branding. Rubbing.

I couldn't prevent a gasp. Or arching my back and hissing like a cat as he went in on that torment. I didn't even realize I was close to climaxing until someone knocked.

"Mommy!"

The twins banging on the door froze me momentarily. "Oh my God..."

Feeling like Jezebel Junior, I rearranged my clothing and my hair, trying to look holy.

Tavares actually laughed. "Bae, relax. The boys won't know you were in your room getting nasty with a man."

Swatting his arm, I opened the door to my sons accompanied by one of the teenaged "care providers," and Princess of the Crooked Afro Puffs.

"Hi, Daddy!"

That man was instantly at my back, an arm about my waist, using me to hide his semi-erection. "Hey, Nubs."

"Miss Yazmeen, Miss LaVelle texted to tell you I was bringing the triplets."

I laughed at the kids' new moniker. "Thank you."

"We appreciate it," Tavares added, handing Quinton's cousin a folded bill.

Unfolding it, she whooped and strutted off, waving new money.

"Mommy, we had fun!"

"I'm so glad, Malcolm." My heart rejoiced, seeing my babies happy.

"Now, we're hungry again," Malik announced, looking at me like I needed to get busy making food appear.

"Who wants room service?" Sir Sexy asked, still at my back.

"What's that?"

"You push a phone button and people bring any kind of food in the whole wide world that you want," Aniyah answered the boys' simultaneous question.

"Cool!"

"Go wash your hands, please," I instructed our cheering children, waiting until they'd left the room to whirl on Mister Magic. "You're on restriction from touching, kissing, licking, or even looking at me."

Heading to supervise bathroom behavior, I left him laughing.

Bellies stuffed, tired from the days' festivities, the kids snuggled between us on an oversized lanai chaise. Jazz streaming from my phone, they were asleep within minutes. Lying on my side looking at Mister Magic, I interlaced our fingers, positioning our hands against the cushion, above the kids' heads. Without projecting into the future, I relaxed and enjoyed our cozy unit.

Jazz and the ocean providing sweet melodies, we were too content.

"If I don't move now, I'll be asleep in a minute and I need to get this little girl to bed."

I glanced at Aniyah curled up against me. "She's already asleep. She's welcome to stay. You are, too. But only here. With the kids between us," I added at his mischievous grin. "And no touching."

"Yeah, I touched you enough. Question? Is your body normally hypersensitive, or is that compounded by abstinence?"

"Got to sleep, Tav."

"No shade, baby. I'm just saying. And I'm sure not complaining." His voice lowered. "I like you that way."

"I'm going to renege your sleepover invitation."

His fingers were warm against my throat as he laughed. "You got that neck tagged."

"Huh?"

"You have a hickey."

I sat up half-way. "I don't."

"Yeah, bae, you do. I do designer work. It looks good on you."

"You got my neck telling our business?"

"Yep. Let these fools out here know you're off limits. That neck belongs to T-Alva Alvarez."

"You're a mess. But I love you."

"Say, huh? I can't hear you."

Leaning across sleeping kids, I punctuated every word with a kiss. "I. Love. You."

"Convince me. Do all that again and add some tongue to it."

I gladly kissed him the way he wanted before laying back, feeling cherished, protected as he resituated the blanket over all five of us.

My bestie was on her honeymoon and not caring about text messages any time soon, but just to mess with her mind, I sent a text the next morning.

I slept with Tavares.

Technically, I had. Even if fully clothed and in the company of our children.

CHAPTER TWENTY-SIX
THAT ROCK
Tavares

G uess what, Mister Tavares!"

"What, Malik?"

"Our used-to-be daddy's going to hell."

"Malie, he's going to *jail*," Malcolm corrected. "But he has to get out of the hospital first."

"And when he does, he'll probably have to live in a wheelchair like GramGram," Malik decided, looking wide-eyed and innocent on our video chat, "'cause Mister Sydney hurt him in his back."

"GramGram doesn't have to live in a wheelchair, "Malcolm clarified, an arm around his twin's shoulder. "Mommy says GramGram only uses one because she's lazy and crazy."

Lord, don't let me laugh.

"Can Aniyah come over after her soccer game tomorrow?"

I'd enrolled Nubs in soccer to teach sportsmanship and to burn up some of that wild child energy. "Thanks for the invite, Malik, but your mom's still not feeling well." From my vantage point it was the combined fallout from recent stressors and running herself ragged with her dance group's upcoming fundraiser, but Yazmeen came down with something a few days back. It flattened her to the point she'd been unable to travel with *Step-N-Style* to their Monster's competition in the Bay Area. Their winning second place had lessened the disappointment. "How about next weekend?"

"Okay. We'll wait."

"Mister Tavares, MoMo let us bake Get Well cookies for Mommy yesterday."

"Really? What kind?"

"Peanut butter oatmeal raisin with gummy bears and graham crackers. We saved some for you."

"Umm, okay. I look forward to trying one," I falsified.

"You can't," Malik apologized. "We accidentally ate them."

"They were good," Malcolm added, "except the eggshells."

Hearing *Mariposa* reentering her room kept me from hollering-laughing.

"Okay you two, off my bed and go get your homework out of your backpacks."

"Bye, Mister Tavares." Malcolm waved, complying. "Mommy, you should close your bathroom door."

"Whatever you did really, *really* smells like death and destruction."

I had to mute my laptop microphone, I was howling. When I sobered up, Yazmeen was sitting, arms over her chest, sporting a surgical face mask and too large pajamas—braids all Pocahontas-ish, trying not to laugh. I unmuted myself. "Hey, baby. How're you feeling?"

"Whatever, Tavares." She was mask-muffled. "You don't care."

"That's not true." I still had the chuckles. "I'm just glad I'm not there."

"I don't like you."

"But you love me."

"I really do. And thank you for Miss *Abuela's* soup."

In my family, my grandmother's *asopaos* had near-legendary healing properties. Knowing she always kept some frozen, I'd asked if she wouldn't mind Yazmeen benefiting from it. She didn't, having fallen in love with *Mariposa* when they first met. Reina had played delivery person for me.

"You're the sweetest."

"Yet you were about to let your kids kill me with those cookies."

"Oh, my Jesus! *Babe.* Never again." She sneezed.

"Bless you."

"Thanks. My babies' whole hot mess cookies're probably why my stomach's killing me."

"The twins ate some and they're fine."

"That death and destruction was selective—'destruction' being their new word of the week."

I laughed. "On the real, how're you feeling?"

Even makeup-less, she was my beautiful butterfly, but that usual Brown Girl glow had slid beneath some paleness. Her eyes were puffy, and she was nasal as heck.

"Better, but not my best. Lethargic. Congested," she remarked, lifting that mask meant to keep the kids germless and sipping the sugar-free sports drink I'd recommended for electrolyte replenishment.

"And now you have me drinking this liquid death."

"You can thank me later," I commented, feeling sympathetic. Her illness was minor compared to the ish that transpired after returning from Joy and Que's Caribbean wedding. Things had gotten over-the-top ridiculous and, of course, involved Roadkill.

M.I.A. since abandoning Malcolm, Roadkill lived up to that name and nearly killed someone last week.

It started as a routine traffic stop. Eluding kidnapping charges, dude fled the scene. A high-speed chase ended when his reckless weaving in and out of traffic caused two other cars to collide head-on—resulting in one of the drivers being air-lifted to a hospital.

Roadkill? Like cats, dogs must have nine lives because he escaped.

But as *Abuela* liked to say, *"Todos los perros mueren alguna vez."*

All dogs die some time.

He might've eluded law enforcement, but Sydney wasn't playing.

That's where dude was headed when ish transpired.

He'd found out where he was holed up and was *en route* to deal with the deceit and Sydney's taking that ransom money. He tried that beatdown routine. Left Sydney flat on the floor before tearing up the space looking for that cheese. That's when Sydney went in with a bullet, shooting him in the back and ending that. Now? Sydney was on lockdown and Roadkill was still in I.C.U. with a prognosis of possibly living life as a quadriplegic.

"How do you feel about that?"

"I don't." She adjusted her oversized pajama top. "I made it clear to his mother that I wish harm on none, but I can't ingest any more Roadkill Jones. She's welcome to communicate with her grandsons, but he no longer exists for me. I'm done. Hold on a moment..." She disappeared from view long enough to close her bedroom door. "I don't want the boys overhearing. The woman airlifted from the collision passed away this morning."

"Awww, *man!*"

"I know. It makes me sick just thinking about it. Sweetie, she was a young mother with four children." She wiped a tear. "I can't even imagine what her family's experiencing."

We shared a momentary silence. "If it's alright by you, I'll ask Reina to look into making a charitable donation in her name, or reaching out to the family to see if they need help financially. Whatever the donation, it'll be from both of us."

"Thanks. I'd like that. So, now on top of kidnapping, he's complicit in her death and looking at vehicular manslaughter."

"I'm curious how the penal system handles disabled inmates."

"Brandon thinks Royal's mother'll seek an injunction citing the system's inability to provide proper care in hopes of preventing incarceration if he's convicted," she answered, sliding her fingers into her braids and massaging her scalp before exhaling. "Who knows? Forgive me if I sound heartless, but who cares?"

I couldn't fault her being human. She'd gone through more hell with that ex than merited. "And Sydney? I'd think he'd catch some clemency as an abuse victim—"

"Right! But he shot him. *And* taking that ransom money made him complicit. Did the authorities return it yet?"

"Yeah, what was left."

"So sketchy."

"Trust, with all the stank on it, I didn't even want what came back. In fact, let's pray sanctification over it and round out that donation to the victim's family with it. How're the twins?"

Removed from their prior daycare, she'd enrolled them in a Montessori-like program more focused on academics than the former fit. More importantly, they offered topnotch safety and security.

"The art therapy's helping. Their therapist is pleased, and they almost seem their normal selves; but I'm opting on a few more sessions. Don't you need to leave to get Aniyah from school?" she asked, suddenly removing that surgical mask and coughing so hard her eyes watered.

"You okay?"

Nodding, that cough continued until ending with a loud toot.

"Wait! Did you pass gas?"

Her laugh was phlegm-filled. "Leave me alone, Tavares. I'm sick."

"God, thank You I'm not there to inhale it."

Hard laughing, a wad of mucous flew from her mouth onto her chest.

"Oh, *heck* naw! You is the *nastiest* woman I know."

That sent her sideways, wheezing and laughing with tears rolling. She tried righting herself, but had to lay a moment, cracking up. "You just made my headache worse." She sat up, giggling, probably wondering why I was slack-jawed and saying nothing.

Swallowing hard, I managed, "Uhh...bae...you might wanna handle that too big pajama situation."

Looking down, she saw what I saw. All that falling over laughing had her top tangled sideways and fully exposing the lushness of her left breast. *"Oh, God!"*

Propping a pillow in front of her laptop camera, she fixed herself—blushing when returning. "I'm so sorry, Tav."

"I'm not."

"I bet. I'd better go. The boys should've been back with their homework, so no telling what they're into."

"Yeah...alright."

"Tav. Eyes up with mine."

Grinning, I refocused, still seeing her breast in my mind. "I'm just saying, baby. Them is some pretty tit—"

"OMG, I can't do premarital phone sex with you, boo."

I laughed. "Okay...holla if you need anything."

"I will. Tell Aniyah I miss her."

"Mos' 'def. Yo, bae."

"Yes?"

Leaning in, I whispered, "For real. I love your breast. Can I accidentally see its twin?"

That earned me a disconnect.

Chuckling, I got up from my home office desk. Bojangles, who'd been asleep on his bed across the room, was ready to roll when hearing my keys. "Sorry, Bo, but you gotta go to your crate. I got things to do." Crating him, I headed out happy, salivating and praising God for dark chocolate-dipped nipples.

Seated in a line of cars in the pick-up zone of Nubs' school, I wrapped up communication with Reina. "I appreciate you, Cuz, for handling that."

"Not a problem. I just wish there was more we could do for the family besides a donation."

"We can keep them in our prayers."

"For sure. Do you have the date for Yazmeen's getaway?"

After all my baby had been through, I wanted to treat her to a spa weekend all to herself. "Two weeks out, after she's feeling better. I'll confirm and get back to you."

"Sounds good. It's on your calendar, but don't forget Lex needs to move your conference call back an hour on Monday."

"Got it. Thanks again and have a good weekend." Disconnecting just before the school bell rang, I had a few seconds to respond to a text from Lex, confirming an upcoming board meeting for *Athletes & Academics.* Seeing Nubs' teacher approaching the gate, her students behind her like a trail of ducklings, I got out and opened the right rear door. Waving, her teacher high-fived Nubs and cautioned her against running.

"Hi, Daddy!"

Squatting down, I scooped her up in a hug. "*Hola, Princesa.*How was your day?"

"It was great! We had story time and a man came from some kind of something. I forget what he called it, but it's where they take care of butterflies."

"Habitat?"

"Yes! He brought some butterflies with him, and they were really pretty." She was all excitable as I helped her into the back. "And we had cupcakes for Kailey's birthday, but mine sat on timeout," she admitted, hopping into her seat and buckling up.

"Why? Talking too much?"

She had the decency to look semi-embarrassed. "Yes. But I got quiet when I saw those cupcakes coming."

Giving her my best no nonsense stare, I closed the door, shaking my head.

"Yo, Nubs, wanna go to a fancy store with me?" I asked once situated in my seat and pulling away.

"Sure! What am I getting?"

"Do I reward bad behavior?"

"Not yet."

Glancing in the rearview mirror, I managed not to laugh.

Despondent, she was quiet. "Who're we shopping for?"

"We need to pick up something I ordered for Miss Yazmeen."

She suddenly had her life again. "Yay! What're we getting her?"

"You'll see."

My daughter well-fed, bathed and in bed, I chilled in the game room that night, watching the Lakers bringing heat, trying to make the playoffs when an alert scrolled across the screen.

Incoming call from Quinton Daley.

Pushing the remote, I accepted the call via the T.V. "Why you calling me, Mister Three Weeks Married? Don't you have wifey work to put in?"

He chuckled. "Trust. I'm handling Joy Daley. Or maybe she's handling me 'cause I need vitamins."

We cracked up.

"How's that married life?"

"Thank God, it's good. We're adjusting. Settling in. Thought I'd peek out from beneath these sheets and check on a homey. How you? Last I saw, you were ready to go in on a wedding guest for dancing with your woman."

"That wasn't dancing. That was grinding."

"True. So, you and Yazmeen: you good? Or you gone?"

"We're good," I answered, sharing a few things and bringing him up to speed.

"I accept cash, check, and food stamps."

"For?"

"That prayer I put in. That's what brought y'all through. So, show that appreciation with a love offering payable to Quinton Daley, your ride-don't-die prayer warrior."

"For sure. Soon as you open a church or become a bishop. On the real," I continued when we'd finished chuckling. "Que-D., it's done."

"What?"

Sitting up and grabbing Yazmeen's gift from the coffee table, I opened it. "I bought that rock."

"Serious?"

I nodded as if he could see through the T.V. screen. "Yeah. Not sure when, but the knee is bending."

"Look at God." He ended a brief silence with, "Well, welcome to the copulation club."

"Man, you stupid."

He snickered. "On the real, T., big congrats."

"Don't celebrate 'til she says 'yes.' And whatever you do, don't tell your missus."

"I'm not that kind of stupid. So, you nervous? Not just about the proposal, but marriage?"

"Mos def. I need to take my time and do this right 'cause I'm—"

"One and done," we finished together.

"Everything'll be fine. You're a good man and you've been blessed with a right woman."

"That she is. And, hold up. It's," I glanced at my watch, "past midnight in Philly. You're calling me because?"

"Man, pregnancy has Joy's internal clock all off. She's in the kitchen making homemade caramel sauce."

"Y'all got ice cream?"

"Ice cream, nothing. My baby's pouring that caramel on me. Get that sticky licky."

"Bruh, bye."

"Peace."

We disconnected, laughing.

Holding Yazmeen's ring, I studied it, impressed by its clarity and cut of the ring I'd had designed, hoping it fit and that she'd like it.

Father God, I'm moving in line with Your timing, right?

I'd been praying about us even before Mariposa and I got in deep. Those prayers intensified after returning from Joy and Que's wedding. I had heaven's confirming peace, and all of me screamed she was my one. I simply wanted to know I was moving in God's timing, not my own.

Whoever finds a good wife obtains favor from the Lord.

Memory might've misquoted Proverbs 16:22, but its depth still moved me. God had kissed my life by gracing me with Yazmeen. Having dismantled her own wall of secrecy, she'd been open, newly accessible in amazing ways, filling our relationship with a richness that didn't previously exist. Our conversations were deeper. Our moments together sweeter. We were real about us and spent time studying the Word, conversing, digging into each other's souls and psyches. She had quirks and idiosyncrasies like me, but the woman was beyond belief. A boss mother to her sons, she'd embraced Aniyah with real love. She treated me with respect and tenderness. She was legit. Authentic. She was my woman, my friend, enhancing my life in ways I'd never envisioned. I'd done what I could as a man to show her she was valued, cherished. But above things attainable through cash money, I was ready to put the work in, wanting her to have everything.

The only thing left I have to give is me.

Assuming a position that had become my normal I got on my knees, bowed my head, and prayed. Simply.

"Father, if I'm the right one for Yazmeen, please let her accept and be my wife for life."

CHAPTER TWENTY-SEVEN
BASKETBALL & BALLET
Yazmeen

M ommy, is gumbo still your favorite?"
"Mmm-hmm," was the best I could do. It was too early
on a Saturday to be discussing food. My whole life was
about to be hyped with *Step-N-Style's* fundraiser that night. Head half
under my pillow, I resisted wakefulness, preferring delicious dreams
starring Mister Luscious.

After recovering from whatever that recent illness, I'd been treated
to a solo weekend of blissful pampering at an exclusive spa resort in
Sausalito courtesy of my love who'd met me there for dinner my final
night, treating me to the luxury of his time. Any and everything wanted was mine. I'd come home spoiled, thinking I had a right to sleep
in on weekends. Which was what I was doing when the twins entered
my room with culinary questions. Their quick exit allowed me to get
to round two with Tavares. Or so I hoped. Instead, my mind did some
trickery with a fish dream.

Knowing old wives' tales claimed fish dreams were connected to
babies, I didn't trip. Sasha and Brandon had just welcomed our newest
family addition, my niece Deja, and Joy was pregnant. That dream had
nothing to do with me unless it was the Holy Spirit's forewarning I was
about to immaculately conceive. Or maybe the smell from downstairs
filtered into my psyche.

"Mommy, we're using tuna since we don't have crab or shrimp."
"Okay..."

Weeks of preparing for tonight's performance, and getting my little family back to normal after that child abduction chaos, had been
intense with art therapy for the kids and rehearsals for me. I must've
been truly exhausted, because the boys' check-ins weren't registering.
Much later, deep asleep in more fish dreams, I felt someone shaking my
shoulder. "Hmmm?"

"Mommy, do you put sugar in stew?"

"No..."

"Told you, Malkie."

"Malie, it's 'roux,' not 'stew!'"

"Roux! Blue! We still can't use sugar!"

"Okay, we'll use honey. Let's go. We left the microwave boiling."

That terminated my sleep paralysis. "What's happening?"

"We want you to never get sick again—"

"And you need good nu-tri-tion," Malik slowly, carefully managed, "for tonight so we're boiling your breakfast."

Lord, I prefer to live until lunch.

"What's that smell?" Hopping out of bed, I headed for the stairs.

"It's your gumbo," Malcolm proudly informed just as a smoke alarm sounded.

That had me running downstairs and into a war zone that used to be my kitchen. I had two words. "Jesus. No."

My microwave was kicking out funky fumes and flames.

Grabbing the extinguisher, I went in like a weekend firefighter. Flames extinguished, I disarmed the alarm, opened windows and turned on the exhaust fan before standing there shook by twin shenanigans. *"What the heazy!"*

"That's a bad word, Mommy."

"Are you mad 'cause we cooked without permission?"

"Malik, you did it! You didn't say 'vermission.'" Malcolm's hugging his twin left me wishing I could barter them both on Craigslist.

"Honeys, just what? Why?" Milk carton on the stove, canned goods on the floor, ice cream and cheese in the sink, and the refrigerator door and practically every cabinet and drawer open, my kitchen was a whole wicked wreck-of-a-mess with unidentifiable matter oozing from my microwave, smelling and looking like oppression and madness.

I had to sit.

The twins immediately worked their way onto my lap.

"Mommy, are you mad?"

What I was, was speechless. I had to take several breaths. "I'm glad you wanted to do something nice for me, but we follow rules in this house for a reason. No playing in the kitchen is one of them."

"We weren't playing. We have real chef aprons."

"And we didn't waste anything. We put leftover tuna *and* a whole new tuna can in our gumbo pot. Unopened!"

I let crickets chirp for me. "Go upstairs and get my phone, please."

I dispatched them, needing an alone moment and a hazmat team. I heard India.Arie's classic, "Steady Love," on their way back in.

Loving the lyrics, that basketball reference, and the video with her and David Banner, I'd replaced Mister Magic's former ringtone with my girl's sexy-smooth groove.

"Mommy, it's Mister Tavares."

"Steady Love" had stopped by the time Malik handed me my phone, which was good because I was beyond an intelligent conversation. Launching my camera, I videotaped twin-created chaos and texted my mother the video with a caption: *I Blame MoMo.*

My mother's constantly letting the twins create edible havoc in her kitchen had resulted in this.

"Okay, we're playing the clean-up game. I'll handle the microwave. Everything else is your responsibility. You have six minutes. If the timer beeps before you finish, I win."

"If we win, what do we get?" Old Man Malcolm had the nerve to ask.

"The ability to live here. Ready. Set. Clean this mess!"

They took off. I sat and sideline supervised *after* grabbing a spoon, that carton of ice cream from the sink and treating myself to a breakfast of champions.

Twin trickery had us rolling up to my parents' ten minutes past my targeted time. I didn't even bother to do my normal walk them inside. I sent the boys ahead, waiting at the curb until my mother opened the door. She took one look at me and busted out laughing.

"Inez Williams, I'm through with you," I hollered heading to my side of the SUV.

"Love you, too, Babycakes. See you at tonight's finale."

"MoMo, we made gumbo for Mommy!"

"But the microwave burned it up."

"That's okay. You can always try again," my mother had the nerve to encourage.

Waving and driving away from The Sabotaging Three, I put the music on for *Step-N-Style's* Summer Dance Fest finale, dancing out the routine, mentally.

Needing to raise that one-thousand-dollar-per-student down payment for next year's summer camp, my troupe had brainstormed the Summer Dance Fest—a four-week series we'd launched the first Saturday in June. The first three Saturdays had featured a different era each week: Harlem's Cotton Club scene, disco, and New Jack Swing/90s. Tonight's final performance was devoted to Hip Hop.

The prep proved so intense that I'd had to get a sub to take my Zumba classes. Despite the demands of choreographing four different routines, I loved that my dance kids had come up with the idea of opening each program by performing a piece reflecting the evening's era before we opened the floor, turning the facility into a virtual dance club for audience and community. And only music and dances indicative of the era or theme of the evening were permitted. They'd even talked me into quick, on-the-spot tutoring each Fest night: teaching a dance step or two from the era so participants had something to work with. I hadn't exerted the energy this project demanded in years, but seeing various generations coming out and enjoying themselves while aiding a wonderful cause made it worthwhile. But let me not lie: a sista was tire-RED!

After Joy's wedding, we'd jumped feet-first into it. Since the end of April my life had been consumed by all things dance. My only exception? Mister Magic's birthday weekend.

The "triplets" and I served him brunch on the beach, an afternoon of miniature golf and laser tagging, ending with a surprise party at his parents' that Miss Perla helped me coordinate. Gifting him a basket filled with his faves—white cheddar popcorn, sports drink, chocolate-covered pretzels, and turkey jerky—I'd included a black tee made by Kyle, India's husband, featuring one word in holographic lettering: Taken.

"You staking territory and letting chickenheads know," he'd teased. "Try me!"

Other than that celebratory reprieve in May, production prep was everything. Choreography. Costumes. Lighting. Deejay. Security. Promotion. Ticket sales. Refreshments. Community volunteers. Sponsorship and donations. And whatever else cropped up. We had to handle it.

There was absolutely zero way we could've pulled it off without the support of Mister Clarence, community volunteers, and *Step-N-Style* parents or guardians. Thankfully the community center had an incredible events coordinator, Miss Evelyn, who'd adopted the project without hesitation.

"What could really make this pop, Yazmeen, is endorsement or participation from community leaders or even a local celebrity."

I had that.

Thank You Lord, for a good man.

That night in the Caribbean had opened me completely—leading to deeper, richer experiences for Tav and me. I felt good not being closed off and secretive; loved being able to do nothing except love and trust him. Freedom was everything.

Despite the busyness of the month intruding on Team Tav-Yaz time, he'd been completely supportive, even offering to pay my troupe's twenty-thousand-dollar tuition in full.

"I will write that check just to get back moments with my woman," he'd half-jested.

Not wanting to deprive my dancers of a sense of accomplishment, I'd declined. We fussed it out but eventually compromised, agreeing if there was a shortfall, he'd make up the difference. Further inspired by Miss Evelyn's local celebrity comment, I'd devised a concept for the grand finale night involving my troupe, Mister Magic, and his *Athletes & Academics.*

"You mean something like The Harlem Globetrotters meets the Queen's formation?"

"Exactly, sweetie." I'd modify our Monsters routine a bit, add a little more stank on it, while incorporating space for Tav and his ballers to do drill routines to rhythm and beat. "There'll be moments with *A&A* solely on the floor and we're sidelining and vice versa. But we'll end with everyone together, bringing it."

"Sounds like controlled chaos," he'd teased, "but I'm here for it." Seeing it fit within *A&A's* mandatory community service requirements, he'd approached eight of his best students. Thankfully, they'd been completely with it. With Tav and team in the Bay, and me and mine in Sacramento, the collaboration got interesting, but I'd provided a videotape of our Monster's performance for them to rehearse with. Miraculously we'd managed.

I love me some him.

I'd kept his involvement a surprise, simply telling my dance kids we'd have a new addition for finale night. Showing up for the initial rehearsal, my troupe had gone ballistic seeing Tavares and team entering the gym for practice. Screaming and running across the floor, they'd forgotten to be teenaged cool and unaffected. Mister Magic and I greeting each other with a kiss had them play-fainting and acting straight up stupid.

"Go, Miss Yazmeen! Go, Miss Yazmeen!"

Motor mouthed Kia's "Miss Yazmeen done leveled up!" became Tavares' favorite tease.

Pulling into the community center parking lot, I laughed at the memory while wondering how I'd been roped into performing.

Without question, my troupe had loved the *A&A-meets-Step-N-Style* concept. To quote them, it was "symbiotic." But their suggesting we open the routine with something the audience wouldn't expect and deciding on ballet and that I *would*, not "should," bust out my pointe shoes and tutu for a solo that segued into their piece, had me pausing.

"Come on, Miss Yazmeen, if you don't, we won't!" they'd threatened.

"It'll be fierce 'cause ain't *nobody* expecting pointe shoe action from a sista with a badunkadunk trunk."

Kia's unsolicited comment caught her three laps around the gym, but I'd conceded they were onto something.

Parking and turning off the finale music, I sat, eyes closed, head back before praying.

Abba Father, thank You for having this finale thoroughly in the palm of Your hand. Bless every participant, and those who've graciously supported it. Let everything go according to Your divine plan. In Jesus' name. Amen.

Grabbing my bags from the front passenger seat, I exited my SUV sipping an imaginary cup of optimism and telling myself everything would be everything.

Me, myself, and I lied.

Preferring a quiet moment to center myself before being swallowed by performance energy and frenzy, I'd scheduled my team to arrive an hour after me. I especially needed quiet considering the twins' gumbo nonsense, but walking into the center, I was met by overzealous troupe members.

"We're early, Miss Yazmeen. You need anything?"

Yes, time away from all critters under the age of twenty.

"Give me a minute, but for now check in with Miss Evelyn," I answered, heading for the women's locker room as "Steady Love" erupted from my cell. "Hey, sweetie."

"Hey, we're *en route*—"

"But?" The tone of his voice alerted me.

"A player called saying she's sick. Another's a no-show. Trust he's catching heat when I get at him next week, but right now we're two players short."

Breathe, Yazmeen, breathe.

"Babe?"

My head hosted a party about this Basketball & Ballet concept being idiotic from jump, and why I should've vetoed its foolishness.

"The symmetry might be off, but we've got this." The soothing in his voice was designed to keep me from climbing atop a one-story building and jumping.

"Okay. Lemme think on it. I love you. See you when you get here."

Disconnecting, I wanted to kick something but needed to save my toes for tonight's pointe shoe pain.

Lord, I need—

Before I could finish, two names dropped on me.

I dialed hurriedly. "Taj, can you and Snook be at the community center by four?" Hearing Mister Magic was in, they'd stopped by that initial rehearsal and were familiar with the concept. I explained the situation while texting the video we'd taped that first day, praying baby brother would act as stand-in.

"You putting dollar bills behind your begging?"

"Not, but I heard Kia thinks you're cute."

"Peep you in a few."

"Study the video!" I barely managed before he disconnected. Taj was a knothead, but with basketball he was about the business. "Thank you, Lord." Storing my bags in a locker, I rushed out to find more dance troupe members on the scene.

So much for pre-performance peace.

Between helping Miss Evelyn set up the at-the-door ticket table for those who hadn't advance purchased, to escorting the caterer to the dining hall, or positioning marquee posters they were all over the place, noisy and animated.

"That's Miss Williams right there." One of my dancers pointed a deliveryman my way.

Depositing two large boxes at my feet, he had me electronically sign for a delivery.

"What is this?"

"I don't know, ma'am, you'll have to open it."

I did, and my mouth hung open seeing beautiful, black t-shirts emblazoned with *Step-N-Style* on the front and #we'sewild on the back—the women's cut featuring rhinestone text and the male, foil—all in our signature turquoise and silver. The paid-in-full invoice showed my brother-in-law, Kyle's, company.

"*Snap*! Miss Yazmeen, you bought us shirts for tonight?" One of my dancers was immediately digging through the box.

"I did not."

"Who did?"

I already knew. "Mister Alvarez."

"These're boss."

"They are. Do me a favor. Have someone help you carry these into the gym and separate them by size and gender so we can pass them out once everyone gets here." Yet again, I thanked God for a good man. He'd already arranged the catered light, pre-game meal for my troupe, now this. Not to mention getting *A&A* board members Derek Stallworth and Bilal Shaheedi—NBA shooting guard and power forward, respectively—to participate tonight with an autograph signing. Viewing the poster of Tav, Derek, and Bilal near the door, I had to agree with a dancer's hollering,

"Tonight's gonna be lit! One hundred."

Wanting the finale to be a positive experience, I tried not to go Debbie Allen-ish at missed steps and Snook's going left a few times when he should've moved right during our final run-through. Still, my eye must've been twitching for Mister Magic to lean down and quietly speak in my ear.

"It's gonna come together, baby. Everything'll be alright."

Inhaling his optimism, I thanked everyone for their hard work and gave final instructions. I was about to dismiss them to their respective locker rooms to get dressed when Tav asked me to hold up a minute.

"Mind if we pray?"

"Of course not," I answered, excusing any who chose not to participate for personal or religious reasons. Amazingly, everyone remained, linked hands, and bowed heads as Sir Sexy prayed for the evening's success. The 'amen' had us huddled, hands on hands in the middle, chanting,

"*A&A*!. *Step-N-Style*. We'se wild.Woot, woot!"

Dismissed, the kids left leaving me inhaling peace in the arms of His Fineness. "You good?"

"Mmm-hmm," I murmured against his chest. "Can I stay right here?"

"How long?"

I looked up hearing something so not casual in his tone. There was a light in his eyes I couldn't identify. "Is always okay?"

"Absolutely." His kiss confirmed it.

Entering the dark gymnasium, the rhinestone sparkle on my black leotard and tutu were my only illumination. Positioning myself, I waited for the spotlight to come on in perfect sync with the opening bars of Andra Day's "Rise Up." It was a throwback speaking volumes to my soul, my body as the chanteuse's gritty, uniquely beautiful voice pulled me into the arms of my passion and purpose. Like a testimony and declaration, I danced. For the woman whose life ended because of Royal's idiotic actions. For Sydney and every person subjected to the brutality of domestic violence. For children stripped from parents and never returned. I danced for me. My loves. My life. My liberty. Ending with one leg vertically extended to the ceiling, I held the position as the house lights came up, and the music dramatically changed to a Hip Hop beat flaring with driving rhythm as *Step-N-Style* swarmed the space. Spinning off the floor, I ended my piece with a *grand jeté*, feeling as if I'd been divinely possessed.

Standing on the sidelines watching, trying not to mar my makeup, I patted tears streaming my face with a tissue someone handed me, not just waiting for my queue to return for the final forty-eight counts, but enjoying.

The crowd was crazy. Whistling. Screaming. Totally into *Step-N-Style*, and eating up Tavares and ballers' dribbling, passing—weaving in and out of my dancers' formations. Soloing or on the floor together, the two groups were call and response. Synergistic. When four of my female dancers stole the balls, did a little routine with them before being lifted by the ballers and dunking, the audience went ballistic. Counting down my musical queue, I returned to the floor, doing Hip Hop with my troupe while on pointe. Trust when I say my toes felt broke and every muscle in my thighs and behind hated me, but we were krunk and the audience ate it up. When the final beat exploded, it was outdone by a standing ovation that felt like pandemonium.

My dancers and Tav's ballers were just as bad, high-fiving, dapping, and cheering. Me? I had to wait to be lowered from Mister Magic's shoulder where I sat perched, ankles crossed, like some prima donna while he spun a basketball on a finger of his free hand. Who thought that geriatric cheerleader ending up, I couldn't remember, but I went with it. Based on the crowd's response, it was effective.

Back on my feet, I hugged my man as Mister Clarence joined our group, cordless mic in hand. Waiting for the ruckus to calm, his face was split with a grin.

"*Sacramento! Did these young folks bring it?*"

That retriggered the cheering.

"I'm old enough to have had more than a few trips around the sun, but I've never seen anything like that. *Step-N-Style? Athletes & Academics?* You did that," he praised, as Miss Evelyn walked onto the floor with a framed plaque and a bouquet. My eyes got misty hearing Mister Clarence highlight my dedication and determination. His words moved me. When he finished, my troupe starting hollering,

"Speech! Speech!"

Public speaking was so not me. Quickly, sincerely, I thanked everyone, *Athletes & Academics*, and my *Step-N-Style* parents for entrusting their children to me. Turning to acknowledge Tavares, I was surprised he wasn't present.

"Okay, now. It's not easy to lose a six-foot-six man."

The audience laughed.

"Here he comes," one of his ballers announced as the group parted down the middle as if planned.

"*Mommy!*"

"*Miss Yazmeen!*"

Aniyah and the twins, approaching with Tavares, released his hands and ran to me.

"Mommy, you did good!"

"Thanks, Malcolm." I hugged all three. "Y'all are too cute." They sported white basketball jerseys His Fineness had obviously ordered with "Team Tav-Yaz" in turquoise and silver foil lettering.

"T-Alva Alvarez, everybody!" Mister Clarence announced on the mic as Tavares stopped in front of me.

Expecting thunderous fandoration, I was shocked by absolute silence. Too busy scanning the audience, wondering what the heck was wrong, I missed Taj and Kia lining up the children.

"*Mariposa...*"

Turning to Tavares, I noticed two things: uncustomary nervousness, and the black, zipped-up workout jacket he was wearing. Taking my hand, he stood a moment, looking at me as if searching. His question caught me off guard. "How long do you want us?"

"Huh?" When he repeated himself, I stuttered a response. "Forever, I guess."

"You guess?"

"No. Yes. Forever with you is what I want. Sweetie, what's going on?"

His voice was low and I felt his hand shaking. "You've been dancing your way into my heart since the night we met. Before then, I thought I had 'it.' But you're my 'what's missing.' You open everything inside of me. I want you to infinity. Yazmeen Rene Williams..."

Blood rushing in my ears, I watched as Tavares stepped back and the kids jostled their way between us, grinning until Taj whispered, "Turn around, Short Stack and Twinny Twins."

Synchronized, our "triplets" turned, each bearing one extra-large word on the backs of their jerseys. I read aloud, frowning. "You. Will. Marry."

It felt like some old testament prophecy.

"Ohmigawd, they're in the wrong order," Kia hissed, switching Aniyah and Malcolm. "Read it again, Miss Yazmeen."

"Will. You. Marry..."

Unzipping his jacket, Tavares was the missing link. Emblazoned across the front of his matching jersey was, ME?

When he removed a ring box from his pocket and lowered on bended knee, I lost all my sanity. I cried that ugly girl cry, snotting, bent at the waist, sounding like a cow with cramps.

"Yazzy, you better answer that man!"

Recognizing Sasha's voice from the stands, I screamed, *"Yes!"*

The audience, who'd somehow been in on it, erupted as did our children, including the basketball- and dance-adopted.

My hand was trembling when Mister Magic held it, slipping on a channel-set white gold engagement ring with an *insanely* beautiful princess-cut diamond. "I lov—"

Cupping his face, I kissed him before he could finish. We held that kiss as he stood, wrapping his arms around my waist and pulling me against him, leaving me feeling as if heaven's best had made my heart its residence.

CHAPTER TWENTY-EIGHT
PEANUTS & PEAS
Yazmeen
Three months later…

A wedding in three months? Who does that? Team Tav-Yaz. The night of our engagement, well-wishers congratulated out of one side of the mouth and asked the wedding date out the other. Wanting to sit in bliss before making such decisions, we allowed ourselves a week of euphoria before calendar consulting.

My initial thought was a year-long engagement as my church typically recommended. Mister Magic's response had been, "Bae, we won't make it."

As in maintaining abstinence.

I'd cracked up, but the concern was legitimate. We weren't marrying for sex, yet a prolonged engagement wasn't necessarily to our benefit. We considered spring of next year only to encounter calendar conflicts.

My parents had paid for a cruise next April; his parents were Hawaii-bound for their anniversary in February, his oldest niece would be out of the country on a study abroad program January through June, and Joy and Quinton were relocating to Atlanta somewhere in there. That had us backtracking to the remainder of this year.

Holidays ruled out November and December.

"What about October? That's a year after we first met."

"That's three months away, Tav."

"And?"

My incredibly beautiful fiancé either believed in wedding fairies or wanted our guests sitting poolside in my parents' backyard snacking on hog head cheese and cracklings.

I ran down the list: venue, caterer, photographer, flowers, music, attire, an officiant, marriage license, etcetera.

"Hire a wedding planner, *Mariposa*."

"With what? The eighty-dollars-and-fiddy-two-cents in my account 'til payday?"

"Why're you sitting on eighty dollars and saying nothing?" That led to a fiscal argument. Demanding my bank info in order to make a deposit, he disarmed my pride with, "Listen, woman, I'm not that man balling around on fleek while his fam's struggling."

"Technically, we're not family until married," I'd teased, grateful, but not wanting him to feel like a Sugar Daddy.

"Hence the ceremony. Small. Large. I don't care. All I need is 'I Do' and a bed." Leaning sideways, he missed being swatted with a sofa pillow while launching a bank app and studying me before angling his phone, displaying an eight-figures-before-the-decimal-kind-of-balance that had me sliding off the sofa, play-fainting. "Woman, you're cray."

Maybe, but I had to lay a *long* time, catching my breath, seeing more money than I could thrift shop on 'til Jesus came back. "Tav, we need a pre-nup," I'd suggested as he helped me up. "The eighty-dollars I'm bringing to the game needs protecting."

Laughing, he'd kissed me. "We can talk pre-nup, but divorce isn't in my vocabulary. And no brag, but that's only one account, so hire a planner, Yaz. Did you have the ceremony you wanted the first time?" he asked when I protested.

Standing in Pastor's office, pregnant, marrying someone who was shady and wondering if I was crazy didn't qualify.

"Then get what you want. The wedding's my gift to us."

"You're denying me the thrill of thrifting or finding a boss wedding gown on consignment?"

"I am. Get the gown you want. Fresh, baby. Not secondhand. Level up."

Wedding planning aside, our lives were fast-tracked after our engagement. Still—whether through regular prayer, long conversations, or studying God's Word—we made concerted efforts to grow as one, spiritually, emotionally; and agreed on the benefits of premarital counseling.

Scheduling sessions with Pastor and First Lady was like being in school with weekly sessions and homework on various subjects. Communication. Conflict resolution. Division of labor. Finances. Intimacy and sex. Trust. Decision-making. Relationships with relatives. Family roles, dynamics, and discipline. Being good stepparents in a blended family was extremely important to us, so we included the kids in a session. Of course, that was comical, and segued into a private discussion about extending our unit.

"I prefer a year to acclimate and enjoy us before trying to get pregnant. I'll be thirty-four, you thirty-seven. Prayerfully, we won't have trouble conceiving."

Sir Sexy had gotten up in my ear, whispering, "Baby, bring the eggs, I'll bring the opportunity."

Laughing until I cried, I looked forward to the try.

We had birthdays and births those busy months. I celebrated the big thirty-three. A month later, in August, Joy and Quinton became the proud parents of our godson, Micah; my babies became big boys and turned four—or "two plus two" as Malik proudly informed. Aniyah, my Crooked Puffs Princess, made the big six in September. The time was busy with blessings. Including packing the twins and me for our move to Tiburon after the wedding.

I'd miss working for Pastor and First Lady but, armed with their glowing letters of recommendation, I'd begun applying for positions near my new home. Of course, Mister Magic gave that "You don't have to work if you don't want" speech. Accustomed to taking care of my little family of three, I felt the need to contribute something. Even if it was little more than the tuition for the boys' new school. Thankfully Aniyah's charter started at Pre-K, and we'd enrolled them so all three would be on one campus. The twins were excited about starting once Sir Sexy and I returned from our two-week honeymoon.

"You're still not telling me where we're going?" I asked, riding to our "Final Freedom" festivities a week before our wedding. With neither of us interested in traditional bachelor/bachelorette shenanigans, our families had devised a joint, family-friendly celebration.

"Nope."

"How do I know what clothes to bring?"

"You won't need any. We're booked for two weeks of butt-naked-ness."

"You're a mess."

"I'm saying. Pack light like I did. It took a whole two minutes."

Posted beside him in his vehicle—Mister Bojangles crated in the rear, the triplets on the backseat—I paused what I was doing to look at him. "What're you bringing?"

"Passport, toothpaste, toothbrush, mouthwash, dental floss, some anti-ashy, and deodorant." Glancing at our chattering kids in the rearview mirror he lowered his voice. "That...and the lubricant we probably won't need since you already have me dripping."

"I cannot with you."

"Yes, you can, baby," he countered, squeezing my thigh. "I can't wait 'til you do."

I lowered my voice. "We agreed: no sex talk, no sexual situations before the wedding."

"Did we?"

Grinning and shaking my head, I returned my attention to the large, coffee-table-ready photo book I held, enjoying our engagement pictures. "This save-the-date card was brilliant." I loved the basketball, pointe shoes, and wedding rings composite conceptualized by our wedding planner, Carissa Daniels. The concept of melding our talents was evident in our engagement pictures as well.

Our attire reflecting our eggplant and ice blue wedding colors, the photographer—my godsister, Kayla—hadn't kept things formal, capturing playful and candid shots.

"Kids, this is adorable."

The backseat chatter ceased and it was suddenly, "What? I wanna see!"

Holding up the book, I displayed a shot of the triplets—Aniyah in a gorgeous lavender dress with the boys in short-sleeved white shirts, pale blue shorts and suspenders—sitting after the shoot, legs swinging, giggling, making a game of eating their snack of string cheese.

"Awww, look at these." Photos of Aniyah fixing Malik's bow tie and her squatting, tying Malcolm's blue and white Buster Browns, sat side-by-side. "Niy-Niy, you're going to be a good big sister," I praised, using the nickname I'd given.

"I know, huh?" she agreed.

"She's already really good at being bossy."

Correcting Malik for his comment, I pinched Tav's thigh for laughing.

Turning the pages, I smiled at a photo of Aniyah and I reclining on an elaborate chaise lounge, her lavender dress complimenting my eggplant beaded gown clutching every curve and showing too much cleavage for my comfort. Mister Magic, of course, loved me in it. About as much as I loved him looking like edible yum in a pearl-gray tuxedo, rocking sneakers like only he could. His pics with the boys in their tuxedos with short pants and similar shoes moved my heart, knowing my sons had been blessed with a man who loved them as if his own flesh.

"This is my fave of us." Angling the book for him to glimpse while driving, I showed Tav the photo of him in his tux behind me, me in blinged-out pale blue leotard, tutu, and pointe shoes. Eyes closed, me on pointe, faces angled towards each other, my arms were in fifth position, my hands cupping the back of his neck as he embraced my waist. It was loving, intimate.

"Yeah, that's sweet," he agreed.

"I like those best, Miss Yazmeen," Aniyah chimed when I turned to the casual shots of everyone in sports gear. Tav and the boys in white basketball jerseys featuring pale blue text of Team Hers, complimented the Team His cheerleader uniforms Aniyah and I rocked—she in sparkly sneakers, me in rhinestone stilettos with crystals decorating the straps criss-crossing up my calves—everyone with basketballs in varying shots.

"I'ma need you to bring those shoes on the honeymoon," Sir Sexy commented, glancing from the road at the photo book.

"Mommy, what do people do on honeymoons?"

"Ohhh, they talk and eat," I answered Malcolm, leaving Tav snickering.

"Well, why can't we go?" Aniyah wanted to know.

"They only serve grown folks' food," her father answered, "and I'm eating Miss Yazmeen without company."

"*Tav.*" My neck cracked, snapping my head towards him.

Realizing his blunder, he laughed so hard he nearly had us swerving. "Bae...I meant eat *with...*"

"Just drive. Say nothing," I scolded, reminding self to tell him I'd never experienced oral sex.

Wanting to celebrate without time constraints, we'd rented a private, gated residence further up Tiburon's coast large enough to accommodate both of our families. Owned by Tav's business associate, the home had been vacant since August as the owners were out of the country. Situated on two acres, the architect had taken advantage of the land's natural terrain to add varying levels to the one-story structure. That six-bedroom, four-full and two-half baths home with cathedral ceilings soaring above an elaborate foyer had me slobbering. With formal living-, great family- and dining rooms, chef kitchen, library, sauna/steam room, recreation/media room, in-home gym, and mother-in-law "cottage" larger than my townhouse, the place was magazine-worthy. And beyond my fantasies. Magnificent views. A circular driveway, four-car garage. Manicured lawns. An outdoor kitchen/BBQ area, and basketball court. All lent themselves to unimaginable luxury. But that master bedroom suite with a terrace overlooking an infinity pool that seemingly dipped into the ocean did it for me.

"Can you imagine living here?" Holding my two-month old godson, Micah, I buried my nose in his neck, inhaling his fresh baby scent enhanced by Sasha's new organic baby products.

"Not even," Joy answered. Putting her cake business on pause until relocating to Atlanta, Joy had flown in last week, giving her and Micah time with Miss Lucretia; Que flew in this morning. We were honored at their standing with us as matron of honor and best man.

"I can," Tav's cousin, Reina, insisted. "I just need two billionaire boyfriends, or a problem-free bank robbery."

Surrounded by a cultural hodgepodge of family—by blood and pending matrimony—I laughed with the women about me. Tav's crew was as loud and crazy as mine, but from day one, his family had embraced the twins and me. I didn't take their love or acceptance for granted. I appreciated his aunts, sisters, cousins, but Miss *Abuela*—a feisty little jewel who'd pretended to speak no English when we first met—was one of my favorites. As was Miss Perla. She treated me like a daughter, not someone stealing her son, extending herself in building our relationship independent of Tavares. She and the mature women of their clan had treated me to a "Welcome to the Family Tea." Her sharing photos of Sir Sexy left me laughing at how fat he'd been as a baby.

She'd confided her heartbreak of complications in her seventh month of pregnancy and her twins being delivered by emergency ce-sarean, prematurely. "Taia might've survived if we had today's medical advances." Tav's twin had been born with spina bifida, deformed kid-neys, and underdeveloped lungs. "When the doctor told us my baby wouldn't make it through the night, I demanded the twins be placed in one incubator together. They needed each other." She showed me a picture of two impossibly tiny infants—tubes sprouting from everywhere—holding hands. "Efren spent three months in Neonatal

I.C.U. But look at him now! No one believes he was a preemie."

Recalling that conversation, I looked across the immaculate lawn to the basketball court where a game had just ended. Men were headed in our direction, no doubt, ready to throwback another round of edible abundance. I smiled seeing Sir Sexy, in basketball gear, running from Mister Bonjangles and the twins who were laughing, chasing him.

Good Lawd, that man is delicious.

"Anybody want anything?" Reina was up and headed for the buffet station.

Kissing my godson's tiny hand and watching my man, slick with sweat, looking like everything I needed, my eyes roamed and traveled to forbidden regions. Stuck and staring, I reached for the snack bowl on the table next to me. "Thanks, Reina, but I'll stick with honey roasted penis. It's divinely good. Probably 'cause I haven't had any in a minute, but I'm triple-loving it."

A cloud of laughter exploded around me, leaving me sitting, wondering who drank happy tea.

Joy was screaming-laughing. *"Ohmigawd, Yaz! I can't."*

"What?"

"Peanuts, Yazzy. Not penis," India corrected, head back, holding her stomach.

"I said 'peanuts.'"

"You said honey roasted *penis*," LaVelle countered, face streaked with hilarity tears.

"I didn't."

"You did," Reina and another of Tav's cousins confirmed, barely able to breathe for laughing.

"I'm telling your week-from-now husband," Sasha teased, holding my newborn niece. "Tavares!"

I slapped a hand over her mouth as His Fineness rerouted towards us. "Whaddup?"

"Big ups, T-Alva! Your fiancée *triple-luvvvvvvssss* peanuts." Simulating orgasmic bliss, LaVelle's stupidness left sister-women falling out all over again.

"What did I walk into?"

Handing Baby Micah to his mother, I hopped up, thankful the matriarchs were seated far from our nonsense. "Disregard all lunatics." Grabbing his hand, I steered my love towards the food table, ignoring sister-women's crazy cackling and rebuking curiosities about honey and the human anatomy.

Tavares

I'd had more than enough of strip clubs and bachelor party lap dances, and needed neither to celebrate my "last go-round" as a single man. I was good with the family-centered festivities our clans insisted on hosting. But wanting my baby to enjoy her last weekend as a "free woman," I'd made arrangements. She was clueless to the fact that she and her crew were spending the night at this mini-mansion. What they did was up to them, but I had tomorrow's activities on lock. The boys would share the day with me, Nubs, and family while *Mariposa* and company were treated to a Brunch-Cruise-on-the-Bay-and-Spa-Day followed by lingerie shopping for my baby, ending with she and her girls up front at a Lizzo concert. Okay. Truth. That lingerie spree was for me. I couldn't wait to see my wife in her half-naked glory.

"What're you up to?"

"Nothing." After a day of food and hoops, I was chillaxing, my baby beside me staring like she could see our wedding night on my mind.

"That nasty grinning is saying something different."

Kissing her temple, I laughed. "Aww suki suki, looky looky!"

"What?"

"Your cousin's tryna push up on mine."

She followed my head nod in Reina and Jamal's direction. Seated at the outdoor bar, they'd posted up chitting-and-chatting.

"I keep telling Reina Jamal's interested. She doesn't believe me, for whatever crazy reason."

Watching them, I decided, "They'll work it out," as my middle brother, Rico, rolled up.

"Yo, little bruh, let me holla at you real quick."

"What about?" I demanded. Rico was a clown known for tossing folks in pools at family functions.

"Boy, get up and come on. Yaz, he'll be back. *Maybe.*"

Giving him stank eye, I kissed Yazmeen before walking into the house, Rico's hand clamped on my shoulder, keeping me from escaping whatever his trickery. Turning and closing the patio door,

I glanced back to see a squad of women suddenly surrounding my fiancée. Fam was definitely up to something.

"Welcome to the King's Court," Rico announced, dramatically opening the rec room's pocket doors, revealing a line of men standing in silence, including Taj and other young bucks.

"What's this?"

"No questions. Just sit." He pushed me towards an empty chair in the room's center.

"Hi, Mister Tavares."

"Hey, Twins." Sitting, I smiled at the boys holding Mister Williams' hands, wishing I knew twin talk and could communicate telepathically to know what was happening.

"Tavares Joselito Efren Alvarez, did I raise you right?"

My father's unexpected question and no-nonsense tone had my attention. *"Sí, Papi. Absolutamente."*

"Then don't embarrass me. Treat your wife like a diamond. Show these youngsters how a real man loves a woman. I pray for your union strength. Juan?"

"Endurance," my oldest brother added. "Rico?"

"Faithfulness. Quinton?"

"Honesty."

"Patience."

"Satisfaction."

One-word prayers flowed man-to-man, like a candle being passed, ending with Mister Williams. "Son, I wish your union every good thing because that's what you're marrying. My daughter and these boys mean the world to me. Like I told you when you asked for Yazmeen's hand in marriage: hurt her or them and I'll resurrect my military combat skills. Are we clear?"

"Yes, sir."

"You have my respect. I can't add anything to what these fine men already said except—"

"G-Daddy, we didn't get a turn," Malcolm protested, pulling his grandfather's arm. "We have a special word."

"Malkie, Mommy said we can't say that 'til after her wedding."

"Oops. Sorry, Mister Tavares. We gotta keep our secret word 'til Saturday. That's when you're marrying Mommy, right?"

"It is."

"See, Malkie. Mommy bought us a good countdown calendar.

Saturday's next week."

"That's when we get to call Mister Tavares 'Daddy!'"

My whole heart got messed up seeing the twins jumping around, impromptu singsong-chanting, "One week....one week...we get the best daddy."

"Son, you crying?"

"Something like that," I answered *Papi* when the twins stopped celebrating to climb on my lap.

Laughing, that line of men moved in, forming a tight circle. When they laid hands on us and my father and Mister Williams took turns blessing the bond of our new family, I couldn't do a thing except praise God.

That was three days ago, and the experience still produced a smile. With the old heads vacating after that prayer, I'd been roasted by my peers and subjected to comical tips on how to make love to a woman. Gonzalo ended it with, "Cuzzo, if she talking and ain't snoring two minutes after y'all finish, you ain't done nothing."

Snickering, I pulled off Highway-99 and gave a voice command to dial my woman. *"Hola, chica."*

"Hey, sweetie."

"Why you sounding stressed?"

"Because! The movers broke a leg off my purple chair. I still need to pick up my dress, and drop my engagement ring off to be cleaned. The weather's not cooperating, and my feet are *dying*."

I knew better than to laugh or remind her our oceanside wedding venue had an indoor back-up plan, or that she'd bought that broke-leg chair secondhand. "We'll handle it. Why're your feet dead?"

"From trying to break in these bridal shoes. I'ma 'bout to wear some Converse, I'm so through. What's your ETA? Carissa'll be here in an hour."

"I'll be there. Did you eat?" The closer the date, the deeper she dived in all things Wedding Central, sometimes neglecting herself in the process.

"No comment."

"That's what I thought. Your energy's off."

"Am I bridezilla-esque yet?"

"No, but you're a candidate."

She laughed.

"We have a wedding planner for a reason. Chillax and let Carissa do what she do. I have a couple of stops and I'll be through. *Te amo.*"

"Love you, too."

Disconnecting, I mentally attacked my own to-do list. Final fitting. Haircuts for me and the boys. Pick-up Nubs from her afternoon in Miss India's chair. Pick-up marriage license. Practice vows. Finish playlist for our first night as husband and wife. "Yeah...that."

I couldn't let my head go in too deep unless I wanted my body reacting. When Que called last night asking how I was holding up, I told the truth. "Man, I haven't had a hot shower in weeks."

He'd cracked up. But he knew. Icy water helped tame a thing or two.

Deciding my stops could wait, I pulled up at a smoothie joint and got two with protein supplements. Seeing a bagel shop next door, I grabbed a bag to help tame bridezilla gremlins and headed to wifey-to-be.

I had a key for use in case of emergencies. Still, I rang the bell while unlocking the door, versus walking in unannounced. "Bae!" My voice echoed in the emptiness.

Electing to lease her townhouse as a stream of income, her belongings had been packed and moved to my joint in Tiburon. Only bare essentials or elements designated for donation to a women's shelter remained.

"Tav?"

She exited the kitchen rocking *killer* heels that must've been the shoes she was breaking in. Triple ankle straps dripping with crystals, accentuated the shapeliness of her legs. It might've been cool and gray in the Bay, but Sacramento's weather that week had been some hot testament of global warming. Ergo the mid-thigh sundress she sported. Sexy didn't fit the description. That wild mass of hair flipped things to dangerous.

"I didn't expect you 'til later."

I stood there staring.

"Sweetie...you okay?"

What I was, was mesmerized by the effortless nature of her desirability stroking raw need in me.

I must've been stalking, not walking, because she backed up, watching me like I was something she'd never seen. Depositing the food on a counter, I approached, admiring. Wanting. "Can I?"

My hand was already immersed, touching, twirling thick, dense curls. Damp. Natural. Released from braids. I loved it, and how responsive she was to me. How my nearness and unexpected need affected her breathing.

Her voice was husky. "My appointment's tomorrow. I needed my braids down before then."

Her hair had been without braids during our courtship, but always twisted up in what she called protective styles. This damp, shoulder-hanging halo was new to me and dangerous-sexy.

"I'm liking." Her unconsciously licking her bottom lip told me she heard something in my tone that wasn't casual. But carnal. "Where're the twins?"

She stalled, studying me, clearly feeling my pent-up hunger and heat. "With my parents. Tav—" She didn't get to finish.

Leaning down, I had those lips. Like I liked. Juicy. Open.

We'd diligently refrained from sexual exchanges and situations since our engagement, but her moaning left me wanting to be done with delay. Gripping her hips, I lifted her onto the counter, keeping her near its edge so she was forced to lean into me, feeling my hard need for Marvin Gaye kind of healing. Kissing a path down her neck, my hands in her hair easing her head back, I was sucking and licking as she sighed thirstily, wrapped those killer shoes about my back.

Ease up, Alvarez.

Hands pushing up her dress and creeping over her thighs, my saved-son-of-God-self was a nuisance. I wasn't tryna hear my spirit when my flesh had my fiancée positioned the way I wanted—my hardness against the heaven between her legs, my hands straying, inching towards her breasts.

"Tav…we…can't."

We could. And maybe we would've if not for divine intervention called the doorbell.

I released her enough to look into her eyes, finding a Yazmeen I hadn't met. She was serious business dipped in fire and desire. But she was also stronger than me, refusing to satisfy our bodies' sexual pleas that had gone zero-to-sixty in a heartbeat.

She gently pushed me away. "Help me down, please."

Complying, I watched her remove those killer shoes, head to the freezer, grab a bag of frozen peas and return to me.

"Bae!" I yelped when she placed those peas against my parts.

"Four days, sweetie, and we can make *all the love* any way, every kinda way we want. *After* you put a ring on it and my name is Alvarez." She kissed my cheek. "I can't wait to be with you."

Opening the door to our wedding planner, she left me to cool down aided by frozen food.

CHAPTER TWENTY-NINE
MISTER & MISSUS ALVAREZ
Yazmeen

Sometimes things in life come together seamlessly, confirming they're God-kissed, -ordained.

That was our wedding.

The Tiburon venue overlooking the ocean. The caterer. Flowers. Music. Photographer. Videographer. The favor of God shone through everything and everyone. From hired professionals to family, it was impossible to repay the outpouring of excellence and love.

We'd wanted family to simply sit and enjoy. But the artisans among us weren't having it, refusing to let anyone else touch their God-given niche.

My beloved bestie wasn't "eating somebody's dry, crumbling cake." How she managed to care for Micah and craft lifelike sugar flowers that she shipped in advance was nothing short of astonishing. Still in touch with the Sacramento-based master chef she'd studied under, Joy's collaborating with her team of cohorts the week of our wedding resulted in a five-tiered work of art that left us speechless.

Lex Ryde, Tav's venture capital partner and proprietor of a transportation service, provided limos and sedans for our bridal party and guests. But his wife being an award-winning makeup artist with her own, Queen of Shades, cosmetic brand specializing in products for dark complexions proved my personal blessing. Senaé Dawson Ryde's team beautified my bridal party, while the makeup guru, herself, transformed me.

"You're sure you don't need a break, Senaé?" Nursing mother of a five-month-old son, I didn't want her exhausted.

"Honey, this is my passion and purpose. I'm good. But thanks," she answered, glancing at the baby carrier where Little Lex was sleeping.

"Okay...so...can I get a peek? *Please.*"

"Yazzy, stop begging. You'll see yourself when Senaé finishes," Sasha fussed, nursing my niece so Deja would sleep through the ceremony.

"This room's Titty City," LaVelle joked, seeing Joy finishing with Micah.

"Enough, Yazmeen."

My laughing caught me a reprimand from Senaé who'd already told me to stop my nervous chattering. Closing my eyes, I complied, practicing meditative breathing.

"Sasha, I'm loving the new products," Joy complimented. Rustling tissue paper let me know she was digging through the gift bags Sasha had distributed.

"Thanks. I'm toying with a sensual line of edibles. Yazzy has samples in her bag."

"Girl, Tavares is coming home from the honeymoon obese after two weeks of eating Yaz."

Joy's quip had folks laughing as Carissa entered the dressing suite. "You're looking good, ladies," she complimented the bridal party of my two sisters, and LaVelle in deep purple, fitted dresses that slightly mimicked mine. Joy's ice blue version distinguished her as matron of honor. "Does anyone need anything?"

"We're good."

"Okay, but my team's here for you. Yazmeen looks serene."

Eyes closed, I smiled, feeling her approaching.

"Relax your mouth."

I obeyed Senaé's instructions as Carissa took the empty seat next to me, answering questions without my asking, finishing with,

"Your luggage is at the hotel and things're laid out the way you wanted. Everything's in place here. Some guests have already arrived, and Reina and Jamal sound like *life*. This ceremony's going to be amazing."

I still didn't know what Reina was singing. At last night's rehearsal dinner, she'd performed a different piece—accompanied by my cousin, Jamal, on keys—keeping the song my husband-to-be had insisted on choosing for my entrance a secret from me.

"Am I the only one who peeped some serious heat between Reina and Jamal at last night's rehearsal?" India asked.

"Girl, naw. Chick almost sang me into an orgasm. And the way Jamal was tearing up that keyboard, I wanted to ask if they needed condoms." LaVelle was out-of-order as always, but undeniably something was brewing between the two. I decided to keep Reina's declining Jamal's recent dinner invite to myself. I had a feeling God wasn't finished with them, and they certainly didn't need this crew in their business.

Velle's sudden, "Aniyah, you're so pretty," had me wanting to risk Senaé's popping me just to see. India had apparently finished with final touches on my daughter-to-be. Oohs and ahhs trailed her as she came to stand by me.

"Do you like my hair, Mom—" She censored herself, remembering she had to keep that special term until after the wedding.

"Little Miss Flower Girl, come sit by me," Carissa invited, shifting to share her chair as I blindly reached out, embracing Aniyah's hand, happy that Deja wouldn't be the only granddaughter in my parents' grandchild crew, and that I was gaining a little girl.

With her year-round school off-track, Aniyah and the twins would spend the first week of our honeymoon with my parents, the second with Tav's. It was an opportunity for them to bond with their new set of grandparents, as well as experience living under one roof with each other.

"*Voilà*, my dear, we're done," Senaé announced, misting my face with finishing spray.

"I can see?"

"Not until we're finished with everything," India announced, probably still wanting to choke me for switching gears at the last minute. After that frozen-peas-to-chill-that-beast-in-my-kitchen incident, I'd opted out of microbraids, electing to have the wet waves of my natural hair snatched into an intricate upsweep with a bun hairpiece around which she'd secured a jeweled headband designed like a crown, veil attached at the back.

Carissa spoke into her headset. "Ask Missus Williams to come in."

My mother wanted to participate in helping me into my gown. When she entered, took one look at me and started tearing up, I panted to keep from crying.

"My glorious baby," she murmured, kissing me before leading me to my wedding dress and helping me out of my satin robe with "Almost His" embroidered across the back.

It was an emotional experience.

Kayla, my godsister photographer, who'd been in the suite from the start, snapped away as my mother and beloveds helped me into the sleeveless, ivory gown with intricate lace appliqués, jeweled embezzlements, and halter-style neck connected to a gorgeous rhinestone choker/collar. The curve-caressing mermaid fit flowed into a trumpet

skirt of large ruffle waves flowing into a detachable train. Finishing
with jewelry, garter belt, those shoes that almost got me de-virgin-ized
a second time, there was absolute silence.

Aniyah was first to speak, voice hushed in amazement. "Miss Yazzy,
you're a princess."

Carissa and Senaé were in place, fanning my face as a rolling mirror
was positioned in front of me.

My mirrored self left me speechless. She was me, not me. A woman
loved. Delicate. Cherished. His wish and want. A queen. Not a princess.

"Don't you dare cry," Sasha warned, blotting her tears and mine.

"No worries. I use only waterproof products for weddings," Senaé
teased, air-kissing my cheek. "You're absolutely breathtaking."

Unable to speak, I squeezed her hand, conveying my deepest thanks
as Carissa's team took the now sleeping infants to designated caretak-
ers, leaving me circled by the women who'd shared the hills and valleys,
mountains and mercies of my life's journey and were there to celebrate
God's goodness with me.

"We love you, too, Yazzy," India whispered, as if responding to my
heart's silently speaking as our mother moved to stand in front of me.

Taking my hands, Mama nearly had me bawling with her, "The full
sum of your existence is far greater than this one day, but right now it
feels as if I birthed you for this moment and this man."

"Mama, why?" Sasha fussed. "You got her doing the ugly cry. Hold
your head back, Yaz."

Laughing, Senaé was there, assuring that my face was still beat and
everything was everything as a knock on the door corresponded with
Carissa's, "Ladies, time to take your places."

Opening the door, she granted my father entrance. "Perfect timing,
Mister Williams."

Daddy walked in, looked at me and went to sniffling in his hand-
kerchief.

My mother laughed while handing me my bouquet. "Only his
baby girls get to that ol' crusty military man like that." Pressing her
cheek against mine she left to be escorted into the ceremony by Taj.

"You ready, Babycakes?"

"I am."

"I'm honored to share you with this man. He's your right husband."

Escorted into position by my father, I closed my eyes, hearing Pastor asking all to rise. When the doors opened and Jamal—joined by an acoustic guitarist—played a sweet melody, my eyes traced a trail of purple petals to where Aniyah and my ring bearer twins stood smiling, waving. Acknowledging my three babies, I deeply inhaled before allowing myself the pleasure of focusing on my groom at the top of the aisle, waiting. Standing wide-legged, hands folded in front of him, drop-dead delicious in a pearl gray designer tuxedo, he was everything. When our eyes connected, a universe of love passed between.

Caught up by Tav thumbing away tears, I wasn't ready when Reina began flawlessly rendering Carol Riddick's "Beautiful," the entry song he'd chosen for me.

Those lyrics slayed, had me leaning against my daddy, crying like a baby as I moved towards destiny.

⁕-⁕-⁕

Tavares

I fell in love again when those doors opened.

Embodying the song's lyrics, leaving me breathless, my exquisite bride was everything God could gift me.

Humbled at her father's presenting her to me, I stomped the need to kiss and claim *Mariposa* immediately. Instead, I whispered words for her ears only until her song ended and, together, we approached the altar, surrounded by God's holy presence. From the opening prayer to the end, my whole self was moved. Exchanging personalized vows, my entire integrity spoke for me, promising my heart and love unending. As the ceremony ended and Pastor granted permission, I cradled her face and saluted my bride beneath that warm October sky as if that kiss itself sealed our eternal union.

"Aiight, bruh, let her breathe," Quinton, my best man, teased, forcing me to let go of those lips and allow Pastor's,

"Ladies and gentlemen…friends and family…I present to you *Mister and Missus Alvarez.*"

Snatching another quick kiss, I wrapped her hand about my arm. "Ready, baby?"

"Always."

Jumping that broom, we strutted up the aisle with our children, cheesing, family cheering.

From countless pictures to the receiving line and well-wishes, dinner and our first dance, toasts, speeches, and cake-cutting, that day was one big party celebrating the blessings of God Almighty. Through it all, I was never far from my love for life, her touches, kisses and that subtle warmth in her skin whispering she was as ready as I was. For love. For us.

"Let's get this and be gone."

Backed by my boys, complete with canes and brims, I'd already pantomimed my way through Zacardi Cortez's old school, "Oh How I love You," faux serenading my bride and getting that standing ovation at the end. Now, I was ready for Missus Alvarez.

We'd spent a quiet moment with the kids, prayed over them, answered their last-minute questions before goodbye hugs and kisses. As far as I was concerned, whatever routine my wife had up her sleeve was the last thing standing between us and that consummating.

"Are you in a hurry?" she'd teased, forcing me onto a throne-like chair centered on the dance floor.

With a near decade of abstinence between us? "Straight skippy, yeah!"

Laughing, she took the floor, her girls behind her, acting out India. Arie's "Steady Love." I held it together, through all her lip-syncing and semi-sensual moves. But when she sat on my lap, purring those lines in my ear, naming me a boss in the streets and royalty between the sheets, I was done.

Scooping her over my shoulder, I waved at our guests. "Say 'good night,' Missus Alvarez."

Folks were howling-laughing.

Pausing and lowering her long enough for one final round of kissing the kids, I walked out with my wife hanging half-way over my shoulder, ready for grown, married business.

I'd never been nervous in sex. Except when ending my virginity and the encounters immediately after. Making love, however, wasn't something I'd done. I sensed the difference. That had me juggling hungry anticipation with uncustomary anxiousness.

I was disinterested in simulating past experiences. I wanted my wife like I'd never wanted another woman. Not as some random pop-off, or boast of sexual skills. My whole goal was communicating pure love, physically expressing that she was my one.

Thanks to my father's relentlessly preaching, "no glove, no love" since I was a teen, I'd practiced safe sex, used condoms *religiously*. Yazmeen's electing birth control pills had me pulsing at the thought of being inside of her, latex barrier-free.

Showered, fresh, I stood on the balcony of our hotel suite, letting that ocean breeze cool my bare chest while hosting a quick Come to Jesus conference.

This ain't the Orgasm Olympics. Touch her right. Take your time.

After a five-year celibacy? And the way I loved my wife? That wouldn't be easy.

I wasn't a saint or superhuman. My want for *Mariposa* had always been extreme. Truth? I. Was. *Starving.* That prompted my booking our honeymoon flight, intentionally opting on a red eye for tomorrow night. Our honeymoon destination was still a surprise to Yazmeen, but trust, that villa on a secluded private island in Tahiti would be there waiting with its white sand and turquoise water *after* consummating.

Leaning back against the rail, queuing our playlist with my phone, I checked progress.

Twenty minutes.

That was our agreement. Carrying her across the threshold, I was ready to get that gown off. Instead, I'd bossed up at her request for personal time in one of our two bathrooms, handling her bridal business.

"I'm serious, bae," I'd warned, caressing her curves, tagging that neck. "Twenty minutes-one second? I'm busting doors open."

I laughed seeing nineteen minutes-and-fifty-plus seconds had passed. Watching that final countdown on my phone, I counted along against a backdrop of smooth jazz.

Three, two, one. And done!

Slipping the phone in the pocket of my pajama pants, I pushed off the rail and forgot how to function.

Good GOD...

Approaching silently, Yazmeen Alvarez reduced me to visually eating every curve and swerve that slightly see-through, two-piece lingerie set served.

Speechless, I was stuck watching that walk, her floor-length ivory skirt riding low on hips that were a whole party waiting to happen. That centered, thigh-high split treated me to legs and loveliness. A cropped, keyhole halter top teased me with cleavage and her bare midriff. Barefoot and rocking some rhinestone toe-to-ankle jewelry, diamond navel piercing and crystal waist beads sparkling against that satin skin, her entire fit was *killing*. I wanted to forget foreplay and just get it.

Her sultry but shy smile put the choke on me, had me glancing at my wedding band, reminding myself to satisfy my wife before getting mine.

Stepping to my bride, taking her in my arms, I whispered my father's language in her ear.

"Translate, please." Her voice was breathy.

"You're beyond belief," I murmured against her lips. Kissing her with everything in me, my hands leisurely strayed down her back until molding that epic behind that I could have and hold for life now that she was mine.

Moaning, she pressed into me, our bodies connecting in places previously forbidden. She felt my hard want. I felt her readiness. That was invitation enough to lift my bride and carry her to bed.

Caught in some *insane* choreographed delay, I posted up beside the bed as she knelt on it, knowing the moment I got in it I was gone.

Her fingers gliding over every part of me within reach, I stood there, aching. Straining. Clenching my teeth, her incessant touch—like fire and silk—left me throbbing.

"My beautiful husband," she breathed against my neck, kissing a slow path down my chest, her tongue flicking my nipples before licking her way to my abdomen. Tonguing my abs, she reached beneath my waistband, guiding those pajama pants off with both hands. Sitting back on her heels, she stared at Beast, eyes full of some kind of admiration-love-lust thing. Smiling, she looked up at me, hesitating slightly.

"I'm yours, *Mariposa*. Do what you want to me."

Licking those lips, she gently slid her fingers up and down my length. Even her butterfly-like touch was too much. Torturous. Leaning forward and licking my tip, she slowly ran her tongue around the rim. Head back, I was hissing, hurting to be inside my wife, riding for life.

"Bae…"

Needing her to stop but not, I wrapped an arm about her waist and pulled her to me, my hands hungrily wandering her curves. Thirsty. Discovering. Hungry to taste and see her everything, I unfastened that top, let it drop.

Her wardrobe malfunction last spring? Zero justice to her full, naked breasts.

Good double dammmn!

Skimming the valley between, I held, caressed, but denied myself the pleasure of tasting, needing to see her completely naked.

I reached for that waistband. She guided my hands to hidden clasps. Undoing them and seeing my wife in nothing but that navel piercing, waist beads and some lacy thong-thing had me fifty-one-fifty. When she shimmied out of that thong, offering all the brown sugar I'd ever need, I swore in Spanish and lowered her onto the bed—both of us way past ready.

Situated above her, I kissed every place I could. Filled my mouth with her taste. Introducing myself to deliciousness, I nipped and licked my way to that diamond-studded belly button. When I reached her thighs, my baby was panting and purring, affirming that hypersensitivity. Kissing the insides of her thighs, I wanted to plunge my tongue in and taste her.

Save something *for later.*

Checking myself, I reversed a path to her breasts, treated my tongue to dark chocolate. Testing. Tasting. I caressed one while licking, sucking its twin.

"Oh...gawddddd...yasssss..." Her breathing was accelerated.

Don't ask how I took my time. Torturing one nipple, then the next. Over and again. Until her back was arching.

I didn't relent pleasuring those twin treasures while sliding my grip down her hip, pausing at the paradise between her legs. She was warm. Wet. Easing a finger gently inside my wife, I stroked her, finding and working that spot while thumbing that jewel throbbing at the juncture of her thighs. Her hips came up off the bed, head flailing side-to-side.

"Tav, baby please, I want you inside of me."

My love didn't need to ask twice.

Even so, I worked that brown sugar, bringing her to the edge of peaking before backing down, letting her catch her breath and possess me.

Fingers sliding down my shaft, she held me, widened her thighs in welcome and guided my slow entry. Lubricant wasn't needed. We were both juicy.

Raising her hips, she took me in completely, slaying me with that absolute flesh-on-flesh immersion wanting to devastate my sanity.

"Awww...shiii..." I clutched her behind to keep from exploding at her tightly enveloping me.

Breath choked in our throats, we lay paralyzed by profound pleasure. Being inside of my wife was divine. Pulsating about me, she was hotness and honey. Together, we were heat and hunger, need and greed. Touching. Exploring. Wanting each other's everything.

"Te amo, mi novia." Whispering in her ear the blessing my bride was to me, I slowly moved in and out of my wife, committed to not leaving her behind. Feeling her sweet gyrations, *Mariposa* was right there with me. Matching my movements. Syncing in pure unity.

Those luscious hips were rocking. Reaching. Getting it the way she wanted. Unleashing that dancer's grace, her undulating was wicked—had me thrusting up when she slid down on me.

She moaned. I groaned.

Stroking her fingers down my spine, over my buttocks, her touch was shiver-producing.

"Yes…baby." Her throaty encouragement was a natural accelerant.

I withdrew halfway only for her to meet me with a hard, upward tilt when I slid back in.

Somebody forgive me, but my wife had me cussing. Grinding. Plunging. Squeezing sheets just to postpone climaxing as we moved in perfect tandem.

Wrapping her legs around my waist, she sighed as I kissed my way to her breasts. Toying with one nipple then the next, I wanted to make her scream, suck her senseless. But when she positioned one leg over my bicep, did some deep, circular rotation with her hips, I was hollering.

That shattered all my hold-back.

Sliding a hand beneath her behind, I grabbed the headboard with the other and let our loving do what it did.

It was criminally *insane.* Deeper than deep. We poured everything we were into the mix. Every want we'd sat on since we met we brought to our marriage bed leaving our loving fierce, relentlessly rhythmic until we skyrocketed in a dual detonation that ripped our universes.

Let a brother confess. I. Was. *Whipped!* Good for nothing except collapsing on my wife after she served me my whole entire tri-racial life.

Her fingernails clenching my back, the sounds of our mutual release reverberated inside of me as long, slow moments passed and I recovered from uselessness, our breathing calmed, and our bodies gently relaxed.

I had zero want to vacate that sweet brown sugar hugging my stuff.

Elevating on my forearms, I gazed down at my bride, touched by the tears of profound contentment in her eyes. Wiping an escaped tear, I kissed her intensely. Reverently. Reluctantly withdrawing, I rolled onto my back, pulling her onto my chest. Holding my bride, I was honored by everything we'd shared.

Bone of my bone. Flesh of my flesh.

That fusion was next level ultimate. *Sonic.* Nothing like I'd ever experienced.

Sated to the nth degree, we exchanged whispered love and gentle kisses while settling comfortably.

Her quiet sigh was a whole other kind of serene.

"You okay, baby?" My wife had me poised for pillow talk?

She smiled against my chest, easing her leg between mine. "How do I say 'I'm slain' in Spanish?"

"You already did." I mimicked her whimpers and screams when orgasming. Quietly chuckling when she pinched me, I tilted her face towards me. "You're my forever, Missus Alvarez. Thank you."

"For?"

"Being strong enough to do this God's way. You're more than worth the wait." Kissing her, caressing her back, my hand slid to her waist, rested on her behind. Rubbing, caressing, I laughed.

"What?" Her voice was fading.

"Bae, this booty's my new best friend."

Smiling, she rested a hand on Beast, stroked that sac underneath. "You have yours. I have mine."

"Te quiero mi corazón." Kissing her forehead and feeling drunk, I drifted into some seriously euphoric sleep, with my wife, snuggling.

Her pinging phone or her absence woke me. Either way, it was past midnight and my wife was missing.

"Bae?"

"Hmm?" Exiting the bathroom, she reentered our suite wearing nothing. "You okay?"

"Come *through*, boo." Watching those hips swaying in moonlight like magic, I felt some twitching downtown. "I'm cold without you."

"You're spoiled already?" she teased, sliding into bed.

"Heck yeah." An arm about her waist, I pulled her to me, lay on her chest, snuggled against her breasts. "Check your phone. You got a text."

Her fingers playing in my hair, she did only to laugh. "These idiots."

"What?" I asked around a yawn, reading the screen angled towards me, showing a group text from her girls.

Did you get that honey roasted?

Is your back cracked?

Or snapped?

Like in half?

"Y'all a mess. Check the nightstand drawer."

"For?"

"Just check."

Turning on the bedside lamp, she sat up and eyed me before extracting the ribbon-wrapped jewelry box Carissa stashed for me. "Sweetie, what's this?"

"No idea," I joked, stroking her hip.

"Awww, the key to your heart," she cooed, holding up a diamond-encrusted key-shaped pendant.

"You already have that. That represents the key to your new address." Finding my phone, I pulled up a pic of us fooling around in that oceanfront backyard at our "Final Festivities." Knowing the owners were permanently relocating to Greece, I'd rented that property to gauge her interest. On sight, she'd loved it. The following Monday, I'd had that earnest deposit in the agent's hands.

She inhaled sharply. *"Tavares, what did you do?"*

"We need room for eggs and opportunity." I kissed her stomach. "Gimme the rec room for my man cave? The rest is yours to do what you want. Happy wedding day, baby."

Teary-eyed, she stared at me. "You are *so* unbelievably beautiful. *Thank you.*" Cupping my jaw, she funneled her happiness into a deep, erotic kiss that had the south rising.

Easing her onto her back, I accepted all that bliss until she started feeling around for something. "Whatchu need?"

"My phone." Finding it, she queued our playlist to Carol Riddick's sensual assertion that round one wasn't enough. She needed seconds.

"That the way you want this?" I asked, hovering over her.

"It's the way I want you," my bride breathed. "Without end."

"Let's get it, Missus Alvarez. Your girls're in the business? Tell 'em…" I kissed a hot trail down her body, speaking one word in Spanish whenever my lips touched her flesh.

"English," she breathed, back already arching.

"Exquisite. Matchless. Delicious. Complex." Entering my wife a second time, feeling that pleasure down in my bones, I joined my one-and-done in lovemaking that was slower and more controlled than our inaugural voyage. Equally intense, round two was straight mind-shattering. Climaxing so hard, my abs ached, my one thought was,

Lord, I'm loving marriage.

EPILOGUE
TEAM ALVAREZ
Yazmeen
Seven months later...

Rae, get outta your head and stop dismissing the man."
Seated on my bed, my cousin-in-love played with the fringe of a decorative pillow. "Yaz, you see how fine he is?"

"No, he's my cousin."

"He's F-I-N-E and can have any woman. Why me?"

Aniyah's "Mommy, look!" kept me from answering.

My heart dropped seeing my children and Mister Bojangles running to me, Aniyah's mouth bloody. *"Niy-Niy, what happened?"*

Reina's, *"Dios mío,"* didn't help.

"We fixed my loose tooth!" Aniyah yelled excitedly.

I examined my child's mouth for triplet-created damage. "Define 'fixed.'"

"The Tooth Fairy's slow, so we ate a buncha baby carrots," Malik cheerfully added, hopping onto his Auntie Rae-Rae's lap.

Shame on me for thinking I could pack an overnight bag and chat with Reina while my babies ate their lunch that was, mind you, carrot-free. Or for thinking that tooth Aniyah proudly held might've survived another two weeks without triplet interference.

"Mommy, watch this." Aniyah poked her tongue through her new twin-assisted gap, leaving the boys oohing and Bojangles angling his head.

"Mommy, can we take our teeth out, too?"

"No, Malcolm Amir, you can't." Grabbing a tissue from my nightstand, I scooped up Aniyah's toothy treasure and cleaned her hands. "And no more "assisting" today. Clear?"

"Yes, Missus Mommy Ma'am."

My caution was a pause button for them.

With these three life'll never be minus shenanigans.

"Let's rinse your mouth, *mi hija.*" Leading my daughter to my bathroom—the twins tagging along with questions and suggestions—I needed bass power like Tav. My husband was "that dad." Gentle, loving, patient and protective, he didn't coddle, but brought out the best in our babies. Even our shy guy, Malik, was less pouty and more confident, thriving from the love of a strong man who'd get on the ground and roughhouse with the kids in a hot minute. But when they were out-of-line? Tav dropped that bass and the kids miraculously got their lives right. On my watch? Our children devised miscellaneous mayhem.

That's 'cause you're part marshmallow.

Smiling at Tav's constant tease, I mixed a solution of peroxide and warm water. "Here, Niy-Niy. Swish. Spit. Don't swallow."

"You're gonna miss this marshmallow mom when I get a job," I'd tossed the last time he'd teased.

Months into marriage, despite multiple job interviews, I'd remained unemployed, floating.

Bae, maybe God's gifting you an opportunity.

To?

Chillax. Can you do that?

I couldn't. I'd worked since my first fast food job at fifteen, was accustomed to self-sufficiency. Other than earnings from my classes and that little rent-my-townhouse-profit, I was incomeless. Which made me dependent. I didn't know how to be that. Particularly after the instability of my first "marriage."

So, you all tight behind the money games Roadkill played? Get a gig. Or don't, Mariposa. That's your choice. Either way, I'm a different kind of man.

That! My spirit was checked and challenged to trust my husband and our union. There was zero need to worry about myself or my sons. God and my husband had our family. Laying pride aside, I'd hugged my love, humbly accepting that rare gift of time to contemplate next steps in life.

That's when I admitted negative-zero interest in continuing as an admin. I'd forever appreciate Pastor and First Lady for bestowing that blessing when they had. But that wasn't me. My amazing husband handed me the chance to do what I hadn't in forever: dream.

Sir Sexy's ringtone blared as if I'd summoned him.

"*Daddy!*" The boys and Bojangles took off. "Mommy, can we answer on your laptop?"

"Yes. And no running." I examined Aniyah's freshly cleaned mouth. "Does it hurt, Niy-Niy?"

"Nope. Can I show Daddy?"

Not needing an answer, she took off squeezing in with her brothers so that all three piled up in the chair at my sitting room desk talking Tav's ears off.

Sliding Aniyah's Kleenex-wrapped tooth in my pocket, I exited the bathroom, inhaling ocean air and serenity, thankful for the blessing of my family. "About you, Miss Rae-Rae. Make some moves already," I encouraged, dropping my toiletry kit into my overnight bag.

"Yazzy, I can't."

"Because?" I loved our growing relationship, but chick had a gift for theatrics.

"I'm big," she complained, flopping back onto my bed.

"You're gorgeous, and we're not debating that. Ehh!" Hand in her face, I stifled her attempted clapback. "I'm here to help however you need. I'll be your exercise buddy, in person. Virtually." Tav had given me space, rent-free, at the *Athletes & Academics* campus where I taught Zumba and dance, both twice weekly. I missed *Step-N-Style*—who by the way earned every dollar needed during that fundraiser—but they were in excellent hands with my replacement. They inspired my next step: starting my own dance company. I was serious about targeting "thick" dancers whose voluptuousness defied mainstream notions of beauty. Reina's ongoing struggles to accept Jamal's interests as legit was like reinforcement for that decision. "Be clear: fitness is for *you*, not him. Jamal's interested in Reina Kingsley. As is. Period*t*! Next topic."

"You make me sick."

Laughing, I pulled my red leather mid-thigh trench and matching thigh-high boots from our walk-in closet bigger than my kitchen back in Sac. "Rae-Rae, stop stalling and handle your business. Like I'm about to handle His Fineness." I wiggled my hips for emphasis.

Clutching her throat, she gagged. "Color me disinterested in booty business between you and Tav."

Swatting her thigh, I zipped my overnight bag before digging my wallet from my purse and handing her several bills. "Mind playing Tooth Fairy?"

"*Two-hundred-fifty?* I'm like Malcolm. Take my tooth, please."

"Girl, quit. Slip a dollar or two beneath Niy-Niy's pillow tonight, but the rest is for the weekend. Pocket whatever's left. Thanks for staying with the kids." Reina was that fun cousin-auntie indulging our babies with treats and countless activities. Ensuring she had enough funds for the frenzy, I knew how blessed I was to go from struggling to abundance.

"Anything for my triplets," Reina insisted, sitting up and accepting Aniyah's tissue-wrapped tooth. "Thanks for listening. I'll deal with Jamal. *Eventually*," she murmured, frowning when her cellphone rang. Eyes wide, she held it up. "Speaking of..."

"You better get him," I teased, silently praying for her confidence while heading for the kids. The triplets leaning across my desk video chatting with Tav, triggered a flashback.

Married to a man worth multi-millions, I still loved thrifting. Haunting consignment shops, public auctions, garage and estate sales in Tiburon and surrounding deep-money vicinities, snagging high-price treasures for pennies on the dollar and blogging my finds, and teaching others how to do likewise, was an adrenalin kick for me. Seeing strong potential in that neglected desk, I'd purchased it last month at an estate sale despite various nicks and dents, studied DIY refurbishing videos, and tried my hand at it. Staining it a smoky gray to contrast with the sitting room's light decor, my first refurbish project was a success.

Bae, you tricked the heck outta that. But...can it stand the test of Tav?

High on accomplishment, I'd accepted my husband's risqué dare and wound up with my legs over his shoulders, butt-naked on my back. Mr. Alvarez worked his magic, leaving us both screaming wickedly. But that desk earned its keep. It didn't collapse.

Mmm, that man.

Missing him, my eyes strayed to the plethora of framed photos lining the fireplace mantle. The kids. Our engagement. Our wonder-of-a-wedding. The pictures captured its majesty, had me remembering that night, and *becoming* my husband's wife.

That first love was engraved on my mind. The moment Tav laid eyes on me next-to-nude in my bridal lingerie, I knew I was about to be slaid. Masking nervousness, I put on some grown woman confidence that kept me from fainting when seeing *him* naked. Praying for elasticity and my ovaries, I let need take the lead and treated myself to my husband. Treated like his treasure, he'd touched me with reverence and greed, shook my everything. That man's lethal loving did exquisite things to my flesh that absolutely wrecked me. Seven months later, Mr.

Magic was still slaying Yazmeen.

Fingering a photo of Sir Sexy and me in swimsuits on that white sand beach, I smiled at the thoughts of our indulgent honeymoon that was *everything*. What I saw of Tahiti was breathtaking but, admittedly, our time was consumed with sexual activities.

Sequestering ourselves that first week, our loving was inferno-kind-of-hot and hungry but tender, sweet. It was all about discovering, acquainting ourselves with each other's bodies. And his? Built to perfection, that man was six-foot-six inches of sculpted magnificence. I couldn't get enough, loved every inch, and was still happily addicted.

Week two of our honeymoon, we actually made it outdoors, toured parts of the island, spent time on that private beach and played in the ocean. But trust, like captives freed from celibacy, we made wild, crazy love at every opportunity. I was greedy for that man, his skills, finesse, and unquestionably lethal loving. Bold, relentless, my baby brought his best to bed. Yes, he cracked my back. Blew it out. Snapped it in half. All that. But he also cherished me. Addicted to my pleasure as I was to his, he went to school on all things Yazmeen and learned my body. Attentive, generous, he catered to my every whim. By the time we left Tahiti and headed home, I was dizzy in love, worn out and needing a vaginal vacation.

Laughing at myself, Malcolm's question brought me back to the present.

"If we catch the Tooth Fairy can we keep it?"

Tav's laugh warmed my belly. "No, son, you can't. Other kids need the Tooth Fairy, too."

"Oh...okay."

"Daddy, we miss you."

"Miss y'all, too, Nubs, but I'll be home tonight. Who wants something from San Diego?"

"*Me!*"

"Aiight, I'll see what I can do. But right now, I need to talk to Mommy."

"Mom—" Swiveling my chair and seeing me behind them, Aniyah giggled. "Here she is."

"Triplets, let's finish lunch and clean up," Reina suggested, having ended her call. "*Hola, primo.* Bring me something, too. Like a better boss."

"Whatever, Rae."

Laughing as she closed the door, I dropped onto my desk chair. Seeing my husband on screen had my whole body happy. "Hey, sweetie."

"Bae, I've been gone two days and my kids are toothless and bleeding?"

"You already know those three. I miss you."

"Apparently." He laughed at the I Love Peanuts t-shirt I was rocking courtesy of India. "You wearing panties?"

"Maybe. How's the conference?"

"Dry. I'd rather be home in my wife."

"You miss this warm-and-wet?" I slowly licked my lips.

"Mos' def'. You might wanna take a nap, 'cause I'm coming home and getting that. How're you feeling?"

"Thanks to you: horny." We snickered, knowing he was referring to my getting dizzy at Zumba yesterday. With Tav out of town and the kids on break, I'd been occupied with them and forgot to eat. The protein bar I'd devoured on the way obviously hadn't been enough. "You talked to the producers?"

"I did. A reality T.V. show's too up in the personal business, and I'm not down with exposing our family like that, so I thanked them and declined."

"I appreciate you, Mister Overprotective, but admit "Basketball & Ballet" had a nice sound to it."

"I prefer the sounds of Missus Alvarez." He mimicked me. "'Ooo, baby, yes. Right there. *That. Please* don't quit. Take care of it.'"

"That's not how I sound."

"Deny you've moaned it."

"I can't." Enchanted by the myriad ways my husband made love to me, I'd become wildly free. Boldly telling him how and what I wanted, I got more than I needed. "I heard you speaking Spanish with the kids. The twins are getting good."

"Stop deflecting. It's getting hot in the crotch, huh?"

Lifting one leg on the desk, I sucked my finger and slowly trailed it down my body until out of camera range. "Maybe. Care to see?"

"Heck, yeah."

I sat up, laughing. "We better quit while we can. Oh, real quick: the guest room's ready for Miss Carmen." Aniyah's grandmother was coming for a two-week visit. "Wait. What if she prefers the mother-in-law cottage?"

I had instant images of being in our guest cottage doing X-rated things with Sir Sexy.

Loving the hardwood floors that were perfect for dance, I'd pushed living room furniture aside one afternoon while the kids were at school, cranked the music, and freestyled to my content. Despite having space at the *Athletes & Academics* complex, Tav kept his home office. Caught in my flow, I hadn't noticed he'd walked in until the music ended. Finding him, expression filled with multiple layers of appreciation and heat as he stalked towards me, a thrill sped through my body. Lifting and bracing me against a wall, he proved he *didn't* need a bed to do what he did to me. After that? The cottage became our sneaky-freaky hideaway. I'd have to ensure a thorough cleaning to make sure Miss Carmen didn't stumble up on anything. "Boo? Are you listening?"

"Not really. I'm waiting on that hand to get in them panties."

"I can't with you. Sweetie, we celebrate your birthday in two days!"

"Did I get my wish list?"

"A stripper pole? No." Pulling up emails, I double-checked his flight itinerary. "Are you having dinner before you leave, or when you get in?"

Those lips lifted in a wicked grin. "Yeah, I'm eating wifey when I get home."

"I'm talking about food."

"I'm talking about you."

"You're *so* bad." With my husband, I was uninhibited, willingly tried new positions and methods. That oral ministry? Yum and yes! Knowing what that man's mouth was capable of, my voice was breathless. "See you soon. Love you."

"I'll text when I'm off the plane. Pick me up with them panties off. Love you, too."

Closing my laptop, smiling at thoughts of my insatiable spouse, I slipped his gift into my oversized purse. Having boudoir pictures made into a photo book for his eyes only was a new kind of bold for Yazmeen. But I loved surprising my husband, expressing the woman he brought out in me, and the lushness of our marriage. Married life was real. It was work. Was our union perfect? Absolutely...*not*. But my husband was my heart, my prayer partner, provider, protector; earth angel, supreme lover, confidant and rock. I wouldn't trade him *ever*.

Lord, thank You for Your unfailing love, my life, my children, every gift You've ever graced me, and most definitely, for my incredible love, Tavares-him-fine-and-mine-Alvarez.

Grabbing my purse and overnight bag, I exited our bedroom, ready for sneaky-freaky birthday business.

Tavares

Invited to be a panelist at a minorities' venture capitalist conference, I'd been in San Diego two days and was ready for *La Casa Alvarez*. I thought I'd enjoy the quiet of a hotel suite to myself. I did but didn't. Was too busy missing my luscious wife and loud kids.

We were a good team: Yaz, the kids, Bojangles, and me. It took a minute to blend and sync. Once we did, we had it. Now? Team Alvarez was in full effect.

I liked teaming up with my wife. Our cohesion showed itself even in basic things like my taking the kids to school, while she picked them up. Naturally an early riser, I got up with the triplets, occasionally letting her sleep in. She was that mom bathing the kids, readying clothes and making lunches the night before. All about that teamwork, when she cooked, I cleaned. To quote my wife, we had "synergy." Not that Nubs and I hadn't been good alone, but with my wife and sons, we were full family.

Texting Yaz when the plane landed, I headed for the exit, leather garment carrier slung across my back containing the kids' souvenir bag.

I'd only traveled periodically before marriage, but had decreased even that. I wasn't trying to live that absentee father life, and I definitely wasn't down with neglecting my wife. After the mess the twins had gone through their stability, Nubs' stability, and my being a reliable father was priority for me.

Speaking of: Yazmeen rarely heard from Roadkill's mother, had severed ties with him, but last we heard despite multiple procedures he was assigned to life as a quadriplegic. Their domestic violence history reduced Sydney's charge from attempted manslaughter to assault with a deadly weapon. On lockdown, Sydney sent *Mariposa* a three-page letter apologizing for his part in the twins' abduction. She forgave him while burning it. My wife was tender, gentle, but when she was done she was done. And she was.

As for my deadbeat? Kryshelle was tearing it up in Tampa Bay, living her best ratchet life, still forgetting she'd ever birthed a child. Seeing that better-than-blood bond between my wife and daughter, the heat over Kryshelle's neglect was long gone.

Gladly bypassing baggage claim, I headed outside, thanking the Lord, yet again, for gifting me Yazmeen Renee.

Where's this woman?

Expecting to see Yaz and the kids pulling up to the curb, I looked around for her Range Rover. Loving that Christmas gift, she'd lured me into the garage Christmas night after the kids were asleep, reclined my seat, climbed on my lap and "christened" her whip. That Rover was solid.

"Mr. Alvarez?"

Turning, I found one of Lex's dudes, posted up, a silver tray in hand.

My V.C. partner had made moves, expanded his transportation outfit to northern Cali. That old school set up of black suit, chauffeur cap, gloves, and gold signature tie easily tagged the limo driver as Lex's employee.

"Sir..." Extending that tray, he waited.

Seeing a familiar white and silver envelope with a purple embossed Y.A. on top, I extracted a notecard, finding *Mariposa's* handwriting and a hint of her scent.

Don't be late.

Curious about what she was up to, I pocketed the card, entered the limo grinning like a fool.

My wife was demonstrative. She put surprises in the kids' lunches, left love notes on my pillow, my desk. Liked coming in my home office giving massages, or wearing sexy lingerie that guaranteed a spicy interruption in my work day. She got off on surprises. But this was a twist.

I shot her a text.

Y the limo?

Her response was the same: *Don't B L8.*

Control wasn't something I relinquished easily, but I'd worked on analness and takeover tendencies. Regardless, I already knew. Getting more 4-1-1 from my wife wasn't happening. Sweetness aside, the woman's stubbornness was epic.

I texted.

Playing the game ur way.

Sitting back, relaxing on a ride to God knew where, I responded to business emails, and checked next week's calendar before scrolling my extended family's private social media group that Reina started in an effort to keep everyone connected. I commented on a few posts until a pic of Team Alvarez on the triplets' spring break at Disneyland last month popped up.

No, sir, we're not paying that!

Yaz practically passed a kidney seeing the cost of our hotel reservations. Admittedly, I customarily paid whatever because I could. Not my coupon-clipping, I-can-get-it-cheaper-thrifting boo. She'd gone online and found less expensive lodging at an equally nice hotel.

And breakfast is included!

That was my wife.

She braided our daughter's hair, didn't trip when our housekeeper quit due to relocating, and shopped at Costco-like bulk joints to lower our expenses. She'd devised a monthly budget, and her tactics saved us a grip. Sometimes I checked her, told her to sit her hips somewhere. She didn't have to grind constantly. Every purchase didn't have to equal massive savings. Compromising, a new housekeeper came twice weekly and before holidays for deep cleaning. Still, I appreciated my wife's organization skills, how she tightened up our lives and kept our household running right. We didn't see eye-to-eye on everything, but I had her back and she had mine.

A text pinged. I cracked up at Jamal's crying emoji.

Your cousin's driving me cray-cray.

Bruh was grinding to get that green light from Reina. I wanted to tell him to buy countless cases of patience like Joy told me when I was thirsting over Yazmeen. Instead, I encouraged him to hang in there, that Reina's crazy would end.

Feeling the limo stop, I looked up, finding a hotel entrance instead of home. Into whatever game my wife was running, I tipped the driver and headed indoors.

"Good evening, Mr. Alvarez."

A smiling front desk clerk greeted me with another Y.A. embossed envelope.

Give the concierge your luggage & meet me @the bar.

Arriving separately at a restaurant as if strangers, my wife and I had roleplayed before, acting out a scenario of lusty attraction that led to animalistic loving. Ready for whatever, I entered the bar expecting to find *Mariposa* sitting up sexy.

Ten minutes later I was still waiting.

Woman, where r u?

As if in response to my text, the bartender handed me what I hoped was the last envelope. I was down for roleplay, but the delay was getting crazy.

U'r L8.

Seeing an enclosed keycard and designated room number, I paid for my Arnold Palmer and headed for the elevator. Yazmeen was an excellent mother, incredible wife, and good money manager. As a lover? That woman was my it. The business. Adventurous. Athletic. Our marriage bed was sacred, but I loved that my wife had zero hesitation in expressing herself, and appreciated every way she kept it fresh.

And she's still tryna prove dancers have more stamina.

Chuckling, I exited the elevator conceding once or twice she won that endurance thing.

Finding our room, I entered a suite prepped for loving.

"Bae?"

Dim lighting, smooth music, whispers of my wife's perfume and whatever was beneath that cloche on the dining table was the room's response. Kicking off the shoes and tossing my suit jacket on a chair, I grabbed a handful of nuts from a tray and headed for the bedroom hungrier for *Mariposa* than food. I was greeted by an empty room and a gift box atop an oversized chair. Opening it, I wasn't ready.

"Whhhaaattt...ttthhhe...?"

I dropped on that chair, seeing some swank picture book featuring page after page of my wife in provocative poses and risque lingerie.

Deep in that book, I was hot, hard, and barely heard,

"Hola, mi amor."

My head snapped up.

Rocking that red leather boot-jacket set I'd gifted on Valentine's—hair loose, wild like I liked—Yazmeen sashayed towards me, radiating sensual heat. Her Spanish was still laugh-worthy, but that fit made it good for me.

"Welcome home," she purred, cradling my face and kissing me deeply as my hands inched up the back of her thighs, beneath that jacket, feeling nothing but silky skin.

I groaned when her mouth moved to my neck. "I should go away regularly just to come home to this."

"No, you shouldn't," she whispered. Unbuttoning my clothing, she slowly removed my everything like some reverse strip tease, leaving me naked and needy. "Happy pre-birthday, baby."

Untying that leather belt cinching her jacket, she parted it, treating me to a single strand of rhinestone waist jewelry, that diamond navel piercing, and whatever had her naked skin glowing. I reached for her. She backed away. "Move an inch and this ends," she softly challenged, cueing the sound system to an old, familiar beat. The rhythm had been slowed down, but it was definitely Pantha's "Purrrfect."

Smiling sexily, my wife let that jacket drop and morphed into Miss Purrrfect, working the sheazy out of a video routine I remembered too well, wearing only killer boots and body jewelry.

It was *cray-zay!* Left me brick hard, hotter than I'd ever been.

My breathing was raggedy when the final bars faded, she turned her back to me and sashayed to the bed. When she perched on its end and licked her lips while slowly opening her legs, I was finished.

That dance the foreplay, I strode across that floor, wrapped an arm about her waist and repositioned my wife further up the bed. Feeling between her legs, finding her wet and ready, I plunged into her hot heaven. She screamed as if that entry was everything. Those red boots over my shoulders, we ripped that ride until we were yelling, shuddering, shaking.

"Do I need to kill a photographer for seeing my wife half-nude?" Drunk from love, enough time had passed for me to semi-recover and toss threats. Sounding half-asleep and playing with my chest hairs, *Mariposa* assured me her godsister, Kayla, had taken those boudoir pics. "Good. Otherwise a dude was about to die."

Laughing lazily, she slid a leg between mine. "I can dispose of it if it's stressing you."

"Bae, it's stressing and pressing." One arm around my wife and holding that book in my free hand, I was still enjoying the decadence. "Turn the page for me, boo."

Snuggling against me, she laughed. "I'm not. Wait!" She sat up. "You have another gift…"

I couldn't want more. That dance. The book. That *loving*. "Yeah… naw, bae, I'm good." Laying there, indulging in my wife's pics, beast made me a lie and started twitching.

"You'll want this."

"Mmm-hmm." Distracted, I felt her leave the bed. She returned a moment later, pried my book away, handing me an easily identifiable box of Joy's cake truffles instead. Smelling Kahlua Chocolate even before lifting the lid, inside I found a half-dozen, perfectly replicated ballet slippers and basketballs. "Bae, your girl's got *mad* skills."

I downed three with my wife, sitting simply staring at me. Her appearing nervous, yet serene, eventually penetrated my greed. "What's up?"

"We said we'd wait until after our first anniversary, but…love happened. I don't know if we'll be buying balls or ballet gear…" Placing that box on the nightstand, she took my hand, kissing it before holding it against her stomach. "You're a daddy again."

Unable to process the indescribable miracle she'd just gifted me, my whole world got warm. I was incapable of anything except looking at my wife, her smile soft as butter, sweet as sunshine.

"Sweetie…are you okay?" she whispered, wiping the tears I didn't feel sliding down my face.

"This is why you were dizzy the other day?"

Emotional, she nodded.

"You're having my child…" Looking at her, I cupped her face, roamed my hands over her body as if seeking confirming changes. Her breasts were slightly heavier. Her stomach seemed puffy, but that waist was still snatched. Pulling her towards me, I repositioned her until kneeling atop the bed between my legs. Staring at her, I stroked her hips.

Too moved to speak, I kissed her stomach. Reverently. Repeatedly. But reverence melted and fire flared until I was full-mast again.

Pushing me onto my back, she straddled my lap. Slowly taking me in, she sighed contentedly. "We're having a little Taia or Tavares."

"Or maybe both," I murmured, feeling beyond blessed as I gently thrust up, praising God for all good things, grateful for the beautiful new life cradled inside my wife.

Before Basketball & Ballet
CALIFORNIA LOVE, BOOK 1

Joy Matthews isn't afraid of risks. She's quit her Fortune 500 job and enrolled in culinary school, chasing her dream. Joy wants her own couture cake boutique. Pursuing her dream by day, Joy pays the bills working nights at The Hourglass—an exclusive gentlemen's club catering to patrons who enjoy "a little extra fine on a woman's frame." Joy's catching up to her dream when a chance encounter reconnects her with Quinton Daley, a childhood friend. Mutual attraction throws the proverbial wrench in Joy's relationship-phobic, happily agnostic life. A goal-oriented woman who "doesn't do men with Bible breath," Joy sees in Quinton a whole lot of what she likes but doesn't need.

Tall, chocolate-skinned, and born-again, Quinton's Christianity poses a risk even the tenacious Joy isn't willing to take. Quinton Daley isn't fazed. He's a man of faith who will willingly wait on Joy to come to God…and him. When love and lust heat up, Joy and Quinton face a predicament. Will they indulge? Or abstain? Join this wild mix of custom cakes, a saved, sanctified and sexy man, and an obsessed patron from The Hourglass who's determined to make Joy's life a sticky mess. It's a recipe for a read that's wickedly witty and delicious.

SUGGESTED DISCUSSION QUESTIONS
For Book Clubs and Reading Groups

1. *Basketball & Ballet* touches on various, overarching subjects. For example: single-parenting, divorced dating, blended families, dating while saved-&-single, child endangerment, celibacy, multiculturalism, etc. Did any of these topics strike close to home for you?

2. When Yazmeen and Tavares first meet she is extremely hesitant to further their acquaintance. Why? Did you understand her reluctance?

3. Tavares admits to being bullheaded. How did that personality trait serve him in getting to Yazmeen? When the twins were abducted? How did it hinder him during the course of the story?

4. What attributes were most appealing to you about our heroine and hero? What characteristics were annoying?

5. What values did Yazmeen and Tavares share?

6. Discuss how, and the extent to which, substance abuse/addiction impacted both the heroine and hero.

7. Whose parenting style resonated most with you, Yazmeen's or Tavares'?

8. In your opinion, did Tavares ever misuse his economic advantages in gaining ground with Yazmeen?

9. Yazmeen was a virgin prior to Royal. In what ways did *his* sexuality impact her female identity and sense of femininity?

10. Discuss the reason(s) why Yazmeen discontinued ballet.

11. Yazmeen and Tavares manage to maintain abstinence until their marriage. Discuss their struggle to do so ('cause it was real!).

12. Aniyah, Malcolm, and Malik (aka the Triplets) are something else! Do you think they'll continue to blend harmoniously? How did their presence add to the story?

13. Child abduction is a loving parent's horrific nightmare. Both Tavares and Yazmeen experience it. Discuss the individual incidents.

14. Aniyah is not Tavares' biological daughter, yet he loves her as if she is. How did that impact your opinion of him?

15. Are you interested in Reina and Jamal's yet untold love story?

16. What, if any, questions were left unanswered for you?

ACKNOWLEDGEMENTS

I always start at the top, which means with *Abba Father God*: thank You for gracing me with the gift of writing. I'm humbled. I'm honored. And I pray I use this gift in a way that pleases the ancestors and heaven.

I never had a hero until I had *my husband*. Thank you, Baby, for being you. Quirky. Crazy. A genius to the extreme. You are the gentleness in every hero I'll ever pen.

My children: I can't even begin to describe what you are to me. Thank you for loving me flaws and all, and for allowing me to be your mother for eternity.

June R.P. Mays: my beautiful, legal eagle. Thank you for your generosity and patience in answering my countless family court questions so Yazmeen could win!

To my *fellow sister-author-friends* and the *literary community* that keeps me going: I appreciate you for always.

WONDERFUL READERS...

Thank you for being the backbone of the literary community. Without your support, writers' works would collect dust and go unnoticed. So, I thank you for noticing me!

I have a secret to share: I absolutely *love* hearing from and interacting with readers and book clubs in person or via Skype and Facetime. Let's connect via any of the following:

EMAIL: sdhbooks@gmail.com
FACEBOOK: Suzette Harrison or Suzette D. Harrison Books
GOODREADS: Suzette D. Harrison
INSTAGRAM: suzetteharrison2200
NEWSLETTER SIGN-UP: www.sdhbooks.com
PINTEREST: Suzette D. Harrison Books
TWITTER: SDH Books
WEBSITE: www.sdhbooks.com
YOUTUBE: Suzette Harrison

If you enjoyed *Basketball & Ballet* I'd be honored if you'd share that enjoyment by posting a review on Amazon.com and/or other venues such as Goodreads. If you're using a Kindle, the app lets you post a review when finishing the book. How cool and convenient is that? So, please take a brief minute to share your perspective. Your review can be as brief as a sentence, but it has tremendous impact. And by all means, please tell a friend!

Thank you for joining my journey! Until next time...

Blessings & peace,
Suzette

ABOUT THE AUTHOR

Suzette D. Harrison, a native Californian and the middle of three daughters, grew up in a home where reading was required, not requested. Her literary "career" began in junior high school with the publishing of her poetry. While Mrs. Harrison pays homage to Alex Haley, Gloria Naylor, Alice Walker, Langston Hughes, and Toni Morrison as legends who inspired her creativity, it was Dr. Maya Angelou's *I Know Why the Caged Bird Sings* that unleashed her writing. The award-winning author of *Taffy* is a wife and mother who holds a culinary degree in Pastry & Baking. Mrs. Harrison is currently cooking up her next novel…in between batches of cupcakes.

CPSIA information can be obtained
at www.ICGtesting.com
Printed in the USA
LVHW051339100620
657784LV00001B/136